Everyone is talking abo[ut]

KINGDOM OF EXILES

"A powerful new voice. Keep an eye on Maxym M. Martineau. If I'm not mistaken, we have a bona fide genius in our midst."

—Darynda Jones, *New York Times* bestselling author

"Original, breathtaking, absolutely fabulous."

—C. L. Wilson, *New York Times* & *USA Today* bestselling author

"A fresh new fantasy. Left me with a happy sigh and a fervent wish for a beast of my own. Highly recommend!"

—Jeffe Kennedy, RITA award-winning author

"Maxym Martineau weaves an irresistible blend of adventure, magic, and romance. Prepare to be charmed!"

—Amanda Bouchet, *USA Today* bestselling author of The Kingmaker Chronicles

"*Kingdom of Exiles* captivated me with its distinctive fantasy world of exiled Charmers, enchanted beasts, and alluring assassins. A fantastic tale of magic, romance, and adventure—I can't wait to read more."

—L. Penelope, award-winning author of *Song of Blood & Stone*

"A strong female lead and a band of lovable assassins? Count me in! I cannot wait to see what more Maxym has to offer."

—Alexa Martin, author of *Intercepted*

KINGDOM OF EXILES

EXILES

MAXYM M. MARTINEAU

sourcebooks
fire

Published by Sourcebooks Fire, an imprint of Sourcebooks
P.O. Box 4410, Naperville, Illinois 60567-4410
(630) 961-3900
sourcebooks.com

Library of Congress Cataloging-in-Publication Data

Names: Martineau, Maxym M., author.
Title: Kingdom of exiles / Maxym M. Martineau.
Description: Naperville, Illinois : Sourcebooks Casablanca, [2019] |
Identifiers: LCCN 2019033548 | (trade paperback)
Subjects: GSAFD: Fantasy fiction. | Love stories.
Classification: LCC PS3613.A786329 K56 2019 | DDC 813/.6--dc23
LC record available at https://lccn.loc.gov/2019033548

Printed and bound in Canada.
MBP 10 9 8 7 6 5 4 3 2 1

For my family and husband.

Thank you, Mom, for teaching me at an early age that it's okay to dream, to find joy in a good story, and to believe in the worlds others might not see.

Thank you, Dad, for teaching me the meaning of perseverance. Without you, I wouldn't have the work ethic I do, and this book wouldn't be here.

Thank you, Chaz, for being the world's best brother, for showing me what it means to dedicate yourself entirely to your passion, and for always making me smile.

Thank you, Jacob, for being the husband I always dreamed of and for supporting me and loving me with everything you have. Just remember, I will always choose you.

To the rest of my family near and far, I love you, too.

Glacial
Springs

Silvis's Ruins

Luma Lake

Wilheim

The Gaping Wound

Tyrus's Ruins

Eastrend

Lightwood Forest

Ortega Key

Kings Isle

Yuna's Ruins

Queens Isle

ONE

LEENA

By the time evening fell, three things were certain: the gelatinous chunks of lamb were absolute shit, my beady-eyed client was hankering for more than the beasts in my possession, and someone was watching me.

Two out of the three were perfectly normal.

I slid the meat to the side and propped my elbows against the heavy plank table. My client lasted two seconds before his gaze roved to the book-shaped locket dangling in my cleavage. Wedging his thick fingers between the collar of his dress tunic and his neck, he tugged gently on the fabric.

"You have what I came for?" His heavy gold ring glinted in the candlelight. It bore the intricate etching of a scale: Wilheim's symbol for the capital bank. A businessman. A rare visitor in Midnight Jester, my preferred black-market tavern. My pocket hummed with the possibility of money, and I fingered the bronze key hidden there.

"Maybe." I nudged the metal dinner plate farther away. "How did you find me?" Dez, the bartender, sourced most of my clients, but brocade tunics and Midnight Jester didn't mingle.

I shifted in the booth, the unseen pair of eyes burrowing farther into the back of my head. Faint movement from the shadows flickered into my awareness. Movement that should have gone unnoticed, but I'd learned to be prepared for such things.

"Dez brought a liquor shipment to a bar I frequent in Wilheim. He said you could acquire things." He extracted his sausage fingers from the folds of his neck and placed his hands flat on the table.

Believable. Dez made a mean spiced liquor that he sold on the side—a cheap yet tasty alternative to the overpriced alcohol brewed within the safe confines of Wilheim. But that didn't explain the lurker.

Hidden eyes followed me as I scanned the tables. Cobweb-laden rafters held wrought-iron, candlelit chandeliers. Every rickety chair was occupied with regulars in grubby tunics, their shifty gazes accompanying hurried whispers of outlawed bargains. Who here cared about me? A Council member? A potential client?

My temple throbbed, and I forced myself to return my client's gaze. "Like a Gyss."

The man sat upright. Yellow teeth peeked around chapped lips in an eager smile. "Yes. I was told you have one available."

"They don't come cheap."

He grimaced. "I know. Dez said it would cost me one hundred bits."

One hundred? I tossed a sidelong glance to Dez. Elbow-deep in conversation with a patron at the bar, he didn't notice. One hundred was high for a Gyss. He'd done me a solid. I could've handed over the key right then and there, but I had a rare opportunity on my hands: a senseless businessman in a dry spell looking for luck. Why else would he want a Gyss?

"One-fifty."

He launched to his feet, nearly upending the table, and his outburst grabbed the attention of every delinquent in the place. Dez raised a careful eyebrow, flexing his hands for effect, and the businessman sheepishly returned to his seat. He cleared his throat, and his fingers retreated to the thick folds of his neck. "One-fifty is high."

Crossing my arms behind my head in an indolent lean, I shrugged. "Take it or leave it."

"I'll find someone else. I don't need to be swindled."

"Be my guest." I nodded to the quiet tables around us. "Though none of them will have it for you now, if ever. They're not like me."

He hissed a breath. "Are all Charmers this conniving?"

I leaned forward, offering him my best grin and a slow wink. "The ones you'll deal with? Hell yes."

"Shit." He pinched his nose. "All right. One-fifty. But this Gyss better work. Otherwise, you'll have to find a way to make it up to me." With obvious slowness, he moved his fingers to his chin, tracing the length of his rounded jaw with his thumb. A faint gleam flashed in his eyes, and I crossed my ankles to keep myself from kicking him under the table. I needed the money, and I didn't want to dirty my new boots with his groin.

I barely kept the growl from my voice. "I can assure you the Gyss will grant your wish. One every six months."

"Excellent." He extended his hand, waiting for the shake to seal the deal.

"You know Gyss need payment for every wish, correct?"

His hand twitched. "Yeah, yeah. Fulfill a request, get a wish."

"And I'm not responsible for what the Gyss requests. That's on the beast, not on me."

"Fine. Get on with it already before Sentinels ransack this shithole."

Sentinels? He wished. The capital's muscle-bound soldiers wouldn't come near this scourge. The festering dark woods of the Kitska Forest were crammed flush against the west side of Midnight

Jester. The errant, bone-shattering calls of monsters scraping through the air were enough to deter even the bravest of men.

No, Sentinels would never come here.

I clasped the businessman's outstretched hand. Clammy skin slicked along my palm, and a chill crawled up my arm. He moved away, reaching into his pocket for a velvet coin purse. As he pulled at the leather strings, a handful of silver chips and gold autrics clanked against the table.

One hundred and fifty bits. Funny how pebble-size pieces of flat metal carried such weight. Those of us living outside of Wilheim's protection had to fight for our coin. Ration our supplies. My last bits had gone to a much-needed new pair of leather boots. This man probably had fine silk slippers for every occasion.

With this kind of money, I'd have the chance to get something much more important than footwear. But the beasts I sold... This Gyss wasn't bonded to me yet, so she'd be fine in his care. Even so, the thought of giving something so precious to this stranger turned my insides to cement. And yet I had to do it. I had to survive. Sliding my hand into my pocket, I extracted a bronze key. Power vibrated from the metal into my palm, and I shot the businessman another glance. "Are you familiar with the Charmer's Law?"

His eyes skewered the key. "Buying and selling beasts is strictly forbidden—I know."

I rolled the key between my forefinger and thumb. "Not that. The Charmer's Law is meant to protect the beasts. If I find out you're mistreating this Gyss, I have the right to kill you. In any way I deem fit."

The man's face blanched, sweat dampening the collar of his tunic. "You're joking."

"I don't joke about beasts." I dropped the key on the table. Offering him a wolfish smile, I cocked my head to the side. "Still interested?"

He wavered for only a breath, then made a mad dash for the key. Thick hands pressed it flush to his breast pocket. "That won't be necessary. I'll treat the Gyss right."

As he pushed away from the table, he offered a parting nod. I jutted my chin out and kept my expression tight. "Think twice before wishing. The consequences can be extreme." A familiar sliver of unease threaded through me. I hated dealing in Gyss, but his needs seemed straightforward enough. Money. Power. He'd never be able to fulfill the boon the Gyss would require for more.

This Gyss wouldn't be used against me. Not like before. The breadth of their ability was dependent on their master, and this man didn't have the aptitude for true chaos. No, my exiled existence would be safe a couple hundred years yet. There were Charmers who lived well into their late two hundreds. I had plenty of time.

The invisible daggers, courtesy of my mystery lurker, dug deeper into my back. Maybe I was overestimating my life span.

Tracking the businessman's escape, I settled into the booth's cushions to count my coins. No need to rush with the stalker's eyes on me. A thief, maybe? Bits were hard to come by, and I had enough to get me to the south coast and back with room to spare. The Myad, and the opportunity to prove my worth to my people, was within my reach.

I just needed to acquire the blood of a murderer—given freely, with no strings attached. It was a necessary ingredient for the Myad's taming, and something that wouldn't happen in Midnight Jester where bartering patrons couldn't distinguish favor from paycheck. I'd deal with it in Ortega Key. For now, I needed to get there before the beast disappeared.

"You taking off?" Dez sidled into the opposite side of the booth, a toothy grin pulling the jagged scar running from his earlobe to his chin tight. With a square jaw and a nose broken one too many times, he had a rugged charm about him. "It's nice having you around."

I toyed with one of the silver chips. Living above the tavern had its perks, like building a relationship with the bartender who was easy on the eyes. "I'll only be gone for a short while. Think you'll survive without me?" My lips stretched into a flirty smile.

He rolled his eyes before placing a thick hand over his chest with an exaggerated thump. "Just the thought of you leaving has my heart aching." Despite the playful lilt to his tone, there was a glimmer of something deeper in his gaze. I glanced away, and he cleared his throat. "What has you running off, anyway?"

"There's been a rare beast sighting in the south, and if I hang around here, I'll miss it." I reached for my coin purse and slid my earnings off the table.

"You know you don't have to prove anything to anyone here." Playful banter gone and voice low, he let his gaze wander from head to head. "Hell, you're easily the best person in this establishment."

"In your eyes." My people would rather welcome a flesh-eating Tormalac into their homes than allow me back into our sacred grounds. "Charmers are only as strong as the beasts they keep. I have to be prepared."

"Prepared for what?" Dez asked. I knew what he wanted. A little bit of honesty. An ounce of trust. I just couldn't cave. There was a reason I was the only Charmer for miles around, and telling him the truth meant he could be used to find me. The Charmers Council had worse rulings than exile.

"I'll come back. You know I love this place."

"You know you love me." Another glimmer of hope.

"And you know I don't do love." I leaned in, trying to soften the words with a smile. "But that doesn't mean I don't enjoy your company."

His eyes shone. "I'll take that. For now."

Heat crawled down the back of my neck. Maybe I should cool

the flirting for awhile. It was fun—I thought both of us had been having fun—but Dez seemed to be taking it a little too seriously despite the number of times I'd made it clear things would never go farther than that. "You're a pain in my ass, you know that?"

He didn't bother to look properly abashed. "Just don't get yourself into any trouble before you come back and mend my poor, lonely heart."

This time, I laughed. "Deal." As I made a move to stand, a high-pitched whine sliced through my mind, and my feet cemented to the floor. Iky—my camouflaged beast I kept on hand during all black-market dealings. With senses sharper than a Sentinel's blade, he would've been able to discern any shift in the tavern's close quarters. We'd had a few brushes with two-bit murderers and thieves before. Nothing he couldn't handle. But it looked like my unseen stalker was going to make his move after all. "Actually, trouble might have already found me."

I scoured the tables. By all appearances, everything was fine. No one jumped. No one made a move to block the bar's only door. The regulars I'd grown to know over the years were neck-deep in their own worlds and not the least bit interested in my dealings. But with the weighted stare abruptly gone and the body count the same, something was definitely off.

"What? Why?" Dez stilled, all humor wiped from his voice.

"Any shady characters in recently?"

He raised a brow. "Seriously?"

"Shadier than usual."

"What's going on?"

"I'm being watched. Or I was. Iky noticed a shift."

Dez's hardened gaze spied the lopsided coatrack tucked against the wall. Forgotten threadbare coats clung to the hooks like leaves that wouldn't die. It was Iky's favorite place to lurk. Dez discovered

Iky once when he unceremoniously tossed another left-behind cloak and missed. A floating red garment gave even the regulars a scare.

"All right. Promise me you'll take care?"

"Of course." I rested my hand on his shoulder. "I'll be back before you know it."

"Sure." Dez stood, spreading his hands wide and gesturing to the crowd. "I just came up with a new special, folks! Cured pig with red flakes." A signal only local outlaws would truly understand: danger, potential spy.

For a moment, everyone stiffened. Eyes darted in erratic patterns before the slow murmuring of mundane conversation—weather, the royal family's upcoming ball, anything other than what we were all here for—flitted through the air. With his coded warning in effect, Dez took up his place behind the counter, polishing glasses with one eye on the door and the other on his patrons.

Always assume they're snitches. Dez's previous warning rattled through my brain as I reached for the busted iron doorknob, a still-invisible Iky right on my heels. How long had my deal with the businessman taken? I'd stationed Iky behind me before that, which meant his hours in our plane were waning. I'd have to send him back to the beast sanctuary soon. With no time for delay, I pushed through the door and met the evening air with guarded eyes.

Staying in the tavern now wasn't an option. What if the Charmers Council had finally caught on to my crimes? I couldn't jeopardize Dez or his establishment.

I glanced east in the direction of Wilheim, our capital city. I'd never had the opportunity to pass through those gleaming white walls of marble and diamond. Stretching tall to kiss the underside of the clouds, the concentric towers guarded an impressive mountain where the royal family lived.

Shaking my head, I quickened my pace. Though the royal family's jurisdiction technically covered the small island continent of Lendria, everyone knew that law didn't apply past those glistening stones. Out here, magic and darkness and questionable dealings reigned supreme. Iky let out another private whine, and my gaze jumped to the forest line. My stalker was back. Invisible to me, but not hidden from my beast's senses. My destination was the train station, but if this lurker was from the Council, I didn't want them getting a whiff of the Myad and stealing my beast. I needed to deal with the threat first.

I know you're there, creep.

Flipping the collar of my jacket up, I picked my way down the winding dirt path away from Wilheim and the train depot. Lure them out, trap them, free and clear. Easy enough. The descending sun crept toward the riotous treetops of the Kitska Forest. Steeped in shadows, the dark leaves shivered in the dusk air, and a small whistling met my ears. The sheer density of the woods invited a certain level of hysteria to the unfamiliar—out here, one couldn't tell the difference between a pair of eyes and oversize pinesco pods.

Needles and mulch crunched beneath my knee-high boots, and my feet screamed at the ache of unbroken leather pressing against my joints. Soon enough, I'd wear the boots in and be wishing for more bits to replace the holes.

A twig snapped in the distance, and I splayed out my right hand. One of the forest's many monsters, or my stalker?

The Charmer's symbol, a barren rosewood tree on the back of my right hand, exploded to life. A crisscross network of roots inked down my knuckles and wrapped around my fingertips in gnarled directions. Iky responded to the flux of power and distanced himself from me. Searching. Pursuing. The lack of his watery scent left me unnerved, but I needed to give my lurker a chance to strike. Then Iky would snare him.

A frigid breath skated along the back of my neck.

I whirled, thrusting my hand forward and focusing on the well of power humming beneath the surface. But Iky had done his job without fault. Just beyond my reach stood a tall, slender man dressed entirely in black. With a voluminous pompadour, thin-rimmed silver specs, and freshly polished dress shoes, he looked suited for a night in Wilheim—not a stroll in the Kitska Forest. With his arms pressed flush to his sides, he was rendered immobile, and an unused, glittering black knife limply dangled from his gloved fingertips.

I dropped my hand, and the ink work along my skin receded. "Iky, be a dear."

Iky materialized at last. Tall and amorphous with see-through skin, he adjusted his body constitution, color, and shape to suit my needs. With elongated arms, Iky had wrapped the man in a bundle, pressing him so tightly his chest struggled to inflate.

"Give him a bit more breathing room."

Iky loosened his arms, and the man let out a sharp gasp. The shadows clinging to the forest's limbs seemed to darken.

"Who are you?"

No response. Harsh ice-green eyes speared me. The high planes of his face sharpened, and a small vein throbbed along his temple.

"Why were you trying to kill me?" I glanced pointedly at the knife. He dropped it to the ground, and Iky nudged it toward me with a newly formed extremity. It receded as quickly as it appeared, folding back into his body mass with a quiet splash.

The man pursed thin lips, and a rattling breeze ushered in more thin shadows. It was no secret that these woods were cursed, but this darkness was thicker. Unfamiliar. Something else was going on here.

Deal with the threat, and get the hell out.

"Iky?" I nodded toward my beast. Iky's arms tightened, and the man sputtered. "If you don't tell me something, this is only going to get worse."

He wheezed, words I couldn't make out intermingling with pained gasps. I glanced at Iky, and he stopped. In the past, I'd never pushed much further than this. The mere presence of my beast had always been enough, coupled with my threats that he'd do more if I didn't get what I wanted.

Murder dripped from my would-be killer's glare. "I'd never dream of telling you a damn thing."

This criminal, it seemed, wasn't afraid to see just how far I was willing to go.

My brows furrowed. "That so? Iky, you know what to do." A new extremity formed, wrapping its way around the man's pinky finger. With a sharp and fluid motion, pulled it back toward his forearm.

The man swallowed a cry, face gone parchment-pale as I studied him. He wasn't a familiar presence in Midnight Jester. Most of the men and women who stumbled through the tavern were scarred, reeking of bad choices and worse fates, but this man? From his immaculately trimmed hair to the smooth glow of his clean skin, everything about him screamed privileged.

I resisted the urge to glance back toward Wilheim. "Who are you?" Taking a few steps forward, I studied his black garb. Long-sleeved, button-up tunic. Slim-cut trousers hemmed just about his shoes. Not nearly ethereal enough to be a Charmer. Certainly not brilliant enough to be a Sentinel. Their armor threatened to outshine even the brightest diamond.

He glowered. "I don't see the need to repeat myself." In my peripheral vision, onyx tendrils slithered across the forest floor and edged toward me. A heartbeat pulsed from their swirling depths. Whatever monster watched us from the forest, we were clearly running out of time.

"You're too scrawny to be a Sentinel, though you certainly

have the arrogance of one." I inched away from the cursed wood. "You don't have the emblem of a Charmer, so you're not one of my kind." Thank the gods for that.

"Are you done fishing?"

"No." I chewed on the inside of my cheek. I didn't want to hurt him, but he wasn't exactly innocent, either. "You were trying to kill me, which means you're likely a murderer for hire."

A slow smile dared to grace his lips. "You won't make it out of this alive."

Oh, but I would. And a new idea was brewing in the back of my brain. One that had to do with favors and blood and the golden opportunity standing right in front of me.

I started to circle him, assessing his potential. The problem was, offering freedom in exchange for his blood didn't exactly mean the blood was "freely given." Semantics, but in the game of taming beasts, semantics were everything. "And why is that?"

"Because I'm a member of Cruor."

The world slipped out from beneath my feet. Heavy ringing filled my ears, and the treetops spun together. I'd assumed assassin from the get-go, but *Cruor*? Who would go to such lengths as to hire the undead?

Realization struck hard and fast, and my gaze jerked to the pooling mass of darkness near his feet. He leached shadows from the corners and hidden crevices of the forest. Even the once-solid blade had dispersed, joining the curling tendrils around my captive. They licked his skin and gathered in his aura, waiting to do his bidding. That wasn't some Kitska monster gathering the darkness—it was *him*.

He'd been toying with me all this time, and I had seconds to react.

"Iky, serrated. *Now*." Iky shifted, coating his arms with thousands of miniscule barbs that punctured the man's clothing and skin, and locked him in place. Blood trickled from a multitude of pinprick holes. Gleaming red droplets that wormed their way out and oozed down his ink-black coat like veining through marble. Blood I couldn't use. The first wasted rivulets dripped from his fingers and splattered against the gravel path. He watched them with fierce eyes, and the dark wisps receded. Good. At least he had enough sense to realize when he was beaten. "If you try to dissipate on me, you'll end up as mincemeat. Why am I on Cruor's shit list?"

Irritation tightened his face as my beast and I so deftly turned the tables. "I'm not going to dignify that with a response. As if I'd tell a *job* the details of my work."

Egotism, even in the face of death. The Charmers Council had to be behind this. If they'd somehow caught on to my underhanded dealings, they'd sooner hire someone to kill me than leave the sanctity of Hireath. But Cruor? Charmers valued all life. Execution was rare. Hiring someone who walked with the shadows all but guaranteed my death. With me already sentenced to a lifelong exile for a crime I most certainly did *not* commit, they must have felt a more extreme response was appropriate. No chance to plea my case. No chance to return to my people.

Gripping my hands into fists, I glared at the assassin. "Gods be damned. Killing was not on my agenda today."

A brittle laugh devoid of humor scraped through the air. "You don't have it in you." Even with my threats, he hadn't been phased. "Even if you did manage to kill me, another would be sent."

He was right, of course, and I prayed my next words wouldn't be my death sentence. I needed this bounty gone. I had business in the south I couldn't postpone. The Myad was my only hope of ever going *home*. "Then take me to Cruor."

His green eyes widened a fraction. "Your logic escapes me."

"Good thing it's not your job to understand how I think. Take me to Cruor, or Iky will end you. Plain and simple."

"Like I said, you don't have—"

Iky snapped applied more pressure to his chest without my prompting, causing his barbs to dig deeper, and the man hissed.

"What were you saying?" I asked.

"Fine." He rotated his head, peering around trees before jutting his chin to the left. "You won't like this."

Tendrils exploded in a swirling vortex that blanketed out the Kitska Forest. Rivers of black surged beneath our feet, and my stomach turned itself inside out. We were thrust forward, and yet we hadn't moved a muscle. Intertwining shadows sped through us, around us, careening us toward a destination I couldn't even begin to pinpoint. Tears pricked the corners of my eyes, and I sucked in a breath.

And then we came to a screeching halt, the outside world slamming back into us as the darkness abruptly receded. I white-knuckled a fist against my stomach and glared at the assassin in Iky's arms. His smirk was maddening.

The comfort of Midnight Jester was now what felt like a world away.

Slowly, I unfurled my hand and caught sight of my Charmer's symbol, weighing Iky's branch and my apparent insanity against his time. Every beast had a weakness, and his was a shelf life. Two hours of strength for every twenty-two hours of sleep. With every minute that passed, Iky's limb retreated to the base until it would fade from existence, forcibly returning him to the beast realm to regain his stamina.

I had fifteen minutes, give or take.

Stepping to the side, I gestured to the woods. "Let's get this over with. Iky, pick him up." His hooks retracted a fraction, and Iky cradled the man to his chest like an overgrown child.

The assassin scoffed, unintelligible curses dropping from his lips.

The void had transported us close, but I still couldn't see the hidden death grotto known as Cruor. Yet I could feel it. The weight of eyes and shadows. My hairs stood on end as we made our way through the suffocating foliage, darkness dripping from limbs like tacky sap. Above us, birds squawked and feathers scraped together as they took flight, swirling upward and chasing the setting sun into the horizon. A heavy branch creaked. A shadow more human than night rocketed from one tree to the next. The assassin stared after the figure without saying a word, but smugness laced his expression. One of his brethren, then, going to alert the others.

Icy hands wrenched my heart, and I gripped the book-shaped locket hanging about my neck—the miniature bestiary all Charmers carried—and begged the gods for favorable odds. I could have waited. Could have called forth another beast, but Iky's strength took a serious toll on my power, and my arsenal that could fight off the legendary might of Cruor was small. Besides, summoning another could be the difference between a peaceful negotiation and a declaration of war. The latter I would surely lose. I needed every chance to run I could get, in case negotiations went south.

Mangled iron fencing battled against the overgrowth of the cursed forest, marking the edge of Cruor's property, and I paused at the gates. In the distance, the evening sky birthed a manor shrouded in darkness. Alone on a hill and two stories tall, with more windows than my eyes could count, the guild was just shy of a castle.

Slate black and covered in vibrant red gems, a rycrim core glittered from between neatly trimmed hedges and the side of the house. Magic energy pulsed from it in an invisible dome over the mansion.

I'd begged Dez to invest in a rycrim core for months. Changing every candle by hand, warming the bathwater over a fire—I wanted the simplicity of self-lighting fixtures, a faucet that immediately poured scalding water. But convenience cost more bits than we could afford to spare. Murder apparently paid well.

Iky whined aloud, a low vibration thrumming through the air. Less than ten minutes left.

With a heavy breath, I pushed the gate open and tried to shake the eerie grating of hinges as I stared down the winding path leading me straight to death's door.

TWO

NOC

The wooden double doors banged open, and a breath of cool air swirled into the foyer. Wild, dark eyes lit with anger found mine. Slamming the doors in her wake, an assassin sped toward me.

"Sir, it's Kost."

All sounds, save the fire, died. Even the voices bleeding through the walls halted. With their senses heightened by death, the rest of the assassins living in Cruor would've heard the sentry's panicked entrance.

I stared at the woman. A rare glimpse of fear threaded its way through her gaze, setting my pulse on high alert. I'd only passed along the bounty to Kost, my second-in-command, yesterday. "What about him?"

Emelia hid behind a sheet of glossy black hair. "The Charmer. Somehow, she got the best of him. She's at the gate."

My blood cooled. "Are you certain?" Jobs weren't without risk, but given our talents, we rarely encountered issues. Fueled by fear and dark rumors, we were often met with stunned terror instead of the wrong end of the blade.

Calem, a top-tier assassin and one of my closest friends, turned to stone beside me as he glowered at the front door. "Want me to greet them?"

"No." I fought for control. Cruor was the only family I'd ever be able to claim as my own, and Kost was the first of my newfound brethren I'd grown to call *brother*. "Is he still alive?"

Emelia cleared her throat. "Yes. She's held him hostage somehow. I can't see... There's so much blood."

My mind reeled. Shadows pooled in the dark corners of the room, crawling along the floor and snaking toward my quaking fingers. I was their leader. I had to protect my own.

"Where's Ozias?"

Perma-smile wiped clean from his face, Calem only turned his chin away from the door long enough to offer me a quick glance. "Out back. Training some of the new recruits."

Calem's stiff spine told me he wasn't going anywhere, and I couldn't blame him. Kost was a brother to both of us. Slipping my hands into the pockets of my trousers, I hid my balled fists to keep the calm facade in place. "Emelia, get Ozias immediately."

Emelia disappeared in a plume of shadow and smoke, calling on darkness to speed through the night unseen.

Calem fidgeted. "Can I murder the Charmer?"

I understood his sentiment well. I'd lost too many loved ones not to acknowledge the unease in my gut. We might have been agents of death, but that didn't mean we welcomed it in our own home. Killing was a by-product of a centuries-old decree left from the time of the First King. Exiled from cities sanctioned by the king, yet forced to fulfill his contracts simply to survive. Death was necessary.

But not like this.

"Let the Charmer come." The manor kicked into full gear, bodies appearing out of every nook and cranny as members rushed to get a glimpse of Kost's captor. They pressed firmly against the iron railing lining the second story, fingers wrapping around metal flowers welded to the bar. Thorns among roses.

I needed to protect them, as our former guild master, Talmage, had done. Tossing a quick glance to the fireplace mantel, my gaze snagged on a framed oil painting of him. The first time I'd seen him had been from the flat of my back after he'd raised me from death.

"You chose your death. Kost found you without armor, without weapons, and with a smile on your face. I can't say this life will be easier, but it will be new. We leave everything from our past in the ground."

I thought death had wiped my slate clean when I followed Talmage and became a member of Cruor. I didn't realize how wrong I was until it was too late. If death couldn't cure me, then nothing would. All I could have was Cruor, and even that required a delicate balance between love and loss.

Never again would I trigger my curse, I vowed. Never again would I lose someone important. And now some Charmer with an army of beasts had Kost.

Careful footsteps thudded against wooden planks. Sinking into the black tufted armchair beside me, I capped the fear and anger in my veins and hid my ire beneath absolute stillness. The bronzed handles jerked, and the doors swung open.

A woman stepped inside.

Wide hazel eyes flashed from left to right. She looked every bit the scoundrel I believed her to be. Faded leather breeches worn from constant use. Formfitting violet tunic with an errant thread dangling from the hem. She probably thought bringing Kost here could net her some extra bits.

She wouldn't live to spend whatever meager amount she kept in her change purse.

My brethren waited, completely still save their heavy stares and the subtle rise and fall of their chests. She studied each one, the color of her face fading with every passing moment. Behind her, a transparent beast with the build of a slender man cradled Kost to its chest. Thousands of infinitesimal barbs anchored him in place, and blood dripped to the floor from his fingertips.

Kost.

His green stare found mine, and his familiar stoic demeanor cracked to one of remorse as he lowered his gaze. He would view his capture as a failure. His downcast eyes sent a surge of rage deep into my bones, and I resisted the urge to lunge from the chair.

I couldn't break my composure in front of the Charmer. In front of my people.

"Now, what do we have here?" I said, as cold as any shadow.

Her head whipped to me, and a few strands of hair clung to her high cheekbones. She pulled her leather jacket tight around her and took a careful step forward. "I mean no harm."

My gaze slid to Kost. To the dried-on bracelets of blood circling his wrists. "I don't wholly believe that."

"Are you the leader of Cruor?" The slender beast sidled in closer to her. She dropped her gaze to her hand, and the frown pulling at her brows deepened. Interesting.

"Perhaps."

"I want the bounty off my head," she said. A few laughs rolled through the crowd before silence once again settled over us. She shifted her weight from one foot to the next, casting another quick glance at her hand.

I kept my tone even. "You're a long way from home, Charmer. I will neither remove the bounty nor permit you to leave here safely."

A peculiar sheen soaked her hairline, and the beast by her side shivered. She touched her chin to her shoulder, concern bleeding from her eyes, before taking a deep breath and meeting my gaze head-on.

"If you move to kill me, this man will die."

The beast tightened its grip, and Kost's sharp gasp was a fist around my heart.

Gods, Kost.

I dragged my gaze from Kost to her. *Control.* Expressing too much concern would threaten Kost's life in ways the Charmer would never be able to understand. It was a careful calculus drilled into me by years living under the pall of my curse. "Kost does not fear death. He's been there before."

When Talmage was in charge, he'd insisted we leave fear behind for the sake of our work. I agreed, but there weren't any rules about loyalty. Standing slowly, I gauged the distance between Kost and me. What kind of powers did this creature have? Would I make it in time?

Shadows gathered in my peripheral and flung themselves to me. Swathed me in a cool darkness that made movements lethal and nearly impossible to track. I lunged before doubt had a chance to freeze my muscles. Thick tendrils flared outward in a puff of black smoke, and suddenly I was before her. I wrapped my hand around the soft flesh of the woman's neck, yanked her from the floor, and held her suspended above the ebony tile. She was so fragile. Breakable. Hard to believe she'd somehow managed to trap my second-in-command. What made her so dangerous that she warranted a bounty? No matter: one swift jerk and I could end her life. Fingers wrenched between mine, and her watery eyes widened.

Behind her, the monster reacted. Arms shifting and tightening around Kost's ribs, the hooked barbs sank deep into his skin. Blood spattered outward. My fingers tightened, and the woman's muscles spasmed beneath my grip. Flicking my wrist would cut off her airway, but there was still the matter of her beast. I wasn't sure I was fast enough to break her neck before it stole Kost's life.

A gruff whisper squeaked through the woman's lips. "I'll give you a beast."

I loosened my fingers a fraction, and my gaze snapped to her. Charmers didn't offer beasts lightly. "You'd trade your monsters? What Charmer would be willing to do such a thing?"

"Negotiate. Please." Her vocal cords flared against the palm of my hand. I could end her right here...but beasts were a rare find.

Like the monster caging Kost. A beast like this could execute the more dangerous jobs, the ones that could get us captured and carted back to our door—or worse, dead. There were also tales whispered from drunken lips, rumors of a beast that could fulfill anyone's deepest desires. I'd tested every manner of a cure except this one. Charmers were too hard to find, too hard to subdue. And they never parted with their beasts, no matter the price—or threat.

The toes of the Charmer's feet skated above the floor, and her creature shuddered. Kost moaned again, and Calem inched closer. In less than a minute, I wouldn't have the opportunity to bargain. He would strike to save Kost.

"Release him. As a show of good faith."

She lifted her right hand to the side, and a soft light emanated from her Charmer's emblem. Rosewood markings flared, and the grating of a heavy door scraping against floorboards cut the air. My eyes peeled away from the woman for a moment in search of the sound, but the hidden realm remained invisible.

"Iky, return," she murmured. A soft hum droned as the beast exhaled. Dropping Kost to the floor, Iky disappeared in a flood of light, and her insignia returned to normal.

Unlatching my fingers, I released her neck. "Kost. Medical wing. Now."

"Noc—"

"Now," I said. He nodded once before taking his leave up the stairs. "Calem, stay with me and the Charmer. Everyone else, leave us. Immediately."

Murmurs of discontent drifted down the stairs, but misty darkness curled around their ankles like the thick vines of the forest ensnaring its victims, and they left.

Calem's muted-red eyes targeted the woman. "Hell of a show. You've got guts, that's for sure."

I couldn't fathom how he found it in his heart to compliment her. Not when she'd strung up Kost like a scarecrow and set him on display. "Calem."

"Yeah, yeah." Quick to anger, quicker to cool. His tense jaw relaxed, and his stare shifted from murderous to an intrigued, slow-moving appraisal. I fought the impulse to send him away. The gods only knew what she could summon, and I wouldn't be caught off guard.

"What's your name?" Boots clipping against the tile, I circled her in a slow walk.

Her voice cracked. "Leena." Purplish bruises swelled in the shapes of fingerprints along the paper-thin skin of her neck. Guilt didn't even bother to rear its head.

"Noc. Welcome to my home." I nodded toward the other open armchair and stepped back, waiting for her to pass. The confident jerk of her chin threw me, and I fought to keep my brows from raising. She carried herself like an assassin unafraid of death. After sitting in the chair, her gaze slanted from me to Calem.

"Most Charmers would sooner die than part with their precious beasts," I said, pulling her attention back to me.

Something dark flickered behind her eyes. "What beast do you want?"

"Before we discuss what you'll be handing over, we should touch on the quantity. I require four."

She shifted uncomfortably in her seat. "Two beasts. Clearly you don't understand the difficulty involved with managing more."

"You manage more than one."

Rotating the rose-gold ring around her pointer finger, she ground her words through clenched teeth. "Ensuring my beasts are happy and healthy is vital."

"*There's* the Charmer blood in you." So not just a black-market scoundrel trading for bits. There were morals tucked away beneath that hardened expression. "I can assure you the beasts will be well cared for, but I still require four. One for myself and one for each of my closest votaries." Kost's stricken gaze played on repeat in my mind. Never again.

Her eyes shifted to Calem, and he winked. "Kost will be thrilled to have a permanent reminder of his unfortunate meeting with you."

"Enough, Calem." I waved him off, turning back to Leena. "B-Class or higher."

She scoffed. "Fuck off."

"Are you incapable of procuring B-Class beasts?" I finally took the seat opposite her and met her heated glare head-on.

"No." She fingered a strand of hair the color of ancient oak trees—layered with rich browns that deepened in color at the crown of her head.

"B-Class it is, then. Shall we see what you have available in that bestiary of yours?" The book resting just beneath her collarbone called to me, sparking a flare of intrigue. So much hidden knowledge just begging to be discovered. And I had the potential to gain access to it.

Parting with her beasts, wandering far from the Charmers' sacred homeland—she was anything but an ordinary mark. Curiosity burned brighter. It was my job to unearth secrets, to use them to further my agenda if needed.

After a moment that stretched for what felt like an hour, a log on the fire split in half, and she looked up at me through her lashes. "I was heading south for business. I'll tame four B-Class beasts during my travels and bring them back once I'm finished." Her tone wavered at the end, just a slight dip in her timbre. She was hiding something. Then again, she was bartering with an assassin, so she'd be a fool not to.

Sighing, I reclined in the chair. "No."

"It's that or nothing at all."

"I think you forget who holds the cards here. My guild has a bounty on your head. Your life is mine to bargain with. You follow my rules."

She gripped the arms of her chair, a defiant glare threating to bore twin holes through my skull. "How do you think I've come to earn this bounty? I make a living dealing with people like you, and I always set the rules." A low whistle slipped past Calem's pursed lips, and I shot him a murderous glare. "You want beasts—that much is obvious—so I think I've got more bargaining power than you realize."

I rested my elbows on my knees and leaned in, intent on the minute changes in her expression. "What happens to your beasts when you die?"

Her boldness fled in an instant, leaving nothing but cold fear in its wake. "What?"

Her reaction said it all. "If you don't comply with my demands, you die. It's as simple as that. I can live without your creatures. So can my brethren." I gestured to Calem, his lazy smile dangerous as he studied her. "But the question is, can your beasts live without you? What kind of fate would they endure if you died? A fate you *chose* because you were too stubborn to negotiate?" Her lips trembled, but guilt wasn't something I was about to entertain. I stood, looking down at her. "Go on, then. Tell me again how I don't hold all the chips."

The air between us sparked, and she clenched her hands into fists before finally lowering her gaze to the floor. "I don't have any on hand to give you. Those I do have are already bonded to me, and breaking that connection would kill them. What do you propose?"

There was a certain level of satisfaction that came with outmaneuvering an opponent, mentally or physically, and I couldn't stop the smirk. "I'm so glad you asked." I turned to Calem. "It seems we're taking our work on the road."

"Awww yes." Whatever remaining anger simmering in his veins disappeared completely, and he clapped his hands together. "This time of year, the south will be brimming with beautiful women. What part, exactly?" He peered around me toward Leena.

"Wait, what? No. I don't need an escort. I promise on my life I'll return with your beasts." Gripping the hemline of her tunic, she stood slowly.

Calem's eyes dipped to her cleavage. "Sorry, sister. Noc doesn't change his mind."

I tilted my head to the ceiling, tracking the invisible path to the medical wing on the second floor. "I'll have Kost make travel arrangements for us."

"Wait—" Leena's voice faded in the wake of Calem's excited holler. She banged her fist against the oak mantel, the board vibrating from the force of the hit, and we turned to stare at her. "I. Am. Not. Taking. You." A rosewood glow erupted from the symbol on her hand, and roots stretched toward her fingertips.

I effortlessly slipped into the shadows and reappeared behind her. Wrapping my fingers around her wrist, I applied gentle pressure and reminded her exactly who was calling the shots. "Think twice before you do something you'll regret."

Gooseflesh trailed down her neck, and she went completely still beneath me. Her pulse thrummed against my fingers, and in spite of the danger, she didn't pull away. There was strength to her stance. The kind of determination and grit that came from battling against terrible odds and somehow coming through it all alive. "I have one more...request."

"Oh?" I released her, but didn't move. Her eyes darted to my neck, gaze lingering on the collar of my tunic. Did she want to strangle me? Payback for what I'd done to her? There was intensity in her eyes I couldn't place. As if she was debating, but unable to come to a solid conclusion.

Finally, she shook her head once. "Never mind."

Before I could probe further, the crash of double doors banging against masonry erupted through the empty halls. Swirling darkness swept through the room, and Emelia and Ozias appeared. Leena leaped a few inches backward, crashing into me, and then scrambled away yet again beyond my reach.

Chest heaving, Emelia spoke first. "Sorry for the delay—he was out farther than anticipated."

"It's fine, Emelia. Please return to your post."

She sank into a wave of shadows, returning to her overlook in the high trees of the Kitska Forest. She'd stay until her shift was over, only to be replaced by another. Members of Cruor could effortlessly summon a path to our shrouded home, but it was still possible for intruders to trek through the cursed wood and find us. We had plenty of enemies.

Spine rigid, Ozias clenched his hammer-size fists by his sides. "This her?"

"Easy, big guy." Calem strolled toward him and placed a hand on his shoulder. "Noc's sorted it out."

Dark-brown eyes jumped from Leena to me, and the heavy

folds across his forehead smoothed. Relaxing his hands, he brushed them along his sweat-stained work shirt. "Emelia filled me in. I should have been here, but the recruits—"

"I know." We only raised those we couldn't live without. Dead loved ones. Lifelong friends. Not everyone had been a criminal prior to the change, which meant our activities—and the powers we used to execute them—were hard for some to grasp. "Give them time. For now, meet Leena. She'll be providing us with beasts."

Ozias's thick brow shot into his cropped hairline. Leena offered him a tight nod, taking a small step back. Dominating in presence, his hulking frame outshadowed every assassin in Cruor, and yet he was the least of Leena's worries within my walls.

Kost's face bled to the surface of my thoughts. He'd want to murder her on principle. Time to make this deal official. "Once we have all four beasts, I'll handle the bounty. Until then, you're stuck with us."

"And by handle the bounty, you mean refuse to execute it, correct?"

Clever woman. If she'd never placed a hit with us, then she likely didn't know about the magic attached to her bounty. And yet, she'd scrutinized my words in the span of a breath. Her survival instinct was admirable. Pity she wasn't one of ours.

Feigning dismissiveness, I started to make my way from the room. "Follow through with your end of the bargain, and I can assure you one of my men won't come after your head."

One of my men, no. Me? That was another matter. This time, she didn't catch on, but she threatened me just the same.

"You should know," Leena warned, "all beast trades are subject to the Charmer's Law. Meaning, if you or any of your assassins harm the beasts I give you in any way, I am permitted to kill you."

I paused, glancing back at her. The heat in Leena's glare was warmer than the fire, but an unhurried grin claimed my face. "I welcome you to try."

Pallid pink anger tinged her cheeks. "I want our deal in writing. Not some verbal agreement that can't be used as proof."

I raised a brow. Verbal, handwritten, signed by the king himself—it didn't matter. The magic of Cruor's Oath couldn't be stopped. "Fine. Though that doesn't stop someone outside my guild from coming after you."

"If that happens, I'll deal with it." She toyed with the flaps of her black jacket. "We need to leave immediately."

"Day after tomorrow." I ignored her obvious frustration. "We need time to prepare."

"Sign me up for some beach time!" Calem danced in place, tossing a grin in Leena's direction. "Bringing any bathing garments?"

She scowled. "Keep your imagination to yourself."

I turned to my third-in-command. "Ozias."

"Yes?"

"Show Leena to her room. East wing."

She stilled. "Wait. How do I know you won't come for me in the night?"

Calem couldn't resist. "If I come for you in the middle of the night, I can promise you won't regret it."

I frowned at Calem. "Go pack."

"Yeah, yeah." He spun around and took the stairs two at a time, whistling the whole way.

"No one will kill you while you stay in my home. That's an order for all my brethren, and you can rest assured they're listening. Now, Ozias, please take Leena to her room."

Tremors of fear touched Leena's body again, but she angled her chin up in defiance and followed Ozias without turning back once.

So much for those survival wits. She should have watched her back the whole way to her room. She had no way of knowing I'd keep my promise.

After they disappeared, I took the stairs and hooked a left at the loft, heading toward the west wing to check on Kost. Palms flat against the worn wood, I pushed open a set of double doors without a glance to the bronze plaque reading *Medical*. The sharp aroma of bleach and lemon assaulted my nose.

Kost sat shirtless on a cot, gloves and tattered dress tunic discarded on the sheets beside him. A spare lingered untouched on the pillow. The medical attendant was missing, but a silver tray next to Kost brimmed with needles and thread. Not like he'd need stitching. His skin would resew within the hour of its own accord.

He pinned me with a strained stare the moment I entered. "I'm sorry. I underestimated her."

I blew out a low breath, parking my hip on the desk by the door. Parchment crunched beneath my weight. "I hope that's not an oversight we'll make again."

Kost stilled. "What do you mean?"

"I made a deal with her."

He stood slowly, anger working its way through the muscles of his forearms. "You know I won't question you."

"Good. Because she traded beasts to have her bounty removed."

Kost's hands went slack, and his brows dipped toward the frames of his glasses. "Does she know about the oath?"

I shrugged. "No. Does it matter?"

"I guess not."

"Good." Pushing off the desk, I reached for Kost's arm. "Transfer ownership."

He froze, stricken. "I can handle it once the deal is complete. There's no need to take on the job yourself."

Again, the sight of Kost skewered by the beast resurfaced.

This job should have been mine to begin with. Not to mention I'd promised none of my men would take her life. Not lying, but not telling the whole truth, made for clean work as an assassin. My voice level, I placed a gentle hand on his shoulder. "This isn't a reflection of your ability. I made the deal; I carry out the task. Not you. Not anyone else."

"But—"

"This isn't up for discussion."

Kost relented, turning his inner wrist upward and revealing an inked scythe the size of a silver chip. Grasping his forearm, I pressed my skin to his and the mark sparked to life. Flesh seared, and I grimaced. When the sizzling faded, I dropped his hand. The magical oath now binding me to the bounty gleamed up at me, sharp black lines neatly cutting across veins.

Now, if I didn't kill Leena, it was my life on the line. Such was the agreement for all bounties placed with Cruor. Folklore suggested it was the god of death's doing. When Zane, the first of our kind, had escaped his clutches and returned to the land of the living, the god of death had been enraged. All our contracts were steeped in his magic so he wouldn't miss his opportunity to claim us a second time. True or not, it didn't matter. All I knew was the oath couldn't be broken, and that level of assurance welcomed the darkest of dealings. "The woman who ordered the hit—did she contact you with any more details after I assigned you the job?"

Kost shook his head once. He'd take this personally as a mark against his perfect record. "No. She wore a mask and was covered from head to toe, even wearing gloves. I did notice a currant-colored glow around her hand when she summoned a beast after the deal was done."

She was smart to keep her identity hidden. The right amount of bits could convince anyone to spill any manner of secret. "A beast?

Interesting." So Leena's own people were after her. "What about the job itself? Any specifics?"

"Yes. The woman wrote down the job's details on parchment: Bones must be delivered within six hours of death." He glanced at the silver watch cradling his left wrist. "I was supposed to meet her within the hour at Devil's Hollow."

I didn't blink. It wouldn't be the first or last time we were asked to do something strange with the remains. But Devil's Hollow was dangerous. Tainted by dark magic and even darker omens. "Devil's Hollow?"

Kost grimaced. "Unfortunately, yes. I requested we meet elsewhere, but the client insisted."

"All right. We'll keep the meeting brief."

Black tendrils of shadow slunk toward me. Kost nabbed the spare tunic, slipping into it with ease, and followed suit, his own power lashing out against mine. Turning our backs on the medical wing, we rushed on the cold wind through the double doors and set out to meet our employer.

Three

NOC

Devil's Hollow wasn't far from Cruor, but we didn't visit the clearing often. We knew better than to tempt the magic of the damned. If the Kitska Forest was a festering wound, then Devil's Hollow was the poison that made it that way. Milky fog drifted across mulch and brown grass, stretching out to meet the gaping mouth of a cave with stalactite teeth. The cursed wood came to a screeching halt in a perfect circle around the opening, as if the whispered wails echoing from the cavern's maw were spells even monsters dared not trigger.

A single barren tree with ashy bark and decaying limbs entrenched its gnarled roots around the opening. Upright spikes of blood-red flowers shooting out from the tips of branches were the only splatters of color—save the client cloaked in a mercury robe standing with his hands clasped before the cave's opening.

I shot Kost a quick glance. Shoulders tense, he only offered a tight grimace. Surprise visitor, then.

I kept my voice low so as not to disturb the dark magic of the cavern. "I expected a woman."

"She has other matters to attend to." The man glanced back and forth between us. With his cloak pulled tight, his features remained hidden. "Where's the Charmer?" Leather fingerless gloves hid his hands and wrists, and he folded his arms across his chest.

"There was an unexpected mishap. I take full responsibility for the delay, and I'm now handling this job personally." Beside me, Kost flinched.

The man tilted his head, and the cloak moved enough to reveal a close-cut beard. "I see. And you are?"

I slipped my hands into the pockets of my trousers. "Noc. I'm the guild master." A haze of shimmering magic brewed at the opening of the cave in response to my claim, and my pulse thundered in my ears. I did my best to ignore the silky murmur of power.

Seemingly unaffected, a nasty smile crept over the man's lips. "Interesting. May I ask what happened? Your colleague seemed capable enough."

Kost fisted his hands. Taking a small step forward, I drew the client's attention to me. "Nothing of note. Any additional details you'd like to share about the job?"

"Other than the fact that Leena Edenfrell is extremely danger-ous? It sounds like you've already discovered that."

I narrowed my eyes. "Indeed."

"You're aware of the conditions?"

"Yes. You'll have your bones within six hours of death. It won't be an issue. And the bits?"

A sneer dominated the lower half of his shadowed face. "Ten thousand bits. Enough to fuel your quaint little manor for a few solid years."

I gave him a tight nod. "Then we're good."

He flexed his hand, and an invisible door groaned open. A beast unlike any I'd ever glimpsed appeared at the man's feet. With a head the size of a boulder, its lizard-like mouth stretched open, and a formidable air current sucked at the space around it.

A swirling white portal flickering with electricity sparked in its unhinged jaw.

With a harsh laugh, the man reached down and stroked the beast's scales. "We'll be 'good' when you deliver on your promise. Just remember that while Leena Edenfrell is formidable, your client is far, far more powerful. The last thing you'd want is for something to happen." He angled his chin toward Kost. "Again."

With that, he passed through the sparking portal and winked out of existence, along with his beast.

Anger swelled in a rush of heat, and the calm facade I'd maintained exploded with his absence. I paced in front of Kost and gripped the back of my neck. Two threats against my people in one day. Both by Charmers. Just what were we really dealing with?

"Let's go." I turned on my heels and welcomed the odd relief that came with the swirling onyx vines and knotted trees of the Kitska Forest. We'd have to put distance between ourselves and the dark magic of the cavern before we could let the shadows carry us home. "We need to work. Fast."

Kost matched my stride and side-eyed me. "Something's wrong."

"Of course something is wrong." Twigs snapped beneath my feet as we walked, and I focused on the sound to stay calm. "Our client is brazen. Our mark is brave. We've never had so much inter-action before. It's unsettling to say the least."

"Our mark is brave?" Kost pursed his lips. "Bravery means nothing in our line of work. You know that. We've killed honorable people for less." He pushed aside a branch laden with pinesco pods and stepped through, holding the leaves back until I passed. "Tell me what's really bothering you. Is it the curse? I'm fine. I can assure you, I—"

"I have it under control."

Competing emotions flickered across his expression. Relief. Hurt. Something I couldn't place. For a moment, I set aside my usual frozen detachment and placed a hand on his shoulder, letting the smallest measure of my true feelings show through. "I'm glad you're unharmed. It would have killed me to lose you."

And I swear I saw it at my words. The first signs of my curse. The subtle darkening bags beneath his eyes. Skin chafing and faintly cracking around his lips. Next would come the cough flecked with blood. Then a fever. Then death. I'd seen all those symptoms play out before in my past. Twice with people I loved romantically. Countless more times with those I loved platonically.

Once with Kost, when I let the true depth of my brotherly affection show. He'd nearly died, saved only by my ability to wrestle my emotions into an icy cage and detach from my feelings. It'd taken weeks for him to recover, and the callousness I'd been forced to exude still hung heavy over my head. But it'd saved his life.

Chills skittered down my neck, and I removed my hand. Kost tracked the progression with keen eyes. Only he and Talmage knew of the curse and what it meant: anything beyond the most tenuous bonds always ended in death.

"Let's get back. We need to prepare for our journey." Shadows began to fester beneath us as the vortex to Cruor opened. I could keep up this distance from my brethren for the rest of my life if need be. Anything to keep them safe. But there was a glimmer of hope now.

One that bloomed from a bestiary belonging to a curious Charmer waiting for us back home.

———◆———

The moment our feet crossed Cruor's threshold, my pulse returned to acceptable levels. My foul mood, however, did not dissipate. The quiet halls whispered of Leena, of her presence in my home, and assassins stuck to themselves to avoid my fried nerves.

Sinking into the armchair, I stared at Talmage's portrait. There were still matters left unattended. "Who stays to run things while I'm gone?"

Kost's voice wavered. "As your second, I understand it's my duty to rule in your stead. But we don't know what she's capable of." He ghosted his fingertips along his forearms where her beast had pinned him.

"Not to mention our clients." Bile soured my tongue. "You're coming. So are Calem and Ozias."

With a tight nod, he settled back into his usual calculated demeanor. He retrieved a white cloth from his breast pocket, removed his glasses, and began to polish his lenses. "As much as I hate to admit it, that leaves Darrien in charge."

Pinching the bridge of my nose, I groaned. "I was afraid you'd say that."

"If it's necessary, I'll stay—"

"No. Like you said, we don't know what kind of arsenal she has. I'd rather have my strongest with me. Darrien will be fine. If not, I'll kill him." Shrugging, I pushed out of the chair. My legs itched to move. To act. To do something, anything, to get this deal over with. Somewhere in my halls, Leena was settling in for the night. In my own damn house. "She was surprisingly bold."

Kost cleared his throat. "There you go again. Bold, brave... Since I wasn't there for the bargaining, is there anything else I need to be aware of?"

It'd been fifty years since I'd been raised. Thirty since he'd watched me pine over someone I couldn't have. Twenty since the curse had nearly claimed him. He was perpetually poised for me to cave again, no matter how absurd the notion was. "What are you really asking?"

His expression remained indifferent. "I simply wish to be prepared. I shall begin travel arrangements, then. We'll have to take the train to Eastrend and find mounts there."

"Perfect." I started to pace.

"Noc." Kost's tone rooted my feet in place. "Be careful. If something happens while we're gone, I won't be able to contact a mage quickly enough." With a pointed stare, he targeted the ring on my finger. Silver scales layered upon a heavy band surrounded an intense emerald in the center. The key to my secret and the life I had before I died.

"Understood." Fingering a strand of black hair that should've been white, I let out a tight sigh. Leave it to him to unearth something better left buried without even mentioning the topic. "Go. Get everything together so we can leave the day after tomorrow."

He was gone in a flurry of darkness before I could finish my sentence.

The fire crackling in the hearth seemed to laugh. A job in my home. A job that would take me away from Cruor and leave Darrien in charge. A job with clients more sinister than the job itself.

But also...a chance to be free.

My moment of solitude was shattered by the sudden swell of shadows slinking across the floor. They pooled at the foot of the stairs and burst outward in a flood of dark mist. Darrien appeared, steel-toed boots clacking against tile as he strode toward me. Smoky tendrils lingered in the curls of his shoulder-length brown hair, and a smile pulled at the edges of his lips.

"So I couldn't help but overhear—"

I repressed a snarl. "Sure you could have. Yes, you'll be in charge while I'm escorting the Charmer. It's only temporary. Don't get any ideas."

His grin deepened. "Of course not. Talmage named you our leader, and so out of respect for him, I will obey." Amber eyes sparked, and he folded his arms across his chest. Darrien was the oldest member of Cruor. Everyone, myself included, had expected him to inherit the guild when Talmage passed. He had been loyal. Efficient. A friend, even, to Talmage. But when I was named, something snapped. Something I couldn't prove or pinpoint, but I knew he considered our late guild master's last ruling a betrayal. He knew nothing of my past or how I came to be, but if he did, he'd use it against me to divide our ranks. To take what he thought was his.

Possessiveness, heated and angry, simmered beneath layers of iron control. Cruor was *mine*. I couldn't deny Darrien his place here. He'd never overtly stepped out of line, but calculated indifference was almost as dangerous as a formulated attack.

Darrien shifted under the weight of my stare. "Any specific tasks I need to be aware of?"

"You'll need to assign any jobs that come in. Make sure you review them carefully."

One of his brows arched. "Wouldn't want a repeat of this mishap, now would we?"

"Careful. I'm not in the mood for insubordination."

Darrien raised his hands in mock apology. "Right. Though I wonder what Talmage would think of this. A job in his home. I bet the very notion has him seething in his grave."

I ignored his baiting. "That will be all, Darrien."

He eyed me for a moment, then chuckled. "Understood."

I turned away from him and stalked to the kitchen to pour myself a stiff drink. He wasn't entirely wrong. A job in my own damn house. Darrien at the helm. But a cure... There was a possibility. An avenue I'd yet to test. I just had to see if there was a beast that could do it, and then I'd take care of the woman and go back to leading my people.

One job, two paychecks, no harm done. That was a deal I'd die for.

FOUR

LEENA

Standing in the center of my temporary room, I'd never felt so claustrophobic. Not because it was small, but because Ozias's frame squandered all light from the outside hallway, blocking my exit. He leaned against the doorframe, and the wood gave a soft creak. How he ever survived as an assassin baffled me.

"Thanks." Flush with the wall was a monstrous bed draped in down blankets. Heat spread from a small, coiled structure in the corner of the room. A low orange light simmered around it. A rycrim heater. Yet another thing I'd longed for during the cold nights at Midnight Jester. I shrugged off my jacket. "I'll need to stop by my place tomorrow to grab my things."

"That won't be necessary." Ozias folded his arms. "Kost will account for everything."

I glanced at the oil-rubbed oak dresser to my left. "Clothes?"

"Kost will handle it." Amused brown eyes bounced from my face to the armoire and back again.

"That seems unnecessary."

Ozias shrugged. "Do you need anything specific?"

I pulled out the gray stool from the vanity and sank onto it. Slowly, I began the arduous task of unlacing my boots. "Toiletries?"

Pushing away from the doorframe, Ozias sauntered over to a door tucked along the far wall. "You share this bathroom with another woman." He pushed it open and candles lit, muted yellow bouncing off mirrors and silver furnishings. He nodded toward a similar door on the far side of the restroom. "Just be sure to lock both handles when you're in there. Unless you're in the mood for some unexpected company."

"Noted." Standing, I pushed both boots to the edge of the bed. A soft moan escaped my lips as I curled and uncurled my toes.

Humor danced across Ozias's broad features. His skin was a flawless, rich brown with cool undertones, and he had a dazzling smile. "Long day?"

"Just breaking in new boots."

He kicked one foot out, displaying tan work boots with brass eyelets and faded laces. "I buy a bunch at once so I can break them in at the same time."

My voice fell flat. "Not all of us get the luxury of multiple pairs of shoes."

His smile disappeared, and my mind spun. His regret was instant and surprisingly human. He placed his foot back on the floor. "Sorry. Anything else you need?"

My brows drew together. Cruor was full of famed assassins. Their power over the shadows gave them the reputation of being legendary agents of death—nothing more, nothing less. The fact that there were people beneath that darkness...

"No, thanks." I didn't want to spend more time than necessary around these potential walking contradictions.

"All right, then. If you change your mind, just poke your head out in the hall and call for me." With a warm smile, he opened the door. "Someone will find me."

It was an effort to keep my shock veiled. Maybe my Charmer's lure was stronger than I'd anticipated. I'd assumed their own dark magic would make it harder for these assassins to feel at ease around me, and yet Ozias hadn't hesitated to ensure I was comfortable. My entire existence was dependent on my ability to charm things. And while taming a human was impossible, our bodies still produced an undetectable aroma that put other living things at ease.

Eyeing Ozias's lax shoulders, I wondered just how much of his nonchalance was my magic, his demeanor, or worse—him lulling me into a false sense of security. Stiffly, I gave him a nod. "Night."

"Night." He closed the door behind him, and I let out a heavy breath.

With Ozias gone, my gaze immediately targeted the window overlooking the back lawns of Cruor. It was only a two-story drop, and the manor was crawling in thick vines. Shimmying down to grounds below under the cover of night was possible. Crossing the room, I flung open the window and was met with a breath of cool air. The moon was obscured behind thick clouds, and hope welled inside me. Even more chance for me to escape sight unseen.

My hands went to the thick, ivy-green vines growing over the masonry. With a tug, I tested their sturdiness. A few weaker tendrils dislodged, but for the most part, it held true. It'd have to do.

A warning howl bellowed from somewhere in the Kitska Forest, and my gaze shot out to the dark tree line. But instead of a monster lingering in the overgrowth, I was met with handful of human-like figures all swathed in shadows. They watched me, bodies unmoving but their heads definitively riveted to my open window.

A curse slipped through my lips. So much for escape. Taking an exaggerated breath, as if I were merely opening the window to enjoy the fresh air, I lingered for a moment before closing it. And fastening the lock.

I'm not getting out of here. Pressing my forehead to the cold panes, I screwed my eyes shut. Even if I did somehow make it past the sentries, I'd be running right into the Kitska Forest. I *could* try to navigate the swirling maze of vines and trees, but I didn't have the faintest idea how we'd arrived. The vortex had winnowed us here in no time at all, but we could've traveled miles from Midnight Jester. Maybe more.

Wandering alone in the forest at night, low on power from Iky's drain and without food, was not a smart decision. Not with monsters hiding in the cursed wood waiting for easy prey like me. Panic clawed at my throat. Assassins, Charmers... Everywhere I turned spelled danger.

If Wynn was coming after me now with the power of the Council at his back, the only thing I could do to survive would be to clear my name. Even if I escaped Cruor's bounty, another would be placed. But owning a Myad would help. The legendary—and impossibly rare—creature's trust alone would give them pause. All I needed was one moment, one chance to tell my side of things.

But first, I had to get out. I had to make myself invaluable to these assassins and protect my head at all costs.

Angry tears pricked the back of my eyes, threatening to spill over. *If only I were home.* No. I shook my head, sinking to the floor and firmly pressing my back against the wall. My people cast me out long ago. I couldn't think like that anymore. Relying on them did nothing for me in the past, and it'd do nothing for me now. I would get through this on my own.

Splaying out my right hand, I channeled power into my emblem and watched as the rosewood markings bled to life. I sifted through the list of available beasts in my mind and settled on Poof, an E-Class creature the size of a child's kick ball. When the light receded, Poof appeared at my feet, circular pink eyes blinking up at me.

I shouldn't have called another beast. I should have held on to some of my power reserves in case danger reared its head in the form of an assassin. Law of hospitality in place or not, I didn't trust them. I was alone in a den of murderers, each one appraising my body and abilities as if I were a weapon and not a person. I needed a little comfort.

"C'mere, you." Poof was a Groober. A round, fluffy beast with white fur softer than rabbit's fluff. With stubby arms and legs, he wasn't much of a fighter, but he was a mean cuddler, and his scent glands emitted a potent mixture of lavender and valerian to aid with sleep.

Wrapped in my arms, he nestled in the crook of my shoulder, purring into my neck. Fat tears broke over my lids. "You're just as special as any A-Class beast." Kneading the space between his ears, I worked my fingers over his fur. Oils perfumed the air.

I never imagined a life where I'd sell the very things that made my existence bearable. And yet here I was, doing exactly that. All because I'd trusted Wynn. So much devotion and love, and for what? To become a scapegoat? My exile was his fault, and yet I had been the one to lose everything.

And now Noc.

A chill raked over my skin. He was exactly the wrong kind of person to be around. Deadly and intriguing and too damn cunning. The type of person who could coax secrets from lips that had long since been sealed.

But not me. Not ever. If I could survive Noc, use him to get what I needed—blood from him or one of his brethren, just like he was using me to get his beasts—I might have a chance to clear my name.

I might still have a future.

FIVE

LEENA

Even with the help of Poof, sleep was fitful. Dreams toed the line between memories and reality as I once again walked the familiar paths of Hireath. My home. Charmers and beasts roaming through the open meadows. Children's wild laughter floating down from the trees as they raced across bridges. The brilliant indigo night dotted with stars and a hand wrapped in mine.

Wynn.

But his grip turned angry, and suddenly I was cast out and running, alone and trapped in the Kitska Forest with monsters nipping at my heels.

And then I ran straight into a pair of open arms that were as cold as ice. Caged in a frigid prison, I should have been scared. But that unnerving chill exploded outward in a sheet of snow, and the Kitska Forest was gone. Fears destroyed. Until I looked up and found sharp black eyes as distant as they were menacing. Noc took one look at me trapped in his embrace and smiled, canines elongating to deadly fangs. Shadows devoured us whole. I lost sight of him and tumbled into an endless pit, flailing until I'd moved so much in my sleep that I rolled right out of bed and crashed onto the floor.

Early-morning light sliced through the space where curtains

met, and I groaned. Cool tile bit through my clothing and sent a
shiver down my back. I pushed myself up and rubbed the back of
my head, wincing.

At least I was alive. I'd half expected to wake up with a knife
to my throat. *Something.* Anything that would've indicated I'd taken
up with a guild full of murderers. But aside from the self-induced
lump forming at the base of my skull, I was unharmed. Maybe they
honored their promises. I could only hope they'd do the same when
it came to my bounty.

I made my way to the bathroom to relieve myself and bathe,
rushing through the process so as not to leave myself vulnerable for
too long. When I emerged with a fluffy towel wrapped tight around
my body, I came to an abrupt stop at the foot of my bed.

Clothes? A coffee-brown corset with thick straps and a buckle
was laid out beside a pair of tan breeches. My nerves prickled. I was
sure I'd been in the bathroom for less than ten minutes, and I hadn't
heard a sound from my room. A scrap of parchment was neatly
folded on top of the pants. I opened it to find a single line written
with loopy flourishes:

These should fit.

Part of me wanted the clothing to miss the mark. Too snug on
the hips or too loose around my waist. Proof that these assassins
couldn't care less about my comfort. Anything that made sense and
matched the whispered warnings about their kind.

The outfit fit like a second skin.

Mumbling, I shoved my feet back into my boots and ignored
their angry protests. I paused at the door, hand poised just above
the knob. Where exactly was I going? What could I even do? Escape
wasn't an option. If they could assess when it was safe to enter my

room without me knowing, then they most certainly had eyes and ears pinned on me at all times. Not like escape was really *valid* anyway. I needed the bounty gone. I had to work with them.

I pulled the door open and stepped out into the quiet hall. The long corridor was marked with rows of doors, some with light slipping beneath the cracks and others entirely dark. A few assassins walked together toward the stairs. They paused when they saw me, easy smiles strained and words caught in their throats. After a moment, they nodded a hello and kept moving, voices lower than before.

Where was the threat? The promise of death? Sure, Noc had said I'd be safe in his home, but was that really all it took? Scratching my head, I followed their path downstairs to find the foyer crowded with life. Four members of the infamously deadly Cruor were huddled around a low coffee table with a tiered game board stretched out before them. Ebony, ivory, ruby, and emerald pieces of varying sizes were stationed across the levels. My brows inched together. A game from Wilheim? I didn't recognize it. One man knocked over a tower with a glittering ruby knight and laughed as the person next to him scowled.

A few more assassins loitered near the mantel, talking with animated hands and wide grins. Another sat alone at a writing desk, scratching words on yellowing parchment with a quill.

It was all so...normal. One of the gamers knocked out another tower, and the howl of laughter mingled with the skittering of glass across tile. The tower tumbled against my boot, and I bent down to retrieve it.

"Sorry about that," one of them called. Earnest eyes searched my face with obvious curiosity. "Do you mind?" He stretched out his hand.

"Oh. Sure." I walked toward him and dropped the game piece into his waiting palm.

"Want to play?"

"Um." I glanced around at the four of them. Not an ounce of trepidation was visible on their faces. Blatant interest, maybe, but that was common when people met a Charmer. We never left the safety of our hidden city. I studied the game board for a moment, but then my stomach struck with an audible growl. "Maybe after I eat."

Their answering smiles were genuine, and the man nodded. "Sure thing."

I edged toward the hall leading to the kitchen just as another piece hit the floor. Rumbling laughter followed me out. When I passed through the open archway, I stilled at the sight of a curvy woman leaning over a cookbook. Her canvas apron was dotted with pastel flowers, and various utensils stuck out from her deep pockets. A stray bit of flour dusted the tip of her nose. Freckles covered her face, and she reached up to adjust a bright-red bandanna that held back a mess of springy espresso-colored hair.

One of those strange living shadows drifted from her frame and slipped toward me, halting just before my chest. Glancing up from her book, she followed its path and met my gaze with a warm smile. "Hello. I'm Naomi. You must be Leena. Are you hungry?"

I resisted the urge to touch the shadow. "Yes. I can just get a piece of fruit or something."

"Tsk. Nonsense." She straightened, and the shadow dissipated. "What do you like? I'll whip you up something."

"Like?"

"Yes. Like." She placed her hands on her hips. "Go on. Spit it out."

"Eggs?"

She snorted. "You don't sound sure. What about an omelet? Do you like spinach? I have some fresh greens that are just to die for. And there's always bacon. We can dress it up with some scallions and cheese, and it will be scrumptious."

"You don't have to do that." I glanced past her to the mountain of dishes lingering in a sink big enough to call itself a bath. Clearly, she'd served others and had enough tasks on her hands.

"I'll happily cook if it reduces the number of bounties I'm assigned. Which it does." She yanked open the icebox and started extracting ingredients. Closing it with her hip, she beamed at me. "Besides, I like it. Now, grab yourself some coffee and have a seat in the dining room. I'll bring it out when it's ready."

When I opened my mouth to argue, she wielded a whisk with the precision of a weapon, and I backed off. She stared at me with firm but kind golden-brown eyes, nodding once to a silver kettle steaming over a low-burning stove. I grabbed one of the ceramic mugs and poured some coffee, retreating in the direction she'd indicated before she could chastise me further.

Cup in hand, I followed the sound of voices and silverware scraping against plates until I reached the dining room.

Fog-colored paneled walls were laden with oil paintings in stark white frames, and an impossibly long tarnished platinum table was centered beneath a row of chandeliers. High-back chairs with the same finish and steel-blue cushions lined the sides and ends. The three closest seats were occupied; two by assassins I recognized and a third I couldn't place.

Ozias grinned. "Stomach calling? Come on. Have a seat." He patted the open chair beside him.

"Thanks." I sat down and took a sip of my coffee—then nearly died of pleasure as the rich undertones of caramel teased the back of my tongue.

"This is Emelia and her twin brother, Iov." Ozias gestured to the pair sitting across from us.

Emelia I recognized from the night before, and even if Ozias hadn't mentioned her relation to Iov, it would've been obvious. They offered the same, uncertain smile that hinted at dimples and brought a warm glow to their sepia-toned skin. Off-black hair framed their oval faces, and they shared similar widows' peaks and full lips.

"Hi."

"Hello." Emelia's plate was empty, but she twirled her fork across it anyway as she studied me. "So you're a Charmer?"

"Yup." I took another sip of coffee. "And you're an assassin."

Iov's grin turned genuine. "Quick, aren't you?"

"Only because of this." I lifted my mug. "Catch me before coffee, and I'm more or less insensate."

Emelia arched a brow. "You shouldn't share information like that with us."

Ozias rolled his eyes. "C'mon. Enough of that."

"What?" Her gaze slanted to Ozias. "It's true. Our whole job is predicated on collecting information that makes it easy to eliminate our marks." Her lips pressed into a thin line. "Besides, you didn't see what her beast did to Kost."

Iov leaned into his chair and cradled the back of his head with his hands. "Ah, Kost was fine. He could've taken her." A flash of humor sparked through his eyes.

My grip tightened on my coffee. "That so?"

Before he could answer, the chef entered the dining room with a plate in one hand and a carving knife in the other—the tip of which was pointed at Calem's back. He sauntered forward with a lazy sway to his step.

Naomi glowered at him. "If you try to take someone else's food again, I'll cut you."

Calem plopped into the chair next to me with his own steaming mug. "Yeah, yeah."

Turning a sweet smile on me, she set the omelet down and handed off silverware. "Here you go. Enjoy." With one last parting glare at Calem, she sashayed out of the room.

"It just looked so good." He draped an arm over the back of my chair and sipped his drink. "Coffee is enough for me, though. What'd I miss? More riveting conversation from the dynamic duo?"

Emelia's fingers twitched. "I was just saying how it doesn't make sense that Noc is letting a Charmer wander freely through our home."

This is what I'd expected. Some kind of tension or concern or thinly veiled threat. Had the roles been reversed, I would have acted the same. I dropped my gaze and speared a forkful of omelet.

And then I paused, half-chewed food coming to a standstill in my mouth. I'd almost forgotten where I was. What job they'd been hired to do. I hadn't watched Naomi prepare the meal, and with Emelia being rightfully hostile, it reminded me that she likely wasn't the only one opposed to my presence. Maybe Noc had thought twice about our agreement and decided he was better off without the hassle. Delivered secret orders to Naomi to do away with me when I least expected it. I should've called Tila from the beast realm to test my food.

"And I was saying it didn't matter because Kost was—is—fine." Iov frowned at his sister, ignoring my sudden stillness.

"Always the same with you two," Calem muttered before glancing my direction. "Something the matter?"

"No," I said, speaking around unswallowed food. The savory burst of flavor lingered on my tongue, taunting me.

Calem narrowed his eyes. Dropped his gaze to my steaming food and then dragged it back up to my lips. With a chuckle, he shook his head. "We wouldn't poison you. Seems counterproductive to our deal, doesn't it?"

"Yeah." With all their eyes on me, I finally swallowed. Death averted. Once I forked another bite, Ozias turned his scowl back to the twins.

"See what you've done?" He leaned forward, bracing his forearms on the table. "Now she's going to second guess everything. She's a guest in our home. Treat her like one." It took me two tries to swallow more of the omelet. Not for fear this time, but because this assassin had placed my comfort above his comrades' concerns. "If you're done eating, clear your plates so Naomi doesn't come after you with a knife, too. Then, be outside in five to help with the new recruits."

Iov side-eyed his sister. "I had today off before this."

"Shut it." She pushed away from the table and grabbed her plate without so much as a backward glance. Iov did the same, filing out behind her with a wave over his shoulder.

Ozias shook his head and reached for his mug. "Those two never quit."

"And you're surprised by that?" Calem set his mug down.

"Nope. We'll run them through some extra drills to tire them out. Maybe then they'll be too exhausted to argue."

"Don't punish them on my account," I said. "If it were me, I might have acted the same." After forking the last bite of omelet into my mouth, I set my silverware across my plate and relished the feel of a good meal. How long had it been since I'd eaten something that wasn't questionable at best? Dez meant well, but he was forced to scavenge for bits like the rest of us. It didn't always make for the freshest of ingredients.

Ozias stood and reached for my plate, stacking it on top of his. "Practice doesn't hurt anybody. We need to prepare them for jobs. You never know when we might get another bounty like you." His voice was light, if not a little teasing.

I shrugged. "I'm not one to go down without a fight."

"That's the spirit. Want to join us for training? I promise I'll go easy on you." Calem's grin was pure mischief.

I hid a snort by draining the last of my coffee. He certainly had an allure about him, thanks in part to his bronzed skin, solid build, and long, golden-blond hair. But I wasn't here for fun. I had a job to do and beasts to tame.

"I'll pass."

Calem shrugged. "Your loss. I would've made it worth your while."

Ozias smacked the back of his comrade's head. "You're relentless. C'mon, Leena. Give him a chance to lick his wounds before he takes it out on the recruits."

Calem muttered something about "licking" beneath his breath and leaped out of the way before Ozias could slap at him again. He fled the room, his laugh still rattling through the air even after he disappeared. Ozias and I tracked back through the kitchen, where he handed off our plates to Naomi, and then he led us out into the foyer. The assassins from earlier had dispersed, leaving behind no trace of their earlier activities.

Coming to a halt, Ozias ran a thick hand over his shorn hair. "I know Calem was teasing and all, but you're welcome to join us. It might be a tad boring, though. We're working with newly raised assassins, and the training is more a mental grappling of sorts. Shadows don't obey in a day."

"What about Emelia and Iov?"

His grin kicked up on one side. "I've got a few ideas."

I shook my head to hide a smile. It was too easy to feel relaxed around him. A ploy? Were they trying to make me let down my guard? Or perhaps Ozias was particularly susceptible to my Charmer's lure? It was possible, and yet... "I'm not sure my presence would help. I'll find another way to keep myself busy."

"There's a library down that hall." Ozias jutted his thumb over his shoulder. "If you're into that sort of thing. Otherwise, feel free to roam." Then, after a beat, he added, "Just be sure to stay on the grounds. You're safe unless you try to leave."

My stomach solidified into cement, and I managed a nod. "Got it."

His grin returned, and he offered me a parting wave before backstepping into a flurry of shadows. Tendrils devoured his frame, and he was gone. Just like that. The double doors leading to Cruor's front lawn taunted me in my peripheral vision, but I stalked away in the direction of the library. I couldn't leave even if I wanted to. I needed something from these assassins, just like they needed something from me. I needed leverage without it actually being leverage, otherwise the blood wouldn't be considered "free."

And therein lay the problem.

Chewing on the inside of my cheek, I opened the doors to the library and forgot to breathe.

And I thought the dining room was large.

Vaulted ceilings with curved walnut rafters held wrought-iron chandeliers fashioned like globes, and buckets of light spilled from countless windows. A maze of shelves packed to the brim with books was laid out before me. Ladders of the same dark varnish leaned against the frames, perched on wheels for easy movement.

For the most part, it was quiet. A handful of assassins were parked in overstuffed armchairs, their noses lost in thick books. Another sat at a large oak table and was scribbling on parchment with several tomes spread open before him. My gaze bounced from head to head until I spied a bay window at the far end of the library. One with plush cushions and a view overlooking the yard behind Cruor.

It was occupied by a dark-haired man I almost didn't recognize.

Back propped against a stack of pillows and legs stretched out before him, Noc lounged with a sizable book in his lap. One hand cradled the worn binding while long fingers toyed with a page. His lips occasionally formed silent words, as if he were reading the text to himself. At one point he frowned. Turned the page. Smiled.

He was entirely engrossed. How could he be so different from our initial meeting in the foyer? Here he seemed warm, intriguing, approachable. As familiar as Ozias and Calem seemed to be. Was that what it meant to be an assassin? Able to flip a switch with a moment's notice? Making a wide circle so as not to draw his attention, I moved closer.

Noc continued to read, his gaze visibly tracking the lines of the story.

Late-morning sun softened the harsh edges of his expression. It was so jarring to see him like this. Relaxed. At ease. A complete and total juxtaposition to the assassin who'd nearly killed me the day before. This man was almost...human.

I inched closer, trying to catch a snippet of text. I wanted to know what he was reading. What story made his lips shape words of their own accord. What pulled him in and gave him such peace. If I could glean that information, it'd be that much easier for me to get on his good side. And being on his good side would not only further guarantee my safety, but also get me that much closer to acquiring what I needed to tame the Myad.

A snaking thread of frost licked my exposed arm. I glanced down, startled, to find a shadow curling around my bicep.

"You're not very quiet."

Noc didn't look up from his book. I expected his expression to harden, but the only recognition I got was a slight tremor in his jaw. He turned another page.

I swallowed. "Guess not."

Finally, Noc glanced up. Obsidian eyes burrowed into me, and with a minute flick of his finger, the shadow dispersed.

"Do you need something?"

"Just passing the time. We could've been on our way to Ortega Key by now."

He closed the book. "Kost is gathering supplies. We'll leave first thing tomorrow." He made a move to stand, and I found myself searching for a reason to keep him seated. My gaze slid to the bold silver title printed across the navy cover of the book.

"*A Chalice of Lies?*"

His feet touched the floor, but he didn't stand. "You've read it?"

"No."

He looked disappointed. "Pity. It's good."

"What's it about?"

A glimmer of warmth bloomed in those dark eyes. "A young man who finds a box of letters left for him by his late father. They contain information about the reigning queen. Some are true, some aren't. It keeps me guessing. The best stories do that. Make you search for the answer. Leave little clues."

"Kind of like a puzzle."

"Exactly like a puzzle." His expression lightened a fraction.

This I could work with. Of course he'd been hard to read the day before. After all, I'd barged into his home making threats and demands. I'd hurt Kost. It wasn't exactly the most welcoming of introductions. Noc's icy demeanor made sense when put into context. Maybe I'd misread him. All things considered, I wouldn't trust me, either.

Trust was exactly what I needed to spark, at least on his end, if I ever had a chance of surviving.

Noc tilted his head and pressed the book flat between his palms. "Something else on your mind?"

"I'm just interested." I rotated the ring around my finger.

His eyes tracked the motion before he returned his gaze to my face. "In the book? Or something else?"

I needed to keep him talking if I wanted to understand him, and I needed to understand him if I wanted to survive. "A bit of both. The story sounds interesting, but I'm more curious about what you want."

His interest in books was obvious, and I'd seen the way he'd looked at my bestiary before. Perhaps I had just the thing to keep him intrigued. "What kind of beast are you interested in?"

Noc frowned. "I'm not overly versed in the beast world, but I'll be sure to study up on our way to Ortega Key."

Tipping my head back to the ceiling, I let out a low hum. "I can show you my bestiary. It's far from complete, but that will give you a good idea of what you'll have access to."

Eyes dipping to the locket dangling below my collarbone, he leaned a fraction closer, the full overwhelming weight of his attention focused on me. "That would be fascinating to read."

Heat followed his intent stare—and more nerves than I'd anticipated. I could still feel the burn of his grip on my neck, and yet the adrenaline I felt had nothing to do with his ability to end my life and everything to do with the way his intensely curious gaze unraveled my resolve.

Maybe getting close wasn't such a good idea after all. This felt remarkably like playing with fire.

"How does it work?"

I grazed the chain of my necklace and swallowed, unsettled. Maybe I'd made a mistake by thinking Noc would be as easy as Ozias or Calem. Something about his focused attention had fight or flight thrumming through my veins. "Only a Charmer can remove it or open it. You'd have to have one nearby to turn the pages, too."

"Good thing I have one nearby."

I grappled with the urge to turn on my heel and run...and the more confounding impulse to open the book for him right there. But if I played all my cards too quickly, maybe he'd find another way to get what he wanted. The black market had its options. "I'm not about to just hand it off. It's not a quick read, and there's a lot of information to digest."

"I don't mind taking my time." His mouth lifted at the corner. "If you don't feel comfortable removing it, I can always read over your shoulder."

Heat flushed my skin, and his attentive stare locked on my cheeks. And then he blinked, and the curious, almost warm man before me was gone. Lost. Noc leaned back, a cool expression carefully masking any emotion.

Before I could probe the sudden change, a plume of black blossomed beside me, and Kost emerged with several bulging bags tied tight with string. He glanced back and forth between us, jaw set and green glare damning. He gave me one quick appraisal before turning so I was just shy of his line of sight. Dismissed.

Irritation spiked my pulse. "Hello."

He didn't dignify me with a response. "Noc, we have some things to discuss. Immediately."

Standing, Noc set the book on the window bench. "All right. I'll be in my study. No need to bring the supplies; I trust you got what we needed."

"Of course." Kost's lips thinned. "I hope I'm not...interrupting."

"Not at all."

"Good." Shadows swallowed Kost before I could get a word in, and he was gone. Noc angled his chin in my direction, his face once again devoid of warmth.

Then, he slipped his hand into the back pocket of his trousers and extracted a folded piece of parchment. "Here."

"What's this?" I took it from him, and my fingers just ghosted his.

"Your written agreement." He pulled his hand back and shoved it in his pocket. "Keep to yourself today. The rest of us have work to do."

I expected him to disappear like Kost had, but instead he

turned and stalked down an aisle of books, veering out of sight as the shelves guided him through the maze. His rigid back was just as affronting as his words, and I ground my teeth in annoyance.

At least I had my agreement. I unfolded it and scanned the meager lines:

> *This contract serves as an agreement between Cruor guild master Noc and Leena Edenfrell, Charmer. Noc hereby agrees that none of his assassins will fulfill the bounty associated with Leena's life, so long as she provides four B-Class beasts to him after traveling to Ortega Key.*
>
> *Signed,*
>
> *Noc*

My eyes narrowed. Thin on the details, but a contract nonetheless. At the very least, it would keep me safe from other assassins within Cruor, so long as I did my job. Which I planned to, because I sincerely hoped I'd never see them again. These murderers were cruel and intelligent and capable of horrendous things, and yet...

My gaze flickered to the man huddled over parchment and books. To the couple reclining in armchairs. And I thought of Ozias's gentle smile. Calem's easy banter. Their actions were so human.

But even humans could do terrible things. And that was a lesson I would brand into my brain if I had to. I needed to make it out of this alive—and with some blood for the Myad taming.

SIX

OZIAS

Training new recruits was like babysitting kittens. And as much as I loved the fluffy little furballs, there was no telling when they'd turn on the crazy and come at you claws and fangs first. The same could be said for newly raised assassins and their shadows. One moment they had control, and the next…

"Watch it!" I ducked my head just as a poorly formed shadow blade went shooting through the air. Wrapped up in some more advanced exercises with Emelia and Iov, Calem hadn't heard my warning. The blade sliced his cheek before dissipating, and a thin, red line of blood welled to the surface of his skin. He whipped his head around, threatening murder with his glare, and the new recruit responsible for the errant blade shrunk behind me.

"Don't mind him," I said, shifting a little to hide the newbie from Calem's unnecessary glare. "He'll heal in a matter of minutes. Plus, he's more bark than bite."

Calem offered me an obscene gesture before turning back to the twins. They both took a quick step back, obviously aware that they'd now be the recipients of Calem's misplaced frustration. Sturdy, ink-black blades formed in their hands, and they took a defensive stance with their shoulders pressed together.

"Sorry," the young woman whispered, and I turned to face her. She had smooth beige skin and round amber eyes. Her dark hair fell to her shoulders in subtle waves and curled upward to her chin. She was dressed like the rest of the recruits in a loose, sleeveless white tunic and fitted breeches with knee-high boots.

"Don't sweat it." I looked over her head to check on the groups I'd sectioned out. We didn't raise new members of Cruor often, but training was a constant activity. I'd grouped together some of the more senior members with our new brethren, and they were running through simple drills of summoning shadows, solidifying them into blades, and then tossing them at scarecrow targets along the forest line.

But for Zara... I smiled down at her. She was having a tough time. "Let's try that again. But this time, hold onto the blade once you form it."

She nodded, and her brows angled sharply downward as she focused her gaze on her open palms. Muscles quivered and tensed along her forearms. Even her fingers twitched. After a moment, a bead of sweat formed along her right temple and threatened to race down her cheek.

"You're trying too hard." I placed my hands on hers, dwarfing them entirely.

"But you told me to focus." She yanked them away with a huff and folded her arms across her chest.

I couldn't fight the grin that spread across my lips. I'd been equally frustrated during my early training sessions with Kost. Of course, he'd never been the patient type, which only made things worse. The moment I'd gotten a grasp of what I was doing, I'd gone to Talmage and asked to train new recruits in his stead. Neither had objected.

"You're right," I said, pushing away the memory of a red-faced Kost as he repeated the same useless instructions over and over again, as if they were the easiest notion in the world. "You have to focus so you don't accidentally take someone's head off, but you also have to relax."

"Because that's not contradictory," she mumbled.

I placed a gentle hand on her shoulder and turned her toward the small groups of assassins running through their drills. "Tell me what you see."

She squinted, then shrugged. "A bunch of people much further along in this process than I am."

A deep laugh rolled through my chest. "Don't tell me what you think. Tell me what you *see*."

I waited, staring out over the open clearing and taking in the sight as if I were her. The lawns were freshly cut, and the scent of grass and dew hung heavy around us. Midmorning sun baked the air, and yet I could still detect the shadows. They lingered in the shade of Kitska Forest. Slithered through the blades of grass, answering the call of whatever assassin had summoned them. Took shape and solidified into something only death could craft.

Only *we* could craft.

She gripped the back of her neck and rocked on her heels. "I see shadows. More than I used to before I died."

I nodded. "They're always there. That's why you don't have to focus so hard to call on them. They're already waiting." Slowly, I turned her back toward me and grabbed one of her hands. Physical contact helped ground new recruits. Most of the time, they were still too shaken from death to discern what was real and what wasn't. Which made it difficult for them to control something intangible, like the shadows, and turn them into something solid. "They'll never fail you. Now, try again."

She took a deep breath and then let it out slowly. Her hand relaxed against mine. She kept her eyes open, but her gaze turned distant, as if she were focusing on something no one else could see. Slowly, a swirling mess of shadowy tendrils gathered in her palm.

"Good." I kept my voice low, steady. "Now, think about the shape you want it to take. A blade is easiest."

She gave a minute nod and lowered her gaze to her palm. The shadows responded, knitting together to form a shaky knife. The form wavered at the edges, wisps of errant smoke dissipating and reappearing as she struggled to picture her weapon.

"Keep it simple." With my free hand, I summoned a blade and let it float beside her creation. "Mimic this shape. Pay attention to its length, imagine its weight. How it will feel in your hand."

Sweat gathered along her brow, but she didn't break. Her blade continued to solidify, growing more realistic by the second. Finally, the last tendrils knotted together, and a blade darker than the night settled into her palm. She blinked. Then inhaled so sharply in surprise that the blade nearly disintegrated, but she regained control before it could slip through her fingers.

"I did it!"

A broad grin claimed my lips. "Way to go!"

"Now, where do I throw it?" She tightened her grip and cocked her arm back, head looking from side to side as she tried to find a suitable target.

I thrust my hands forward. "No, don't throw it. Not yet, anyway."

She pursed her lips, failing to mask her disappointment. I knew she wanted to be with the other recruits. Feeling left out or left behind never sat well with me, either. I knew all too well what that was like.

Before I could stop it, the memory of Jaxson surfaced in my mind. It took me years to grow into my body, and I'd been a scrawny, gangly-limbed kid with zero coordination. I had even less finesse when it came to making friends. But somehow, Jaxson had picked me. I went from sitting on the sidelines as the village kids played their made-up games to creating new ones with him until everyone wanted to be part of our crew. Best friends easily transitioned to partners in crime, and just like he'd done when we were young, he'd protected me when I'd needed it most.

And lost his life for it.

From that moment on, I swore I'd be the one protecting those around me. Not the other way around.

"Ozias?" Zara asked, her concerned voice chasing away the memory. "I'm sorry. I don't need to throw it." She worried her lip, and guilt threaded through my gut. She wasn't responsible for my past, and I sure as hell shouldn't have let my mood sour her training.

"What are you apologizing for? You did nothing wrong." I pulled my hand away so I could give her shoulder a warm squeeze. "I just don't want Calem coming after us if one of these blades gets a mind of its own again."

She smiled and tucked a strand of hair behind her ear. "Is he always like that?"

"Calem?" I tossed a glance over my shoulder. He had stripped his tunic and was fighting bare-chested, for no good reason, one-on-one against Emelia. Blond hair whirled outward as he spun away from one of her attacks, and he maneuvered behind her with deadly precision to press a blade against the nape of her neck. She stilled, and he let out a triumphant laugh.

Rolling my eyes, I turned back to Zara. "He's *always* like that. Shirtless and everything."

"You don't practice shirtless on occasion?" Her smile was wry, eyes alight, and suddenly I forgot how to swallow. Words died on my tongue, and I averted my gaze. Jaxson never did figure out how to make me loosen up around women, but he sure as hell tried. Failed, but tried.

Stiffening, I let my hand fall away from her shoulder and took a careful step back. Cleared my throat. "Uh, no, not really."

"How come?"

My pulse ratcheted to an uncomfortable level. I hated the way it made my hands tingle. "I don't know."

She inched closer. "I bet you look better than Calem does."

And there went my entire ability to form a rational response. It was as if a mage had set fire to my brain, blowing my vocabulary to unsalvageable letters that rearranged and formed words that clearly had no business being words.

Which, of course, resulted in me emitting a strange grunt that probably was supposed to be "Thanks."

Zara laughed, and that only made everything worse. "Go on. Prove me right."

My gaze shot skyward as I tried to remember what it was like to speak. I didn't know *how* to flirt. And stripping off my tunic would only make things worse. I could barely function as-is with the protection of clothing. No, it would be better if she just went back to her training. I swallowed thickly, dislodging unspoken words and finally finding my voice.

"Why don't you try forming another shadow blade?"

She stilled, then let out a disgruntled sigh. "Sure."

Better she be disappointed now than later when I would only inevitably make things worse. After a moment, the blade in her hand melted away in a wispy pool. Then she called the shadows back and began the task of knitting them together once again. Her frustration faded as the minutes passed, and my unease lessened.

I just didn't know what to say or how to act. I'd never be like Calem, able to go from dalliance to dalliance without a care in the world. I even got the feeling that Kost and Noc were different, that they could have whoever they wanted, they just decided not to act until the timing was right. But me? My gaze drifted to the recruits who'd finished their drills and were gathering on the lawns, making their way back toward me.

I was better herding kittens. Plus, the family I'd found, the friendships I'd developed, they were what mattered most. Stretching my neck from side to side, I let the leftover tension fade away and slipped back into my familiar role of teacher and protector.

A barrier would always be there, and that was the way I liked it.

SEVEN

NOC

The five of us stood on the outskirts of Wilheim, the preposterous white wall towering at our backs. The train station was packed with travelers. Their bags brimming with clothes and personal items, they stumbled on unsteady feet, shoes scraping against the beveled ground. Metal carts with cog wheels moved from one vendor stall to the next, delivering packages wrapped in linen cloths—no operator required.

Wilheim's elite wouldn't set foot in the station. With rail transportation free, all manner of patrons flocked to the train for travel. If wealthy Wilheimians ever decided to leave their sliver of paradise, they'd fork out the extra bits for a more luxurious, private means of transportation. Less opportunity to sully their appearances.

Leena eyed the closest stall and tilted her nose toward the fruitcakes and muffins tossing vanilla and citrus aromas into the air. Every new noise seemed to pull at her attention, and her wide eyes swallowed up the whole street and its occupants.

This was nothing compared to the Royal Bazaar. Beyond the train station and crammed cobblestone houses, as if it were the center of all eternity, stood the Violet Castle. Carved out of the lone mountain that had once been there, it was home to the royal family. Massive in size and hollowed out for use, the first floor was dedicated to the bazaar. I'd never forget those riotous colors. Gold-trimmed tents of burgundy, emerald, cerulean, and amethyst all competing for attention, wares from other lands glinting in the magic glow of the walls.

Leena's stare followed my gaze to the castle. "It's huge."

"Indeed." I turned my back on what had once been my home. The castle, the people, all of Wilheim. But the longing I'd felt for that life had disappeared with my dying breath. Even with the grace of Mavis, the First King's sacrificed daughter, extending the life spans of Wilheim's inhabitants, my family had long since passed.

Beside me, Kost pressed his lips into a fine line as he searched my expression. He was the only one who knew what I'd been before. Who I'd been.

"It's not purple, though," Leena mused to herself.

"Violet, not purple." Kost glanced down his nose as if the distinction should have been clear to everyone. "When the first full moon of spring appears, the white stone transforms. A violet sheen covers the castle and lasts for a few days. It's truly a spectacle to behold. Have you not seen it?"

She turned her back to Wilheim. "No."

Slipping my hands into my pockets, I tossed her a sidelong glance, but Leena's eyes were transfixed on something I couldn't follow. Longing, perhaps. Did she know her own brethren were after her? Was she searching for a home she couldn't go back to? Wilheim wouldn't have been any better. To an outsider, I suppose the allure was undeniable. But to an insider... There was almost an air of constant panic lingering in the aura of the castle. As if the very thought of losing their precious city coaxed paranoia from normally sane minds.

I peered out at the daggerlike treetops of the Kitska Forest cresting against the horizon. As easy as life would be inside the damning white walls, I'd grown to prefer the shadows of Cruor.

Leena stared at the tracks, brow furrowing. "Remind me why we're traveling this way if you can just move from place to place with the shadows? Seems like we could get there faster with your magic."

Ozias offered a kind smile. He always had a soft spot for someone in need. It's why he was one of the faster assassins, completing jobs before his emotions could even dare to get in the way. It seemed he was already taking a shine to Leena. "It doesn't work like that. Over a great distance, the most we can do is project our awareness. We can hide in a small area as long as we want, but actual shadow travel is limited. It takes considerable power to go more than a few miles, and it's draining."

Kost hissed, rounding on Ozias with a tight glare. "Stop spilling Cruor secrets."

Ozias lifted his palms in apology. "Sorry, Kost. Not like she could do anything with that knowledge, anyway."

"You don't know that." He spared Leena one disdainful look while adjusting his glasses. "No matter. The train is coming. Better rein in Calem before he misses it."

Leaning against one of the vendor stalls, Calem chatted with a woman selling hand-stitched tunics. He bent low to whisper something in her ear, and she giggled.

"Calem." My voice was no more than a murmur. Through the hustle of people and barked calls for sales from vendors, no average person would have heard it. But Calem's back straightened, and he sauntered over to us with a lopsided grin on his face.

"Is it time?" He pulled at one of the loose strands dangling from the sloppy bun on top of his head.

Leena buried her hands in the pockets of her leather jacket. "How can you tell? I don't see it." Black calfskin pants were tucked into knee-high onyx boots, the only smear of color on her a teal cotton camisole Kost had acquired. I'd stopped asking long ago how he knew things, like Leena's clothing size.

Kost barely deigned to give her a glance. "We can hear it. Our senses have been heightened by death."

"I guess you don't consider that a secret." A smile touched her lips.

Kost twitched. "If anything, it should be a warning."

She prodded further, and I had to admire the way she didn't back down in the face of Kost's obvious distaste. "Then why do you wear glasses?"

"Preference. Ozias?"

Ozias grunted and slung four of the five bags over his shoulders, tossing the other one at Calem. "Here you go. I left the light one for you."

"Fuck off." Calem's harsh words didn't reach his eyes, and he strapped the bag on with a smile. "I'm so ready for this. Ortega Key, here we come!"

Leena's gaze slanted to his sleeveless arms. "You know we won't get there today, right?"

"One can dream." He winked, rocking back on his heels, and a strange frustration brewed in my chest. I turned back to the tracks. A low hum vibrated through the air, signaling the train's approach. On the horizon, a black mass appeared. Running on a mixture of rycrims and steam, it barreled to select cities across our continent. Traveling everywhere else happened either by foot, mount, or boat.

The train came to a screeching halt before us, and a gust of wind following in its wake blew Leena's hair right into her face. She swept away the haywire strands and slipped through a staggering mass of bodies.

And just like that, she was gone. Carried away with the wind. My limbs froze, and my gaze tore through the crowd. I should've been more attentive. I'd assumed she'd stay put now that she'd received her contract. But maybe she'd seen through the loophole. Decided her fate would be better without us.

It wouldn't have been a wrong assumption.

"Noc." Kost's eyes darted from person to person. Calem's face blanched. Ozias shoved forward, creating space where there was none, and we followed him into the parted sea.

"I know. We'll find her." She could run all she liked, but we'd catch her. It wouldn't be like before. This time, we knew what we were dealing with.

She, on the other hand, didn't.

People flooded around us, jabbing elbows into sides and grunting half-hearted apologies. Had she gotten on only to slink off to another set of doors? Black shadows pulled from hidden corners of the train, pooling around my feet and circling my ankles.

"Hey, over here." Leena's voice broke through, and my eyes were at once riveted to hers. Legs stretched out across five seats along the back of the cab, she waved. "If you don't hurry, someone will take them, and we'll be left to fight for spots until the next stop."

The shadows lingering around my frame receded. She hadn't broken her word. Hadn't tried to escape.

Calem was the first to snap out of it, his wicked grin spreading a mile wide. "Smart thinking."

"It will be several hours before we reach Eastrend. Make yourself comfortable." Kost shot Calem a stern glare when he dropped into the seat right beside Leena, stretched both arms to the ceiling, then draped one behind her head and the other across the empty space beside him. My fingers twitched, a high-pitched whine groaning from the bowels of the train as steam covered the windows. "But not too comfortable."

Calem grinned. "You're the boss, Kost."

———◆———

A quiet giggle broke my peaceful sleep, sparking something light in my chest. Without moving, I slid my eyes open. The cab had since emptied as the train barreled farther south, leaving only a slumbering couple huddled together at the far end of the car. Kost had moved to a row ahead of me, his back pressed firmly against the windowpane with his legs stretched out before him. Nose-deep in a book, he hadn't noticed I'd woken. Calem snored from a few rows up: mouth open and neck craned at an impossible angle as his head jostled between window and headrest. Ozias...

Another small laugh. An easy grin graced Leena's face, and she mumbled something to Ozias while cupping her hands. It was impossible not to want to smile despite everything as I watched them. A groaning, invisible door signified the opening of the beast realm, and Ozias brought his forehead in close, squinted eyes deciphering something in her palms.

"She's cute, isn't she?" Leena cooed, and a miniscule monkey leaped from her hands and landed on Ozias's cotton work shirt. A snaking tail longer than his torso curled behind her. Leena tossed a furtive look at the sleeping couple before giving a quick nod. "Hold out your hand."

Palm flat, he gestured toward the creature. Tawny in color with three blue eyes and hands too big for her body, the creature gripped one of his thick fingers and hoisted herself up. A soft clucking bubbled from her throat, and Ozias beamed. "You think she likes me?"

I snorted softly to myself, but Leena pressed her elbows to her thighs, dipping her face to meet the monkey's. "Of course. Her name is Tila. She's a Dosha, a D-Class beast. She's immune to any poison and can detect whether food is safe for consumption. She's also incredibly nimble, as you might imagine."

Tila cocked her head before suddenly launching herself onto the handrail above them. A tacky slime oozed from her fingertips. A tremor of concern tugged at Leena's brows, and she glanced again at the couple. Beasts weren't illegal, but their rarity drew attention.

Leena extended her hand and tickled Tila's underbelly. "C'mon, get down from there." Her voice was soft and tender, and the warmth in my chest hinted briefly at longing. Exuding that type of emotion with my friends, my family, would only get them killed. The way Leena and Ozias interacted... Perhaps soon enough that would be me. If there truly was a beast that could eradicate my curse.

"The pores in the pads along her fingers exude the world's strongest adhesive. They accept their Charmer by gluing themselves to the Charmer's side." Leena waited as Tila unstuck herself and crawled over her jacket before nestling into the crook of her neck.

Ozias placed a gentle finger on the beast's head. "Thank you for sharing her with me. How many beasts do you have?"

Leena's smile widened. She was more alive, more intriguing with every second she spoke of her beasts, and it was too much. She couldn't be anything more than a mark. Not when she'd threatened my second-in-command. Spilled Kost's blood. That thought pushed away the whispers of warmth, and I settled back into my chair.

Leena happily sighed. "I have a lot of little guys like this. When Charmers first start out, they can only tame E-Class beasts, and so on and so forth as their abilities develop and they climb the ranks. In Hireath, many creatures naturally flock to the surrounding meadows. We very much have a symbiotic relationship."

"Hireath?"

Silence weighed down our cab, punctured only by a poorly masked inhale from Leena. It was as if the word broke her. As if she hadn't realized she'd even said it until Ozias repeated it back to her.

A wistful kind of sadness played across her features. It was something I knew well. I'd gone through that very phase after rebirth. And even though I didn't know her, even though she'd threatened Kost, I didn't like the thought of Leena—or anyone—ever feeling like that. I didn't like wondering if there was something I could say, some knowledge I could share, to make her feel better.

"Hireath is the Beast City tucked in a hidden valley to the west." Kost spoke without breaking his gaze from the pages before him. "It is a sanctuary for Charmers, a home they can always return to. Unless, of course, they've been banished."

Face flushed from his verbal slap, Leena nodded once. "Exactly." Rosewood glow burst from her hand, and she called Tila back beneath her breath. Pain-filled eyes locked on Kost and skipped away, dancing toward me and widening once she noticed I wasn't asleep.

For a moment, I simply held her stare. I knew what I saw there. Remorse. Homesickness. Sacrifice. For those of us who lived on the outskirts of society, hard decisions often left too-deep scars and a lifetime of memories we'd rather forget. Whatever she did to get this bounty, I didn't care. Judgment made work sticky, and I knew I'd done worse with my days. Not that she could ever know that. Not that I would ever tell her.

Not that I could comfort her.

Wanted. Not that I *wanted* to comfort her.

With light fingers, Ozias placed his hand on Leena's forearm. "Next time, can I see something bigger?"

"Of course. If you'll excuse me..." She stood and moved down the center of the train, locking herself in the nearest bathroom.

Ozias frowned. "Harsh, Kost."

Kost snapped his book shut. "Harsh? Two days ago, this woman wanted to murder me, and *I'm* harsh?"

Ozias winced. "I get it. It's just that, if we're going to work with her, maybe we should try to let things lie."

"I was only answering your question to the best of my knowledge."

"But you're always so cold. If you could just soften up a bit, it'd go a long way. We're used to you, but she's not." Ozias turned to me, yanking his thumb over his shoulder. "Aren't you going to say something? He only listens to you."

Leena's stricken gaze flashed in my mind, warring with the image of a bloodied Kost. I buried both beneath years of training and the reminder that I still had an active bounty on her head as I fingered the smooth inked-on scythe on my wrist. "He didn't do anything wrong. Don't get too attached."

Ozias relented and relaxed back. "All right."

"We should be arriving any minute now." Kost brushed invisible dirt off his jacket and nudged Calem's dangling foot from across the aisle. "Get up."

"Hrrrrmm?" Calem stifled a yawn before doing a quick head count. "Where's Leena?"

"Bathroom." Ozias cracked his neck and stood, pulling out the duffel bags one by one.

Late-afternoon sun slanted through the windows. The sprawling city of Wilheim had disappeared, leaving a vast rolling wilderness. Grassy plains stretched into a horizon of forests and mountains, peaks topping out against the clouds to the south.

The metal bathroom door slid open and Leena emerged, eyes dry. Her unfocused gaze found Ozias before she nodded once, gripping the handrail a few feet away.

I straightened the cuff of my tunic. "We should stay in Eastrend tonight and set out first thing in the morning. No use trying to make ground now only to camp in a few hours."

"Agreed. I'll search for a mount dealer right away." Kost stood as the train slowed, a shrill whistle signaling our approach.

"See you boys at the inn." Leena's words bit the air, and she turned without another sound, slipping through the doors the moment they parted.

I made a move to follow, but Calem leaped into the aisle. "On it."

"This ought to be fun." Ozias shrugged past, duffel bags smacking into the backs of seats. He followed Calem out, and I fought the urge to sigh. "Fun" wasn't the right word. Challenging, certainly. Maybe even...interesting. But in the end, none of it mattered. Leena was a mark. Once we had our beasts, her life would end. It had to.

"C'mon." I rested my hand on Kost's shoulder, and he tensed beneath my touch. "Let's go find the mount dealer."

EIGHT

LEENA

From the window of my room in the Braying Donkey, I watched Noc and Kost haggle with the only mount dealer in town. Corralled in a large stable built out of tree trunks and gated in with wood fencing, mounts kicked up dirt while munching grass. Through the floating dust, I made out a few generic horses and a handful of Zeelahs. I prayed they coughed up the extra bits for the latter.

Once wild magical beasts, Zeelahs had roamed the plains across Lendria. Twenty hands tall with the frames of deer, they had tan hides with thick white stripes across their backs. Nestled between oversize ears, a morganite stub cast a faint peach glow across each of their ivory manes. They were hardier than horses, even though the magic had been bred out of them over the years. If we took the horses instead, our two-day trek would stretch into three. Maybe four. Which meant less time dedicated to finding and taming the Myad and more time with these assassins. A predicament I did not want to face.

Turning my back on the outside world, I stared at a more immediate concern—our shared room. Eastrend was a logging town. Bordering on Lightwood Forest, its primary export was wood, and only a few hundred locals lived here. They survived off game from the forest and fresh vegetables grown in the few farmland plots on the outskirts of town. Buildings were sparse. It wasn't exactly lively, and because most only visited Ortega Key by taking a scenic and much costlier route via ship, lodgings weren't a high priority. The inn was a mere two stories with half a dozen rooms, only one of which was available.

Supposedly, it slept six.

My eyes traveled over the two sets of bunks and a floor-bound mattress covered in calfskin hides and down blankets. I sank into the bottom mattress of the first bunk bed, and the springs creaked beneath my weight. Arms spread wide, I could graze both opposing bunks with my fingertips. Shiplap with black swirled patterns ran horizontally along the walls. Candlelit iron fixtures clung to either side of the door, casting a flickering light that made shadows dance at my feet.

Those shadows. I couldn't shake the way they clung to Noc. If he wasn't so damn menacing, he'd be attractive. I'd swear he'd peeked at my soul on the train, the way his obsidian eyes burned right through to my core. He knew pain, that much I could tell. There was a level of understanding in his gaze that couldn't be faked. Certainly he'd done things, horrendous things, as an assassin. Did he regret them? He didn't show any reservations about his role as the leader of Cruor. So what was it? What had he suffered that made it so easy for him to recognize that pain in me? Whatever it was, it hadn't lasted. That same gaze had gone cold once I'd reemerged from the bathroom, and I was instantly reminded of his power. Of the nonchalance he so effortlessly wielded. His beauty didn't outweigh his danger, and I wasn't in the game of putting myself in harm's way.

The bedroom door swung open, Ozias and Calem strolling in. Ozias came to a full stop. "When he only gave me one key, I thought he'd already given you a separate room."

I shrugged. "Nope. This is all we've got."

Calem shut the door behind him and dropped his bag on the floor. "Dibs on the top bunk."

Ozias rolled his eyes. "I'm sorry, Leena." He leaned against the wall, and the shoulders of his white tunic turned brown with dust.

"It's all right." I eyed the mound of blankets stretching across the mattress on the floor. Before anyone could claim it, I slid off the bed and dropped into the pillows.

"Here." Ozias flipped over the tags on each bag before finding one with my name on it and setting it before me. "I don't know what Kost packed, so whatever you do, don't blame me."

I smiled. "Thanks."

"No sweat. I'm going to find the bathroom and clean up." Slinging his duffel bag over his shoulder, he left.

"You know, sharing rooms ain't all that bad." Calem winked and yanked off his tunic in one fell swoop. Heat traveled from the back of my neck to my cheeks at the display. The sun god had blessed him. Even with the low lighting of the wall-mounted candle fixtures, his tanned skin somehow glistened. Carved muscles flexed as he grinned and leaned toward me. "How about it?"

How about it? Out of all the murderers available to me, he might have been the easiest to work. Whether it was my Charmer's lure or just his demeanor, or some combination of both, I couldn't say. But in the end, it didn't matter. Flirting with him could lead him to handing over what I needed: blood.

"Well—"

The bedroom door swung open before I could consider the thought further, and Noc and Kost froze in place. Murderous—there was no other word for the expression that solidified on Noc's face as he skewered Calem with his gaze. Calem stiffened for a moment before sighing and palming the back of his neck. "You're no fun."

"Watch yourself." Noc's words were low, almost inaudible, and a chill swept down my arms. Distancing myself from Calem, I sank farther into the blankets.

"Yeah, yeah. I called dibs on the top bunk by the way." He tossed his bag onto one before shouldering past Noc and Kost, reclaiming his tunic along the way. "See you guys in a bit."

"He's getting worse." Kost's eyes bounced from bed to bed. "Though these arrangements could be better."

"Take the top bunk. I'll take the one just below you."

"All right."

Leftover tension knotted in Noc's shoulders, refusing to dissipate. He riffled through his bag without speaking. Slowly, I slipped out of my jacket and peeked inside my duffel. I ran my fingers over an array of tunics and breeches. All clean. All seemingly new. Finer fabric with sturdy thread, but still soft like Poof. Garments like this didn't make their way to Midnight Jester.

The bits these must have cost. I tied the bag shut, ignoring the errant desire to run to the bathroom and try everything on.

"There's food downstairs." Kost hung his trench coat over the wooden railing of the bunk. Neatly pressed, his tailored tunic showed no signs of travel. He rolled up his cuffs, revealing embroidered jacquard print underneath. Every assassin dressed differently, but none as sharply as him. "Shall I get us a table?"

"Do that." Noc didn't look up from his bag, and Kost left without another word.

With Noc and I alone in the room, silence stretched on for what felt like hours until he sighed, abandoning his duffel and pinning me to the wall with his gaze. "Calem can be a handful."

"It's fine." Untangling myself from the blankets, I stood and brushed lint off my pants. The space between us didn't make his stare any less unnerving.

"I suppose I'm not here to tell you what to do with your spare time..." Straightening to his full height, he added, "But keep in mind, you have a job to do."

I lifted my chin. "I'm capable of saying no. I do it all the time." Being a Charmer had its downfalls, one of which was attracting less-than-reputable men. Present company included.

Noc studied me without moving closer. His short-sleeved, fitted tunic allowed me to make out the cut of his muscles. So much tension knit tightly beneath that fabric. I doubted he would ever strip his tunic without a care like Calem had.

And yet... There was a flash of skin visible just beneath Noc's collarbone. A hint of his chest.

A glimmer of appealing vulnerability under all that strength.

"Be careful with Calem," he said suddenly. "The last thing we want is to make this...situation more awkward or uncomfortable than it needs to be."

"That would never happen," I said immediately.

"Oh?"

I lifted a shoulder. "He might be fun, but...not really my type."

"Oh. I see." Rubbing his jaw, he studied me with wary eyes. Was I really that dangerous to him? The thought was almost laughable, considering how easily he'd almost ended my life. He dropped his arms to his sides and walked to the door, wrenched it open. Paused for a beat, then angled his chin in my direction. "Dinner?"

Maybe not so dangerous. "Sure."

"Good." He pulled away without looking back, heading out and taking the stairs down two at a time.

For a moment, I simply stood in the open doorway. Sounds of the first-floor tavern, clanking silverware scratching against plates, mumbled conversations among friends, and intermittent laughter floated up to me. And still, Noc's voice rang in my mind. His emotions were a moving target, and I didn't have the slightest clue where to aim. Despite his frigid detachment, though, he'd inched closer. Expressed concern about Calem. About me.

It could've been my Charmer's lure starting to kick in, but it felt different than that. As if there was more beneath his frosty words and bitter stare. I just needed to find the right kind of heat and see what thawed.

Because if he started to care about me, then I'd make it out of this alive. And hopefully with some blood on my hands.

———◆———

Dinner was anything but relaxing. Sitting at a four-top table with Noc, Ozias, and Kost, I chewed on lamb stew and freshly baked bread. Kost was a case study of efficiency, eating in record time with more table etiquette than I could ever muster. The moment he finished, he extracted maps of the woods and discussed possible camping locations with Ozias. Calem never joined us, opting instead for a barstool, a brunette, and several rounds of ale.

And Noc... I took a long drink of water, washing down the remainder of my food, then pushed my plate to the side. Noc never spoke. He occasionally nodded in agreement to some of Kost's questions, but whatever he was thinking he kept carefully locked away. Occasionally he'd glance my way, only for his gaze to skip over to Ozias or Kost.

So much for interest. Getting Noc to befriend me was going to take time. And patience.

"You all done, hon?" The bar maiden nodded toward my plate before wiping her hands on a floral-patterned towel at her waist.

"Yes, thank you."

The tavern was only a few notches cleaner than Midnight

Jester, yet it reeked of home. Dust-covered windowpanes turned the black sky a weird ruddy brown. Thick candles dripped hot wax on tarnished silver holders. And yet the bartender slinging drinks to Calem and his date had none of the rugged charm that Dez so easily wielded, and the warmth was missing.

Maybe that was because of the sheer force of the ice wall sitting across from me: Noc leaning back in his chair, idle hand gripping a near-empty glass.

Ozias pushed his empty plate to the middle of the table. "Hopefully, Calem doesn't wake us when he comes back." He stood slowly, bones creaking as he stretched his hands to the ceiling. "I'm going to hit the sack."

Kost rolled up his maps. "Me too. Noc?"

Noc stared at his empty glass. "You go on ahead. I think I'm in need of another drink." Kost hesitated for a fraction of a second before nodding, then turned to follow Ozias across the tavern toward the stairs. Settling further into my chair, I hoped our lack of an audience would prompt him to speak. To give him reason to open up. After a minute, Noc's stare shifted to my face. He opened his mouth to speak at the same moment the bar maiden returned and caught his attention.

"You two calling it?" She set her hands on her hips. "Or can I get you something else?"

I had to fight every instinct in me not to glare her into the next room.

Noc fingered his tumbler glass. "I'll have another."

Thank the gods. "Just some more water, please."

"Sure thing." The bar maiden strolled off. She snagged a heavy bottle of spiced acorn whiskey from the bar, then made a quick stop for a fresh glass of water before returning. With skilled hands, she poured a heaping amount of amber liquid into Noc's tumbler. "Enjoy."

When she moved away to another table, I finally braved words. "So..."

"Why don't you know about the violet sheen of Wilheim?" The question burst out of him as if he'd been holding it back for hours. Curiosity, it seemed, was Noc's weakness.

Rotating the ring around my finger, I had no option other than to stare right into those unyielding pools of black glass, remembering the way he'd smiled as he talked about his love of puzzles. He was a collector of sorts, finding stray bits of information to store away in the brilliant puzzle trap of his brain. It was an uncomfortably appealing thought, but I welcomed his intrigue. He could store whatever information he wanted if it meant I'd survive this journey. "I've never been."

Exile carried a nasty price. It wasn't enough to be excommunicated; my people had to go ahead and put an asterisk next to my name, making it impossible for me to find reasonable employment within the safety of Wilheim.

Noc braced his forearms against the table and caged his drink between his hands. "I guess that's to be expected if you've spent most of your days in Hireath."

I stiffened. So I wasn't willing to let him store *everything* in that brain of his. I never should have mentioned Hireath. It was a place of both beauty and abject terror. My home and the source of my pain. My only chance at ever going back lay in convincing the Council I was worthy of a hearing. Which would be nearly impossible even with the Myad, given Wynn held a seat of his own. But if I could just get the beast... If I could show up and take them by surprise, even the Crown of the Council would have to listen. A Myad wouldn't bond with someone as evil as they believed me to be.

Dropping my eyes to the table, I ran my fingers along the smooth wood grain. My exile was a farce. A by-product of Wynn attempting to charm a forbidden creature and then using a Gyss to make the Council believe it had been me all along.

Noc cleared his throat. "I wonder what other sights you've missed."

My head jerked up. Taking a slow sip from his drink, he peered at me over his glass, empathy there and gone in a flash. Was he going to drop it? Just like that? A swell of gratitude bloomed in my chest, and a soft smile captured my lips. "I've seen enough. Beasts live everywhere."

He set his glass down. "Really? Let's see what you know."

"What?" I eyed my untouched water, suddenly wishing I'd ordered something stronger. The table beside us burst into laughter as a pile of whittled sticks toppled over. One man cursed, shoving a mound of bits to the center and breaking a stick in half. They'd go on like that until only one stick remained and the pot reached astronomic proportions.

"True or false—Kings Isle is guarded by two warrior statues at the mouth of the bay."

I blinked. "Seriously?"

The ring on his pointer finger clinked against his glass, and he offered me a nearly boyish grin. "You don't know?"

My heart fluttered, and I folded my arms across my chest as if that would somehow hide what his unexpected smile did to me. "False. It's three women—the child, the mother, and the elder."

That smile only grew. "Excellent."

"My turn." I leaned forward, resting my chin in my hands. Noc's raised glass paused in midair, and a spark flared behind his normally distant gaze. "The Kitska Forest is littered with monsters Charmers can't tame."

He pursed his lips before taking another sip. "True."

"Damn it." Tipping my head to the ceiling, I hid my smile from him.

"Point for me." His sharp stare contrasted with the lazy dance of his fingers across the rim of his glass. He was almost catlike in the way he approached our conversations. Aloof and distant, but when the right thing struck his interest, he was suddenly warm, if not a bit mischievous.

Calling him a beast would be too high a compliment, but he was close.

"What was the First King's name?"

I rolled my lower lip into my mouth. The First King wasn't exactly a talking point in Charmer society. He was responsible for the only war our people had ever been forced to suffer through and, as such, deserved nothing more than his title. "I can't say."

He sucked an ice cube, let it fall back into his glass. "It's Huxley Farnsled. By the way, I would've also accepted 'King.' He despised his name, so he forced his subjects to refer to him as such at all times. Even his wife."

I couldn't help but laugh. "Really? How do you know all this?"

"I like to read."

My mind raced. I needed practical information, then. Something he couldn't possibly pull from a book in his library. I drummed my fingers on the table. Stopped. "What beast has the ability to change its constitution depending on its master's desires?"

He arched a brow. "I already told you my beast knowledge is thin."

"Giving up so easily?"

His grin sharpened. "If you want to play dirty, sure. I'll give. But I won't play fair, either."

My pulse kicked up a notch as heat bloomed down my neck. "Okay."

"Which assassin is responsible for the bloodletting of Sloane Saint-Germant?"

So much for dirty. "You got me."

Leaning forward, he laughed—low and a little rusty, as if he didn't often get a chance. "I know. Shall we go back to an even playing field?"

Gods, what that look could do to a person. It was impossible not to dip my face toward his. Everything about him was magnetic. "Yes, please."

His gaze flitted to my mouth and then back to my eyes. And then he abruptly sat back in his chair, smile strained and voice cool. "Let's see…"

I cursed at myself for moving in too quickly, but sent silent thanks to the gods that there was still lingering interest in his eyes. Not entirely lost, then.

Pressing my glass to my lips, I took a slow drink just as he spoke. "True or false: you're being extra…friendly with me and my men. Namely Ozias and Calem."

I choked on my water, spewing a few droplets across the table. "Excuse me?"

His lips kicked up at the corners. "I think you're making it a point to go out of your way to get us to like you. Perhaps to ensure your safety?"

Heat scampered down my neck as I placed the near-empty glass a safe distance away. "I'm being nice to Kost, too."

"Let me rephrase: you're flirting with us. True or false?"

That damned heat crawled onto my cheeks and gave away everything. I tried to hide it by cupping my face in my hands, but Noc had already seen enough. His chuckle did weird things to my insides, and I tried to get a grip on my suddenly uncontrollable emotions.

He waited, eyes alight and teasing. Silence wouldn't get me out of this one. "Okay, yes. True. I needed to ensure I was safe, all right?" Letting out a breath, I studied the patterns in the wood beneath my fingers rather than meet his gaze. "You gave me a contract, but how am I supposed to know that you'll be true to your word? But if you liked me, if I were *friendly*..."

Slowly, I raised my chin so I could meet his eyes. His smile had turned strained, and something foreign and dark clouded his expression. He chased it away with a drink that emptied his glass. "Your contract stands, regardless of whether or not we like you. But I applaud your efforts. You're much cleverer than you let on."

"Hey!" I slapped my hand against the table. "I resent that, thank you very much."

He laughed and signaled for the bar maiden. "Keep proving me wrong, then. I believe it's your turn to try and outsmart me."

We continued this game of wits through two more drinks. His questions shifted as history bled into personal preferences, and he leaped at every opportunity to turn a seemingly normal answer into a tease. There was something light to him, something genuine that blurred the severity of his role as an assassin. As the leader of Cruor.

He sipped quietly while he rifled for answers to my questions, never once breaking his gaze. And aside from that question about beasts, he never answered incorrectly, no matter how badly I tried to stump him. He was a wealth of knowledge and culture, and as the minutes dripped into hours, my fingers inched closer to his unmoving hand on the table. Even with my ploy out there in the open, I couldn't stop myself. There was an errant thought now, one teasing me from the back of my mind that made me wonder...what if this wasn't just a tactic? What if the flirting actually meant something?

He didn't draw away. Didn't close the gap, either. But his stare had drifted to that seemingly insurmountable space. Against my better judgment, I wanted him to reach out and claim my hand in his. It didn't make sense, how much I longed for that simple touch. Just a graze of his fingers. The promise of something more.

Gods, what the hell am I doing? Physical. It was purely _physical_. I was only in it to convince him to give me some blood and assure my safety. Nothing else.

Absolutely nothing else.

"True or false—you can never go back to Hireath."

The space between our fingers became hot as a forge, and I jerked my hand away. So this, _this_, was what he was up to. Baiting me into a game to unearth the answers I didn't want to give. He'd sensed my pain and reluctance to talk about Hireath on the train, and yet here he was. Bringing it up again, wielding insight like a knife between my ribs. A minute ago, he had been something more than a cunning assassin. He'd been warm. Human.

Shame burned my insides. I knew better than this. Hadn't he used his wits against me already? He was an assassin both in words and weapons. For a moment I had forgotten.

I pushed away from the table, and my chair smacked into the back wall. "Good night."

Noc blinked, miniscule creases in his forehead momentarily giving the impression of confusion. I knew otherwise. He was craftier than I'd realized. Spinning on my heels, I didn't give him a chance to speak, and I stormed toward the stairs to feign sleep before he could return.

NINE

NOC

We left early the next morning on five Zeelahs. Judging by Leena's approving nod, we'd made the right decision in purchasing them over the horses. Not that she would admit it. The only acknowledgment she gave me came in the form of a handful of unnecessary bits as she insisted she pay for her own mare.

Had she been one of my assassins, I would have ordered her to keep her funds. It was my job as guild master to provide basic needs for jobs—food, shelter, and in this case, travel accommodations. Whatever leftover bits remained after the monthly collections rolled in went to the assassins who worked, and their money was theirs to spend.

The oath on my inner wrist simmered. I did what I could to avoid handing bounties out to those who couldn't stomach the work. Gave them tasks in our home so they could provide for Cruor in another fashion. But sometimes, I didn't have a choice. Even cooks and gardeners had to get their hands bloody from time to time.

But Leena was none of those things, and so when she'd curled my fingers over a pile of gleaming silver chips, I could only stare in shock. She'd mounted her Zeelah with ease and led her into a canter, leaving me rooted in place to catch Calem's hushed snickering.

Since that moment, nothing. Save the steady cadence of beating hooves against soft dirt, we rode in silence well into evening. The road to Ortega Key was a constant backdrop of massive moss-ridden trees. The branches of willows, pines, and firs reached above us, threading together through a sea of green leaves and creating a canopy that blocked out the sky.

I hadn't meant to offend her, but I had, and there was a small knife worming in my gut because of it. A stab of guilt that shouldn't have been there. But she'd thrown me with her admission of guilt, of flirtation. Of course that had been her tactic, but her outwardly stating it, and then still acting on it throughout the night... My grip tightened around the reins of my Zeelah. Her hand had been so *close*. Was she still thinking that she needed to try? Or had it been genuine? The latter had me retreating so fast I hadn't thought to censor my questions. I asked her the first thing that came to mind, the thing I'd been pondering since her reaction on the train. Curiosity had blurred the lines of detachment, and I'd gone a step too far. For both of us.

I needed to speed up this process, get my men their beasts, find me a cure, and send us home.

Moonlight broke through a clearing in the treetops, basking a hidden meadow in pale glow. The soft calls of nightingales intermingled with the strained chirps of insects so vastly different from the cacophony of bone-shattering whines in the Kitska Forest. Here, the darkness was fainter—like weakened smoke rather than a smearing of black ink.

"Let's make camp." Kost broke away first, steering his mount into the open air before sliding off and leading him to a far tree.

We followed suit, looping reins around trees and giving our mounts food and water. Within minutes, Ozias, Kost, and Calem set to work on the tents, and Leena stared listlessly into the night. Loose hairs framed the angles of her face, and a strange urge to brush them away jolted through my fingers.

"Noc, dinner?" Kost stared through me, and I nodded, turning away from the group to find game in the woods. Shadows sprung to life at my ankles and crept up my legs, enveloping me in darkness. I snuck through Lightwood Forest without making a sound.

Some say Zane, the first of our kind, acquired the power to control the darkness when he ripped the god of death's cloak and came back with it fisted in his hand. The material had diffused into his skin, and a portion of death's endless realm became his to control.

And while there were some at Cruor who found the wasteland of darkness terrifying, the shadows were my home—a soothing, familiar relief that blanketed out the rest of the world. Here, I could breathe. Think. Assess. Everything was precise and finite—no varying shades of color to paint a brighter picture when there wasn't one to be seen in the first place. The darkness was even tender in its welcome. Like standing underneath a gentle stream without actually getting wet.

Killing comes easy when you leave no trace. I brought my focus back and searched for game. Five rabbits gave their lives to my swift hands. No more than what we needed. I peeled back the shadows a fraction, seeing reality as the gods intended without revealing myself. I wanted to linger a moment longer in my sanctuary. Drifting along the outskirts of our camp, I stepped around gnarled roots and patches of violet toadstools. Plumes of green spores and dust skirted over the forest floor. Harmless, but they reflected the light of the moon like tiny emeralds in the night.

Leena and Ozias's voices captured my attention before they came into view. Hushed whispers were barely audible on the evening breeze, but it was enough for my ears. I should have left them alone. Should've walked away or made my presence known. But I wanted to know things about her without putting myself on display. Last night's dinner had been too much. She was too intriguing for her own good. For *my* own good. Disarming in the way she smiled and made me forget about the problems that came with forming deeper connections. Even her honesty was disarming.

"How did Noc get to be the leader of Cruor?" Leena pressed kindling flush to her chest and peered into the darkness. I swear she saw right through me. She had the kind of stare that threatened to unearth every secret, every lie. My stomach churned.

Ozias paused, kneeling to unearth a fistful of edible mushrooms at his feet. "The former guild master, Talmage, named him leader before he passed."

"How does that work?"

Such curiosity in her voice, and yet I'd remained hidden for the hopes of learning about her, not to have Ozias spill details about me.

Before he could reveal more, I emerged from the shadows. "We already had our game of questions."

Spinning on her heels, she showered the earth in a layer of branches and twigs. "Gods, you scared me."

"So jumpy."

She hissed, scooping up the kindling and turning her back on me. "I think you've done enough prying lately." Without so much as a second glance, she stormed back to camp.

Ozias cleared his throat. "Are those rabbits for dinner?"

I nodded, tossing them his way and following him back to the fire. Ozias sprang to life around food, his surprisingly dexterous hands prepping the rabbits and mushrooms with ease. He splattered oil in a skillet, setting it on blazing coals, and rotated the game on a makeshift spit. His passion for cooking, even in the restricted setting of the woods, was admirable.

Dead air stretched between us as we ate. I hadn't realized

how much I'd enjoyed Leena's banter until I was met by a stone wall of silence. Her sharp wit and eagerness to try to outsmart me. She could've, had she only known what to ask. If she had dared to question who I had been before, the kind of life I used to lead, I would have been forced to lie.

Nothing you're not used to. I ran a hand through my black hair, half expecting smudges of ink to cover the pads of my fingers. Of course, they were clean. Kost and Talmage had worked together to find the best mage in Lendria for my disguise. Anything to keep my past hidden so I could have some semblance of a normal life. A normal life for an assassin, anyway.

Calem cleared his throat, snaring my attention. "So, Leena, let's talk about beasts."

Sitting in front of the dying embers, Leena's gaze flickered to him. "What about beasts?" Her inked hand flew to her locket, toying with the book-shaped charm dangling above her cleavage. Clenching my jaw, I kept my gaze level. I never knew where to look with her. Every potential option was beginning to feel like a trap, and I'd never been one to take the bait.

"What choices do we have?" Calem's eyes tracked Leena's fingers.

Kost looked up from scratching notes in his notebook. "I, too, would be curious to know what is available to us."

"Must you always talk like that?" Calem let out a quick laugh. "Join our century, buddy."

"Proper speech should not be dictated by time." Kost barely spared him a look. "Now, as we were, Leena?"

She shifted, pulling one knee to her chest and kicking the other leg out toward the fire. "I can show you what I've documented."

Ozias set his empty dinner plate down and scooted closer to her. His broad grin smoothed the worry lines touching her eyes, and a soft smile graced her lips. My temple throbbed. I shouldn't be bothered by Leena. By the way Ozias assuaged her fears and brought a smile to her face. I shouldn't focus on the way she rotated her ring when she was anxious. How I was beginning to find myself wanting to reach out and stop her every time.

"Noc." Kost's voice shattered my thoughts.

"What?" Tilting my head in his direction, I raised an eyebrow.

A flare from the fire glinted across his specs. "What do you think?"

"Yes. The information would be helpful."

Leena's hazel eyes scoured my face. I didn't know what she was searching for, but that look was damning. Not because she condemned me with her gaze, but because it was too warm. Too intent. Sometimes she reminded me of Amira, of the person responsible for my hidden identity, and that was a memory I could never let surface.

I clasped my hands together. "Go on. Show us your bestiary."

"All right." With the barest touch, she brought her middle finger to her pendant. "Open."

Faint rosewood light exploded from her sternum, showering the air with thousands of glittering dust particles. As the magic settled, the projection of a book floated above the fire. Inscriptions in loopy gold lettering dripped down the binding of the tome, but the language was foreign to me. The only thing I recognized was the tree branded on the worn leather cover. The Charmer's symbol. A deep, antique pink on Leena's hand, but here? Molten gold, freshly heated with an underlay of fiery orange.

Power pulsed from the bestiary's pages, and Leena offered it a smile I'd only ever seen on mothers' lips. The projection had expanded to the size of a large history tome, and when her fingers met its cover, ripples of magic pulsed from her touch. The book floated in the space before her chest, waiting. She flipped it open and angled it toward her body. It held steady as if propped on a stand.

"What would you like to know?" She ran her hand above the text. Magic reacted to the motion, turning pages, and the whisper of parchment scraping together kissed the air.

Riveted by the sight of the tome, Kost spoke first. "Demonstrate a B-Class monster, please." It was the first time he'd shown Leena even a morsel of respect.

Leena noticed, too. Her smile deepened. "Sure." As she swiped her hand from right to left, pages flicked before her. The tome creaked when she came to a stop, and she bent her nose to the pages. A wondrous mixture of papyrus and ink perfumed the air. "I'll start with one you know."

The book widened, and a mirage of Iky appeared. Shapeless and tall, he hovered in place, hieroglyphs bleeding to life around him. She dragged her fingers across the symbols, and they transitioned to a floating script we could read. Kost leaned forward, and sparkling words about Iky's powers reflected off his glasses.

Alters its constitution to suit its master's needs.

The beast she'd questioned me about over dinner. I forced my face to remain impassive. That evening had come and gone. I needed to put the memory out of my mind. Not endlessly ponder the way she'd used knowledge to her advantage. Cunning as well as brave and bold.

"All Charmers have a bestiary that fills each time they capture a new beast. If you have anything in mind, I can search through the pages and let you read the specifics for yourself." The script disappeared along with the image of Iky as she mindlessly flipped a few pages.

Read for ourselves? My fingers itched to run the length of the pages. I wanted to sidle up to her, examine the passages she shared, and store that information away.

"Any beasts that could improve my chances with women?" Calem stood, inching closer to Leena. His comment brought me back, and I stiffened. Distance was always better.

"You sure you need that?" She paused, and a new image sparked to life in the space above her book. A small, genie-like creature with a wispy tail and mischievous eyes glittered against the navy night. No bigger than a mug, and yet the devilish grin spoke volumes about her power.

And so did the floating text surrounding her mirage.

Ability to grant one wish every six months. No limitations, so long as payment is met.

No limitations. The text pulsed with implications. *This* was the beast. The one drunken men longed for when their ales and fortunes ran dry. An answer to my curse. I had resigned to living a life full of distance and detachment. But there was always the chance I could slip up. All it took was a glimmer of longing. A display of too-honest affection. If anyone reciprocated in any way, they would die. Painfully. I'd continue to build a barricade around me if it meant keeping those I cared about safe. That was fine. But if there was a possibility of changing that, of preventing myself from accidentally killing another loved one again... "Tell me about this beast."

Leena turned, dragging her gaze away from Calem's grin to examine the floating text. Her right eye twitched. "You don't want a Gyss. The payments for wishes aren't worth the cost of receiving them. Plus, it's a C-Class beast. Doesn't meet the terms of our agreement."

"Could I *wish* for more success with women?" Calem's flirtatious grin eased the sudden stiffness in Leena's posture. "Or perhaps just success with you?"

Leena rolled her eyes. "For payment, the Gyss would probably ask for your junk on a silver platter. You ready to part with that?"

Calem's face blanched. "No."

"Sounds like you know the pros and cons of each beast best." Kost spoke to Leena without ever meeting her gaze. Instead, he studied me with measured levels of concern and frustration, turning blades of grass to green pulp between his forefinger and thumb.

"Agreed." Ozias stretched toward the sky. "I'll leave it to you, Leena. I'm not much of a reader. I'd rather see a beast in person and judge from there."

"Oh, I like that idea. How about it, Leena?" Calem bounced on the balls of his feet.

She touched her middle finger to her pendant again, and the book disappeared. The afterimage of the Gyss seared the night air. I could still picture the creature's grin, the way her eyes burned with a magic I'd yet to test.

Leena tilted her head to the side. "What do you mean? There aren't any beasts in the area right now." She gestured to the chirping woods and wide-open meadow.

Calem's grin widened. "I have an idea."

Brow furrowing, she stood before him. "I'm listening."

"Let's have a little sparring match. But you can't use any beasts we've already seen."

"A sparring match? It's been ages since…" She trailed off, and then placed both hands on her hips. "Any other rules?"

A protest caught in my throat. This had *bad idea* written all over it. If Calem lost control and hurt Leena, we'd be down a Charmer—and this Gyss I needed to know more about. Or worse, she'd hand Calem his ass like she did with Kost. My gaze darted to the first of us she'd encountered, and Kost's carefully placid expression failed to mask his clenched jaw.

But Leena stood tall, a subtle grin tugging at the corners of her lips, and a light sparked in her eyes. This was a chance to see what she had in her arsenal. A glimmer into who she was. And that was knowledge I could always keep in my back pocket. Kost had been alone before, but if she tried anything drastic here, I'd kill her and convince another Charmer to find me a Gyss.

But Leena's fire... Where did it come from? I wanted to know. *Needed* to know.

Kost flexed his hands. "I strongly advise against this."

"What? Why?" Calem tossed him an annoyed glance. "I'll go easy, I swear."

"You can't control yourself. You'll end up hurting her."

Leena jutted her chin. "I can take care of myself."

"This isn't about your abilities," Kost snapped. "This is about Calem and his *inability* to exhibit self-control."

"I promise it'll be fine. This is just for practice."

Kost and Calem looked to me. I stood slowly, and Calem's expression faded to one of remorse as if he expected me to banish the idea altogether.

"No life-threatening injuries." Turning to Leena, I caught sight of her hazel eyes. Mischief touched her smile, but she turned back to Calem without saying a word. "No other rules."

"This should be good." Without standing, Ozias scooted in place to face the empty meadow on the other side of our camp. "That big enough?"

"Works for me. But you know I'm good in confined spaces." Calem bent his head toward Leena's.

She smirked. "So am I."

For the first time in my life, I witnessed Calem blush. Ozias exploded in a fit of laughter as Leena stalked toward the clearing, a slight sway to her hips. Kost mumbled to himself as he moved to join Ozias, his spine tense. Adrenaline hummed through my body, and an anxious, infuriating desire to protect her stirred. She had no idea what she was getting herself into. Catching Kost off guard was one thing. But taking Calem head-on? His deadliness was bar none—he had no moral qualms with his work. There were even times he reveled in it.

Shadows fled from the forest to cling to him as he chuckled. "You're in for it."

They positioned themselves on either side of the clearing, and Leena settled into the weight of her heels. Every sound stopped. Nightingales halted midcall, and the lightning bugs scattered for safety. It was as if they knew. As if they could feel the sudden swell of power emanating from her emblem. Her Charmer's symbol ignited in a brilliant display of rosewood light, roots and branches climbing the expanse of her hand and arm—a beautiful interlocking filigree of leaves and flowers. Fingers twitching, she studied the space between her and Calem.

"Go ahead. I'll give you a chance to call forth your beast. Otherwise, it will be over before you know it." He was nothing more than shadows and red eyes, a terrifying mockery of a man.

The heavy groan of a door opening shattered the silence of the night, and an influx of magic encircled Leena. Wind mussed her hair, and my heart stilled. Something was different. Beside me, Kost's eyes widened and Ozias stiffened. Power unlike anything she'd demonstrated streamed from her, lashing against the night air and sending a charge through the wind.

When the breeze receded and the rosewood glow died, all the breath left my body.

Not one monster, but three emerged from the beast realm and clung to their master.

Leena grinned. "You said no rules." Twin serpents with dragon-like heads and whiskers trailing the length of their scaly bodies glided through the air around her, constantly moving, constantly assessing. Electric blue in coloring, the first one growled, barring heavy fangs in Calem's direction. The other, white as fresh snow, simply watched: sharp gray eyes trained on its target.

"Assassins don't fight fair, either." He winked out of existence, only an empty space where he used to be. The serpents tilted their heads, nostrils flaring wide as they searched for his scent. The third beast remained motionless. Child-size and sitting cross-legged at her feet, six arms with humanlike hands spread wide around its frame—two palms facing up to the sky, two flat and parallel to the earth, and the final two firmly pressed against the ground. Its cow-like head swiveled in our direction, ears going taut, and ten white eyes locked on us.

Shadows naturally began to fester around my feet. Safety in darkness.

Ozias rubbed his hand over cropped hair, back to front. "Leena might have strength in numbers, but Calem doesn't like to lose. Ever."

Calem crept through the dark, visible only to us. Her serpents hissed and groaned as they failed to flush him out. Leena only smiled, occasionally encouraging them with a soft clucking. Kost shifted into a low crouch, muscles tense, and waited for me to give the command—only I didn't know if he'd be targeting Calem or Leena.

Calem moved before I could think. Leaping from the shadows and barreling toward her with unmatched swiftness, he had a clear shot on her unprotected neck. The world slowed as I remembered the way purplish bruises had immediately swelled against her skin when I'd held her suspended above the ground.

As Calem's hands sliced through the air, an invisible, bubble-like shield rippled to life. He smashed into it, ricocheted off, and landed on the ground a few feet away from Leena. One of the cow beast's eyes closed.

"Kinana, now," Leena said. The blue serpent sped toward Calem, flying over the grass with the fluidity and grace of liquid. Dislocating her jaw, she opened her mouth wide, and an ocean of water blasted Calem deep into the ground. Leena flicked her wrist. "Kapro." Kinana peeled off, and the snow-white serpent bulleted toward Calem. Snowflakes and tiny crystals trailed behind it, frosting the blades of grass beneath its underbelly. Like Kinana, Kapro unhinged his jaw.

Calem was spurred into motion and leaped away just as Kapro unleashed a blizzard of frosty air. The droplets of water in the grass cracked and froze, an icy imprint in the ground where Calem had landed. He bounded out of reach onto a nearby branch, dusting icicles off the edges of his trousers. He laughed, a croak from the back of his throat. Flashes of oily black blades winked in his palms. "Missed me."

"Calem." We needed her alive. I needed to know more about the Gyss and the wishes it could grant. Only after... I flexed my hand, and the binding oath on my wrist seemed to smirk at me.

He flinched, but didn't acknowledge me. He'd certainly heard me, but the drive that made him so unbelievably lethal had started to take hold. He was by no means an old member of our guild, and yet he'd completed more jobs than any assassin. Including me.

Calem sped forward again, and a barrage of jet-black shadow blades cascaded from his hands. Crafted from darkness by the god of death, those blades could pierce almost anything. They careened right toward Leena's unmoving body. One by one, they crashed into her shield.

The beast by her feet closed six more eyes.

Leena shuddered as another blade smashed against the dome. A sweat broke out across her forehead, and the beast closed yet another eye. Two milky orbs left. What would happen when all lids sealed shut? Was that good? Or bad?

"Calem!" This couldn't go on. A dead Charmer was only good once we got our beasts. More than that, I couldn't stand the thought of her hurt or, worse, gone.

No. That wasn't it. That *couldn't* be it. It was about responsibility. I'd promised that my men wouldn't hurt her. That was all. The fingernails along my left hand sharpened to fine points, and my fingers trembled.

Kost's gaze dropped to my hand for a flash. Grimacing, he turned back to the fight. "Are you sure?"

No. I wasn't sure at all. My nails sharpened further, and my pulse throbbed in my empty palm. Beckoning. I didn't want to answer it, but if Calem couldn't follow an order, if he was too lost in the thrill of the hunt to obey...

I already had to keep my comrades at arm's length. Something like this would only push Calem further away. I needed this delicate balance I'd found—a leader, but not quite a friend, close and yet not close enough—to survive. If I destroyed his trust, I'd lose him. There wasn't enough between us to keep him around. I had made sure of that, if only to keep him safe.

His dark laugh floated in the air and coaxed my fingers to move. He wouldn't stop. Not until he won. If he killed her, I'd never have the chance to close that distance, anyway.

With daggerlike nails, I slit a thin line across the palm of my right hand. Blood pooled in my heart line, waiting to do my bidding.

The blood of a guild master. It swirled and formed a hardened blade much stronger than the shadows, hovering at the edge of my fingers.

"Noc." Ozias gripped my shoulder, his worried gaze darting to my weapon.

The tip turned serrated. Dangerous weapons to enemies, but to my brethren... If my blade met Calem's skin, the call of his leader would shock him into submission. He'd have to follow my command until the remnants of my blood cycled out of his system. To be stripped of free will... I'd only seen Talmage use the power once, and the horrid screams of the affected assassin still haunted me. To do that to Calem...

Bile gathered in the back of my throat. He'd never forgive me, not really, but if he wouldn't listen, I'd have to compel him to follow my orders. I needed that beast.

I needed Leena alive. *For now*, I forced myself to add.

In the meadow, Calem fled from Kinana and Kapro. They chased after him, spiraling around each other and spewing water and frozen air. Each shot missed, just barely kissing the soles of his shoes rather than ensnaring his foot. Winking out of existence, he snuck through the shadows to appear behind Leena. Forceful hands drove a blade into the barrier all the way to the hilt. A sharp crack flooded the meadow, and Leena's knees hit the ground. Unperturbed, the monster closed another eye, and the knife in Calem's hand skittered across the grass.

He raced toward it, and the blade hovering above my palm rose inches higher. "If he breaks through..." I couldn't explain the rising need to protect her. I wanted to run out into the clearing and restrain Calem myself. Use the damn blood blade if I had to.

"Calem!" Ozias shouted. Kost went rigid beside me. He'd seen a blood blade in action before, too.

I took a few steps forward. Crouched low in my heels. Prepared to lunge.

Calem didn't respond. Eyes focused on the glittering blade before him, he even ignored the serpents in the grass. They didn't forget about him. Kinana had flooded the space with water. As Calem bent low to snatch the weapon, Kapro unleashed fury. Ice formed in the span of a breath, immobilizing Calem's left leg and bringing him to a complete standstill.

Pulling more knives from the shadows, he sank blade after blade into the column of ice encasing his leg, but with every crack that appeared, Kinana and Kapro were there. "For fuck's sake!"

The breath I didn't know I'd been holding left me in a ragged exhale. Safe. She was safe. I straightened and called the shadows to me. Let their cool touch douse the anger and fear in my veins. I'd nearly lost it. Lost control. For her.

Leena walked toward him, an unmistakable shake to her steps. The cow beast followed, one milky eye trained on Calem. "What do you say? Should we call it?"

His wild red gaze threatened to rip her to shreds, and he gnashed his teeth as she inched closer. Muscles popped along his neck and shoulders. "I'm not done yet."

She rested her hands on her hips, frowning. "Can you get out?"

He hissed and called forth more blades, smashing them against his cage. Crack after crack snaked through the ice, but her beasts were there. Poised and ready. He had no chance of escaping, but the fury in his glare only burned brighter. Forfeiting wasn't an option.

I whispered his name, and his stare found me before spying the suspended blade floating above my right hand.

All the fight died in his eyes. He took a breath. "You win, Leena. Let me out."

She raised her brows. "Not trying to trick me, right?"

Fear, barely detectable, strained Calem's tone. "No."

Puzzled, Leena turned to us. The blood blade dissolved and my wound resealed before her eyes found mine. "You heard him. It's over."

With a quivering hand, she extended her palm outward and called back her beasts. They disappeared in a rosewood glow, and the ink along her right side retreated. Calem leaped into action, carving away at the ice with an unending supply of blades until he broke free.

"C'mere." Ozias patted a space beside the fire. "You need to thaw out."

"Say one word, and I'll end you." Calem dropped to the ground, muted eyes trained on the flickering flames.

"You were foolish." Kost sank onto a tree stump and braided his fingers together. "You should have listened."

Calem snarled. "Fuck off. She bested you, too."

Tension rippled between them, and Kost's lips trembled. Before he could respond, Ozias held up his hands. "Don't go there. Either one of you."

Calem's chin dropped. I'd almost stripped him of free will because of this woman. Turning away from the fire, I strode out to meet Leena as she approached.

She beamed up at me, strands of hair clinging to the sweat-slicked skin of her neck. "Well? How did I do?"

Part of me wanted to encourage her. To commend her ingenuity. But that was a step down a dangerous path I couldn't follow—one that was tantalizing close and so hard to ignore. "I almost hurt one of my men because of you." The truth of my words burned against my tongue. She'd gotten under my skin. I needed detachment. Separation. Distance.

Leena cocked her head. "What?"

I circled her, each step a warning I desperately needed her to heed. I'd been so worried for her. Calem hadn't been able to contain himself after all, and that look in his eyes... That sheer determination...

I pushed concern to the back of my mind. Caring about her safety was a dangerous notion.

"If this had been real, you'd already be dead."

She shivered, but set her jaw tight. "How do you figure?"

"Assassins are not warriors. We don't fight fair. We don't battle, and we don't give forewarnings. We strike when we know we'll win. In the silence, when you least expect us. You survived Kost because Iky was concealed. You survived Calem because he gave you the opportunity to summon your beasts. But let me tell you something, Leena..."

I positioned myself directly in front of her.

She froze, not backing down but visibly wary.

"No matter how hard you try, no matter how many battles you win, you will never survive me."

And that was the honest truth.

TEN

LEENA

Much to Kost's frustration, we started late the next morning. I'd maxed out my talents by calling forth three beasts at once, and the heavy fatigue in my system was determined to keep me rooted in place. We were only a day's ride away from Ortega Key, but if I didn't get my ass in gear, we'd have to make camp again.

When the unbearable midmorning rays smashed against the canvas of my tent, baking me alive, I finally packed my things, ignoring the weight of Kost's eyes inking a healthy target between my shoulder blades. Zeelahs already waiting, he led the way, leaving Noc and Calem to ride in front of Ozias and me.

"How you holding up?" Ozias reached into his pocket and offered me a handful of almonds.

I popped a few salty morsels in my mouth and chewed slowly. "I'm tired."

Several feet in front of us and engaged in their own conversation, Noc and Calem spoke softly, quiet words laced with something I couldn't place. Heavy shoulders and dark clouds in his eyes, Noc was beyond approach.

"I'd be tired, too, if I summoned three beasts at once." Ozias pulled me back, swapping almonds for a canteen, and I accepted.

"Yeah." I swallowed water tinged with the distinct tang of metal. "What's up with Calem?"

Ozias shrugged. "Wounded pride?"

"Is that all it takes to get him to leave me alone?"

"Hardly." He rubbed the back of his neck. "He'll be back at it in no time."

"He's a flirt, but nothing I can't handle." My gaze slid past Calem to Kost's stiff frame. "Kost, on the other hand..."

Ozias chuckled. "You did threaten to murder him." I grimaced, and his grin deepened. "He certainly has some wounded pride going on, but you'll never have to worry about him flirting with you like Calem does. He's not interested in women."

"Oh, okay." I brushed a stray leaf off my bare arm. I'd changed into a fresh sleeveless tunic and linen pants right after waking, but the grime of fighting Calem remained on my skin.

Sunlight filtered through the thick canopy of broadleaf trees. Giasem brush lined the crumbling dirt path, and their curved leaves held crystalized droplets of water. With each passing breeze, a wondrous mixture of jasmine and lavender with a hint of lemon escaped from their bell-shaped flowers.

A stray beam of light illuminated Ozias's face, and he closed his eyes and tipped his chin to the sky. I couldn't help but smile. "Oz, is anyone waiting for you back home?"

"Oz?" He opened his eyes, a tease lingering in his gaze. "That my new name?"

"If it doesn't bother you."

"No, I kinda like it." He smiled to himself and patted the striped hide of his Zeelah's neck. "But to answer your question, no. Definitely not."

"How come?"

"I'm too shy."

I blinked. "No, you're not."

"You're the only woman outside of Cruor I've talked to for more than five minutes without putting my foot in my mouth." He paused, tossing me a sidelong glance before gripping the reins of his Zeelah. "I'm not an easy guy to approach to begin with. I know that. And then…I dunno. It's like my mind goes blank. With you, it's different."

Oz was a dominating figure—there was no denying that. But beneath his hulking frame was a friendly and sweet gentle giant. His eyes searched my face for an answer, and I exhaled a low breath. "Call it a Charmer's perk."

His brows drew together.

"My whole existence is based on my ability to charm things. I'm a living lure. My body produces an undetectable aroma that puts others at ease."

"Can you control it?"

I shook my head, staring at the patchwork knitting of branches and leaves. "It's not a switch. I forget it's even a thing sometimes." I used to detest it—the first year of my banishment was littered with men and women making advances, eager to flirt. But the emotional attachment wasn't there, no actual connection. It wasn't until sometime later that I realized I preferred it that way. No strings attached. No chance of getting hurt. Dez was the closest anyone had come to even toeing that gap. Between the lure and the Charmers Council, I had no desire to test out trust again. Not when it was so hard to glean anyone's true intentions.

Especially Noc's.

My gaze found him again without even trying, despite his warning still ricocheting through my brain. *No matter how hard you try, no matter how many battles you win, you will never survive me.* His words were so menacing, and yet it was as if he were referring to something else. Not the way he could incapacitate me without a second thought, but something more dangerous, if that were even possible. A shiver spider-walked the length of my spine.

Oz steered his Zeelah closer. "You okay?"

"Yeah, enough about me." I just couldn't let it go. "What about Noc? Who's waiting for him when this trip is over?"

Something foreign darted across Oz's face. "No one. To be honest, I've never seen him bring anyone home."

"No one?" The wheels in my brain turned. I couldn't imagine *no one*. No lasting attachments, sure. But not a single person? What would cause him to create such a barrier? Or was it more a barrier he was trying to tear down...with a wish, perhaps? Noc's reaction to the Gyss played on repeat in my mind. I could gift a mischievous beast like that to a scoundrel with ease. A Gyss's power was dependent on its master. Those with more grit, determination, magic—whatever driving force it may be—could successfully wish for anything. Those with weak wills or flimsy desires? A Gyss wouldn't have the amp necessary to make the truly chaotic possible.

But someone like *Noc*?

Danger.

"Do you know why he wants a Gyss?"

Oz side-eyed me. "No. You could ask Kost. He's known him the longest."

"I'll pass."

A soft, lyrical trill broke through the other birdcalls. It was musical in the way the pitch carried between octaves, and it didn't fit. Craning my neck to the treetops, I scoured the branches. I knew that sound—it was the contact call of a Femsy.

A twig shifted, and the bird appeared. Steely gray with a violet breast, the Femsy inflated its chest once more to let out a string of notes. My bones went cold. This non-native beast was far from home, and those three beady black eyes could easily be telegraphing information to its master.

Adrenaline ignited in my veins, and my symbol sparked to life. The bird homed in on my hand. Was it simply lost? Carried away by an errant wind stream and just trying to get back to its flock? Or was it owned? It was too far away for me to sense a connection. But if it blinked... If the protective films slid over its eyes and glinted an ominous yellow, then I'd know. That unique hue was a by-product of taming. No wild Femsy would have that coloration.

Gods, I needed it to *blink*.

"Leena? What's wrong?" Oz's voice broke my concentration. The Femsy chirped once more before launching into the treetops. As the flapping of its thin wings died, my heart sank.

I hadn't glimpsed the film. But deep down, I knew. A Charmer was watching.

"Leena?" He reached over and gripped my knee, and I jumped. "Sorry, thought I saw something."

His saddle creaked as he turned to look behind him. "What?"

"A spy. But there is a hit out on my head, so I guess I shouldn't be surprised."

Oz frowned. "Who did you piss off enough to warrant your death?"

I swallowed the bile gathering in my mouth. "My guess? An ex."

"Why hire us, then? Seems to me like you Charmers can handle yourselves."

"Charmers don't believe in using their beasts for anything other than companionship. Sure, we'll spar and they'll defend us if needed, but to send them out on the offense... It's unheard of. Even for this man." I tossed Oz a sidelong glance. Ahead of us, Kost and his Zeelah broke through a dense patch of the forest, following the path into a sun-bathed field. A short break from the constant canopy.

"What's his name?"

The sun chased away the last of my chills, and I sighed. "Wynn. I found him doing something illegal, and he pinned the crime on me. Guess he decided exile wasn't punishment enough."

"I'm sorry." Oz's gaze found mine, and I believed him.

"He wasn't always that way." I rotated my ring. "Something happened to him. He went on a hunt for beasts, and when he came back...he was never the same. He never told me what happened."

I didn't know why I was telling Oz this. Even now, years removed from our golden days, the memory of who Wynn used to be tormented me. He'd done enough damage to ensure I'd never return to his arms, but I still wondered. Still retraced those nights to determine what happened to him so long ago. Why he traded love and compassion for power and dominance.

Oz's soft voice brought me back. "Still, you deserve better."

Something inside me shifted. Something warm. I smothered it the second it appeared. "Yeah, yeah." Following the trail, our Zeelahs cut into the knee-high wheatgrass before us. A breeze worked its way through the field, beating the strands of grass against my mount's legs. Another jarring birdcall taunted my ears.

There was no way for me to track the Femsy. All I could do was get on with the job—quickly. The sooner I found their beasts, the better. I needed to get to the Council and clear my name before Wynn did anything more drastic.

As if hiring an assassin wasn't drastic enough.

Chewing on the inside of my cheek, I studied each of the men. I wasn't even certain whether these assassins would turn on me the second they received their beasts. Maybe, just maybe, if I provided them with creatures so perfect for their needs, they'd feel obligated to honor our arrangement.

Assuming assassins even cared about respectable things like honor.

Another heavier breeze coursed through the plains, shifting the grass and rustling the trees along the edges away from the dirt path. Tracking the wind's progression, something white caught my attention. There, lounging at the base of a thick oak tree overlooking the meadow, sat a Poi.

White fur with one black stripe running the length of his spine, the fox-like Poi studied the open field. He was probably hunting for mice, and I only had moments to act. Smack-dab between his oversize ears sat a jewel-like purple orb, and if he decided to pull his focus from his hunt for one moment, if he tapped into his ability to check the future before him, he'd see me coming.

No other beast was as perfect for Kost, the control freak.

"Oz." I pulled my mare to an immediate halt and kept my voice low. "There's a beast along the edge of the forest. Hold on to my Zeelah. I don't have time to explain, but don't follow me."

He blinked, taking my reins as I shoved them into his hands and slid out of my saddle. I only had minutes, maybe seconds, before the Poi sensed me. Crouching low, I weaved my way through the grass out of the creature's direct sight line.

Pausing roughly twenty feet away, I centered myself and focused on the dormant well of power. I tapped into it, letting warmth and joy spread through to my fingertips. A bond offering between the beast and me, a display of love and kindness. My body emitted a peaceful rosewood glow, and I inched forward.

The Poi's head riveted to my direction. Round brown eyes peered at me, and a cloudy mist obscured the once crystal-clear gem atop his head. A new future was brewing, and soon enough he'd be able to see what was about to pass. He licked his chops.

Palms up, I beckoned for him. "Come on. It's all right." I tried to push more power outward, to dazzle him with the possibility of the Charmer's Bond, but fatigue struck hard and fast. Adrenaline fled my system, and darkness tinged my vision at the sudden expense of power. At once, the warm light dissipated, and the Poi saw me only as an intruder in his territory, one within reach of his jowls.

He snarled, lips pulling back to reveal finely pointed teeth coated in venom. Darting forward on precise feet, he already knew the outcome—I was just late on the uptake. He bit the soft flesh of my hand and shredded skin as he dragged down toward my fingertips.

A high-pitch curse burst through my lips, and I stumbled backward into the field. Exhaustion and pain claimed me as I crashed heavily onto the ground. I'd failed. I should've known better, trying to charm a beast so soon after depleting my power. It'd been ages since I'd been this foolish. What was it about these assassins that made me push myself beyond my limits? Black spots bloomed across my vision, and my limbs grew heavy. These men were taxing and damning and annoying and…and I wanted to do right by their beasts. That's why I'd pushed myself.

Before I could examine that thought further, harsh ringing sounded, and I settled into the wave of night that followed.

———◆———

"Why would you let her run off by herself?"

"She saw a beast. What was I supposed to do?"

"Stop her."

Between the cotton in my ears and the crackle of a distant fire, I vaguely recognized the hushed tones of Kost and Oz. Weighed down by fatigue, I couldn't force my lids to open. I'd overclocked myself. Used too much power in too short a span. Kost was right: I shouldn't have tried to tame the Poi.

"How's she doing?" Noc. Was that concern lacing his words? Or just the fog doing weird things to my senses? Slowly, I peeled my eyes open. Three shadows bled against the canvas of my tent, wavering in the orange light of a fire.

"We bandaged her hand, but that doesn't cleanse the poison." Kost's words were clipped.

Poison? Oh. With sluggish and clumsy fingers, I pulled back the edges of my calfskin hide to get a look at my right hand. Poi venom. Black sludge oozed from the bandages, and an onyx matrix of darkness tracked my veins. "Shit."

The three figures outside went ramrod straight before peeling back the entrance to my tent and clambering in.

My gaze fell to Noc first, and my pulse went from canter to full-blown stampede. Wild jet-black eyes pinned me in place. I sank deeper into the blankets to put distance between us. "What?"

Edged words forced their way through his clenched teeth. "What were you thinking?" Behind him, Kost pressed his lips into a fine line. Oz didn't make a sound. Sad eyes lingered on the fluids seeping through the bandages of my hand.

"Where's Calem?"

Heat of a different kind flashed through Noc's hardened features. "Hunting. Presumably better than you."

I forced myself into a sitting position. Dark sludge drained to my fingertips. "No need for quips. I saw a beast. I tried to tame it and failed. End of story."

"Is this what we should expect of your taming abilities?" Kost folded his arms across his chest. With his sleeves rolled past his elbows, I spied the tense muscles of his forearms. He was a harbinger of disappointment. I wanted to throttle him.

Instead, I bit back a growl. "The beast was for you."

Silence stretched between us. Anger fled from Noc's face as he crouched before me. "I see."

"Do you?" I cocked an eyebrow at him, trying to get a grip

on his ever-changing mood. "I was trying to fulfill my end of the bargain."

Kost scowled. "I haven't told you what kind of beast I want. Your efforts were futile."

Oz ran his thick hand across his cropped hair. "Kost..."

"You're insufferable, you know that? You would have wanted this beast, trust me." I clenched my hand and fought back a yelp, pain spiking through my arm and speeding toward my shoulder.

Kost tensed. "Don't presume to know what I want. You know nothing about me." Without another word, he stalked out, heels meeting the earth with more force than necessary.

A weight settled in the pit of my stomach. I needed Kost to want this beast. More than that, he needed to love his creature so he'd be inclined to honor Noc's promise. A beast worthy of erasing the bounty for good. Maybe they'd never accept another hit on me again.

Someone in the good graces of Cruor. I slumped back into the makeshift bed of tan hides. I wasn't stupid enough to think that would ever happen. Pay anyone enough money, especially an assassin, and the whole deal could change. But by then, I'd be worlds away with a Myad in tow. No one would dare attack me with that beast by my side, and hopefully it'd be enough to grant me a meeting with the Council.

"I'll check on Kost." Oz tossed me a half-hearted smile before slipping through the green flaps of the tent.

Noc side-eyed me, the high angles of his face sharpened by his profile. "What kind of beast were you trying to acquire?"

"A Poi." I felt another surge of pain, and I brought my arm flush to my chest. "Trust me, it's the beast Kost wants."

"Why do you say that?"

"Aside from their nasty bite"—I flexed my fingers to fight back the stiffness—"they can see two minutes into the future. No more, no less, but extremely useful when it comes to strategic planning. It's a B-Class bordering on A-Class beast. Meets all the requirements."

Noc inched closer until he was within arm's reach. A rare bit of softness touched his gaze. "I'm sorry."

"For what? You didn't do anything wrong." I winced, but didn't dream of moving. He was so close. Tension roiled thick between us. So much like that insurmountable space that had been between our fingers the night we had dinner and talked for hours.

"For Kost. I think you're right… This beast suits him." He leaned forward, and my breath caught in my lungs. "What are we going to do about this?" He cupped my injured hand, and a droplet of poison splashed against his palm. My heart squirmed at his touch. I knew nothing of fortunes. My own peaceful future had been savagely ripped from my grasp, and I'd been left ostracized and alone. But looking at Noc's hands, at the network of creases and callused fingertips, I wondered if one of those crossing lines had anything to do with me.

No. I couldn't think like that. His future was his and mine was mine—we'd never cross paths again after this. That's the way it had to be.

"There's only one way to fix this." I couldn't bring myself to look away. I knew I should have wrenched free of his grasp, put some distance between us, but his voice was so low. Pained. He was the last person I could ever trust, but the soothing heat from his touch, so at odds with the usual chill from his demeanor, burned away the sting of the poison. "I have to tame the Poi. He can pull the venom out."

Noc's fingers brushed higher up my wrist, almost reflexively. "Do you have the strength to do that?"

"Tomorrow."

His touch froze as if he'd only just realized what he was doing, and his eyes stuck to the place where his fingers met my wrist.

Unease stirred in my belly. "Are you okay?"

Darkness sharpened in the tent. A range of emotions fought for control over his face. Some I recognized, some I didn't. But I noticed a glimmer of longing. A beat of despair. Was touching me really so painful? Why?

He dropped my hand and pinned me to the ground with a stare cut from granite. "I'm fine. Will your hand last until tomorrow?"

I blinked. "Yes, but—"

"Good night." He rose, the tent flap shuddering as he stalked out.

I stared helplessly after him. Understanding Noc was not part of the bargain. Get his beasts, get out. But he had a way of consuming me without even trying, and his honeyed scent lingered in the air as sleep tugged on my consciousness.

ELEVEN

NOC

Leena left her tent at first light. We followed a short distance behind her, quiet. Onyx lines scratched across her skin like patchwork stitching, spanning her shoulders and reaching toward her cleavage. A slick sheen clung to her, dampening the fabric of her blouse.

"Noc—"

I shot Kost a glare, and he buried his words with a subtle gulp. Shadows hugged us, masking our presence to give Leena the best possible chance of taming the Poi. She trailed left and right, studying patterns in the dirt I couldn't see. A dance between Charmer and prey. Eventually, she came to a standstill, and her head snapped toward a tree along the edge of the wheatgrass field.

Nestled among overgrown roots, the Poi lorded over the edge of his territory. Brown eyes speared her, and Leena smiled. Endless minutes stretched on as neither of them moved, a battle of wits. Then, without preamble, Leena's skin burst into a pale glow so vibrant and pure that my breath caught in my chest.

"She did that yesterday, too," Ozias whispered beside me, all his weight pressed into the balls of his feet.

I couldn't explain the sudden pull. The insistent swell of energy that begged me to leap across the clearing and take her in my arms.

Was this her charm? Or something else? It was more than a physical drive. She was the fire that threatened to melt the frozen cage I'd constructed. And no matter how hard I tried to keep things distant, every action of hers begged me to persist. Her very existence gave life to something deep and long buried in my heart.

"She's incredible," said Calem, muted awe evident in his voice.

Kost removed his glasses and blinked several times before replacing them. "Is anyone else experiencing feelings of elation? This is quite spectacular."

Calem and Ozias grunted in agreement, but the description fell flat. My mind teased me, dragging up possibilities of a future where Leena and I existed on the same plane. One without cool detachments and lines in the sand.

I clenched my hands into fists. *No.* Thinking like that wasn't an option. Between the bounty and my curse, her fate was set. I tried to force myself to view her as merely another being, another job, and not an impossible future.

She brought herself within a few feet of the Poi, hands outstretched and fingers beckoning. Pain stabbed my gut at the sight of the poison, but the light around her diminished the severity of her situation. She *was* light. Love. A promise. And the Poi had the opportunity to take it.

Slowly, the Poi stepped over the roots to sit directly in front of her. Large ears flicked up to the sky, and he tilted his head to the side as he sniffed her hand. With gentle fingers, she tickled the underside of his chin. The swirling cloudy orb on his head cleared, a sparkling, radiant gem winking in the light of the morning sun.

And then Leena laughed. Pure, untainted, joyous. The Poi made a soft barking sound, and a flare of light exploded beneath her fingers. When the surrounding air dimmed, she turned her head to us and smiled. "Come on, it's safe."

I reached her seconds before the rest, but I couldn't drop the darkness as I so desperately wanted. I needed the shadows to lessen her light. "Everything go as planned?"

She frowned, eyeing the creeping blackness licking my extremities. "Yes. There isn't any danger." She turned back to the Poi. "He's going to draw out the venom now."

Rows of pointed teeth sank into her flesh, but Leena didn't flinch. When he released her, he licked the puncture holes and a thick coating of saliva sealed the wound.

"I need to take him to the beast realm." She stood, brushing dirt off her pants. "When I get back, I'll have a key for you, Kost. Unless you don't want him." She kept her back to him, ignoring his presence and focusing entirely on the creature at her feet.

Kost sighed. "This beast suits me."

"So be it." Rosewood glow erupted from her hand, and an invisible door swung open. Leena and the Poi winked out of existence.

Calem tugged on his hair, pulling it out of its bun. "What do you think the beast realm is like?"

"I'm sure we'll never know." Kost stared at the empty space where Leena used to be. I could sense traces of her in the air. The faint scent of her perfume. The leftover warmth of her charm.

Ozias placed a hand on my shoulder. "You can come out now."

It was meant to be a tease, but I flinched. Ozias raised a brow and tightened his grip on my shoulder. An unspoken question. With a heavy breath, I released the curling darkness and capped my power.

"Everything all right?" Kost studied me with more knowing than the other two.

"I'm good."

His eyes formed fine slits. "Calem, Ozias, go get the Zeelahs and our gear. We should leave the moment she returns."

The two shared a silent exchange before disappearing. We'd

already packed our things, but Leena had demanded we leave the Zeelahs behind so as not to spook the Poi.

"She's getting to you, isn't she?" Kost pressed his hands along his buttoned tunic, searching for nonexistent wrinkles.

"It was just her charm."

"Was it?"

"Yes." *No.* I didn't know. Kost knew that, too.

He adjusted his glasses, eyes boring into me. "You need to be careful. It's been years since Bowen—"

"Don't." A heavy breeze worked its way through the tree leaves, the steady rustle the only sound around us. "Don't say his name."

Kost cracked, a flicker of sadness tugging at his lips. "I'm sorry, Noc. I just don't want to see you hurt again."

"There's no need to worry about that, is there?" I tapped the bounty mark on my wrist. "You know as well as I do that if I don't kill her, my head will roll."

Kost winced. "That can't happen. The guild needs you. We need you. I just worry that if you let emotion take over—"

"I'll be fine. I *am* fine."

He didn't relent. "Ozias and Calem might not know the extent of your curse, but I do. I couldn't imagine your life. Precariously balancing on the edge of caring too much while praying it's not enough to hurt us. Are you saying you're not the least bit tempted?"

I kept my voice low for fear of it cracking. "Do you remember what happened to you?"

Kost stilled. "Of course. But—"

"You almost died." I stared at my hands. "All because I felt, expressed too much. I watched you grow sick. Stood by while purple bruises bloomed beneath your eyes and the skin cracked around your face. When the cough hit, I knew. I knew it was my fault."

"Noc..."

Gripping my hands into fists, I shook my head. "You were my best friend. And then I was a royal ass for weeks. I never visited your bedside. I ignored your dying wishes. I did everything I could to remove my emotions from the equations. By the gods' favor, you survived."

"I don't blame you."

"You should. I still blame myself."

Kost sighed. "That's what worries me. If you get too involved with her, if you go too far... Noc, I...*we* need you. The guild cannot survive without you."

"I'm not going anywhere." I leveled him with one look. "My devotion to the guild is all I have. All I can have. You know that as well as I do. It's a nonissue."

Kost dipped his chin to his chest, hiding his eyes from view. He hadn't been there when my curse had claimed Amira. When I'd proclaimed my love to her and she to me, only to have her die in my arms a few days later, riddled with sickness, courtesy of the high priestess's magic. He hadn't been there when the magic claimed the lives of my brothers-in-arms on the battlefield. When I mistook their failing health for the plague and condemned many, so many, to death without even trying.

I'd become an assassin before I'd even died.

But Kost had seen me with Bowen. He'd watched as I fell in love again, only to have him ripped from my hands because of my own ignorance. His sickness—the same illness that Amira had exhibited—was the wakeup call. The thing that caused me to retrace the months, years, and examine the deaths of all those I cared about.

I'd nearly come undone. But Kost had been there. Had helped me reconstruct my walls and build a safe, if precarious existence. He'd somehow snuck through a crack in my defenses, though, and almost *died* because of it. Just then, the low swing of a heavy door opening overcame the scratching of tree leaves. Leena appeared alone, the Poi nowhere to be found. Ink scampered down her shoulder, receding back to the barren tree on her hand.

She pivoted to Kost. "Do you remember the Charmer's Law?"

Kost didn't blink. "Of course."

"Of course you do." Leena gritted her teeth. "As much as I don't like you, that doesn't mean you'll be a bad owner. But I'll be watching your every move. Got it?"

"I'd expect nothing less."

Muttering to herself, she fished a small bronze key out of the front pocket of her linen breeches. "Use this gate key to open the door to the beast realm, and your Poi will come to you. You won't be able to enter, and only your beast will be able to come and go."

Kost took the key, holding it up to the sun to inspect it. "How does it work?"

Fatigue washed over Leena's features, and she sagged in her stance. "When you want him to appear, hold out the key and call him. He'll come." Another breeze threatened to topple her over, and I instinctively reached out to steady her. Tilting her head back, she smiled up at me. "Thanks."

My heart skipped a beat.

"I may ask for more details later." Kost pinpointed the space where my hand met her back. "But it can wait."

"Oh, and Kost?" Leena's eyes fluttered. "He doesn't like the name you picked out for him. Think of something else."

Kost blanched. "What?"

Leena tapped her forehead, her smile turning lazy as sleep started to take her under. "Two minutes into the future, remember?"

I let out a quiet chuckle and caught Leena just as she sank to her knees. I barely had time to sweep her into my arms before she lost everything to unconsciousness. A soft murmur, and she nuzzled into me. Every muscle in me tensed. The rightness of her weight against my chest was startling, and that dangerous emotion—longing—started to unravel in my heart. I *couldn't* want her, in any way. She was a target. It was my job to end her life. Even if she wasn't, even if we'd met under different circumstances, she was still liable to die at my hands if I ever let anything slip. Yet, as she pressed her cheek deeper into me, the heat of her body threatened to shatter the cage I'd spent a lifetime building.

Kost cleared his throat, eyebrows disappearing into his hairline, but I only shook my head. Her outcome had been predetermined the moment she walked through my door.

——◆——

We hit Ortega Key just as evening shifted to night. A cylindrical rycrim core towered high into the sky, showering the surrounding city with magical energy. Cheerful lights glowed against the night, windows thrust open to welcome the gentle breeze heavy with the scent of salt. A crescendo of ocean waves crashed in the distance, and our Zeelahs' hooves sank into white sand.

Somewhere along the way, pines and firs had shifted to palm trees.

"There's the inn. I'll arrange our accommodations." Kost trotted ahead to the first structure on the outskirts of the city. Ironclad light fixtures lit the face of the bamboo-slatted building. The clanging metal insignia hanging above the door featured a dead pig on a spit with the words *The Roasted Boar* engraved along the bottom.

Calem followed after Kost, Leena's bag-laden Zeelah in tow. She'd been unconscious since the taming, and I'd wisely left her to Ozias.

He rode up beside me, Leena tucked between his chest and the neck of his mount, and he grinned. "I dunno about you, but I'm ready for a good scrubbing."

"Same." The town was alive with seafaring folk. They wandered the streets and docks, belting conversations at unnecessary decibels. They were so different from the people of Wilheim. So...free. Tanned from days in the sun, they wore light garb and buckled, open-toed shoes. Laughter was so joyous and constant that it could have been mistaken for music. But they had that, too—men and women with drums and lutes sitting in circles around crackling bonfires. Their rumbling chorus welcomed the boats ceaselessly docking and departing from the city.

Tilting my head to the sky, I studied the low-hanging moon. A smearing of emerald light stretched across the indigo night—a fissure in the darkness that was brighter than the smattering of stars. We'd left our world entirely for something grander. More alive.

Ozias let out a low whistle. "We should come here more often." A soft moan worked its way through Leena's lips, and she buried her head into his chest. Ozias tucked loose strands of hair behind her ear. "She'll be okay, right?"

Jealousy was a beast, and I feared Leena was the only Charmer skilled enough to tame it. When had things taken this turn inside me? "She'll be fine."

With a heavy yawn, she dug her palms into her eyes. "Where are we?"

"Ortega Key. You slept the whole way." Ozias shifted to give her space, and she blinked up at him. Realization slammed into her fast, and she went rigid in the saddle.

"I'm sorry." Her gaze shifted to me for a moment before skittering away.

"You needed the rest." Our Zeelahs slowed as we approached the inn, and I nodded toward Calem already unloading our bags. "Take it easy."

"Sure." She didn't look my way. Once the Zeelah stopped, she jumped down and pushed through the double doors without another word.

Kost emerged from the inn, irritation lacing his gait. "She just stormed in and took the key without thanking me."

"Did you thank her for the beast?" The words tumbled out before I could stop them.

"Noc's got a point." Calem reached for the Zeelahs' reins. Kost opened his mouth, but Calem cut him off. "And don't even give me that 'She tried to murder me' crap. She bested you. That's all you care about. She bested me, too. I'm over it." He turned his back to Kost's slack jaw. "Ozias, there's a stable up the road. Come with me?"

Ozias pursed his lips in a horrid attempt to hide his grin. "Sure, but let's make it quick. I want to clean up."

"And I want to hit the town." With a wink, Calem prowled down the street with Ozias close behind.

"About Leena—"

"Enough, Kost." Baring my teeth, I flexed my hands. "I'm not in the mood."

Kost dropped his chin. The lantern clinging to the inn's wooden wraparound porch flickered, and I cocked my head to the side. A cloud of shadows spiked around us, and Kost's confused gaze snapped to mine.

"Not me," I said. The slats beneath my feet creaked as I turned, searching the gravel street before us.

"Me." It was a whisper, a grating of dead leaves along jagged rocks, and all concern faded. There, standing in a plume of darkness a few feet from the entrance, was Emelia. Or rather, Emelia's shadow self.

I stepped off the porch and strolled toward her. "Everything all right?"

Kost followed, flanking my side and studying Emelia's apparition. A gust blew through and her frame wavered, but she nodded. "Sort of."

My jaw tightened. Emelia was a damn good sentry, and I'd left her in charge of reporting any issues while we were away. "Is it Darrien?" His wry grin sparked in my mind, and I fought back a grimace. Cruor was all I had. If Darrien tried to take it from me, he'd learn firsthand what it meant to experience a slow and painful death. It would be far worse than his first.

"No, Darrien is fine. As intolerable as always, but nothing of note. It's the client."

"What client?" Kost interjected, folding his arms across his chest.

"Leena's client." Errant tendrils of smoke spiked around her hands. "He wants to see you, Noc."

My fingers lightly traced the mark on my wrist. Such a small, disastrous thing. "When?"

"Now."

"Of course." I tossed a glance back at the inn. Leena was inside, hopefully resting, and here I was, plotting her murder. "Where?"

"Midnight Jester. He's already waiting."

"All right. Get back home. I'll handle it."

She nodded, her shadow dissipating into the night. I headed back to the inn and pushed open the double doors with Kost on my heels.

"You're on the first floor. The rest of us are upstairs. The last door down this hallway."

"Got it." I took the short hallway down to a single door framed by twin lamps. I paused at the entrance, fingers lingering on the handle. "Kost, no need to stand guard. Take the night off. Get to know your beast."

"If you insist." He hesitated, feet angled toward the low-lit hallway, but his gaze still trained on me. There was something unspoken buried deep within him, and he shook his head once before turning away.

With a soft click, I locked the door behind me. Of course, Kost had gone above and beyond for my accommodations. Back doors thrown open wide to the night, the breeze rolled in off the ocean and flirted with the white organza curtains. Lights winked on as I strolled forward, illuminating the shiplap ceiling painted seafoam green. A low, white sofa was pressed flush against the foot of a bed.

I kicked off my shoes and sank into the mattress, eggshell-white sheets molding to my skin. If I was going to be shadow walking tonight, at least my body would be comfortable. My back pressed against the wicker frame, I closed my eyes and called the darkness to me.

Charcoal tendrils swirled behind my eyelids until my conscious-ness detached. Leaving my physical body in stasis, I welcomed the freedom of moving without restriction. Shadows formed without thought or effort, and the world disappeared as I traveled on the wind, picturing nothing more than my destination.

Midnight Jester appeared. Tucked between oppressive willow trees on the border of Wilheim and the Kitska Forest, it was the perfect location for black-market dealings.

It was where Kost had first tracked down Leena.

Pushing that thought away, I moved forward and materialized through the door. A few locals shot me cursory glances, but they went back to their ales and their business without wasting a second glance. Assassins flocked to this tavern for work, but only members of Cruor could walk with the shadows. No one wanted to test their luck with us.

The bartender moved toward me, a careful smile trained on his lips. "Can I help you find someone?"

"No." He most likely meant well, but revealing client information was strictly forbidden.

He didn't seem offended. "Well, I'm not saying you're looking for anyone in particular, but there's a fellow in the back corner who seems interested in your arrival." Turning his back to me, he took up his place behind the bar and began wiping down the counter with a rag.

Crammed in the far corner of the establishment was a rickety table with two mismatched chairs, one of which was occupied by a cloaked figure in those same liquid-mercury robes from Devil's Hollow. Strolling toward him, I bled through tables and people without a thought. Only one person yelped.

"Noc." The man gestured toward the chair before him. "Please, sit."

I slipped my hands into the pockets of my trousers. "Not necessary. What can I do for you?"

Wax dripped from the candle in the middle of the table, puddling around the tarnished holder. He picked at a dried glob of yellow goo, and his snowy Charmer's emblem bleared up at me. Harsh in its vibrancy, it scorched the air with none of the softness of Leena's power. "I would like a status update. We expected the job to be completed already."

"We're working on it."

The man grimaced. "Work faster. She sells beasts on the black market. That's punishable by death." He steadied himself with a deep breath, adjusting the hem of his hood to hide his jawline. "Plus, she's a skilled Charmer. She once used her talents to try to tame a human. For all you know, she could already have you under her spell."

A human? My pulse quickened for a moment. I recounted every interaction, every hidden look or passing conversation and came up empty. If she had tamed me, then she was damn good at it, considering I was still here. Conducting business that involved her death.

I narrowed my eyes. No, this was different. Something was off about his anger. Something deeper. I'd spent enough time dealing with miscreants to know most people hid their true intentions, but it didn't matter in my line of work. Leena had been marked. Whether it was for selling beasts or something else entirely, the result would be the same.

Twisting my right hand to show him the inside of my wrist, I held the inked mark to the candlelight. "You know as well as I do what this means. You think I'm willing to let her walk away in exchange for my own life?"

"Cruor's Oath." His lips quirked up in a wicked grin. "The reason we hired you in the first place. Your assurance is guaranteed."

"Indeed."

He braided his fingers together. A monstrous silver ring with garnet stones winked in the candlelight. "I'm sure you don't get bounties like this often. Don't forget what's at stake here. For you. For your guild."

I didn't need the reminder. Jobs were necessary. They kept Cruor fueled, my brethren safe and fed, and made our extended life a little bit easier. Normalcy had died when I went under years ago, and this was the best I could provide. I would do anything to keep that intact.

Leena's hazel gaze flashed before my eyes, and my heart shuddered. "I will keep you posted."

The man leaned back in his chair. "She's heading to Ortega Key... But you already knew that, didn't you?"

"What are you insinuating?"

He snapped his fingers, and a severe glow ensconced his hand. The familiar groaning of a door dominated the room, and several patrons turned their attention to our table—including the bartender. Gaze stuck on my client, he polished the mug in his hand so hard it cracked.

A soft chirping dragged my attention back to the Charmer. A tiny bird with a violet breast and three eyes stared up at me. It blinked, and a yellow film slid over its irises. "You think I wouldn't keep tabs on my investments? We hired you to do a job, and you're dragging her halfway across the continent. You've even got backup. Why is that?"

I kept my voice level. "The job will be done. If you needed it within a set time frame, your *boss* should have set a limit when she hired us."

"Ah yes, the terms." He snapped his fingers again, and the bird disappeared. "An oversight on her part. Just speed up the process. You have her already, so end her."

I had to rein in my fury to keep lashing shadows from blanketing the entire establishment. "Don't question my methods. You hired us; we'll do the job."

He folded his arms across his chest. "We still need access to her bones within six hours of death, so don't wander too far. Otherwise, I'll be forced to send something to collect her."

I froze, instantly ensnared. I needed to get back to her. He could already have someone, something, lying in wait. If she was in danger... I fisted my hand once before letting it fall slack. I shouldn't *care*. "If there's nothing else, I'll be on my way."

"Quickly, Noc." The way he said my name only fueled my anger. "Whatever promise she's made you is a lie. She's lied before, and she'll lie again. I would expect an assassin to know the difference." He stood slowly and leaned in close so the edge of his cloak brushed my shoulder. "And remember: If you don't kill her, we'll have to intervene. The last thing you'd want is something unfortunate to happen, say, to one of your friends? Think about that." Without another word, he walked right through me, leaving a chill in the air and my heart.

TWELVE

KOST

My feet ate up the space between the foot of my bed and the ottoman as I paced. Calem and Ozias were out drinking, no doubt, completely unaware of the danger their guild master could be in.

Noc was perfectly capable of dealing with our employer without my assistance, and yet leaving him alone to shadow walk to Midnight Jester set me on edge. Yes, he would be safe from physical harm, but there was no telling how cunning our employer was. We needed to deliver Leena's remains soon, lest we face more beasts that were as skilled at killing as we were.

"*Tsk.*" I shook my head once as I remembered the way Iky had snared me. I'd been too arrogant. I should've tracked Leena longer to see exactly what I was dealing with before I struck. Then we wouldn't be in this unfortunate mess.

Sighing, I slumped onto the cushioned ottoman and studied the layout of my room. I'd organized my belongings the moment I'd arrived, leaving me with little to do while the others were occupied. A thick book with red binding sat on the nightstand—a bit of light reading I'd brought in case such moments of reprieve occurred. But with Noc off pretending at niceties with our employer... No story would keep my mind engaged.

I should have planned for this. *But how?* I ran an errant hand over my tunic and paused when my fingers grazed a key-shaped lump tucked away in my breast pocket. Leena had mentioned the Poi could see two minutes into the future. That might seem miniscule to the average person, but I was acutely aware of what such time could do. Two minutes could give someone a chance to change their mind. Two minutes could stop a blade from piercing a heart. Two minutes could prevent a lifetime of distrust.

Clenching my jaw, I pushed away the foggy memory of my past and settled instead on a more recent calamity: two minutes could've stopped me from getting captured by Iky.

Now, more than ever, we could use that foreknowledge. Which meant I needed to practice. Fishing the bronze key out of my pocket, I extended it in front of me and focused on my beast. I heard rather than saw the beast realm door open. The heady groaning rolled through the confined space, and after a brief flash of light, my Poi appeared.

"Felicks," I said by way of greeting as I returned the key. He sank to his haunches and studied me with inquisitive coffee-colored eyes. The crystal-clear amethyst orb atop his head turned cloudy with smoke, a sign he was tapping into his future. Leena had fallen unconscious before I could get a detailed breakdown on how his power worked. Tonight's training would be an exercise in trial and error. But how, exactly, to go about it? What would prompt him to share his visions?

The smoke cleared in his orb, and he tilted his head to the side ever so slightly.

"Waiting for me to catch up, are we?" I asked. While I didn't have the Charmer's symbol sprouting to life on my hand, I could feel the invisible tether between us. It was a slight prickle of warmth that started in my palm and bloomed outward to my fingertips. Given that beast lore wasn't something I'd find in any book in Lendria save a Charmer's bestiary, the feeling surprised me. It was so different from the cool, soothing welcome of my shadows, and yet equally delightful. Reassuring.

Felicks waited without moving. At least he appeared to be patient. Would it be as simple as commanding him to share what he had seen?

"Felicks, show me what will happen in two minutes' time."

While he clearly didn't have eyebrows, he gave me a look that suggested if he had them, at least one would be raised.

"It's prudent to try the most obvious option first," I muttered. Gently, I removed my spectacles and began polishing them with a cloth from my pocket. I knew little about training animals, let alone beasts. Ozias once told me a story of a dog he had growing up and how he'd used bacon scraps as incentive to teach him to bark on command. Felicks seemed far more intelligent than the average canine, but perhaps he was food-motivated as well. Replacing my glasses, I stood and made my way to the bamboo dresser. There, carefully tucked beside my tunics, was a pack of blueberry beast treats I'd managed to secure while acquiring provisions for our travels. Tracking down the underground dealer who was known to carry such rare morsels had been bothersome but not impossible. While I'd hoped for more variety—he only had apple and blueberry, and one of each, no less—it was better to be prepared, in case Leena needed some for taming.

I snagged the pack, returned to the ottoman, and sat, patting the space beside me. "Come on. Up."

That command, apparently, Felicks knew. He leaped onto the soft cushions and settled in, gaze intently locked on the small sack in my hands. I undid the twine and pinched a soft, circular treat between my forefinger and thumb.

"Let's try this again. Felicks, show me what the future has in store."

This time, the orb clouded and swirled as my beast took a deep inhale. His tail swished back and forth. Holding the treat out of reach for now, I fixated on the orb and the unknown future brewing inside. I didn't know what to expect. A voice in my head? A distinct picture or series of events that would play out in my mind? I held my breath until the smoke dissipated. Future determined, and yet I had no inkling as to what it would be.

Do I need to touch it? With my free hand, I ran my fingers delicately over the smooth surface of the orb. The connection of our bond surged, and the tingling warmth radiating from my palm grew. But still, no visions.

Felicks nudged my hand, his wet nose cold against my skin. A small whine eked from his throat.

"Oh, all right." I gave up the treat, and he snatched it with impressive quickness. It was gone in an instant, and he was back to staring at the sack of treats in my lap with rapt attention. Food motivated, certainly. Whether or not feeding him would result in him sharing his visions…still to be determined.

"I have no intention of allowing you to become a gourmand." I ran my fingers along the underside of his chin, and he huffed—a sign of affection or a disgruntled reaction to my statement, I couldn't tell. But it did something weird to my heart—tightening my chest in a way that wasn't exactly unpleasant—and I sighed as I procured another treat. This time, he ate it in a much more civilized manner.

"I've never had a pet before. You'll have to be patient with me." My fingers naturally traveled upward to his scalp, and when I hit the spot between the base of his ear and the orb, he practically melted into my touch. I felt myself smile. "I also never imagined I'd be talking to a beast, and yet here we are."

For a while, I simply sat and stroked the length of his spine, studying the swirling orb atop his head. It clouded every two minutes and cleared shortly thereafter. And while the warmth in my hand grew with every passing instance, the visions never came.

Leena is probably in her room. I should ask her. I balked at the errant thought. Certainly when I saw her next I'd demand more detailed instructions, but seeking her out intentionally? The last thing we needed was to become dependent on the person we were supposed to kill. No, I needed to keep trying on my own, at least for now.

Exhaling a quiet hum, I let my gaze wander about the room. The candles on the nightstands provided a gentle light that cast the space in flickering shadows. Everything was adorned in soft beiges with taupe accents and the occasional pop of canary yellow streaking through the throw blankets at the foot of the bed. The windows were open to let in the evening breeze, still warm despite the darkening sky. The fluttering, sheer curtains caught around a square table set with two chairs. A gridded game board with smooth oval stones, ebony on one side and ivory on the other, sat waiting.

Perhaps a quick game of Gunchess will spark some ideas. Scooping Felicks into my arms, I moved to the table and slid into the first chair. Felicks didn't seem bothered we'd left the beast treats behind, so long as I kept up my methodical scratching.

"Tell me, will I win this game?" I directed the question to my beast, who responded by settling into my lap with his back against my chest so he could stare at the board. No vision. It was a long shot, anyway, seeing as most Gunchess games lasted for the better part of an hour.

On each game piece was a symbol dictating rank, and the etchings sparked with magical white light at my touch. If another player had been present, they would've remained lifeless. But now, I waited as the opposing ivory stones arranged themselves across from me, their symbols glowing as an invisible force took hold. One that would learn from my every move and grow in prowess as the game continued.

As the challenger, I went first, pushing one of my ebony pawns one grid space toward my opponent. Felicks's ears flicked high, and he studied my hand with the same attentiveness as he had the treats. His orb clouded.

"Do you like games?" I asked, my attention divided between my beast and the ivory pawn that slid a space closer to my line. The objective of Gunchess was to checkmate the king through a series of strategic maneuvers, eliminating key forces along the way. Running a few fingers over my own oval stones, I selected another pawn and moved him forward, planning to create a protective barrier for my bowman to emerge. Then, I dropped my hand back to my beast's fur and continued to run my fingers down his spine.

Felicks's orb cleared. And for the briefest of moments, I caught a glimpse of an ivory oval with a dragon marking scooting into position. Not because it actually happened—there was no space on the board for my nonexistent opponent's piece to move that far just yet—but because I saw it in my mind. It was like a highly detailed sketch, or rather two or three pictures rapidly presented in succession, disjointed and hard to follow. A sharp pain sparked through my temple as I tried to grapple with the foreign image at the same moment my hand spurred with warmth.

And then it was gone.

Three moves later, the dragon piece moved and took out my bowman. My hand went still against my beast.

"Felicks," I said, voice quiet. He looked at me expectantly before slipping his snout beneath my fingers, begging for a scratch. "Was that you?"

He let out the softest of barks. A quiet affirmation, and my heart soared. Unable to contain the grin tugging at my lips, I tore my gaze away from the board and focused solely on my beast. I didn't have the faintest idea how he'd managed to project that image—or rather, I hadn't the slightest inkling how I'd received it. But I had. And that was a start.

Instead of pondering my next move, I waited until Felicks's orb began to cloud.

"Let's try that again, shall we?" I watched the indecipherable swirls with fascination, waiting for them to settle. It only took a moment for them to dissipate and reveal the crystal-clear amethyst. And just like before, I ran my fingers along his spine. He closed his eyes in contentment, and again I was hit with a spark of pain in my temple and a flash of images. Perhaps not two minutes' worth—we'd only just begun to connect—but still something that had yet to occur. This time, he'd shown me moving one of my pieces, which would prompt my opponent to move their ivory chariot forward.

Which I could then take out with my prince.

I moved my piece into position and waited, fingers softly massaging tiny circles behind Felicks's ear. If the chariot moved forward three spaces...if it took out my furthest pawn and left itself open to a swift demise, courtesy of my prince...

The chariot moved forward, knocking my pawn to the side and signifying its claim to the space.

Excited, I stood up so quickly I nearly sent Felicks toppling to the floor. But, he must have known that was coming, too, because he deftly leaped out the way just a fraction of a second before I rocketed to my feet. With a harried look, he flicked his tail back and forth while waiting for me to collect myself.

"Apologies." My voice was a breathless rush of air. "This is incredible."

The gears in my mind started to turn as I planned out the rest of the match. I'd study the board and contemplate moves, but withhold from making any concrete decisions until Felicks's visions came through, all the while maintaining physical contact to keep our connection strong. Then, and only then, would I move my pieces into position after learning about my opponent's intention.

He's truly magnificent. My gaze slanted back to my beast, still patiently sitting on the floor. And then he opened his mouth wide, exposing all his sharply pointed teeth as he let out an exaggerated yawn. Some of the warmth in my hand receded. Just a small fraction, but enough that it was detectable, as if it were crawling back toward the center of my palm.

My brow furrowed. "Are you tired?" I flexed my hand, trying to encourage the heat to spread, but nothing happened. All Felicks did was blink, but it would stand to reason that he needed to rest. I glanced back at the board. As much as the idea of finishing the match with Felicks by my side excited me, his well-being came first. He wouldn't be able to help me in the future if I didn't take care of him now. I could encourage him to sleep in my lap—I'd started to grow used to the warmth of him against my legs—but something told me only the beast realm would offer the respite he needed. Perhaps one day he'd be able to snuggle beside me while I read or drifted off to sleep.

"That's enough for tonight." Slipping my fingers into my breast pocket, I extracted his key and held it out before me. "You did well."

He stood up and rammed his head into my calf. An unfamiliar but not unwelcome warmth stirred in my chest. I was ready for the responsibility of owning a beast but unprepared for the pleasing emotions. I was already eager to summon him again. His ears flicked skyward when the realm door groaned open, and then he winked out of existence. Back to his home to recover. I returned the key to

my pocket. There was still so much to learn. So much to *discover*.
The thought brought a smile to my lips. I'd have to prepare a list of
questions for Leena, but at the very least, I'd done this on my own.
We had done this on our own. Felicks and me.

And with his help, I'd make sure my brothers and I—*Noc*—
would always be prepared, no matter what danger we faced.

THIRTEEN

LEENA

Between the hours I'd spent sleeping on the ride and the kicker from the Poi's restorative saliva, I had more energy than I knew what to do with. Freshly bathed and wrapped in a fluffy towel, I dumped the contents of my bag across the four-poster bed. Everything from my clothes and makeup to the hidden pack of apple-flavored beast treats—which Kost must have scoured the black market to find, given only bakers in Hireath crafted such delicacies—was meticulously chosen and arranged. If I'd never met him, I would assume he cared.

I slipped on a pair of cutoff twill breeches and a low-cut, ivy-green blouse, then relaced my boots and paused before the mirror to apply a light go of cosmetics. Dark bags had started to form beneath my eyes. A by-product of stress, no doubt. I didn't want to advertise that weakness, though, so I packed on some powder and called it good before leaving to enjoy Ortega Key's nightlife. Warm air rushed against me as I stepped out onto the gravel road. Lampposts manned the sides of the street, sandy beaches laden with shells coming flush with the roads. A heavy crowd with loud men lingered outside a bungalow down the road, and I smiled. In past conversation, Dez had mentioned a pub in Ortega Key that ran in the black-market circuit.

Guilt soured the back of my tongue as I pictured Dez's face. I'd said I'd come back, but now...I'd been made. If the assassins did let me walk, going back to familiar quarters would make me the easiest target around for any other bounty hunter. Maybe here I could have a new start in warmer surroundings.

Another debate for another time. The sooner I unearthed information about potential beasts in the area, the better. My bestiary only held data for locating and taming beasts I already owned. Anything new, including the Myad, came through hearsay. That, or failed taming attempts until one stuck.

A failed attempt is exactly what would happen if I couldn't get my hands on the blood of one of these men. I'd almost forgotten about it, what with Oz's reassuring grin and Calem's shameless flirting. We were getting closer, and I still didn't have enough answers, enough solutions to the mounting problems clambering in around me.

Maneuvering through jumbling bodies, I held my breath to avoid choking on the stench of sunbaked fish and climbed up the steps to the Drinking Mermaid. Once I passed through the open doors of the tavern, ale and liquor drowned all other scents. A gaggle of women dressed in shift dresses and bathing garments giggled over crystal glasses filled with clear liquid. Nestled between two of them, Calem glanced up at me as I walked in. He offered a leisurely wink before turning to the blond on his right and whispering something into her ear.

"Leena! Over here," Oz called from the far end of the bar, a shaky smile pulling at his lips.

Dodging a pair of tits that threatened to knock me over, I sidestepped the bar maiden and sidled in next to him. Scrubbed clean and dressed in a sleeveless white tunic and loose-fitting, russet-brown trousers, he leaned against the bar and palmed a mug of ale.

"Did Calem drag you here?" I stuck my thumb over my shoulder at the sudden outburst of feminine laughter.

Oz's eyes slid behind me to linger on his friend. "He claimed he'd get me a date."

"Really now? Seems like he's more interested in his own nighttime activities." Signaling the bartender, I ordered a Cockatiel Kiss—a southern specialty—before swiveling on the wooden stool to face him directly. "Not to worry, though. I've got you covered." I took a swig from my freshly poured drink. Pineapples and cinnamon liquor with a hint of nutmeg rushed over my tongue, warming my throat. "You're not great with women."

Oz's chuckle was short. "You're not instilling any confidence."

I set my glass on a black napkin, and a ring of condensation bled to life. "I'll help you. Charming people isn't that different from charming beasts."

Thick eyebrows drew together. "Can you do that? Actually tame people like you would a beast?"

A sudden sharp pain speared my rib cage, and I stared past Oz into a memory he couldn't see. Cool sweat trickled down the lines of my palms. No one had ever *successfully* tamed another human being, but that's not to say it hadn't been tested. Not by me, but by someone I knew. Intimately.

"Leena?" Oz reached out to graze my shoulder, and I flinched. "What's wrong?"

"Nothing." My gaze darted to the dangling light above our heads. Seashells dripped from fish netting in a makeshift lampshade. "No. You can't charm people. I just meant that figuratively."

His eyes narrowed. "Leena—"

A portly man made a move for the open barstool beside me. I turned in my seat, flashing him a dazzling smile, and leaned forward to give my cleavage a good show. "Sorry, hon. I'm saving this seat for my friend."

Grimy hands wiped down his off-white work shirt. "No

problem, doll. Come see me if you want a drink." He moved away, but kept his face angled toward me.

Concern fought with curiosity, deepening the creases in Oz's forehead. Curiosity won out. "Who are you saving the seat for?"

"Your date."

His face blanched, and he drowned his ale in one heavy swig. "Leena, don't worry about it. I'm not alone, anyway. You're here with me."

I glanced back at him. "I'll worry if I want to." I tossed him a smile before once again skimming the patrons for possibilities. Just then, a lone woman entered the pub. With sunset-red hair tied back in a thick braid, she had a pleasant heart-shaped face and wide olive eyes—eyes locked directly on the open barstool beside me. Her gaze jumped to me and I smiled, motioning toward the empty seat.

"Anyone sitting here?" She brushed her hands along her hips, and her gaze caught on Oz. Winner.

I beamed at her. "No, help yourself. I'm Leena, and this is my friend, Ozias. 'Oz' works, too."

He fumbled for a moment before pushing out a rushed "Hey." He hid his face in his mug and tried to fade into the wall at his side.

"I'm Corinne. Nice to meet you." She gripped the edge of the bar as she sat. "I haven't seen you two around here before."

"I'm here on business. Oz was kind enough to escort me."

Corinne peered past me to smile at him. "That's nice of you."

When he didn't respond, Corinne reclined and stared out over the crowd. I glared at him, but he only wilted farther away.

"So." I swiveled back to her. "What do you do around here for fun?"

The bartender dropped off Corinne's drink, and she toyed with the black straw. "Well, fishing is an obvious first choice for most, but I'm more partial to getsa ball."

"Getsa ball?" If this had been one of the questions in Noc's game, I would have failed miserably. Growing up in Hireath had its perks, but we were woefully secluded from the rest of the world. Whatever she was referring to was something we didn't have, and my days of banishment weren't exactly full of leisurely activities.

She gave me an incredulous stare. "You've never heard of getsa ball? C'mon, you're kidding me." She looked past me to Oz. "She's kidding, right?"

He braved a sentence. "It's a sport."

"Oh." I rotated the ring around my finger. "How do you play?"

Corinne lit up, fire practically igniting in her eyes. "The entire point of getsa ball is to get the ball to the opponents' end of the arena three times."

"That doesn't sound too bad." I nudged Oz's knee, hoping he'd weigh in. He only blanched again.

"It's not that simple." Dimples burrowed into Corrine's cheeks, and she launched into a feverous explanation that involved something with shifting terrains, magical belts, and teams that I didn't have the dexterity to follow.

When she paused to drain her beverage and order another, I rounded on Oz. "Have you ever played?"

He swallowed twice. "A few times. I'm always given the defender belt."

Corinne's eyes skimmed his frame. "Makes sense, given your size."

He mumbled something unintelligible into his drink, and I kicked him beneath the counter. Ale lurched from the brim of his mug and coated the bar.

Corinne giggled. "A group of us get together and play in the evenings. You're more than welcome to join us tomorrow, if you'd like. The last ferry from Queens Isle docks right around dusk, so as soon as I help my father clean up, we can head over to the arena."

Queens Isle. All thoughts of getsa ball and getting Oz some action faded in the wake of those words. I scooted closer to her. "Any reports of beasts on the island?"

She tilted her head, gaze dropping from my face to the bestiary dangling around my neck. Charmers were rare, but easy to identify. The bestiaries were a permanent part of our attire, removable only by our own hands. "He hasn't mentioned anything."

There was a question lingering on the end of her sentence, but she pursed her lips. The Myad had to be here. Right before Kost tracked me down, a patron had visited Midnight Jester raving about a black, winged beast in the south.

"What about any of the passengers? Have they had any run-ins?"

Corinne tilted her head to the ceiling. "I usually just run the booth, so I only talk to them when they're purchasing tickets for travel, not after. But I could ask around."

She was my in. My way to the Myad. A burst of sharp laughter erupted from Calem's table across the tavern, and I caught his haughty grin in the corner of my eye. Shame settled low in my stomach. Beside me, Oz had deflated entirely, brown eyes searching for answers swirling in the contents of his drink. I was about to do exactly what Calem had done—ditch him for something I wanted.

Corinne took a sip from her drink. The bartender appeared then, and she pressed her chest flush with the bar. "Can I get an order of fried mushrooms, please?"

Mushrooms. My ears perked up, and I leaned back to lay my hand on Oz's forearm. "Oz makes some mean mushrooms. We traveled here by Zeelah, and he found some along the way. They were the best thing I'd ever eaten."

Corinne's dimples returned. "Really? I love to cook."

I tightened my grip on Oz, and he smiled. "Me too. Back home, I experiment with stuff all the time."

"I've got to visit the bathroom. Be back in a bit." I slid off my stool. His eyes widened, but I winked and darted away, lingering along the back wall to watch the pair. If he wouldn't talk while I was there, he'd be forced to with me gone.

It was only a matter of minutes before Corinne switched seats, abandoning hers to claim mine and lean closer to Oz. My forgotten drink pushed to the side, they bonded over the platter of deep-fried shrooms and alcohol. While I couldn't make out their conversation, at the very least, I'd done better than Calem.

"Seems you have a knack for making people happy."

The hackles on the back of my neck stood on end, and I spun to find Noc leaning against the wall. Faint tremors of darkness clouded the space around him. He could have been hiding in plain sight for hours, and I never would have known.

I strong-armed my racing heart back down to an acceptable speed. "Must you always do that?"

A wry smile teased the corners of his lips. "Do what?"

"Scare the living shit out of me."

He shrugged. "It's not my fault you're...excitable." Glittering eyes sparked with mischief. Shoulders and hands relaxed. Posture open. He'd set aside his usual frosty demeanor for the moment. He really was no easier to understand than a cat. One minute slinking away without an ounce of interest, and the next looking at me as if I were the only thing in the room.

Heat gathered along my neck, and I swept my hair over my shoulders to hide the trail of red. "You're dangerous."

His smile deepened. "You're finally starting to understand. Care to join me for a stroll? I'm not sure Ozias needs your help anymore. Unless you prefer to follow Calem's lead, in which case I'll leave you to pick from the many winners at this fine establishment." As he gestured widely, his frame went unexpectedly tense at his own suggestion.

I shook my head. "Walk sounds good to me."

"Good." Placing one hand on the small of my back, he guided me out to the gravel road. Our feet crunched over loose rocks, and his fingers warmed the skin beneath my blouse. Butterflies took flight in my belly. He'd never touched me like this before. It'd always been with an air of reluctance. Even when he'd cupped my hand in the tent, it'd only been to inspect the poison. But this was different. Deliberate. I didn't want it to end.

After a beat, he removed his hand.

A low hollowness skated around the space where his touch had been. "I'll start gathering information on beasts tomorrow." Lamplight had been dimmed to amplify the beauty of the night, and millions of stars crowded the heavens. We veered off the beaten path toward the sands.

Noc nodded. "All right. I'll get Ozias and Calem to give you more information."

"Thank you." There was enough space between us to fit another person, and rational thought warred with insane desire as I eyed his swaying hand. As if reading my thoughts, he hid it in his pants pocket.

The backdrop of ocean waves kept my nerves at bay. Noc gazed at the deep-blue water crashing beside us. Seashells and glittering pebbles glistened in the moonlight. The beach was relatively empty, save a few bonfires with couples huddled together, cotton blankets with geometric designs draped about their shoulders.

"Actually...I should be the one thanking you."

I stopped, sand giving beneath my feet. "Me? Why?"

"For Ozias. And Kost should thank you for his beast, though I don't think he will, so I'll do it for him."

Slowly, I started walking again. "What did he end up naming the Poi, anyway?"

Noc's lips quirked. "Felicks. He agonized over it, too. He didn't know what name you had been referring to, so for the rest of the ride, he was a bit of a wreck."

"Guess I'm good for laughs. One more thing you can thank me for."

"What else are you good at?"

I snorted. "That's an odd question."

He shrugged, and our elbows brushed. "I'm curious."

"Still trying to figure this puzzle out?" That certainly made two of us. I inched closer. "I don't have the worst singing voice around."

"Really?" He pulled his hands out of his pockets.

"A lot of Charmers can sing. Or play an instrument—something musical. We're trained in a lot of different things that could help us potentially tame a beast." Sand gave beneath my foot, and I unintentionally swayed closer. My pinkie grazed the back of his hand. He didn't flinch.

"What do you do for fun?"

I chewed on my lip. "Not a lot."

Tilting his head to the side, he pinned me with his gaze. "How come?"

For a moment, I paused and simply stared out over the endless expanse of ocean. There were more stars than waves, and their collective light dwarfed that of the moon. We were a world away from Hireath. A world away from Midnight Jester and black-market dealings and scrambling for bits. Out here, with Noc's hand so close to mine, I could almost forget. I could almost pretend that I had the luxury to simply *be*.

"I'm on the run. I don't have a lot of time for leisurely activities. What about you? What do you do for fun?"

"Not a lot." His smile was surprisingly soft. Full of understanding. As if he knew what it meant to fight for just a sliver of peace. He probably did.

"That's not true. You read. What else do you do? I imagine you get into plenty of shenanigans with Calem and Oz."

"Oz?"

I waved him off. "Ozias. Don't avoid the question. You're surrounded by friends and family. I bet you're always having fun."

His shoulders stiffened, and his gaze drifted out over the waters. "Not as much as you'd think."

I could practically *see* the frost gathering in his aura. Feel the building cold that defied the warm humidity of the beach. My pulse quickened. I didn't want him to retreat when I'd finally brought him close. If he shut me out, I wouldn't be able to get closer, to build a relationship that could save my life. And yet...this felt deeper. More instinctual. I wanted to *know* him. Not to gain something, but because it felt *right*.

I tried to shake off that thought. "I can also play the harp."

The chill left with the tide. His eyes found mine. "The harp?"

"Yeah, and I'll brag: I'm certifiably amazing." I knocked my elbow into his side and started walking parallel to the ocean. He kept up with ease.

"I don't play any instruments. Maybe I should learn."

"I can give you lessons." Tilting my chin to the side, I gave him a crooked smile.

For a moment, he said nothing. Then, after a several beats, he let out a cautious breath. "Maybe."

We reached the far end of the beach, and both of us stilled, uncertain what to do next. But I wasn't ready to end our conversation, no matter how difficult it was to get him to open up. Sinking to the ground, I positioned myself before the ocean and stared out over the ink-black waves.

Slowly, as if he were second-guessing his decision, he sat beside me, body tense. I needed something to put him at ease. A safe topic to keep the conversation flowing. He'd shown interest in my beasts before. Maybe summoning one now would keep him intrigued.

Splaying out my hand, I centered myself and focused on the hum of power stemming from my symbol. Flipped through my available beasts in my mind and settled on a Canepine. The realm door groaned open, and out bounded my wolf-like beast. Still a cub, he tripped over too-big paws as he barreled toward me, tongue lolling out the side of his mouth.

Noc smiled and eyed my beast. "What's this?"

"This is a Canepine. His name is Blitz." I scratched between his ears, admiring the ivy-green color of his fur. Tiny white flowers naturally grew from his coat, lining his neck, the underside of his belly, and sides of his face. They produced a subtle aroma reticent of pine trees that intermingled with the salty ocean breeze.

Noc offered the back of his hand to Blitz, who sniffed his knuckles while wagging his fluffy tail. "He's cute. What does he do?"

"Aside from fetch?" I snagged a piece of driftwood that had been washed up on the beach and held it high above my head. Blitz's body went taught, his round, powder-blue eyes riveting to the branch. I threw it as hard as I could, and he took off down the beach after it. "He's a C-Class beast with the ability to purify water for consumption. He's also a phenomenal tracker."

"I bet that comes in handy for beast hunts." Noc's gaze followed Blitz as he leapt onto the twig and began dragging it back to us.

"It does. If I ever run out of water, I just have to find a stream, collect some, and have him purify it. As for the tracking…" I stifled a laugh when Blitz dropped his prize in Noc's lap, showering him in sand. Noc raised a bemused brow, but complied, tossing it farther down the beach than I had. Blitz raced after it. "Let's just say he's got a few years yet before he's grown up enough to put those talents to good use."

"Not focused enough?"

"Unless it's a stick. He can pick the right twig out of a lumber pile, but couldn't care less about the scent of anything else." I shrugged. "Maybe I'm in the wrong field. I could go into logging with his talents."

Blitz came bounding back, happily offering his branch to Noc. But when he went to pull it away, Blitz growled playfully and tugged it back. Noc chuckled. "Maybe not. He doesn't seem too eager to hand over his find."

"You're right. I'm screwed."

Noc finally wrenched the branch free and chucked it again. "I think you're doing just fine as-is."

"You must be, too." I pulled my knees to my chest and draped my arms over them. "Running a guild and taking care of your family."

"It's not without its challenges." His voice was low, almost sad.

"Noc?" I hesitated, unsure how to continue. What could have happened in his past that caused him to be so distant? Forlorn? I sifted for words in my mind as Blitz came back, but instead of asking for another round of fetch, he flopped down before us and started gnawing on the branch.

Noc turned his heavy gaze on me. "Yeah?"

"Why are you so…detached all the time? I mean, not *all* the time. But when you start to warm up a bit, I feel like you intentionally pull back and isolate yourself. Why is that?"

He reacted as if I'd slapped him, jerking back a few inches and clenching his jaw so tightly I was afraid he'd break his teeth.

"Like that. Right now. Why do you do that?"

"I have to go." His voice was cold. Lifeless. When he made a move to get up, I shot out my hand and pressed it firm against his chest.

"Wait. I'm sorry." I dug my fingers ever so slightly into his tunic. "Please, don't go. We don't have to talk about that."

The whole world stilled while I waited for him to respond. Even the constant sound of the ocean waves somehow dimmed, and Blitz's relentless chewing disappeared entirely. There was only Noc and the unsteady beat of his heart against my fingers. After a moment, it began to slow to a normal cadence.

Noc sighed, letting his hands drop to the sandy bank on either side of him. "It's just the way it has to be."

Gently, I moved my hand away and placed it beside his. Fingers only inches away. "Are you sure?"

"I'm sure." He looked at me then with so much heat in his obsidian gaze that I choked on my words. So much turmoil. All I could do was stare. If I wanted to, I could reach out and graze his cheek. Lock my hands behind his neck and angle his face toward mine. And crazily enough...I *did* want to. I wanted to very, very badly.

I tipped my head his direction, heart thundering madly.

Noc inched his hand closer to mine in the sand until our fingers grazed. His expression said so much, and yet I couldn't comprehend it at all. But gods, did I want to. Yes, this had *bad decision* written all over it. He was an assassin. I was his bounty. There were so many things that could possibly go wrong—for both of us. And yet, no matter how hard I tried to fight it, I found myself drawn to him. Pulled to him like the ocean waves were guided by the moon.

"You're trouble." The words were a deep hum purring from the back of his throat, and he dipped his head low, almost as if he couldn't help himself.

I traced the inside of my lower lip with my tongue, and his eyes targeted the motion. For the first time, I noticed a small crescent-moon scar above his left cheekbone, faded bone-white. I wanted to run my fingers over it. To lose my hands in the mess of his hair. To know what it was like to kiss him. "I know."

He was so close now, his lips inches away from mine. "I don't think you realize what you're doing to me." Heat from his breath scorched my skin, and a delicious chill swept across my neck. "It can't be that bad. Right?"

Unable to resist any longer, my fingers skimmed the side of his face, ghosting over that small scar. No way was this just me trying to get close to save my own skin. No, I had to be honest with myself—I wanted this. I wanted *him*. Everything had been bringing me to this moment.

"If you were smart, you'd stay away from me." His voice was pained. I couldn't shake the feeling that he was begging me to give up. To walk away. But I just couldn't. Not when his lips were so close to mine.

Just as I was about to close the gap between us, Blitz let out a loud, playful bark. That jarring sound broke whatever spell had taken hold between Noc and me, and he jolted back. All the heat I'd felt was taken away with the next wave, and he stood without meeting my gaze.

"Goodnight, Leena."

"Noc, wait." I scrambled to my feet.

He didn't deign to answer. Darkness surged, and Noc disappeared, leaving behind nothing more than his honeyed scent.

Angry heat bloomed in my chest, and I scrubbed my lips with

the back of my hand to try to wipe away the feeling of his nearness. But that was the problem with honey—wiping was more like smearing, and suddenly I was covered in the sting of his rejection and wishing I'd thought twice before flirting with a harbinger of death.

FOURTEEN

NOC

Leena had a hidden talent—shadow walking. Throughout the day, our group meandered through the town while she hammered locals for information on beast sightings. And while she was there, walking just in front of me beside Ozias and Calem, she wasn't. She never looked at me. She never spoke directly to me. And I couldn't blame her. I'd left her high and dry, even if it was for her own good.

But gods, had it been hard. I'd wanted to kiss her so very badly.

My stomach tied into knots again at the thought. I just needed to be more guarded around her. Anything more than trivial conversation opened the door for emotions, and those couldn't get involved. Not with a bounty and a curse to consider. The former becoming a more pressing issue, given we were being watched.

My hands curled into fists. I didn't like being monitored, and the mere thought of that smug prick studying us made me want to spend my hours locked in the shadow world.

We'd abandoned the crowded beaches of Ortega Key for a more remote inlet in search of a beast Leena had sensed. The waning sun set fire to thousands of smoothed crystals mixed in with the white sand, and the pastel-lilac sky slipped toward a deep blue. The night air was calm. Quiet. The constant ebb and flow of the ocean waves masked the muted conversation between my comrades, and Leena halted. Gaze lingering on the horizon, she studied an island in the distance shrouded in mist.

Everything around us reminded me of last night. The call of the ocean. The slowly darkening sky and the first smattering of stars. Her gaze, lost and longing, as she looked out over the sea. How close I'd come to kissing her.

"What kind of beast are we looking for?" Calem sidled in closer, and their shoulders brushed. My fingers twitched.

"I can't tell. I know it's here, but it's hiding." Her brow scrunched together. "It's strong."

"Is it a Gyss?"

She shot daggers with her eyes right through my skull. "No." She turned back around and continued parallel to the ocean, searching for something I didn't even know how to look for.

So it wasn't a Gyss, but I didn't want her to forget. I hadn't. She was so averse to the beast that I wasn't sure she'd tell me if it were nearby anyway.

"Wait." Leena froze. Her eyes darted wildly across the beach. Endless rows of sand dunes stretched to our right, and broken shells stood out like teeth against the tan grains.

The nearest dune shivered.

Leena whipped around and crouched low into her heels. "Found it." Power swelled in her aura, and the rosewood glow of her emblem ignited against the evening air. Just as she was about to move, the mound struck first.

Showering the earth in a gritty spray of sand and shells, a monster erupted from the top and landed before us. More than thirty feet long, it stood on four powerful legs that ended in hooked fingers. Its wormlike body was plated in thick, orange scales and slick with a shimmery mucus.

"What. The. Fuck." Calem's words couldn't have been more appropriate. Three eyes on either side of its mandibles snapped to his location. And then it let out a shrill cry that shook the beach and covered us in the stench of rotting flesh. Eight pointed tongues spilled between rows of jagged teeth.

Leena flexed her hands. "It's a Scorpex."

"Like that tells me anything!" Calem fell into the realm of shadows, dodging one of the errant tongues and reappearing behind us. The Scorpex snapped its jaw shut. For a moment, it did nothing but stare at Leena.

"Wait a minute." She dropped her hand, and the glow about her emblem died. "This one is already tamed."

Unease stirred low in my gut. "What do you mean, it's already tamed?"

"I can sense the bond. It's..." Her eyes went wide. Fingers trembling, she barely found her words. "It's his."

The beast shrieked again and lunged. With impeccable aim, it whipped its tail around and struck its stinger in the earth—right where Leena had been. I'd yanked her out of the way just in time.

The bastard Charmer from Midnight Jester. When I hadn't immediately delivered Leena's corpse to his feet, he must have decided we needed some encouragement. Fire sped through my veins, and I slit a deep gash across my palm. "Kill it. Now."

"My pleasure." Ozias's normally calm face was granite, and he glowered at the enlarged insect with heaping amounts of disgust. Shadow blades molded between his fingers, and he formed heavy fists before launching toward the monster. He connected with the side of its neck, and two of the blades drew blood.

The beast's high-pitched screech ripped through the night. Reeling back, it struck Ozias across the chest with one of its feet. He careened through the air and smashed through a dune hill before his spine cracked against the base of a palm tree. Kost and Calem sped forward, calling forth shadow blades as they moved, and flung daggers at the Scorpex's hide.

"Wait!" Leena's voice barely registered above the shouts of my brethren and the beast's cries. "I don't think it wants to be doing this."

Frustration spiked in my chest, and the blood in my palm quivered before shifting to a serrated blade. "And?"

"Don't kill it." Wide eyes locked on my weapon. "Please."

I couldn't believe what she was asking. The smack of flesh meeting flesh reverberated through the air, and Calem's body flew past us into the ocean. Water sprayed the night, and he leaped up. The same ire he'd possessed while sparring with Leena consumed him, and all recognizable traces of Calem were lost in his manic growl. He lunged past us and bulleted toward the beast, thrusting more blades into its hide as he went.

One arm bruised and broken from his earlier crash, Ozias flanked Kost's side. They brandished fresh weapons and charged. But their blades slipped against the beast's thick mucus, dropping to the ground in tacky pools. Between the Scorpex's barb-covered mandibles and the stinger at its back, they dodged life-threatening cuts at every turn.

No more. I stalked away from Leena.

"Noc." She gripped my wrist. "I can feel it. I don't know why, but I can. Let me try something first. And if I fail..." Her gaze slid to my blade. "I won't get in the way."

Everything inside me demanded I say no. But she leveled me with her hazel stare. Those eyes could tear through all of my constructs, all of my careful plans and rationalized defenses. She was an impossible force, and I didn't have the strength to resist her.

Gritting my teeth, I yanked her toward the beast. "I'm not leaving your side. If it makes one move to strike you, it's dead. Understood?"

She nodded. "Call them off."

"Fall back!" I bellowed over the roar of the creature, and Kost and Ozias slipped into shadows. Without hesitation, they reappeared behind me. Calem didn't respond. Lost in his anger, he continued to lash out at the beast.

Blow after blow connected with the Scorpex's hide, but it only had one target now, not three. Sand dunes toppled to the ground as it whipped around and locked its gaze on Calem. And it struck. Fast. Its stinger barreled through the air and punctured Calem's shoulder.

"Calem!" I made a move to run to him, but Leena had already taken off. She sprinted toward him, coming to a skidding halt just as the beast shook him off. Shouldering his body as it slumped to the ground, she placed herself between him and the beast.

Red-hot fury clouded my vision.

If you don't kill her, we'll have to intervene. The last thing you want is something unfortunate to happen, say, to one of your friends? The man's threat ricocheted in my brain. One day. One day I had dallied, and this is what I got. A soft, jarring chirp shattered my focus, and I spotted the same bird from Midnight Jester perched on a broken palm frond.

Fucking Charmers.

The Scorpex shrieked again and shifted in the sand to bring its mandibles within piercing distance of Leena.

Leena. I dove into darkness and charged toward her, praying I'd reach her before this monster destroyed the person who could change my world.

A stunning rosewood light erupted from Leena's frame, the same wondrous glow she'd emitted when taming Felicks. Warmth radiated from her center, and she stood tall before the beast. The fear I'd glimpsed in her eyes earlier had disappeared altogether.

"Go home. You don't want to be here." Hers was the firm tone of a mother reprimanding her child. This beast wasn't even hers, and yet the love in her voice was real. Tangible. Something foreign and long forgotten stirred in my chest.

The beast shuddered. Sand shifted beneath its feet, and it sank lower into the ground.

It's going to pounce. Darkness flowed, and I closed the remaining distance across the sloping sands in an instant. She was within my reach. I just needed to grab her, to bring her flush with my chest, and welcome her into my world of shadows.

Her light sharpened, battling against my darkness, and she reached out to place a gentle hand on the beast's head. "Go."

A heavy moan escaped the creature's mouth and threatened to split my heart in two. Suffocating sadness poured from the Scorpex, and it whimpered beneath her touch. With a sharp gasp, Leena's body started to tremble.

Intensified light shot outward from the space where her fingers made contact, and the groaning of a heavy door opening filled the night air.

"What...?" Leena didn't move. All she could do was stare at the subdued beast beneath her.

Kost sped toward us with Ozias on his heels. "What's happening?"

After a moment, her light faded, and the door creaked closed, taking the beast with it. Slack-jawed, Leena turned to face us. "I tamed it. I shouldn't have been able to do that."

Questions bubbled to the surface of my mind, but they were lost in the sudden wet gurgle spilling from Calem's lips. "Fuck, that hurt," he said.

"Dumbass. Noc told you to back off." Nursing his broken arm, Ozias peeled back Calem's tunic with his good hand and cringed. Dripping with blood and impossibly deep, a gaping hole covered in viscous green venom dominated the right side of his chest. "That will take a while to heal."

Leena kneeled before him. Deft fingers swept across his wound. "He didn't dislodge his barb. Good. Felicks can help seal the wound, but you'll need to crush up some piffa root and pack it in there first. That will take care of the poison."

"Great." He tossed me a sheepish look. An apology for not following orders.

I steeled my anger. "You're lucky it missed."

"We'll take him back." Kost looped one of Calem's arms around his shoulders, then glanced at Ozias. "We need to set your arm so it heals properly. We wouldn't want to rebreak it later."

Ozias winced. "Yeah, all right."

"I need to check on the Scorpex." Leena stood slowly, brushing stray grains of sand off her bare legs. Dressed in cutoff, skintight linen breeches and a sleeveless tunic, her body was covered with sand. A bead of sweat dashed down her cheek, and I braided my fingers together to keep myself from wiping it away. Gods only know where that would have led.

"I'll wait here for you." After everything that had just happened, leaving her alone wasn't an option.

Kost stared at me for a moment before relenting. Calem's pained grunts spurred them into motion, and as one, the three of them disappeared in a plume of shadows. There was silence, save the constant backdrop of the ocean waves. As if the monster had never been sent in the first place. As if we weren't evading bloodthirsty Charmers.

If I didn't act quickly, this was bound to happen again. My comrades or Leena? My curse or freedom? The answer was harder than it should have been.

A quiet trill sounded from a nearby tree, and my gaze snapped to the bird. The damn spy. I summoned the last undried droplet threatening to coagulate in my palm. Sharpening my blood into a fine needle, I sent it flying. It struck the bird square in the heart, cutting off its final chirp with sickly finality.

Leena tracked its descent with her gaze and flinched when it crashed into the earth. She'd probably hate me for killing a beast, but I didn't need her to like me. I needed her alive. I needed my *family* alive, and tonight, some bastard had threatened that.

My bounty, my terms. I hoped he got the message.

Preparing for her disgust, I turned to face Leena. A single tear slipped down her flushed cheek. A mixture of sadness and...relief? She dug her palms into her eyes. "This is all my fault."

I tried not to gape. Her fault? We were the ones plotting her murder. And she was worried about putting *us* in harm's way? Pinching my nose, I steadied my breath. "What just happened?"

"Not sure. Once I get back from the beast realm, I'll know more." She stared at me for a moment, the sadness in her gaze replaced with something I couldn't follow, before she dropped her attention to the ground.

I don't know why, but part of me died. I needed that look. I needed it back. Her worry for us, for my brethren's well-being... It was too much. Between the bounty and the curse, I knew damn well that her company wasn't something I'd ever truly get to enjoy, but I couldn't help the gnawing ache in my gut.

I gripped the back of my neck. "Hurry back."

She peered up at me through her lashes. "You could come with me." She dropped those words as if they were nothing. Like it was a simple possibility rather than the opportunity to see something that was entirely hers. And while I should've brushed her off and put much-needed distance between us, I couldn't.

"Go with you?"

"You can enter the realm with the assistance of a Charmer."

Without any further explanation, she splayed her right hand out to the side. The inked insignia on her hand grew, roots wrapping around her fingertips. The branches of the tree climbed upward, snaking across her shoulder and reaching up her neck. She'd hidden her face from us when she'd taken Felicks, but this time I watched as the magnificent tree grew over the right side of her cheek. Leaves and flowers bloomed to life, framing her temple and eye in an intricate garden meant only for her.

It was the most striking thing I'd ever seen.

She held out her hand. "Come on. I know it must pain you to trust me." Her voice broke, as if she were realizing something deeper about her statement that I didn't have the wherewithal to understand. It was so subtle I barely caught it, but the slight dip in her tone shoved a blade deep in my heart. She was so unbelievably wrong. I would've kept my fingers interlocked with hers forever if our circumstances were different.

Once she wrapped her fingers around mine, light exploded, washing away our surroundings into a blinding-white stretch of pure warmth. A different kind of nothingness. My heart squirmed, and I tightened my grip. When it receded, the world before me was unlike anything I'd seen before.

Thick with the scent of vanilla and lilac, so like the faint aroma that clung to Leena's skin, a gentle breeze worked its way over rolling hills covered in lush grass. Leena released me and stretched her hands wide. Behind her, a dense forest clambered up against the foot of a snowcapped mountain. A brook trickled somewhere in the distance, the gurgling water competing with the whooshing leaves dancing in the wind.

Bright eyes pried open my soul, and she smiled. "Welcome to the beast realm."

FIFTEEN

NOC

Two moons hung heavy in the sky, one slightly larger than her sister. An aurora of aqua blue stretched against the cobalt night. Millions of stars clustered together, creating a brilliance that showered every inch of the realm in fine light. Leena strolled parallel to the woods, her boots leaving soft imprints in the earth. She walked with the certainty of a ruler, moving through the endlessness of this world without an ounce of hesitation. This was her domain, and I was just a spectator.

I didn't have words, and her small grin told me she knew.

We didn't have to go far to find the Scorpex. Curled in on itself in a tight ball, it unfurled its head as we approached. Beady eyes darted from Leena to me. With a gentle hand, Leena ran her fingers across its mandibles.

"Why are you here?" she murmured more to herself than the creature, but it responded with a series of clicks. She shook her head, offering it one last stroke. "The dunes are over there. You're safe now." Standing, she pointed to someplace beyond the forest. The Scorpex followed her gesture. It folded its legs flush to its body and slithered away at breakneck speed.

"What happened back there?" Being in this space with her, in her world, I wanted to know everything. It was a dangerous feeling.

She tilted her head to the sky. "I honestly don't know. I know the beast wasn't happy. I could sense his anguish from being forced to fulfill his master's call. But when I told him to leave... I dunno. It just sorta snapped."

"What snapped?"

"The bond. But instead of disappearing, it reattached to me. I don't know why. I don't even know if this has ever happened before. If I were back in Hireath, I might be able to find answers..." Her words died off, and she started to walk again. It was so hard not to ask. Not to pry. But she wasn't forthcoming about anything to do with her home. If I wanted answers, I'd have to coax them out of her.

She stopped to tangle her hands in the dripping pink strands of what appeared to be a weeping willow. Among the leaves, flashes of bronze caught in the moonlight. She smiled, fingering one before plucking it.

"The key tree. Charmers can gift beasts as they see fit, and so the realm provides."

Taking the key from her outstretched hand, I rolled it between my fingers before handing it back to her. "Why is it such a crime to sell beasts, then?"

Her chest deflated, and she rotated the ring around her finger. "Gifting implies the Charmer has done their due diligence. That we've decided, after careful consideration, someone is worthy of owning a beast. It harkens back to the days when Celeste, goddess of beasts, first shared her creatures with us. Selling negates all that. It puts a price on the things we cherish most in our lives. They should be priceless."

The bounty mark on my wrist throbbed. "Everything has a price."

She shook her head, taking a few more steps along the edge of the forest. "Not to Charmers. Not to our beasts. They may heed our call, but our connections to them are unlike anything else in this world. It's a sacred bond."

She wrapped her arms around her chest and came to a standstill. She had ventured through life on her own for so long, dealing in creatures she loved, that admitting it seemed to exhume a type of pain I couldn't begin to comprehend.

She'd meant to share something beautiful with me, and here I was reminding her of her sins.

"Tell me about this place."

She blinked, and some of the heaviness faded. "The realm alters itself to accommodate the needs of the beasts. Those who thrive in the cold live in the mountains." She stared beyond the treetops to the mountain range in the distance before turning back to me. "The plains house so many different types of creatures that I couldn't even begin to name them all. And if a new beast appears that the realm hasn't seen before, the environment shifts."

Before us, a small pond pooled to life. Bluish-green waters spread outward, and Leena sank to the ground. She dipped her boots in the pond, nudging a newly formed lily pad. Slowly, I sat beside her.

"What beast requires this?"

"All creatures require water. I don't know when, how, or why the realm creates what it does. I just know my beasts are near, and they know I've come to say hello."

Suddenly, the forest was alive with calls. Chirps hummed from the backs of throats as branches groaned from the added weight of the beasts. Deep grunts rolled in on the breeze from the plains, and the ground beneath us vibrated with the cadence of rushing hooves. The world was alive before, but now it was thriving. Reacting to the presence of a Charmer. And Leena flourished. Her skin glowed faintly, a beautiful glimmer that spoke to her power.

Beasts appeared one by one, flocking to her side to bask in her light. It was a procession of all colors, shapes, and sizes. She treated each creature with the devoted love and attention of a mother. E-Class to B-Class, they were the same to her. She stroked chins, ruffled feathers, cooed words of pure happiness, and placed gentle kisses with her flushed lips.

Why anyone wanted to kill this woman was beyond me.

Twin serpents appeared, encircling Leena before tilting their dragon heads in my direction. She stroked the length of their bodies. "You remember Kinana and Kapro? Go ahead. Touch them."

Nostrils flaring wide, Kinana edged toward me. I extended my hand to her, and she rammed my palm and slithered against my body. The soothing feeling of running water flooded my veins.

Leena laughed. "She must like you." I'd never seen her so happy.

Running my fingers down Kinana's scales, I glanced at the dark shadows hidden in the trees. "So, is this a realm just for your beasts? Or can other Charmers come here?"

"All beasts come to the same realm, though it's extremely rare to see beasts that aren't mine." She paused, eyes flickering out across the horizon. After our surprise bout with the Scorpex, neither of us seemed eager to deem anywhere safe. "Other Charmers can come here, too. The realm is endless. Running into one of them is next to impossible—unless they're part of your family."

There it was. Another opening into her past. I just hoped it wasn't a fresh scab over a gaping wound. "Family?"

She nodded. Kinana left me to curl against Leena. Weighted silence, occasionally punctuated by the soft grunt of a beast, passed between us. In my peripheral vision, I watched her fidget. She picked at the hem of her tunic and pushed her hair off her neck, only to pull it around the front again.

Finally, she sighed. "My parents died when I was four." Rotating the ring around her finger, she stared only at the pond in front of her.

"They tried to tame a beast beyond their capabilities and failed. It happens. Anyway, my aunt took me in. But when *she* died…"

Her beasts nestled in closer, providing what comfort they could through simple contact. Something near undeniable inside me begged me to do the same. Instead, I braided my fingers together.

"Kost is right—most Charmers never leave Hireath. I never thought I would, either. But I was young when my aunt died, alone in a house with too many rooms and not enough bodies. I had my beasts, of course, but…it's not the same as a human touch." She looked at me, the saddest smile gracing her lips. A glassy sheen obscured her irises, and my throat swelled shut. The branches sprawling across her face began to recede, disappearing down her neck.

I didn't dare ask why, not when she was finally opening up about her past. "Is that when you left Hireath? When your aunt died?"

Tila, the monkey creature from the train, crawled into Leena's lap. Leena stroked her belly, working soft tufts of fur between her fingers. "No. I fell in love with a man on the Council."

"Ah."

"Yeah." She blew out a short breath. "He was supposed to be the answer to my prayers. Kind and intelligent, and easily the most powerful Charmer I'd ever met. His beasts could last outside the realm for weeks, even months, living off his energy wells." Her gaze returned to the pond, eyes locked on the rippling water stirred by Kapro's tongue. "We were happy for a while. But one day, I found a dying…creature chained in a cage beneath his home. A creature no Charmer had ever successfully tamed. It destroyed me."

Shifting closer to her, I placed my hand on the ground inches from hers. More ink disappeared, fading down her shoulder. "Something from the Kitska Forest?"

She shook her head. "No. Gods, why am I telling you this?"

"Leena, it's okay. You can tell me." My fingers grazed hers.

A small, irrational part of me wanted to cup her hands in mine. I wanted to do about a thousand things that didn't make any sense. She stared at the place where our hands met before letting out another breath.

"It was a human, Noc. A human man." Her voice cracked. *A human.* Warning bells sounded in my mind. Isn't that what the Charmer at the tavern accused Leena of doing? She cleared her throat. "I could never do that. Can you even imagine what that would be like? Controlling another person?"

My gut twisted, and the blood in my body ran cool. Yes, I could imagine. It wasn't something I'd done, but something I'd witnessed. The horror of stripping someone of their free will... I could understand why it was illegal, especially for a race of people with the power to charm.

Bringing her knees to her chest, she rested her chin on her forearms. "When I confronted him about it, he used a beast to convince the Council I was the one harboring the human—not him. And because he was on the Council and Charmers value beasts above all else, my words meant nothing."

Tears spilled over, heavy streams bisecting her cheeks. I'd worked as an assassin long enough to know the burn behind Leena's story couldn't be anything other than the truth.

"The Crown of the Council was away on a beast hunt, so the rest of them held a sentencing and determined my fate. They let me live, but they released my name to the world—Leena Edenfrell, exiled Charmer, unfit for society. Finding work after that was next to impossible, so I did the only thing I could. I sold my beasts to survive."

I sat still, horrified by her words. To be betrayed by the people she loved, the man she devoted herself to? My mind raced back to Cruor, to the loyal comrades flanking my sides and living beneath the same roof. I would do anything to keep that sanctuary, to provide for them. It was all any of us had left. But Leena had been ripped away from the only community she'd ever known, exiled like a criminal so the man she loved could hide his own crimes.

And now he was paying me to murder her.

Slowly, I reached up and brushed Leena's tears away with my thumb. "I'm so sorry, Leena."

It had to be the same man. No wonder he'd been so adamant about the bounty. It was his transgression, his previous act that could come to light if Leena ever tried to speak up. But the woman who placed the hit? The real person behind Leena's bounty? What did she have to do with any of this?

Leena's eyes fluttered closed. "Don't be." She moved away from my touch. Her bow-like lips formed a genuine smile, and then she loosed an arrow I couldn't have prepared for. "I learned long ago not to trust people or promises—only beasts. So when you tell me you're dangerous, it's not a question of believing you. It's simply a universal truth."

I nodded my understanding. "Why come after you now, though? Why not leave you in exile?"

A bitter smile touched her lips. "I *am* selling beasts, even if it's my only means of survival. First attempting to charm a human, and now this? There are no second chances when it comes to ensuring the safety of our beasts."

My hand moved before I could think. All I wanted was to provide her with some comfort. Something to show her that I understood. We all did what was necessary to survive. More than that, I knew what it meant to sacrifice something I loved. But when my fingers were inches from her cheek, I stilled. I couldn't keep doing this. If she caved beneath my touch... If she reciprocated my dangerously growing feelings...

I drew my hand back. Her eyes tracked the motion before she turned away.

She composed herself, burying her head in the soft bellies of her beasts and whispering quiet words of love directly into their ears. Tongues licked away her tears. They gave her what I couldn't: Love. Devotion. Compassion. They held nothing back, and neither did she. It was a bond I could never experience.

It must have pained her beyond measure to give them away.

By my feet, the blades of grass shifted, and a small woman wearing a leaf dress peered up at me. Pointed ears poked out of mossy hair and she smiled, revealing endless rows of dagger-sharp teeth. Where her legs should have been, a trail of smoke billowed beneath her.

A Gyss.

Time itself stopped when she arched her brows. *Hello.* A feminine drawl sounded in my mind.

She was the answer. The beast who could possibly remove my curse. A chance at connection, at feeling, without condemning anyone to death. My limbs tingled, and I forced myself to remain calm. Steady.

Hello. What's your name? I thought back, lacing my fingers together.

Fable. Her wide smile stretched further, splitting her face in half. *I know what you want.*

What I want? I glanced at Leena, but she was absorbed in the comfort her beasts could give her.

The woman hovered above my lap and folded her arms beneath her bust. *Yes. It's obvious, really.*

I raised a careful brow. *Tell me what I want, then.*

Fable giggled. *Are you sure you want to hear it?*

Absolutely.

She cupped her chin in her hands and gave me her biggest smile. *Beg for it.*

It was impossible not to roll my eyes. *Please, oh magical Gyss, tell me my deepest desire.*

That'll do. She winked. *You're cursed. One of my kind can lift it.*

The world slipped out from beneath me, and a dull ringing obscured all sounds. *How do you know about that?*

She cackled, and Leena's head snapped to me. Hard expression set, she was impossible to read. "Ignore Fable. Mischievous little thing." Reaching over, Leena poked Fable right in the stomach. A soft peal of laughter fell from her lips, and she floated out of reach.

"She's a Gyss, right?"

Leena stiffened. "Yes."

Fable wiggled her brows. *Maybe she'll consider transferring ownership. My dear master has never asked one wish of me. It's rather boring.*

My gaze met Leena's. "You've never made a wish?"

"No." She fisted her hands in her lap. "And I don't ever intend to. We should be heading back." Her muscles tensed, but she maneuvered around each beast with care.

"What do you have against Gyss?"

"Nothing. Let's go." She brushed her hands along her tunic, and I caught a glimpse of her diminishing ink work.

"Leena, I don't care if it doesn't meet our agreed-upon requirements. If that's the beast I want—"

"I said no!" True silence followed in the wake of her shout, and her beasts disappeared in a flurry of movement, save Fable. Her sly smile only deepened. Was she really so dangerous? Even with that cunning glint to her gaze, I couldn't imagine her inflicting serious pain. Not like Felicks's bite or Kinana and Kapro's ice prison. But there was obvious fear coursing through Leena's eyes. "Noc, the whole reason I'm exiled is because of a Gyss. Because the man I loved wished the Council would only hear lies from my lips instead of truth. I don't know what his payment was, what he sacrificed to make that wish come true, but clearly my life and love didn't hold a candle to his ambitions."

The anger in her voice died as she stared at her Gyss.

"I love Fable. I do, I promise. But Noc, I only sell Gyss to scoundrels with clear-as-day intentions. Fame. Fortune. Prosperity. Because a Gyss's true strength is tied to its master's power. Someone who cares only about trivial things, who has weak desires, won't be able to unleash a Gyss's true potential. But you?" She turned on me, a sudden uneasy sway to her step. "The truth is, I have no idea what you're capable of. And that could put me in the line of fire. Again."

My mouth went dry. I would never dream of using the Gyss against her, but what evidence did she have to the contrary? An active bounty as a bargaining chip?

Knots formed in my gut, and I dropped my gaze to Fable.

She smirked. *She may change her mind. But for now, you better take care of her. She's stayed for too long.*

Leena buckled forward, knees crashing against the ground. The ink along the right side of her body had all but extinguished, and the last leaves and flowers were bleeding out of existence. Around us, the world shimmered like a mirage.

"Leena." I caught her as she tipped back, her body heavy and colder than a block of ice.

The realm shattered, blinding-white light slipping between fractured glass, and we were thrust back into our reality. Ortega Key bloomed to life around us, and we barreled into a heap of sand.

I sat upright and pulled her into my lap, calling her name more forcibly. "Leena. *Leena.*"

She shivered, unresponsive; her fingers entrenched in my shirt.

The shadows swarmed us in an instant, barreling us toward the inn and her room. I flew through her door, slamming it shut behind us and racing toward her bed. I tried to untangle her, but her muscles had frozen in place.

So cold. I stared at the bed. She needed warmth, but I couldn't get her to let go. I didn't really want her to. That realization was deadly, and yet...

Yanking back the sheets, I slid beneath them and cradled her to my chest. Lilac and vanilla, aftereffects of the beast realm, filled the space between the crown of her head and my nose.

Her story played on repeat in my mind as she slept, her weighted breath tickling the space between my shoulder and neck. She was remarkable. Despite the damage she carried, despite the way she worried the ring on her finger, as if trying to turn back time to a moment when everything made sense, she was so incredibly light. Too bright for my world, yet so strong that she saw through my carefully crafted facade.

The black scythe on my wrist gleamed up at me, a taunting reminder that it was my life or hers. This was why we assassins didn't speak to our jobs. Why we kept everyone other than ourselves, our brethren, at arm's length. If I refused to act on the bounty, I would die. But where would that leave Cruor? If I had enough notice, I could perform the ritual to name Kost my successor, but he'd die himself before watching me willingly walk into the god of death's arms. Again.

Shadows bled from my fingertips and hovered around us. Death didn't scare me. But now that there was a chance for something more...

No. *No.*

The shadows eked away, leaving me all too exposed.

When Leena's grip relaxed, I slipped out from underneath her and tucked the sheets in tight around her body. She looked so frail, and my arms were so unbelievably empty, but she was too deep under my skin. Fable was wrong—the problems of my past couldn't be fixed. There was nothing in this world that could change that. I'd been given false promises of a cure before, after I'd condemned Bowen to death. But nothing ever worked, as evidenced by Kost's sickness that followed years later. I couldn't do that again. Not now. Not to anyone. Most of all, not to Leena.

I couldn't escape my curse, couldn't attempt to have something more with her, but I could try to save her from this bounty. There was another way out of this damned oath, a method to negate the magic that no one had ever stooped to before. I'd discuss the idea with Kost, Calem, and Ozias. If they didn't agree, then I'd have to say goodbye to Leena in the worst possible way—permanently.

SIXTEEN

CALEM

I woke before the sun fully rose, just like always. Warm, yellow light slipped through the windows, and the urge to move, to start the day, hit me with enough force to shake whatever semblance of slumber remained. There was something about spending most of your childhood on the streets that made it hard to sleep in. Dirt roads and pavers didn't make for the best of beds.

Rolling out of the sheets, I padded across the wooden floor and into the bathroom to bathe. In and out, minimal resources, maximum time to get shit done. To grind. I didn't slog in the same way these days, but... I shook my head, then toweled off and dressed in a light work shirt and breeches before leaving my room. A few attendants tiptoed down the corridor, but aside from the smell of meat frying on a pan and the muted clangs of dinnerware and pots coming from the first-floor tavern, the hallways of the Roasted Boar were quiet. Ozias would sleep until midday if he didn't have work to consider, and Kost, well... My gaze flickered to his door. He was probably awake, reading or doing some other boring activity. Gods knew I wanted nothing to do with that, so I didn't bother him.

Taking the stairs down to the foyer, I passed the dining area and exited the building. There were better places to get food at this hour.

The gravel road gave way beneath my boots as I walked toward the main street of Ortega Key, already bustling with early risers and vendors setting up shop for the day. One man was cooking slices of honeyed pineapple on a wire rack over an open flame, and the scent made my mouth water. Fishing some bits out of my pocket, I ordered one—along with a fresh-baked raisin roll his wife practically threw into my hands—and went on my way.

I wasn't quite sure where I was going. Whenever I was away from Cruor, my morning routine was the same: rise early, get the lay of the town, eat. If I was on a job, there'd likely be some reconnaissance, but for something like this... Ortega Key was nicer than our usual haunts. Out of all the jobs I'd received, not one had brought me here. And it was easy to see why—the vast majority of these people appeared to be well-off and happy. Bright smiles stood out against sunbaked skin, and even if they were shouting over one another to try to outsell their wares, their voices carried a lightness. As if hardships weren't all that common.

Lucky bastards. Even day labor couldn't shake their sunny disposition. Shoving the last of the roll into my mouth, I brushed my hands along my trousers. It was too early to head to the Drinking Mermaid for a stiff cocktail, and short of flirting with the blond manning an impressive selection of glass-blown vases—which was a valid option—there wasn't much in the way of entertainment.

Speaking of the blond... She glanced my direction and offered a shy smile, setting a small sculpture on her table that winked in the sun. I felt my lips pull up in a lopsided grin and was starting to make my way toward her when a handful of children dashed by and snagged my attention.

It wasn't the fact that there were children in Ortega Key that made me pause. There was a whole gaggle of them up the road screaming about some rules to a game they'd likely made up. No, it was the fact that these children were dressed in tattered, sack-like tunics that were clearly too large for their tiny frames.

Not to mention they were holding fresh fruit that had obviously been stolen, judging by the way a vendor came hauling ass after them.

"Hey, get back here!" His shout carried over the other vendors and summoned a whole slew of memories I fought daily to forget. Huffing, he raced after the street kids and was about to cut around me when I stuck my hand out and gripped the fabric of his white tunic, dragging him to a lurching stop.

"Something wrong?" I fought to keep my voice level.

The man sputtered, took one bewildered look at my hand fisted in his shirt, and then glared at me over the rims of his glasses. Unfortunately for him, I had plenty of practice ignoring stern looks from men in specs. "Take your hand off me. Those kids stole from my shop, and I intend to get my wares back."

I glanced over my shoulder at their retreating forms. The sun had risen high enough to coax shadows from nearby buildings, and the children had darted into the waning darkness and down an alley out of sight. With any luck, they'd find a quiet space to enjoy their meal.

A strained smile claimed my lips. "How much?"

The man raised a brow. "How much what?"

"How much did they steal? What was the cost?"

"Fifteen coppers."

With my free hand, I dug into the pocket of my pants and fished out the bits. "Here, take this and go back to your stall. And watch your wares. I bet one of them was waiting for you to leave just so they could take more. It's what I would've done."

The man's fingers curled around the coins as his eyes went wide. He craned his neck in the direction of his shop, mouth silently moving as if trying to calculate the amount of fruit still piled high on his table, and then took off as quickly as he'd come. I stared after him for a moment before turning on my heels and following the escape path of the young criminals. I could've let them go—they were likely doing just fine on their own—but every time I saw a street kid, no matter where I was, my insides tightened. It was as if I didn't have a choice. My legs would move, and I'd go after them, hoping I could help in some way. Hoping that by offering them a chance at a different life, I'd somehow forget about the one I used to lead. Slipping between two stalls, I walked in the shadows, following my instincts until I came to the mouth of an alley littered with abandoned crates and trash.

Bile soured my tongue. Every city had a dark side, and Ortega Key was no different.

As I made my way around the mess, a few startled figures exploded from their hiding places. Children rushed past me, bright pieces of fruit clutched in their tiny grasps as they bolted toward the mouth of the alley. I didn't bother trying to stop them. They'd be wary, even if they had no reason to fear me. One child, though, remained behind, and my whole body went stock-still.

There, sitting in a crumpled heap on a makeshift bed of towels, was a small boy with sunken eyes and matted brown hair. The others had been kind enough to leave him a peach, but clearly, he barely had the energy to eat it, let alone run from me. He stared up at me, his gaze a mixture of fear, despair, and determination, and recognition sang through my blood. I *knew* that look. I had worn it often enough, even if it had been some years since I'd been this boy. Forcing a hard swallow, I turned around without a word and headed back out into the bright warmth of Ortega Key.

And I bought everything within sight. A small duffel bag. Canteens of water. Bread. Cheese. Dried meat. Clothes. The woman from the vase shop tried to get my attention with a wave, but I ignored her completely.

This child had no need for crystal decor.

Bags bulging with goods and fresh clothes draped over my arms, I returned to the alley and the kid. He hadn't moved save to devour the peach, and he was gnawing on the pit to get those last sinewy strands still clinging to it. He froze when he saw me, cautious eyes traveling from the clothes in my hands to the bag slung over my shoulder.

I sank to the ground in front of him and crossed my legs. "Hey, there."

He didn't answer.

"I've got some extra stuff." I let the bag fall from my shoulder and opened it, showing off the water and food I'd shoved in there. "Want any of it?"

With narrowed eyes, he leaned closer. I tried to ignore the bruises and cuts, the sharp jut of bones that should've been hidden by round cheeks, the grime that he wore like a second skin. The look of pure hunger, reined in only by distrust. He didn't reach for a single item.

Smart kid. Trust no one, fend for yourself. That's how he'd survived this long, but he wouldn't last at this rate. He was clearly too weak to steal for himself; if he didn't take this now, he'd be facing a fate no kid deserved to stare down.

"I used to be like you." I nudged the bag toward him and leaned back against the hard wall of the building behind me. Familiar anger flickered to life inside my gut, and I braided my fingers together to keep them from trembling. I hated everything about my past, but maybe if he believed me, he'd eat.

"Like me?" His voice was hoarse and full of uncertainty, but he inched closer to the bag.

"Yeah, like you." I gestured to his tattered tunic and bare feet. Then I set the fresh clothes in a neat pile before him. He gave me one incredulous look that told me he had no intention of undressing, and I bit back a chuckle. "I lived on the streets for a long time."

"Yeah, right." Finally, he reached into the bag and snagged a hunk of bread and some dried meat before giving me a pointed look. "You're too clean."

"Now, sure." I waited until he took a bite to continue. "Where's your family?"

He furrowed his brow before jerking his head toward the alley. "They just left. You scared them away."

"Not the kids." I nodded for him to keep eating, and he obliged, shoving a large piece of bread into his mouth. Crumbs dusted his lips, and he ran the back of his hand along them to scrub himself clean. Or as clean as he could get. "Your parents. What happened to them?"

The boy lifted a shoulder. "They died." Wary eyes narrowed. "Is that what happened to you? Did your parents die?"

Before I could prepare myself, the memory of my mother surfaced. Her strawberry-blond hair soaked to the scalp from the sudden onslaught of rain. Her brick-colored eyes cold as the wall at my back. Thin lips pulled tight in a grimace. Even though it'd been raining and the droplets running down her cheeks could've been mistaken for tears, I knew better. Maybe not then, but I sure did now. She held no love for me. She'd left for an "errand" and told me to wait.

She never came back.

Steeling myself against the old pain and rage, I forced myself back to the present and offered the kid a weak nod. "Something like that."

For a long time, he simply stared at me while he ate. Satisfied with my answers, he polished off the dried meat and drained one of the canteens before dropping it back into the bag. He then tied the bag shut and nudged it my direction with a rigid look of determination.

"Thanks. I'm done."

"Keep it. There's more food, water, and some bits in there." I didn't bother to shove it toward him. If he was anything like I'd been, he'd just kick it back and run off with whatever renewed vigor the food may have given him.

He folded his arms across his chest. "I can take care of myself."

"I can see that. Those kids wouldn't have brought you food if you hadn't done the same for them at some point." I gestured to the bag and the clothes, trying to seem noncommittal about the whole thing but praying to the gods he'd be smarter than I'd ever been when handouts were on the table. "I'll make you a deal. How about I give you this bag in exchange for something?"

Tilting his head to the side, the boy studied me for a moment. "What do you want?"

"There's no shortage of trade in Ortega Key. If you promise me you'll use this stuff to find yourself an apprenticeship, whatever you want that to be, then you can have it."

He scoffed. "But what do you get out of that?"

"Peace of mind. It's worth it to someone like me. You're just gonna have to trust me on that."

"Is that how you got out? A job?"

This time, when the memory hit, all I could do was smile. It didn't take much for a thieving street rat to become something else. The older I got, the more brazen I became, stealing from dangerous men and women who weren't afraid to murder over stolen jewelry. City guards were just a hassle they didn't want to deal with. Mercy wasn't a concept the rich entertained. So when I met the wrong end of a blade and found myself bleeding out in the street, I'd only laughed. My mother may have birthed me, but the streets had raised me. It was fitting they'd also be there to welcome me into death.

I just hadn't expected to wake up in a pool of my own blood with a man kneeling over me, his dark eyes full of an emotion I still couldn't place. Out completing a nearby job, Noc had watched the whole thing—from that reckless theft to my last breath—and raised me only minutes later. He'd said I'd reminded him of someone he'd known, someone who'd stolen from him before. I never had the nerve to ask him who, only accepted his terms to live as an assassin of Cruor.

But that wasn't the answer this kid needed to hear. He still had a chance to turn his life around before falling prey to a blade he could've avoided.

"Yes. Now, I have a great family and a job I love. You should do the same."

He reached for the bag and then paused, his fingers only inches from the strap. "But what about the family I have now?"

The group of kids who'd brought him the peach. Perhaps they could use some food and inspiration, too. "I'll talk to them. But only if you promise to do this for me. See? Now you *have* to take this, or your friends won't get help, too." I was lying through my teeth—there was no way I wouldn't track them down and provide them with their own bounty of goodies—but I got what I needed. Panic flashed through his eyes, and he snatched the bag before I could threaten to change my mind.

"There's another alley up the road. At the back of it is our house." He pressed the sack closer to his chest, a touch of sadness lingering in his gaze. No doubt their "house" was little more than a shack constructed of crates, palm fronds, towels, and whatever else they could get their hands on, but it was home in his eyes. "Tell them Astor sent you, and they won't run."

"I can do that." Standing, I pointed to the untouched pile of clothes. "Change before you see anyone about a job. Maybe take a trip to the ocean and scrub some of that dirt off your face, too. Better to smell like salt than the street."

"Okay," he said. I was starting to walk away, a feeling of lightness spreading through my chest, when he called out after me. "Hey, what's your name?"

I glanced back at him. "Calem. Come find me when you're on your feet."

"But how?"

"Ask around. Someone somewhere always knows how to contact a member of Cruor." With a wave, I turned back to the open mouth of the street. "See you around, kid."

He didn't call after me, and I didn't bother to wait around to see if he'd follow through with his promise. He either would, or he wouldn't. Regardless, I'd keep my end of the deal. So as I made my way up the streets of Ortega Key, purchasing food and hope for his family, I could only pray to gods I'd never really followed that these kids would find a way out, too. That they'd find a new family like I had, and that maybe, just maybe, they'd have a chance at a fulfilling life.

Otherwise, they might end up on the wrong side of a blade. And there was no telling if Noc would be there to save them.

SEVENTEEN

LEENA

I must have lost track of the time in the realm, because I didn't remember returning to my room. Every muscle in my body ached. Every breath rattled my rib cage. Every accidental movement spiked pain in my neck. How many times would I overtax myself, physically and emotionally, in the presence of these assassins?

I should've asked Fable to make it impossible for me to repeat my past. I never thought I'd share those intimate details, and yet Noc's unyielding gaze had upended me. Peeled back layers I didn't think I could fold back up, and I was exposed. I needed to understand why. Why he pried into my past. Why his demeanor had shifted from one of detachment to something far more dangerous…

Gods, I really was beginning to *trust* him. Not because I was flirting to save my skin, but because I actually *wanted* to know more about him. He was so damn confounding and yet, I couldn't help myself.

My heart throbbed at his absence, at the heavy weight of our conversation. No closure. No words about his past or his thoughts. I didn't know why it mattered. And yet, I was raw and revealed, and there was no salve to alleviate the ache.

No. I was wrong. I didn't need to understand anything. I needed to get these assassins their beasts, get someone's blood, and get out. End of story.

And maybe convince Noc to take any beast other than a Gyss. I dug my palms into my eyes and groaned.

Noc was right about one thing—he was hazardous.

After the world's slowest bath, I made my way to the mirror. The purple swells beneath my eyes had deepened. These assassins would be the death of me. Reaching for my cosmetics, I hid the dark circles and winced when my hand grazed the cracked corner of my lips.

"Seriously?" I muttered, inspecting the chapped edge. I dug into my bag and found a healing salve, slathered it on. A faint gloss clung to my lips. At least it wasn't obvious. I dabbed a small amount of powder over it to hide the red and dressed. I needed food. Water. Sustenance. My body was falling apart.

Sun high in the sky, I'd missed breakfast entirely, but I managed to shuffle downstairs to eat lunch at the tavern.

The small diner tucked away on the first floor of the inn seated maybe thirty people, and I sat alone at a table made of palm wood. With a bay window open to the baked breeze, linen curtains kissed the edges of the booth. I shoveled fried rice into my mouth and soaked in the sun. Locals chatted aimlessly, carefree smiles plastered onto weatherworn faces. Vendor stalls brimming with glass-blown vases and glittering gems reflected rainbow mosaics on the gravel road. Children's pealing laughter carried lightly over the barking calls of sellers.

Day three in Ortega Key, and I still had no word on the Myad. I needed that beast in my arsenal. With a beast of that caliber by my side, I'd be stronger. Strong enough to stand up to the Council if I never got the chance to clear my name.

Or if the assassins didn't cooperate.

An errant chill grazed my skin, and I forked more food into my mouth. Try as I might to focus on my beasts, or on some way of convincing one of these men to donate their blood, my thoughts wouldn't stay in line. Pushing the plate of food away, I turned back to the vibrant town. A group of children gathered on the outskirts of the market, and in the middle of their congregation was Calem.

The backdrop of canary-yellow vendor stalls couldn't compete with his brilliant, million-bit grin stretching from ear to ear. A foreign light played through his normally muted-red eyes, and he crouched to the ground before slipping a duffel bag off his shoulder. With quick fingers, he unlatched the flap and started passing out hunks of bread.

My heart stilled. Bony-kneed and grimy, the kids clambered around him, eager gazes transfixed by what they likely considered a feast. And Calem delivered. Loaf after loaf, followed by cheese wrapped in brown paper and canteens of water. They danced in place, tattered clothes two sizes too large nearly dropping off their slim frames. I couldn't make out their words as they ran away, tossing smiles over their shoulders and clutching their wares to their chests.

But I could see Calem, and at that moment, his grin turned strained—something dark and heavy coloring his ruby eyes a muddy crimson. And then he was gone. Darkness swallowed him like a vacuum, and I was left to stare at nothing more than the mouth of Main Street with its colorful vendors.

The heady scent of spiced cinnamon struck first, followed by a brush of cool air along the back of my neck. "Spying on me?"

Lurching forward, I banged my knee on the table and knocked over my glass of water. "Gods, Calem. Was that necessary?"

He righted the cup, a wry smile touching the corners of his lips. It didn't reach his eyes. "Entirely. Were you checking out my assets?"

I rubbed my knee and stared at the man leaning over the back of my booth. Something was haunting him. Something was haunting me, too, and resolving that something meant ending this job as quickly as possible—not getting involved with whatever demons Calem kept on lockdown. "You could say I was assessing. I think I have the perfect beast for you."

His brows knitted together. "You found a beast that will help me with women?"

Rolling my eyes, I gingerly scooted out from the booth and leaned against the table. "You definitely don't need that. But trust me, you'll love it. We'll go tonight, after I've gotten some more rest."

"Noc, Kost, and Ozias won't be back until late."

I raised a brow. "Where are they?"

"Training." Calem folded his arms across his chest. "I don't think we should do this without them."

"We don't need them, but we will need some stuff." I patted his chest then strolled toward the stairs leading up to my room. "I'll make you a list. Once you've got everything, we can go."

———————◆———————

When pallid-purple hues claimed the waning afternoon sky, I opened my bedroom door to find Calem waiting, bulging duffel strapped to his back. The muscles in my body protested at the thought of a taming, but the sluggishness was gone. Power hummed beneath my fingertips.

"Got everything on your list." Calem tossed a glance down the hallway as I closed the door behind me. Flickering lights lined the wooden doors, and I spied the two rooms closest to the stairs. Oz and Kost. Calem's jaw ticked. I'd asked a big favor of him, going on this hunt without them. But the Effreft only came out at night, and I wasn't willing to dally any longer.

Reaching out, I grazed his forearm. "Don't worry. Nothing bad will happen. This beast won't physically harm me if something goes wrong. It'll just leave."

His shoulders tensed, but he didn't move away from my touch. "You still haven't told me what this beast does."

"It's a surprise."

Glancing down his nose at me, he huffed. "Let's go." Hand gently placed on the small of my back, he pushed me toward the stairs. Two Zeelahs stood at the ready, tied to a post with leather reins.

We didn't need to travel far—there was an open plain about a thirty-minute ride from Ortega Key. With a full moon raised high in the night sky, it was a prime time and location to lure the Effreft. Crisp air tinged with salt nipped at my skin, and I ran my hands along my arms as we brought our mounts to a stop.

"Leave the Zeelahs here. We need to create the offering." I slipped off my mare and looped her reins around a thin tree before picking my way across the field. Calem followed close behind, bag bouncing in time with his gait.

In the middle of the field rested a flat oval slab. Raised above the grass with a polished surface, it made a perfect offering table. I nodded toward it, and Calem sank to the ground, upending the bag and dumping the contents onto the stone. Fresh fruits, vegetables, meats, cheeses, and fish bombarded our improvised altar, followed by a heaping stack of reeds and broken-up palm fronds.

An apple rolled onto the ground. Calem snatched it and placed it on the precarious pile of food. "Now what?"

"Now we work. Quickly." Grabbing the reeds and stripped palm leaves, I began weaving a basket in the shape of a horn.

For a beast that brought bounties of plenty, a feast was needed as part of the bait. Once the makeshift cornucopia was constructed, we stuffed the food inside, leaving scraps around the mouth for easy visibility.

Brushing my hands along my linen pants, I stood and surveyed the trap. "That should do it."

With Calem dressed entirely in black, it was hard to decipher the shadows from his clothing. But they were there, lurking around his ankles and steel-tipped boots. Following my lead, he wiped his hands across the front of his black trousers.

"Here's how this is going to work." Pivoting to face him, I cracked my knuckles. "You need to stay right next to me. I'm talking inches. Keep yourself hidden until I call you out. And when I do, push me to the side and touch the Effreft as fast as you can."

Calem narrowed his eyes. "I'm not going to push you."

"I'm serious. Effrefts bond immediately. It's not normally an issue for Charmers, but since I plan on handing off the beast to you, you'll need to be its first point of contact. If it sees me first or otherwise associates me as its master, I can't give it to you. Breaking a permanent bond between beast and master could result in the creature's death, and I won't risk that."

I placed my hands on my hips, daring him to contradict me. Shifting in place, he rocked on his heels. The muscles along his jawline ticked as he weighed his options.

"A little dirt won't kill me. Just pretend we're sparring again."

Red eyes skewered me. "That's what I'm afraid of."

"This is the beast I want to give you," I said. He studied my face for what felt like hours before relenting, dropping his hand to his side and taking a careful step in my direction. Sinking to the ground, I positioned my butt on the soles of my feet, laying my hands palm up against my thighs. "Get behind me."

Low and dark, a chuckle escaped from the back of his throat. "I think I've been waiting all my life for you to say that to me, Leena."

A blush ravaged my neck. He crouched behind me, the heady scent of cinnamon thick in the air, and his breath tickled a loose strand of hair on my cheek. Shadows pulled from the earth, flooding the space behind me and hiding him in their void. His scent disappeared with the breeze, and I was left alone.

"Here we go." Lips pressed into a thin line, I willed my power to the surface. Glowing bright to compete with the moon, my skin radiated warmth. An hour ticked by to the steady hum and vibration of energy within me. I could lure the night away on a full tank, but if dawn claimed the sky before the Effreft appeared, it wouldn't matter.

Fortunately, that didn't happen.

A mint-green streak of color dropped from the sky, barreling toward the cornucopia and landing with grace atop the pile of food. Its falcon-like head cocked to the side. Curious eyes rounded on me, pale pink and so endlessly intelligent. The Effreft snapped its beak, and a soft inquisitive chirp filled the air.

She was perfect. I intensified the glow within me, and the pointed ears atop her head twitched. Carefully, she stepped forward. She was built like a small dog with a long and thin feathered tail, and the powerful muscles in her legs contracted as she walked. Talons skewered a piece of meat, and she paused to gobble the morsel.

Wynn had an Effreft.

My mind recoiled at the thought of him. With my body shuddering, the glow radiating from my being dimmed before recovering to full blast. The Effreft stilled, foot frozen in midair.

"Effrefts are flighty creatures. You must be stable." Wynn had bent low behind me, lips grazing the side of my neck as he placed both hands on my hips. His Effreft had sat before us, light eyes trained on her master.

Before the gods cursed my happiness to hell.

Gooseflesh covered my body, and I speared my bottom lip with my teeth to pull my mind back to the present. Blood pooled in my mouth. It'd been so long since I'd allowed myself to think of those warmer moments with Wynn. I'd buried his existence so far beneath the surface, and yet my conversation with Noc had all my walls crumbling. His strength, his cunning, his quiet prodding that was somehow both infuriating and welcoming...

The Effreft stretched her wings to the sky, testing the wind. My eyes snapped to hers.

No. I needed to tame her. I needed to end this deal and get out. Steadying myself, I bent farther into my crouch, submitting to the creature fully.

She folded her wings and took a step forward, beak inches from my forehead. My light grew, temporarily blinding her and showering her body in unending waves of warmth. She knelt to the ground and pressed her head firmly against the earth. When she looked up, the first person she met would be her master.

"Now, Calem!"

Shadows shot outward, fleeing from his body and escaping into the night, and he elbowed me to the side. My face smacked into the dirt, and I pulled my knees to my chest, giving him as much room as possible. Before she could raise her head, he reached out and placed a gentle hand along the down-soft feathers of her neck.

She cooed, raising her eyes to him, and the bond was sealed. Awestruck, Calem stared at his beast. Eyes wide. Lips parted, but slightly curled in the beginnings of a smile. His muted-red stare flared bright like a ruby. The Effreft cooed, and she knocked her beak against his nose. Already totally devoted to her master.

I couldn't help but grin. "Thank the gods." I rolled to my back, eyeing the heavens. Adrenaline left me in a rush, and a cool shiver danced over me. "She's all yours."

Calem moved his fingers down her back, easing the tension between her wings. "I think I'll call you Effie." Effie clucked, rubbing her head along his shins.

I pushed myself up and offered Effie my hand. She nudged it once, but turned back to Calem. "She encourages life," I explained as I studied her nimble body. She was already vibrating with energy, eager to please her newfound master. "Sprouts reach maturity in an instant, plants grow regardless of season or weather, and the dirt beneath her feet is the most fertile soil in the world. Watch." Reaching behind her, I snagged an apple and bit into it, exposing the core. After extracting a seed, I burrowed it in the earth and signaled to Effie. "We'd better take a step back."

Without hesitation, she spread her wings wide. A radiant light streamed from her feathers, and snowy particles of magic floated to the earth. The ground rumbled, massive roots puckering through fresh dirt as a thick and healthy tree reached for the heavens. Apple-laden branches crawled outward, and I snagged one from above my head.

"I guarantee this will be the juiciest apple you've ever eaten."

Calem took it from me, sinking his teeth into the skin. Nectar dribbled, and his eyes went wide. "This is amazing. She's amazing."

"Now you can feed anyone, whenever you want."

My words were barely a whisper, but Calem went rigid, turning his back to me. I shouldn't have said anything. But damn if I didn't want to know why, if I didn't want to help or understand, even though it was the last thing I should have been doing.

Effie flew the short distance to him, circling his feet and leaning into him. Concerned chirps slipped past her beak.

Placing a gentle hand between his shoulder blades, I spoke into the fabric of his tunic. "Calem?" His body convulsed once, and then suddenly he turned, real emotions buried beneath a wall so strong I knew I'd never be able to crack it.

"Thank you, Leena."

I chewed my lower lip and sat with the silence before finally caving. "You know, Calem, I might actually miss you when this is all said and done."

He clenched his jaw tight. "Me too. So what do we do next?"

Tracing the emblem on the back of my hand, I knelt beside Effie. "I take her to the beast realm, make you a key, and then she's permanently yours."

"She can't stay here?"

I shook my head. "Unlike wild beasts, tamed beasts need to return to the realm when it's time to replenish their powers. The stronger the bond between master and beast, the longer the creature can remain at your side. Strengthen your connection with her, and you'll be able to call on her whenever you wish. Though, newer beasts do have a tendency to slip out of the realm on their own, especially if their masters aren't Charmers. Just be careful."

Calem dropped to the ground, sprawling out on his back and casting his gaze to the night sky. "All right, do your thing. I trust you."

Trust. Immobilized by the weight of that word, I fought for control over the sudden spike in my pulse. *Trust.* The lonely and scared girl I thought I'd left behind in Hireath poked her head up, and I winced at the flux of eagerness. I was probably being a fool for liking them, trusting them, so much. The truth was, I was bound to them until they had their beasts, and that kind of relationship didn't encourage hope. If I couldn't even believe in my brethren, in Wynn, how could I ever trust an assassin?

And yet...

Shifting in the grass, Calem turned his head to me. "Well? We'd better get back before the gang tears up Ortega Key looking for us."

My heart squirmed. Yes, I would miss Calem and Oz and... And *him.* But being alone was the safest route, and I wasn't about to change direction now. Hand outstretched, I opened the door to the beast realm and tried to leave my emotions behind.

The only problem was, sooner or later, I'd always have to come *back.*

EIGHTEEN

NOC

So much time away from Leena made me more irritable than I cared to admit. We'd just returned from hours of mindless training, hours of me hoping control of the shadows could counteract the sharp light she'd used to slice my barriers open, and I was already seeking her out.

Slipping my hands into the pockets of my black trousers, I took the stairs to the second floor of the inn. Apparitions of Leena's eyes kept peering at me in the darkness, assessing my weaknesses and deeming me unworthy. Because I'd fled. I'd left her injured and alone, and while nothing could ever happen between us, I couldn't stand the thought of her doling out judgment. I wanted to be worthy.

As I hit the last stair, her bright laugh floated down the hallway. My gaze snapped to her doorway. The flickering light of the wall lamps illuminated her, but there was someone standing before her. A man dressed in all black.

Feet and hips pivoted toward her as he brought a hand to her cheek. "You've got dirt on your face."

Calem.

Gently, Leena brushed his fingers aside. "I should get cleaned up."

"Need any help?"

I was across the hall before I knew the shadows had taken me there. "Am I interrupting something?"

Leena shifted her weight as Calem straightened, a strained smile replacing the flirtatious one that had been there moments ago. "Not at all. Leena was just on her way to the bath. I, of course, offered my assistance, but maybe you could help instead."

"That's enough," I said.

"Why?" Calem folded his arms across his chest. "Someone should get laid around here."

"Noc," Leena started, "really, he was just—"

"You're being disrespectful," I spat at Calem.

He winked. "In the best kind of way."

I wanted to punch him, but I kept my hands lax at my side. Who was I to interfere if this was what she wanted? Never mind that the thought of Calem anywhere near her felt like needles pulling barbed threads through my skin. Over and over again. "Fine. Do as you please."

"Gods, Noc. It was a joke." Calem's gaze darted from Leena to me. Assessing. If she wanted him, I had no doubt he'd say yes. Unless he thought I felt otherwise. His eyes searched my face.

Down the hall, Ozias's and Kost's doors opened, and the pair strolled out to meet us. As much as I tried to hide my frustration, tension rippled across my shoulders, and shadows naturally began to fester near my fingertips.

Kost placed a firm hand on my back. "What's going on?"

Calem hardly breathed until Leena spoke.

"Nothing." Leena held my gaze for a moment before shifting to Kost. She twisted the ring on her finger.

"I don't believe you." Kost narrowed his eyes.

Calem stepped closer to her. "I made a bad joke. Happens all the time."

I longed to fall back into the shadow realm. To allow darkness to wash away the brewing feelings in my chest. Instead, I felt compelled to ask, "What were you two doing, anyway?"

Again, he moved closer to her. "We *may* have been on a beast hunt."

"You were *what*?" The last time she'd attempted to tame a beast alone, she'd nearly died. My gaze raked over her body. Smeared in dirt. A few minor scratches on her hands. Nothing overtly wrong. But that didn't keep my heightened pulse from roaring in my ears.

Kost's calculating gaze tracked my tenuous control. "I can't believe you went without us. Without at least informing Noc. You report to him when on a job, not Leena."

"I swear, Kost, now is not the time." Calem cracked his knuckles, red eyes bouncing between him and me. "She had a beast for me, so we acted. There was no danger involved."

No danger? I couldn't beat the rage building inside me into submission. We'd only been attacked *yesterday*.

Kost's nostrils flared. "I will not allow a *job* to dictate our orders. I will execute the problem if need be."

Shock bolted through Leena, and her stricken face and slack jaw speared my already throbbing heart. She met my gaze for a long moment. Waiting. Accusing. When I didn't say anything, she turned on her heels and stormed into her room, slamming the door behind her.

"Now you've done it." Twin blades forming in either of his hands, Calem toed off with Kost. "Let's roll, Four-Eyes."

Ozias pulled him off, wrapping his arms in a bear hug. "Kid, first you piss off Noc, and now you're going after Kost? Are you sure Noc's the one with the problem?"

"There wasn't any danger involved." Calem glowered at Kost.

"Enough." I ground out the command through clenched teeth. "My room. Now."

Calem pursed his lips as Ozias placed a hand on his shoulder, shoving him after Kost and me. Once we were locked behind the door of my bedroom, exhaustion and disappointment and frustration with myself added weight to my limbs. I slumped into the sofa at the foot of the bed.

"It's weird to see you so...agitated," Ozias said as he took an armchair across from me. Calem followed suit, lips still pressed into a thin line, and dropped into another chair before propping his feet up on the coffee table between us. Kost leaned against the doorframe, and I stared past him through the open windows at the endless horizon, where the ink-black ocean and onyx night met.

"What has gotten into you?" Calem asked.

I formed a steeple with my fingers and rested my elbows against my knees. My silver ring beamed at me, the glint of the emerald catching in the low light of the room. Like Leena, I rotated it around my finger. I had so many secrets. Secrets only Kost knew, but now wasn't the time. Now, I needed to know if they were on my side.

"I'm not going to kill Leena."

A low hiss escaped Kost, but Ozias beat him to the punch. "What about you? The oath?"

Three pairs of eyes slanted to my wrist. I slipped my hands into my pockets to hide the mark from view. "I'm not keen on dying, but there is a way out of this."

Kost pushed off from the wall, fists trembling by his sides. "I strongly advise against this. Think of the guild. Think of everyone depending on you."

"What's he talking about?" Calem stood slowly. "Noc?"

Kost's voice was even. "We'd have to kill the person who contracted Cruor for the job. The bounty would disappear with their life. However..." He tipped his head to the ceiling. "You realize what this would do to Cruor."

"Our reputation would be shot. No one has ever reneged a job before." Calem's shoulders drooped. "We're already not allowed to live in any city sanctioned by Wilheim. If we lose our only means of work, how will we keep the guild afloat?"

Leaning back into the couch, I pinched the bridge of my nose. "The king won't risk cutting ties with Cruor—not when it means his Sentinels stay safe. As far as other private jobs go...we'll manage."

Steely and brimming with ire, Kost pinned me with his stare. "You're forgetting a key element here."

"And what is that?"

"We don't know who placed the bounty."

I opened my mouth to argue, but my words died before reaching my tongue.

You will no longer be dealing with her. Her time is better spent elsewhere.

A woman had placed the hit on Leena's head. Not her glorified lackey. Not the man with the close-shaved beard. A fist clenched my gut and wrung it tight, sending bile up the back of my throat.

Kost kept coming, fury fueling his tirade. "And even if you do miraculously find out who placed the original bounty—which is impossible, given we don't even know what she looks like—how are you going to kill her? Did I mention she's a Charmer? Aren't we all innately aware of what a Charmer can do? Let alone one who's probably living in Hireath with hundreds, maybe thousands, of other Charmers. Tell me, Noc, is letting Leena go worth it? Worth all of this?"

"Kost." Ozias stood, placing a gentle hand on his heaving chest. "That's enough."

Calem rubbed the back of his neck. "It does seem like a lot, Noc. Why?"

Why indeed. Because she wasn't guilty? They'd only want a

better answer. It wasn't on us to pass judgment. We executed orders. Plus, no one wanted to take a step back and evaluate their kills. How many innocents we've likely claimed for the sake of bits.

In our world, innocence wasn't good enough.

Rough and pained with something I couldn't place, Kost's voice broke through my thoughts. "You're developing feelings for her, aren't you?"

My answer was swift, harsh. "No."

"Don't try to deny it."

Burying my head in my hands, I barely had the strength to speak. "Just let me save her, Kost. Please. Let me do for her what I couldn't do for the others."

Ozias's voice was low, curious. "Others?"

I dragged my fingers down my face before dropping my hands into my lap. Some secrets were just meant to be spilled. I'd held the truth back from them because it had seemed safer for everyone that way. Seeming disinterest couldn't be argued against, but a curse? Calem and Ozias hadn't seen the sheer horror it could unleash like Kost had. They wouldn't stop fighting, thinking they could help me overcome it. It had been better to keep them in the dark, but now... Things had come to too much of a head to keep this to myself. "I'm cursed. If I show affection—any kind of deep, true affection—to another person, they die. Always."

Calem stood, pacing back and forth behind the armchairs. "What, you mean like physically?"

"Not strictly speaking, no." I rotated the ring around my finger again, and the restless motion quieted something inside me. Maybe Leena was onto something. "It's more about emotions. Dalliances, passing trivialities, casual interactions—all those are fine in theory. But if anything deeper develops..."

"They die?" Calem asked.

"Yes." I paused, weighing exactly how much information to share, information that could possibly reveal my past. But I trusted my men, and they needed something more if they were ever going to let me save Leena in exchange for the guild's reputation. Swallowing my doubt, I kept my voice calm. "A long time ago, I crossed a high priestess and she cursed me. I've killed...*many*. All because I couldn't keep my emotions in check. The curse causes a sickness that, once it reaches a certain stage, can't be reversed."

Kost's face went cold. Silence stretched between us until Ozias cleared his throat. "How do you manage with the guild? With us?"

My smile was brittle. "Precariously."

"Gods. That's awful." Calem stopped pacing and gripped the back of the armchair. "But what does that have to do with Leena? It's not like you love her."

I could've sworn someone gut-punched Kost from the way he looked at me. I fought to say words that didn't want to come out. "I don't." Not yet. But now there was a line. A line between interest and something deeper, and it was entirely too visible.

Calem's face blanched. "Does she love you? Gods, Noc. Sorry. I didn't know."

My heart did an irrational flutter at the thought. "No. I don't know. It doesn't matter. Unrequited love won't get her killed. Only my feelings have the death sentence attached to them. That's how it happened before."

Ozias's heavy-lidded gaze—his compassion—pierced my heart. "Who were they?"

I shook my head. The truth was, I didn't know how many I'd killed. Amira and Bowen, definitely. But how many more had I condemned to death? The war caused by Amira's passing had lasted years. And for those years, I'd watched my closest brethren die, chalking it up to a plague common in the trenches. They'd all gone the same way: the darkening eyes. Chapped skin. Blood-riddled cough. Fever. Death.

There were too many to count. My parents were only spared because the priestess was bound to protect the throne. She safeguarded them from the curse to fulfill her duty. But Leena... "I just... I can't kill her. Not when it feels like I'm killing them all over again. Whether it's the curse or the bounty, she doesn't deserve it."

After feeling Leena curled in sleep beside me, I knew she had the potential to be something more. That fire in her soul was too real. Too beguiling. I would never get the chance to know for sure, never let myself go beyond cool detachment, but at least I could spare her.

Calem pivoted, facing me with a stricken look in his eyes. "So we let her live."

"Only if we all agree." I glanced at Kost. He was entirely still, but his silence was somehow louder and more demanding than any of Calem's outbursts. "Well?"

"We can still kill her." Kost stared at the floor, fingers twitching. "If her death bothered you that much, you could always bring her back."

"Out of the question." It was hard to keep my voice steady. As the guild master, I could raise her. Intermingling my blood with hers would reverse the flow of time, restoring function to her organs and heart. But what would that do to her? Would she lose her beasts? Would she balk at the cold realities of our existence and turn her back on me?

That would be the better of the two options. Because if she stayed, if she forgave me and remained at Cruor, she'd be an unending source of temptation, and I wasn't sure I'd be strong enough to resist. One slipup. One error, and then she would die again—this time at my hand, and without the ability to be reborn. I couldn't raise what I'd already brought back from death.

I released a heavy sigh and stared at Kost. He refused to meet my gaze. "We should have killed her the moment she stepped into Cruor." Calem hissed at Kost's words, but I shook my head once to keep him in place.

"Kost has seen everything. The way I was before you two joined. He may be brash, but he's just protecting me." Standing, I propped my arms against the back of the couch. "If I have to honor the oath, I will. For the guild."

"What, and have you miserable for all eternity? How is that a fair thing to ask of us?" Kost finally looked at me, no fight left in his eyes. "We need a plan. If you get yourself killed in the process, none of this even matters."

"She had me on her side from the start." Ozias shrugged. "But I never would have stood against you."

Calem nodded, slumping into his chair. "Same."

Gratitude swelled in my chest, and I fought to keep my breathing normal. "Thank you."

Ozias rubbed the back of his neck. "And Leena?"

I stared at them for a long moment. "Leena has a job to do. No need to tell her any of this. Let her gift us the beasts while we work on a way to find the person behind the hit. Then, we'll send her away and hopefully never cross paths again."

Both Ozias and Calem opened their mouths to argue, but Kost cut them off. "That's the only option, aside from her death. If she lives, she lives without us. End of story."

"He's right." I drifted over to the window to look out across the ink-black ocean. "The farther away from us, the safer she is."

NINETEEN

LEENA

Heavy, brooding clouds obscured the morning sky, blotting out the sun and cocooning Ortega Key in a blanket of darkness. Rain poured from the heavens, crashing against the vendor stalls on the streets and turning the gravel to mud. Umbrella in hand, I moved from shop to shop, hounding the locals for information on beasts.

Clutching the handle tight, I sidestepped a deep puddle and continued toward another vendor. I could have stayed at the inn. No one would have faulted me for hiding from this torrential onslaught. But I couldn't stand still. Out here, there was space to breathe. Space to think. Space to encourage distance from the man who, intentionally or not, continued to wreak havoc on my thoughts.

"Hey there. How's your friend doing?"

Lost in thought, I hadn't realized I'd meandered to a stall laden with fresh fish. Gleaming scales doused in rain glistened from buckets of ice, and a fiery redhead peered up at me as she crouched over the nearest one. Wiping her hands on an apron across her waist, she stood and smiled.

"Corinne, right?" I stepped under the awning and closed my umbrella, shaking water on the ground. "And do you mean Ozias?"

Her smile deepened. "That's the one."

"He's fine. Is this a recent catch?" Gesturing to the fish splayed before us, I flashed her a grin of my own.

"Yeah, when we're not ferrying guests, we're fishing. We didn't get our usual haul today. The coast along Queens Isle has the best fish, but the storm hit early and we had to turn back."

A crack of lightning illuminated the sky. "Sorry to hear that."

Corinne shrugged. "Personally, I'm glad. Lots of weird noises coming from the jungle."

"Noises?"

She nodded. "Some sort of yowling. At first, I thought it was the storm, but I swear it's something else."

Sharp tingling stirred in my fingertips. The Myad. She'd heard the legendary beast's mating call. A male, then. I inched closer to her. "Can you take me there?"

She placed her hands on her hips. "What? Now? No. If the storm clears up, we can go tomorrow."

"Deal."

A faint smile touched her lips, and she quickly glanced at my bestiary. "Private charter?"

"That would be best. I'll pay, of course." The thought of emptying my coin purse based solely on the hearsay of this woman sent my stomach reeling, but the Myad would be worth it. He *had* to be there.

"I'll let my father know."

I couldn't keep myself from smiling. "Thanks for your help, Corinne. I've got to tell the others."

"Tell Ozias I said 'hi.'"

"Will do." Freeing my umbrella, I darted out into the street and booked it toward the Roasted Boar. The Myad had probably made the dense jungle of Queens Isle his den. If he'd been away spreading his scent to attract mates to his location, he'd spend the next few days perfecting his lair.

It was either strike now, or wait and possibly face two Myads at once. Or three, if two separate females decided to follow his trail. Chances of taming him were low already. If more appeared, death wasn't just a risk—it was a guarantee.

But I still needed a murderer's blood to complete the taming. My mind reeled at the options. Oz was most likely to comply, but part of me wanted it to be Noc. I didn't dare examine that notion long enough to understand why.

As if my thoughts somehow summoned the damn assassin, I hiked up the groaning steps of the inn to find him already lingering on the wraparound porch. The rain seemed to harden to ice, and I froze in place. Sleeves rolled past his elbows, he wore a black tunic that hugged the hard cut of his body.

My heart thrummed against my rib cage. "Morning."

He parked a hip on the railing, turning his back to the road. "Morning."

I couldn't stand his slate eyes. So sharp and calculating and inquisitive. They threatened to crack me wide open when all I wanted to do was barricade myself shut. "I've got a lead on some beasts. We'll head to Queens Isle first thing tomorrow."

His jaw twitched, and he gripped the railing on either side of him. "Great."

I closed my umbrella. "What are you doing out here?"

"I needed some air." Bone-white knuckles gleamed at me. In terms of proximity, we were so close...

My mind flashed back to the night before. To the sudden maelstrom of darkness when he'd discovered Calem and I had set out on a hunt alone. I'd once thought his shadows were something to be admired. So many varying shades of onyx, like the vast depths of the ocean. But last night, those tendrils had been harsher than obsidian.

Yet still, not as devastatingly terrifying as his blood. A shiver spider-walked across my skin. When the Scorpex had appeared and Noc summoned those blades, I froze. I should have been ecstatic—blood so freely available—but it had coagulated before I could think, before I could weigh the importance of stopping the Scorpex and stealing an ounce for my own needs. As quickly as it had appeared, he'd sharpened it into a weapon that whispered of devastation, and he'd held death in his palms. Controlled it.

"Noc," I started, "can I ask you something?"

He blinked slowly, his grip on the rail no tighter, no looser. "Of course."

"When the Scorpex showed up, you slashed your palms, and your blood..." I rotated the ring around my finger as I searched for words. "Why does it do that?"

I didn't expect him to answer. So much of our conversations had been one-sided; him discovering secrets about me and offering very little in return. And yet, I couldn't help but ask.

"Because I am the leader of Cruor," he said slowly, as if checking each word before revealing it to me. My chest tightened with surprise. "My blood carries a power that acts as both a weapon—the blades you saw—and a tool. Passed on from guild master to guild master, it allows me to raise potential assassins from the dead. My blood mingles with theirs, reversing the stasis of death and giving them life."

I probed further. "Has it always been like that?"

"For centuries now, thanks to the First King of Wilheim. He was...cruel. Ambitious. Craved power above all else. He bartered with a powerful mage in exchange for the lives of his firstborn daughter and son."

There were whispers of the First King, of his crimes against Charmers. But how he came to be, how he garnered power strong enough to force Charmers to barricade ourselves away in Hireath, had escaped our texts. "You're kidding."

Noc shook his head. "The people of Wilheim? Granted unnaturally long lives and powerful Sentinels to protect their homes—a gift from Mavis's blood." His gaze flickered away. "Zane wasn't as lucky."

Understanding took me, chilling my bones. "He was the first of your kind."

"Yes. He was slaughtered and raised again, and his blood was given to the fallen to strengthen the king's army during the First War."

Above our heads, the rain intensified, slamming itself into the thatched roof of the inn. Leaking through with a steady drip along the patio, water gathered on the floor in places where the roof was weak. Noc shifted, the toe of his boot casting ripples in one of the puddles.

I knew of the First War. Even though I hadn't lived it, a slow burn churned in my gut. "Thousands of Charmers died during that war. Their beasts, too."

Dark eyes swallowed me whole. "As I said, ambitious. He wanted Lendria for himself. When Zane learned of his true intentions, he took his men and left. Outlawed from the kingdom, they performed what work they could."

My anger faded. "I can relate."

"It wasn't until Queen Lokelai came into power centuries later that she bargained with Cruor to use our talents in exchange for bits. She didn't want to sully the good name of Mavis's descendants by asking them to do work she saw fit for Zane's kind." Noc's face was surprisingly free of tension. No tremor to his jaw or tight glare. His long fingers loosened around the railing. His openness stunned me and, at the same time, spurred me to unearth more. This was the first real glimpse into his past, his history, I'd gotten. I wanted to learn more about the man who'd found a stronghold in my thoughts and wouldn't let go.

"What's it like, being an assassin?"

His spine tensed. "It's a job. I'm good at it."

"Good at it?" I tilted my head. "What about when you have to kill someone who's innocent? What if you had to kill someone you loved?"

He rose from the railing and stalked toward me, backing me against the wall. Warring emotions, complicated and nearly unreadable, clouded his face. Hands pressed to the wooden planks on either side of me, he dipped his head low. "I'm especially good at killing people I love. No more questions."

I was a mixture of temperatures. Chilling words scraped along my exposed neck, leaving an icy tingle I couldn't ignore. But there was a heat blooming in my chest, a growing, burning need. I *needed* to know more. It was frightening, and yet I couldn't stop myself. Couldn't bring myself to not ask questions when he was around, to not invest in something that was so plainly not meant to be.

Gently, before he could retreat, I traced the crescent-moon scar on his left cheekbone. His eyes fluttered closed. Noc was an open door. Not because he was easy to read, but because every action begged me to walk right into him. To unearth every secret of my own volition and turn it over in my hands. For the first time in years, I wanted trust, both given and received. I wanted him to believe he could share something with me.

Moving my fingers to grip his chin, I brushed a thumb over his lips. He inhaled sharply, but didn't pull away. His breath against my finger burned hot, and my heart raced. Slowly, I angled my mouth up toward his. Felt his breath against my lips. And then I kissed him before he could disappear like he had so many times before.

Noc didn't move. My mouth met hard granite, and time stretched as nothing happened. No reaction. Not even a sound. Embarrassment burned my cheeks. Just as I decided to pull away, something snapped. And then all at once, he rushed over me, his heated kiss rough and hungry. His tongue swept into my mouth, and a broken sound slipped from somewhere deep in his chest. I locked my hands behind his neck and wrenched my fingers in his hair.

My heart thundered in my ears. It'd taken us so long to get here. So many moments of lingering gazes and subtle touches. Unbearable stretches of denial and cold fronts that had threatened to put us permanently on ice. But not now. Now there was nothing but warmth and heat.

And I couldn't get enough. I wanted to be wrapped in him, lost in the way his hands traveled restlessly over my body. In the undeniable fervor of his kiss. Our lips meshed together, and for the first time in a long time, I felt *whole*. Dragging my hands from his neck to his spine, I pressed him against me. Noc gripped the sides of my waist, and delicious pressure flared from his fingertips.

He broke away for a moment and rested his forehead against mine. "Leena..."

My name on his lips only furthered my desire, and I pulled his mouth back to mine. I nicked his bottom lip with my teeth, and he dove into me. I swear I felt every raging emotion inside him in that moment. Longing mixed with pain and uncertainty. It was so visceral and raw that I nearly went limp in his arms. I wanted nothing more than to soothe those battling fears while sating his—and my—desire.

Something clicked then, a brilliant flare of warmth right in the center of my chest. I gasped and pressed my head against the wall while he tasted my neck. A steady hum thrummed through my veins, a new frenzied beat like another heart racing alongside mine. It was the exact opposite of carnal. The exact opposite of what I'd sought out in past flings. Fear and passion battled with each other, and I brought Noc's lips back to mine to keep myself from running away.

Wrapped in the heat of him, I didn't notice the inn door swing open until Noc was thrown off me and into the rain. He barely had time to steady himself before turning his wild eyes to the man in the open doorframe.

Hands shaking, Kost leveled me with his glare before turning his ire to Noc. "Don't be a fool. Cool off."

Hard eyes skewered Kost, but Noc pressed his lips into a fine line. Water dripped down his face, trailing the length of his cheekbones before sliding off his jaw. He spared me one pained look. I could've sworn I saw a glimmer of ice-blue flash from the inky black depth of his eyes, but it faded in an instant. And then came the wall of cold so sudden and violent that I swear the rain turned to sleet around him. Every muscle rigid, he strode past me without a second glance. Slammed the inn door behind him.

So cold. I brought my fingers to my lips, hoping to reignite the heat he had left. Why had he acted that way? With Noc gone, my body ached to follow him. To understand. Had he felt our connection, too? Maybe that's why he'd shut down. It was so intense and unexpected. Even with Wynn, another Charmer, I'd never felt such a pull.

Kost swiveled in place, shined shoes clipping against the wood, and he pinned me with his stern expression. Frustration bubbled over, and I narrowed my eyes. "What's your problem?"

Kost snapped. Baring his teeth and towering above me, he cornered me against the wall. "You, Leena, are my problem."

Pressing my palms flat against his blood-red formal tunic, I shoved him. He didn't budge, so I leaned forward, bringing my nose inches from his. "Get out of my way, Kost."

"Leave Noc alone."

"You don't get to tell me what to do."

Kost formed a fist with his gloved hand and held it tight for a solid minute before uncurling his fingers. "Leave. Him. Alone." The vein along his temple throbbed.

I itched to smack him. To knock his glasses to the ground and mess up that perfectly styled gods-damned hair. "What do you have against me, Kost?"

"You're a *job*," he said. I winced, but he kept going, voice trembling. "You don't even realize what you've done. You've jeopardized *everything*."

"Kost—"

"What is it about you that makes him throw caution to the wind?" He studied my face for answers. And apparently came up empty, because he grimaced. "I hate that you fit."

My body went numb. "What?"

"You're like a gods-damned puzzle piece. And the rest of us? We've been helping him put together the larger, more important picture for years. But there you are, the single piece he can't ignore. The only one that *fits*. There's nothing quite like that feeling of relief and satisfaction when the last piece finds its home." A tight laugh punctuated his words. "It doesn't matter how long the rest of us have been lying around."

"Us?"

"Us! *Me*. I..." His expression cracked, and his shoulders curled toward his chest.

His words shattered like lightning, striking in the small space between us and rooting me to the ground. A quiet ringing followed his outburst, and he slid his fingers between his spectacles and his nose, hiding his eyes. Realization hit me.

"*You* love him." My words were barely a whisper, but Kost flinched.

"Don't act like you know anything about me, Leena. This is for Noc's sake, not mine." His voice hitched an octave higher. Caught on a shuddering breath.

I tried to get a grip on my racing thoughts. "Does he know?"

"Enough." He slipped his glasses from his face and polished the lenses. "Just stay away." Gaze unobstructed by frames, he peered at me. Hurt laced the fields of green, and my throat constricted. How long had he and Noc been friends? And for me to just come in and change their dynamic... To be Noc's missing piece, at least in Kost's eyes... Words shaped and disappeared, nothing substantial enough forming in my mind.

Finally, I managed a weak "Kost, I'm sorry. It's not serious—"

He barked out a fragile laugh. "Where Noc is concerned, everything is serious." He turned away, took several visible breaths. After a moment, he replaced his glasses. Ran his hands over the length of his tunic. Only then did he glance over his shoulder at me. "Tell me, what are you willing to risk? Because if it isn't death, you may as well leave now."

"You'd risk your life for him?"

Muscles jumped along his jaw. "I'd risk anything. Remember, Leena, assassins don't fear death. You'll always be one step behind when it comes to that."

TWENTY

NOC

The next morning, we boarded the ferry heading for Queens Isle. Coated in thick layers of sweat from the sudden onset of humidity, we baked in the sun on the deck of *Arrow's Wind*. The slow-moving ferry churned water through its red wheel and cut through the ocean. Even the sea breeze died with the disappearance of the storm, and we fanned ourselves with our hands as we waited.

Sitting in a slatted white chair underneath a green awning, Kost stared over the open waters. Felicks sat in his lap, orb clouding and unclouding every few minutes. Like his master, he studied his surroundings. Ozias clung to the metal railing of the boat next to the woman he'd met at the bar, who pointed to dolphins traveling in the wake of the ferry to his obvious—if shy—delight. Leena sat next to Calem, straddling the posts and dangling her feet off the edge. Ocean spray coated her thighs, and she rubbed the water into her skin before wiping her hands on her cutoff canvas breeches.

"You're staring."

I ignored Kost's quiet reprimand. Staring at her was all I had. With her hair braided to the side, her neck called to me. I wanted to taste it. To run my tongue along the curve and kiss the shell of her ear. I wanted her lilac and vanilla flavor, tinged gritty and real with salt.

I never should have kissed her. Now she was all my mouth craved.

I formed my hand into a fist and punched the wooden wall at my back. The panel cracked, and Kost raised a brow without meeting my gaze. Slow fingers worked their way through Felicks's fur. "Control yourself. We need time to sort this out."

Gods, she was water in a drought. "Yeah, yeah."

Calem ripped off his work shirt and fell back against the deck, folding the clothing over his eyes. Leena continued to look to the sea. There'd been little chance for the two of us to talk—Kost had seen to that. Jaw set and eyes hard, she studied the island in the distance. Was she mad? Or was it something else? Tension gathered between her shoulders, and she drummed her fingers against her kneecaps. Ozias hollered at Calem and he jumped up, joining the couple at the railing and leaving Leena unattended.

"I'd tell you to stay away, but Felicks tells me you won't listen." He pointedly glanced down at the swirling orb of his beast. Felicks let out a soft bark and nudged his master's hand.

"Well, since you already *know*." I tossed the words over my shoulder as I walked toward her. There wasn't enough time. Before we knew it, the days would be over and Leena would disappear from my life all over again. At least she would be safe. At least she could have a future.

I sank to the deck beside her. "Hello."

Loose strands of hair swept across her face as wary eyes locked with mine. "Hey. How's Kost?" She tossed a quick glance behind me before turning back to the waves.

Considering his foreboding gaze was embedding a knife into my back, not great. "He's fine. Why do you ask?"

"No reason."

A massive wave crested against the side of the ferry, spraying us with a sheet of white water. Leena's face cracked, its stern facade faltering as she giggled and wiped droplets from her eyes. A fist wrenched tight around my heart, and I looked away.

"You're soaked." With an easy smile on her face, she nodded to the sprinkling of damp spots across my typical Cruor ensemble of black on black.

"So are you."

Her smile eased...warmed. She was so gods-damned *warm.* "Guess so." Longing burned within me, and I inched my fingers closer to hers. I was playing with fire. With light. Shadows waited in corners of the ship, eager to do my bidding, but I didn't want to hide. I could at least enjoy my limited time. She pressed herself against the railing and looped her arms around the nearest post, her gaze already focused back on the island.

My heart threatened to shatter when her fingers moved that insurmountable distance from mine. "You seem preoccupied."

"There are a lot of beasts in locations like this."

"Why?"

She shrugged. "Less involvement with people. Jungles, dense forests, caves—we're bound to run into something here that's beyond the norm. Have you thought any more about what kind of beast you want?"

My mind rewound to the night we'd spent in the beast realm. There were so many creatures there, so many possibilities. And yet the only thing I wanted was her. She was strong and brave and cunning and everything I could ever desire in a partner. And yet, she was entirely beyond my reach. And I was dangerously close to letting those emotions take hold and condemning her to a fate she didn't deserve.

I know what you want. A female voice purred through my mind, and Leena's Gyss, Fable, rattled my thoughts. She was such a tiny thing. Could a beast like that truly fix the impossible?

If she couldn't, then what? I couldn't love Leena. I'd felt a spark when we kissed. One I was trying to douse with ice water in order to keep her safe. No, no matter how good she was, no matter how good she could be for everyone—the guild, Ozias, Calem, even Kost—her happiness and her life ranked higher than my selfish need.

The weight of the curse had never felt more unbearable. Love, true friendship, trust, understanding—everything I wanted in an ally, and all the things I could never obtain.

Leena studied me, eyebrows furrowing with concern. "Are you okay?" She dropped one hand from the railing, fingers twitching against the deck just inches from my leg.

"I still want the Gyss." My life at Cruor was satisfying enough. I'd worked hard to form the ranks, to build tenuous relationships. I was able to keep them safe from me. Close in proximity, if in no other way. It was a precarious balance, but I'd keep walking the line to hold on to what I had.

Another wave smashed against the boat, and a fine spray of mist drifted above us. Her frown sharpened. "Noc, we've been over this." Queens Isle loomed before us, and the ferry dropped its speed as we neared shallow waters. Leena stood slowly, shaking her head and avoiding my eyes. "Speaking from experience, nothing is worth the risk. Plus, it doesn't meet the terms of our agreement."

But there was a possibility. A life without shackles. "Those can be modified."

Behind us, clanking chains crashed against the ocean water as the ferry sank an anchor. The ship jolted, and she took another step away. Hands forming fists, she rolled her lower lip into her mouth. "I'm sorry, Noc."

Her voice was so small that the groans of docking threatened to swallow it whole. But I caught the concern. Leena looked at me without really seeing me—stared at my chest and walked away before I could question her further.

"You ready for this?" Calem slapped me across the back, rocking me in place. The rest of the group had already boarded a small barnacle-encrusted wooden boat with oars off the left side of the ferry.

The woman from the bar waved at us to join them. "I made lunches for everyone." She handed us small boxes neatly wrapped in plaid cloth. When she gave Ozias his, her fingers lingered a moment too long.

"Thanks." I jumped into the boat behind Calem and landed between Ozias and Kost, Felicks nestled safely beside him.

A genuine smile graced Leena's lips, and she reached back to scratch Felicks behind his ears. "It's admirable how quickly you've established a bond with him, Kost."

Kost nodded. "I summon him every night to see how long he can stay in our realm. We're progressing nicely."

"Soon you'll be able to stay out for days at a time," Leena cooed to the beast. Felicks let out a contented huff, and Leena dropped her hand. "It helps that your master is strong."

The faintest blush scorched the tops of Kost's ears, and he cleared his throat. Without looking Leena's way, he gripped the oar at his side. "Let's go."

Heavy waves made paddling to the beach hard work. We each manned an oar while Leena sat to one side, fingers drawing patterns in the crystal-clear water. Everything about her called to me.

The bottom of the boat scraped against the sand, and we jumped into warm, ankle-deep water. Ozias hauled the vessel several feet up the beach, securing it beyond the reach of high tide. White sand greeted us, and we trudged toward the forest line of the jungle.

"Corinne and her father will be back tomorrow to grab us. Is that enough time, Leena?" Ozias dropped two duffel bags on the ground. The rest we'd left at the Roasted Boar.

Leena stared up at the midmorning sun. "Hopefully." Palm trees lined the edge of the jungle, and countless caws of eager birds filled the air. She turned toward the chirps, tilting her head as if listening for something none of us could comprehend. The jungle crowded the base of a conical volcano, and rugged peaks of black and brown shot through the rubber leaves.

"What beast do you have in mind?" Kost set Felicks on the ground. His beast cocked his head to the side just as clouds brewed in his orb.

She shrugged, but something foreign passed through her gaze. "I'm not sure."

Lie. I could read it plain as day. "Oh, really now?"

Eyes narrowed, she stepped away. "Really, really."

"I'm good with whatever you pick." Ozias cradled the back of his head. "You did so well with Kost and Calem, I'm sure you'll figure it out."

Exasperated, Leena placed her hands on her hips. "That doesn't help me at all."

Kost looked past her to the retreating ferry. "Well, you must have had something in mind if you dragged us here." By his feet, Felicks's orb cleared. His hackles raised, and a low growl rattled the back of his throat. Kost's face pinched. He crouched down to rest his hand on Felicks's back. "What's wrong?"

Leena stilled, her eyes darting from Felicks to the suddenly quiet surroundings. "He senses something."

"Is it that?" Calem leaned forward onto the balls of his feet and pointed at a reddish boulder some fifty yards down the beach.

My lips quirked into a smile. "That's a rock."

"I swear I saw it move." Calem squinted, and Leena followed his gaze. As if struck by lightning, she froze in place, fingers trembling.

"Stay very still."

I frowned. "What?"

Slowly she touched her chin to her shoulder. "No sudden movements, or it'll charge."

The low groan of something ancient and powerful grated like grinding gears, and adrenaline prickled across my skin. Spurred to life by our arrival, the rock unfurled its mammoth shape. Taller than an elephant and built like a wingless dragon, the creature leaned forward on powerful legs. Thick claws speared the soft sands. A bone headdress with pointed spikes sat like a crown around the beast's head, and gleaming, threatening eyes targeted us. A mirage shimmered around its body.

"What the fuck is that?" Calem asked. Leena stood alone in front of us, one hand splayed outward and the other nervously gripping the bestiary around her neck.

"Laharock." She lowered her voice to a whisper, as if that somehow would keep the beast from charging. "It'll kill us all."

Something violent and angry wrung my insides. She *couldn't* die. Not now. Not after I'd decided to do everything within my power to keep her safe. Sidling toward her, I allowed my hand to brush the back of hers. She looked up at me, and her gaze softened. I'd chase away her fears for the rest of my life if I could.

"We'll handle this. Together."

And with my brethren all offering tight nods of agreement, the trembling of Leena's fingers disappeared. Her answering grin was fierce. Determined. It lit up my world.

"Together."

TWENTY-ONE

LEENA

The Laharock extended its elongated neck, raising its head to the sun, and let out a screech that rattled the treetops. Pupilless white eyes burned with heat. We were staring down the face of death in the form of an A-Class beast. One I had not expected to encounter. My gaze shot past it to the volcano. It should have been lounging at the base, soaking up the minerals and heat from the lava beneath the surface. Far, far away from where I'd find the Myad.

Noc sliced a fine line across his palm, and blood swelled to the surface, pooling in the grooves of his palm and trickling toward his fingertips. "What do we do?" Shadows leaped from the forest, encompassing the band of assassins and delivering ink-black weapons into their open hands.

Think. I flexed my hands. *Which beast?*

The Laharock stepped forward, and the sun glinted off the protective blood-red scales lining its spine, neck, and arms. Edges rimmed in gold, Laharock plates sold for a good amount on the black market, but piercing its hide was damn near impossible.

Iky wouldn't be able to do any damage.

"Look at that." Oz nodded toward the creature's hind legs. Nestled deep into the sand, a baby Laharock blinked up at its mother.

Mother. "Shit." She'd left the steep hills of the volcano to birth her young on easier terrain. Blood blades rose by my cheek, and Noc's hand once again grazed mine. *Together.* Kost crept closer, an endless supply of weapons brimming against his hip. With one hand, he snuck his fingers into his breast pocket and extracted a bronze key.

"Wait." I glanced at Felicks. At the wondrous future unfolding in his globe. "You two have bonded enough for him to share his visions, right?"

Kost's hand froze. "Yes. At least I think so. I don't get full stories just yet. More like images."

"That'll work." I tapped into my power, and rosewood light bloomed around my hand. "Are you comfortable with using him? His ability would help keep us out of harm's way."

Kost pulled in a breath. Released it. Finally, he put his key away. "If anything happens to him—"

The Laharock roared without moving. She was being careful, keeping her young within defending distance while asserting her territory. Her precaution would only last so long. Soon, she'd realize we were easy prey and make dinner out of all of us.

"Nothing will happen to him. I promise." The door to the realm groaned open, and my Asura, Quilla, materialized before us. Her cow head swiveled round until all ten eyes locked on me. She made a move to position herself beside me, to activate her protective shield and keep me safe, but I shook my head and pointed at Felicks. "Protect him. At all costs."

Quilla hugged Felicks to her chest with her middle arms and sauntered toward the edge of the forest line behind us. She sat cross-legged on the ground, nestled Felicks in her lap, and then extended her arms. Shield activated.

"Don't move," Kost said to his beast. Felicks barked, and the clouds in his gem cleared. Future determined.

"Well?" Calem edged forward. His fingers twitched.

"Easy, Calem." Noc glanced between him and me. The blood blade in his hand glistened in the sun and made my gut churn.

"We're not killing her. She's got a child. Which means…"

"Taming," Kost said. He pressed one finger to his temple, brow furrowed. "Felicks doesn't see it yet, but that doesn't mean—look out!"

The Laharock charged and we scattered, the men sinking away into the shadows and me leaping to the side. I rolled against the ground, grains of sand worming into my skin. Unable to see the assassins, the beast turned toward me. Heat sweltered in the space around her. Rocketing to my feet, I launched several yards back. The edge of the ocean kissed the heels of my shoes.

Kost reappeared first, finger still pressed to his temple. "Calem, Ozias—don't try it!"

Both men manifested from the shadows, flanking her sides and aiming blades at the backs of the beast's knees. But at Kost's command, they peeled off and fell back into darkness. If they'd gone through with their actions, the Laharock's heat would have burned their skin down to the bone.

I caught Felicks in my peripheral vision and the swirling glint of vibrant amethyst atop his head. Still telegraphing. Adjusting predictions based on our actions. He was remarkable.

Noc materialized before me, onyx tendrils spreading outward. The Laharock charged, and Noc yanked me toward him, pulling me into the depths of darkness and the safety of his arms. A world as black and endless as the night sky encompassed us, faint gleaming shades of gray weaving through the ink. Between the slate-black color of his hair and eyes, I couldn't tell where he began and the shadows ended. Forehead scrunched in worry, he pressed me closer for a moment before Queens Isle returned, ocean waves and blazing hot sun before us.

My mind reeled as I tried to grapple with the sudden change in surroundings. Noc's grip on my wrist tightened. He'd moved us into the water and the Laharock was standing her ground on the beach, howling and tossing her head to the sky. An ocean wave crested against the back of my knees.

"Are you okay?" Noc positioned himself in front of me, drawing the brunt of the beast's attention.

"I'm fine." Black swirls toyed with the corners of my vision, but they faded with the force of the sun. Still pacing and roaring, the beast tested the edge of the water before retracting her foot. Salt water corroded Laharock scales if they spent too much time in it.

Kost, Calem, and Ozias joined us. *We'll handle this. Together.* Noc was right—this was not a beast I could tackle alone. Kost's rigid stare was locked on Felicks. Quilla hadn't moved. Their stillness made them a nonthreat to the Laharock, who only had eyes for us.

"Kost, tell us what to do." As much as I wanted to take point, this is where Kost excelled: calculation. And with a beast that could predict the future? He needed to be the one at the helm.

He drew his head back, stared. "If you insist." His fingers went to his temple. "We need to separate the mother and child. That's how we win. Felicks is showing me...a water beast? A fish? I can't quite make it out."

A grin tugged at my lips. "Selenis."

Taking several deep breaths, I channeled all my power into my hands, and the door to the beast realm swung open. A tremble disrupted the ocean waves. Selenis would act as a conduit and could divide the beasts.

Light shattered the space around us, and my water beast emerged. Iridescent blue and purple scales ran the length of her torso, and her tail slapped against the water, long fins trailing wide behind her. Webbed hands grazed the waves, and she brought a few droplets to her fish-like lips. Her hair was a mixture of seaweed and tentacles, fluttering behind her as she moved toward me. Her endless oval eyes were the color of rubies. When she extended her palms outward, circular black voids rimmed with pink flesh shuddered.

"What about us?" Oz crouched low in the water, his gaze tracking the mother's path.

"Noc, Calem, and myself will bait the mother. Once she's far enough away from her young, Selenis will erect a water wall dividing them. Then, you will transport Leena to the baby so she can tame it first." Kost dropped his hand. His stare found Felicks, and something like pride filled his expression. "The mother will fall in line after that to be with her child."

"Done and done." Calem leaped into the shadows without a backward glance.

Noc stilled. "Ozias takes Leena?"

Unmoving, Kost didn't meet his gaze. "I don't make the predictions, Felicks does. This is our best chance at survival."

The air was thick with tension. Noc clenched his fists. Shook them out. "Fine." He gave me one parting glance full of so much emotion that my breath caught. "Be safe." Darkness shrouded him, and he disappeared after Calem.

Inky tendrils festered around Kost's fingers. He stared only at his beast. "It really was the prediction."

I hate that you fit.

My heart gave a violent twist. As much as it must have pained him to see Noc's reluctance to leave my side, I knew Kost would always do right by his family. His loyalty to Cruor, to his brothers' safety, came first. After all, in his eyes, I was just a job.

"I know."

Oz looked back and forth between us, thick brow furrowed tight. "Am I missing something?"

"No." Kost closed his eyes. Opened them. "Be careful. We'll be on the other side of a very powerful water wall. I'm not sure our shadows could carry us through something like that."

Oz nodded. "Understood."

"You too, Leena." And then darkness swallowed him whole. My throat ached. *Kost.* I wanted to examine that flare of warmth—of concern—further. Maybe I *wasn't* just a job anymore. Maybe giving him Felicks had done the trick. Maybe... But the assassins had already gone to work, and I wasn't about to be the one who held us back. I pushed my thoughts aside.

"Selenis." I called to my beast, and she slithered through the ocean waves to wait obediently for my mark. "When the mother is far enough away, erect a wall. Don't harm the child."

She smacked her lips in answer. Right hand submerged into the wake, a small whirlpool formed around her fingertips as the vacuum in her palm drew in water. She extended her left hand, pointing it directly at the beast. Droplets leaked from the quaking void, flesh sealed across the opening until she used her power.

"Now what?" Muscles coiled in Oz's neck as he watched his brothers from afar.

"We follow Kost's plan so they don't get injured," I said. Oz flinched, and I placed a gentle hand on his arm. "I'd sooner get hurt than them. Baby Laharocks aren't great at controlling their power, as it's not yet set in stone."

"I don't want you hurt, either."

"That's what I have you for. To protect me." I beamed up at him, and his expression smoothed a hair. He looked beyond me to the Laharock. She'd spotted Calem to her left, and heat poured from her body. Calem grinned, flipping a black blade in his hand. He tossed a knife directly at her chest plate, and it clattered to the sand at her feet. Steam curled from her nostrils and she bared her teeth, inching her way closer.

The heat around the Laharock intensified, and the sand beneath her feet glowed a fiery orange. Tacky strands clung to her claws as she stalked toward Calem. He leaped back, wide eyes glued to the glass forming beneath her heavy tread.

Noc tossed a round of knives at the Laharock, only for them to scatter like pine needles beneath her feet. But it drew her attention. Rounding on him instead of his brother, the beast growled. Calem and Kost reappeared, each one flanking a different side and shooting weapons with ease. They worked together, trading off when the Laharock got too close, and inch by inch pulled her away from her young. It was the long game, but it was the only one that would work.

Selenis waited, ruby eyes judging the distance between the Laharock and my assassins. Unused water dripped from her quivering void. Creeping low through the waves with Oz beside me, I eyed the young.

"Almost," I said. The baby yawned, stretched. Stood and peered after its mother. Far from full grown, and yet still the size of a bear.

And just as ferocious. I scowled. Baby Laharocks were difficult to approach. If they grew up in the wild unthreatened, their magic would result in the ability to summon scalding fires and intense heat, much like the mother. But until then? They were empathic metamorphs—susceptible to any outside trigger that could shift their power. They were in constant flux until that happened, making them impossible to gauge.

One of Kost's blades wedged between two of the Laharock's scales, just a sliver of an opening. She roared, wet spittle coating the ground before her, and charged several feet his direction.

"Selenis!"

A powerful stream exploded from her palm and expanded to a wall as thick and tall as the ones surrounding Wilheim. Impenetrable. The roaring sound of cascading water drowned out the panicked cries of the mother.

"Now, Oz!" I reached for him, and he wrapped his arm around my side. Darkness engulfed us, and he dragged me through the ocean toward the beach. We appeared before the baby, and sable tendrils shot outward, exploding from Oz's frame like lightning strikes. The child startled.

A desperate wail shook the back of his throat, and magic blasted around him. Heat and wind, and suddenly he was running, legs moving faster than should have been physically possible for his size. Stricken by terror, he'd chosen to sprint straight for the roaring wall of water. The force of Selenis's stream would send him barreling into the jungle.

"No!" I lunged, but he lashed out with heated wind. The gust slammed into me, and I fell backward into the sand. All I could do was watch in horror as he ran toward certain death.

Several things happened in the span of a breath.

Oz disappeared in a chaotic mess of shadows.

Selenis saw the charging young and reacted, pulling back on the force of her water wall.

The mother took one look at my beast's weakened stream and decided the risk was worth saving her child. She barreled toward it, ignoring the endless blades and shouts from Noc, Calem, and Kost.

And Oz reappeared, wrapping his body around the child to protect it from the spray of water misting the air.

"Oz!"

The mother towered above him. A roar shook the ground, and grains of sand bounced around us. Fire erupted, and Oz's scream shook the treetops. Heat clawed outward over the beach, bringing welts to my skin. My gaze found Noc. Horrified, he stood before the insatiable maelstrom of fire with Calem and Kost on either side, helpless to save Oz.

And then a different kind of wall burst from the earth. Crystallized black rock as thick as Selenis's stream surrounded Oz in a perfect circle. Simmering red veins drizzled through cracks and cooked the air with enough heat to evaporate the remaining spray of water. The mother Laharock paused, calling back her own fire to stare at the fortress. She blinked. Sniffed it. A worried call rumbled from her chest.

A soft whine answered from behind the stone. Slowly, the walls shuddered until they crumbled, revealing the baby standing protectively over a dazed Oz. His clothes had been scorched to ash, and shiny, burned skin covered his arms and back. He groaned.

Alive. Relief spurred me into motion, and I ran toward him. Slid across the sand and fell to the ground beside him. "Gods, Oz." Noc, Calem, and Kost joined us, varying expressions of panic and anxiety readily on display.

The ground began to tremble, and the baby speared me with wary, pupil-less, white eyes. Then turned his damning gaze to the assassins. Oz's shaking hand found his snout. "S'okay. They're good."

The trembling stopped. The mother hovered above us, uncertain but not aggressive. She shifted her weight between her front legs, left and right. The baby stepped away and extended his neck upward. A snort scorched with fiery heat came from the mother's nostrils.

The child looked back at Oz. Whined.

My jaw hit the floor. "Oz, the baby wants to go with you."

"Really?" He tried to sit up, but recoiled. Tight skin glowed a blistering red. My gaze darted to the mother. All the fight had left her eyes, and she continued to linger. Sad, soft calls working their way through her. She didn't want to leave her child. Not yet.

I stood and walked toward the pair. The mother was wary, but the child seemed to understand. To know that, by going with me, he'd end up with Oz. The child cooed, rubbing up against my leg and nudging my fingers. I stroked his crown gently. Unlocking the well of power in my core, I showered the surrounding area in a loving light. The child leaned in closer, the charm solidifying his connection with me.

Now I just needed the mother. The wet heat of her breath hung over my face, and my heart skyrocketed to the heavens. Lifting her head, she peered at the volcano. At the place that had likely been her home since she was born. *The realm is good*, I thought, begging her to understand. *You will not suffer. You can stay with your young.* She turned back to her child and let out a quiet huff. The heavy swing of the beast realm's door groaned, granting her access to my world. To her world.

I let out a shaky laugh. "Thank the gods."

"Some plan, Kost." Calem crouched by Oz, examining his blistering skin. "Didn't see this coming?"

Kost glowered. "Like I said, what I see is more like images. I saw which tactics would work to draw them apart, and I saw Oz and Leena with a beast. Not this." He jerked his chin over his shoulder and signaled to Felicks. His beast bounded across the sloping sands, tongue lolling out the side of his mouth. Without prompting from his master, he ran straight for Oz. Tongue coated in saliva, he began licking the length of Oz's back.

Oz's face screwed up in pain. "It's so scratchy." The baby inched toward him and watched Felicks work.

"His saliva is numbing. Give it a minute." I slumped to the ground but kept my hand on the mother's maw. Grateful eyes examined me. She wouldn't have to say goodbye to her young. Not now. Not ever.

Slowly, Oz's skin returned to normal. He pushed himself up, rolled his shoulders. "That was fun."

I laughed. "Sure. Fun." Glancing past him, I looked at Noc. Hands hidden in the pockets of his trousers, he stood still. But there wasn't any tension to his muscles. No clenched jaw or signs of worry. Instead, a small smile lifted one corner of his mouth. With his dark gaze perceptibly soft, his eyes drifted among his brothers. Safe. We were all safe. And relatively unharmed, thanks to Felicks.

We'd handled this beast together after all.

Felicks plopped on his haunches, done with his task of caring for Oz, and barked. Reaching out, I tickled the underside of his chin. "Nice work, bud."

Kost stared at the space where my fingers met his beast's skin. "He's spectacular."

"You, too." Noc placed a hand on Kost's shoulder, and Kost's entire frame went rigid. Emotions flared in his green gaze, but he chased them away with a cough.

Sweat gathered above my lip, and my body started to tremble. Four beasts outside of the realm. I thrust my hand outward. "Selenis, Quilla. Return." Rosewood light showered over us, and the realm door groaned. They disappeared, leaving the Laharock and her child alone. Some of the exhaustion ebbed, but I needed to take the child and make him a key for Oz. "I need to go to the realm. I'll be back."

Kost brandished Felicks's key. "You go on, too. Get some rest, and I'll call you out again later."

Calem grinned. "In the meantime, we'll set up camp. And get Oz some pants."

With both Laharocks, I entered the realm and was followed by the warm laughter of my assassins. I'd never loved a sound more.

TWENTY-TWO

NOC

Life filled my brothers' eyes. We camped right on the beach,
tents erected against the jungle line a few yards away. As we
lounged on the white sand around a fire, beasts milled between
us. Effie and Felicks had become fast friends, much to Kost's displeasure. They jumped over our ankles, ran circles around bags, and
barked at each other, ears pointed up in attention. Effie made a game
of trying to pin Felicks, but his ability to predict her moves made him
hard to tag.

Leena leaned against the mother Laharock, who she'd named
Lola, and stroked her scales. Lola's watchful gaze flitted between
Ozias and her son, though her stare was one of interest instead of
concern. Apparently, she'd deemed Ozias worthy of caring for her
child. The baby Laharock watched Effie and Felicks from his side.

"How big do you think he'll get?" Ozias fished out a fistful of
nuts from his pocket and fed them to the child.

Leena hummed. "Males get to be pretty large, but it will be a
while before he's fully grown. He'll be self-sufficient in a month or
two, though. Then you can summon him whenever you want. Until
then, try to minimize the time he's away from Lola, okay?"

Ozias nodded. With a gentle hand, he traced the back of the

baby's spine. Lola let out a contented groan, closing her eyes and sinking her head into the sand. "Lola's not going to cook me, right?"

Leena's smile was light. Peaceful. "Not if you're good to her son. What are you going to name him, by the way?"

He ran a hand over his jaw, looked at his beast. "I think I'll call him Jax. In honor of an old friend of mine who was always looking out for me. Just like this little guy did today."

"Jax?" Calem tilted his head. "I don't know anyone at the guild with that name."

Ozias's eyes darkened. "He was someone I knew before I died."

Silence bubbled around us. I knew Calem and Kost wouldn't pry. I wouldn't, either. I had my own dark dealings from my previous life that were better left unsaid. And judging by the sudden hard set of Ozias's normally pleasant expression, he had no desire to share his memories. Leena studied his face, worry clearly lancing through her eyes, but she kept her lips sealed.

She had her own past to outrun, just like the rest of us.

Shaking away the tension, Ozias grinned and patted his beast. "That work for you?"

Jax emitted a throaty warble and then rested his head in Ozias's lap. A grin claimed my lips. "Seems like he's good with it."

Calem kicked out his feet in front of him and tilted his chin in Leena's direction. "What about Lola? Will she stay with you?"

"She's not fully bonded to me yet. Her primary concern is Jax's safety. Noc could have her." A heavy pause followed her words. The ocean waves lapped against the beach, punctuated by the occasional bark from Felicks or birdcall from Effie.

Kost looked up from his beast and firelight danced across his spectacles. "Noc?"

"She seems pretty attached to Leena already. I'll take something else."

Leena speared me with her gaze, eyes probing beneath the surface to try to root out my intentions. I couldn't shake Fable's words. I think Leena knew, because she set her jaw before dropping her chin to her chest. Kost opened his mouth to say more, but just then Felicks leaped into his lap to escape Effie.

Exasperated, he sighed, but the warmth in his eyes remained. "Get your beast under control, Calem."

"She just wants to play." Extending his hands outward, he called to Effie. She flew the short distance toward him, ramming into his chest with little poise. Soft clucks worked their way from the back of her throat, and Calem laughed.

Leena studied me without moving her head. "It's probably time to call it a night." Rosewood light flared from her right hand, and Lola stood, showering the space around her in sand. She was formidable. Strong and relentless, singularly focused on protecting her young. Battling against her while Leena and Ozias worked had shown me that. And judging by the way Kost kept glancing back and forth between me and Lola, he'd have a word—or several—for me about turning the creature down.

With a loving pat, Leena sent her beast home. My men followed her lead, brandishing bronze keys, and one by one their beasts winked out of existence. The lack of happy cries and soft coos was jarring.

Calem stretched his hands to the sky and rolled his neck from side to side. "See you in the morning."

"Ditto." Ozias stood and followed Calem's footsteps toward the tents.

Kost adjusted his glasses. "If the Laharock didn't suit your desires, I suggest you discuss a suitable alternative with Leena. We wouldn't want her to waste her talents on another beast you're not interested in, now would we?"

Clipped words dropped like weights. I pinched my nose and forced out a steady breath. "Good night, Kostya."

He flinched at his full name. Only Talmage had used it, and Kost turned on his heels without another word, his rigid gait giving beneath sloping sand. Leena stared after him, worry lining her face. She twisted the ring around her finger three times before hiding her hands in the sand.

"What's wrong?"

She jolted, startled eyes finding mine. "Nothing."

She'd changed into fresh clothes after taming Lola and Jax, and the thin strap of her cotton camisole slipped off her shoulder. My fingers itched to fix it. "You're lying. Does it have to do with the beast you had in mind?"

"I didn't have a beast in mind."

I let out an exasperated huff. "Leena, cut the shit."

"What about *your* shit?"

"What do you mean?" I rolled grains of sand between my fingers, and her gaze followed the motion. Dark shadows passed through her eyes.

"Why do you want a Gyss?"

I hesitated. "It's not important."

She leveled me with a discerning stare worthy of a queen, and my chest caved as I fought to keep control of my emotions. She rotated and scooched closer to me. "Wasn't my story enough? Wasn't it proof that there's no guarantee the request is worth the risk?"

"The Gyss is my beast, Leena."

Both of her hands covered mine. A cool sea breeze worked its way from the ocean to us, whipping her hair across her face and obscuring her clouded gaze. Gently, I removed one of my hands and brushed the locks from her eyes.

Cautiously, she leaned into my touch. "And this wish has

nothing to do with me, right? No possible way for it to backfire and make my life a living hell like it did before?"

"I won't use it against you." I wouldn't dream of it. After seeing her curled in my arms, I knew I could never do anything to hurt this woman. I had known for a while, but the irrationality of it hit me as she slept tucked against me and nuzzled my chest. It'd been the most contact I'd shared with another person since Bowen.

And she likely didn't remember it at all.

Dropping my hand into my lap, I leaned away. With her proximity, all I could smell was vanilla and lilac. A dangerous combination. "What do we need to do to get one?"

Trailing her fingers along the space where mine had been, she stared at the ground. "They don't live here. We can find one back on the mainland. They're actually easy to tame—just another part of their conniving nature. They like to grant wishes and watch the results unfold."

"Then we'll leave first thing tomorrow when the ferry returns."

"About that..." Her words trailed off beneath the crashing waves. She rubbed her forehead, closed her eyes. After a long breath, she opened them and met my gaze head-on. "There is a beast here I had in mind. For me."

Chuckling, I tilted my head to the side. "So that's why you've been guarded. You didn't want me stealing your beast."

A deep blush crawled across her cheeks. "I'm sorry. I should have told you, but you're right."

"Why not wait till after we're done?" The thought wrenched my gut, and I pressed my lips into a fine line. *Done*. Done was the only option. Unless the Gyss was right—but I'd held out hope before only to be proven wrong. I'd tried countless remedies, met with priests and mages and healers, all who claimed they could lift the curse. None could. Hope wasn't something I allowed to fester, because if I was wrong, the price was too high.

"Because I kind of need something from you."

My brows arched as curiosity took over. "And what's that?"

She chewed on her bottom lip and winced, touching her fingers to the corner of her mouth for a moment. My eyes narrowed, but when she dropped her hand everything seemed normal. I was about to pry when her words stole all my attention. "Your blood."

I went stock-still. "What? Why?"

"The blood of a murderer to entice the beast. It's a necessary part of the taming process."

All I could do was stare. "Why not make this part of the bargain from the beginning? What if I were to say no?"

Cupping her chin in her hands, she hummed. "The blood has to be given freely. Without coercion. I can't steal it. I can't hurt you to get it. I can't buy it off you. Obviously I can't charm you and make you give it to me. As you can imagine, it's a rather difficult object to obtain when most murderers aren't looking for charity cases." The last log on the fire cracked, and embers simmered a burnt red. With her face angled toward the waves, the dying light washed over her. "I was hoping we'd get to know each other well enough that it wouldn't be an issue."

There were so many different ways I wanted to get to know her, and none of them boded well for her if I couldn't eradicate my curse.

And yet, I couldn't say no. "All right, then."

She tilted her head in my direction and blinked before a wondrous smile claimed her face. "Thank you." Another breeze flirted with her hair.

"Let's see what we can find." Rooting through the closest duffel bag, I maneuvered around clothing until the soft tinkle of glass met my ears. Calem always came prepared. Extracting a small vial of clear liquid, I removed the stopper and poured out its contents. A potent mixture of citrus, pine, and charcoal stung the air.

Leena wrinkled her nose and let out a soft snort. "Imperit? Is he really so concerned about getting someone pregnant that he had to carry a tonic?"

"He's known for his dalliances." Elongating one of my nails, I slit my palm open. Leena watched with curiosity as blood welled to the surface. "I don't know a lot about his past, but I know he's not eager to bring a kid into this world. A lot of us aren't. We don't exactly lead a safe life." I willed the blood to form perfect spheres and sent it into the now-empty vial.

"Oh." She rotated her ring as she searched for words.

"How much do you need?" The vial was halfway full, and the wound on my hand was already resewing.

"That's enough." Her gaze left my hand to linger on my face. "Thank you. Really. This beast..." I handed her the capped tube, and she rolled it between her fingers. "This is really important to me."

My heart stilled. The line I'd drawn in the sand was damn near gone. I knew what not to say. I couldn't tell her what I was thinking, how I was feeling. I only knew that sometimes saying nothing was better than the truth. Even if it hurt her.

She stood, long legs coated in fine grains of sand, and turned her back to me. "I better get some sleep. Tomorrow will be a test for me." She brushed loose hair over her shoulder, exposing her neck. She was so beautiful. So strong and cunning. She knew when to lead and when to defer to others. More than that, she was genuine. *Human.* Despite the circumstances that brought her to my door, she never once tried to harm us once we'd agreed to our terms.

I couldn't help myself. I launched to my feet and closed the distance between us as I came up behind her. I brushed the hair off her neck, and a visible shiver worked its way through her.

If only... She leaned into me, trying to catch my mouth with hers. To replay our kiss from outside the inn.

And I swear there were swelling bruises beneath her eyes that hadn't been there a moment ago. I blinked and they were gone, but it was reminder enough. I couldn't let that happen to her. Tucking my hands into the pockets of my trousers, I stepped away. "Good night, Leena."

Her face crumbled, but I couldn't risk her life like this. She deserved more. *Better.* Slowly, I walked toward my tent.

Voice soft and hoarse, she let me go. "Good night."

TWENTY-THREE

LEENA

As much as I should've slept in and stored whatever stamina I could, the prospect of taming the Myad filled me with nervous energy that had me exiting my tent just as the sun crested the ocean horizon. Aside from the soft ebb and flow of the waves, everything was quiet. Peaceful. Such a stark contrast to what I was sure to face later. While turning to the ocean, I paused when I saw a familiar figure already awake and seated with his back to the tree line.

"Calem?" I called as I approached, soft sand giving way beneath my feet.

He glanced up at me and offered a wide grin. "Hey. What are you doing up so early?" Patting the space beside him in invitation, he turned his gaze back to the warm, yellow sun climbing higher into the sky. Beneath it, the ocean was tinged a wondrous teal thanks to its light.

I sank to the ground beside him and pulled my knees to my chest. "Couldn't sleep."

"Me either." He let out a wistful sigh. "'Course, that's normal for me. But I haven't seen you scramble out of bed at daybreak this whole trip. What gives?"

"I'm going to charm a beast later today, and I've been thinking a lot about it."

Calem's gaze drifted my way. "For Noc?"

I paused, chewing on the inside of my cheek. He'd find out soon enough, anyway. "No. For me." A wave crashed against the toes of my boots, and I reached forward to run my fingers through the tepid water. "A beast I've been after for quite some time."

His brow furrowed. "Is it dangerous?"

"I'm prepared." I hedged my answer, and Calem was too smart not to notice. He waited, his stare impatiently hammering into me as I tried to ignore the weight of his unspoken words. I couldn't tell him, or any of them, what I was about to face. A Myad taming *was* dangerous, prepared or not. If they found out that I could lose my life, that if the beast deemed me unworthy it'd kill me, then they'd try to stop me.

I'd come too far to let something, or someone, stand in my way, no matter what their intentions were. I needed the Myad.

My fingers went to the bestiary hanging around my neck, and I took comfort in the familiar leather cover and cool metal chain. If something were to happen to me, my beasts in the realm would be safe. They'd be able to live out their days without worry, free to roam the endless plains, mountains, and deserts that made up their sanctuary. As for the beasts I'd gifted to these assassins...

Finally, I summoned up the courage to meet Calem's gaze. If I died today, they needed more information. They needed to know how to care for their creatures in case I wasn't around to help.

"Can you wake the others?" I asked.

He blinked before glancing behind me at the tents. "Why?"

"I know Noc doesn't have his beast yet, but the rest of you do. It's high time I fill you in on some key things about beast care." Brushing sand off my pants, I stood and folded my arms across my chest.

Calem hesitated. "You're not instilling much confidence about this being a 'safe' taming." He nudged a seashell into the water with his boot, then sighed. "I can wake them."

"Good. I'll wait." I offered him a smile and prayed that was enough. That he'd stop pestering me about the taming and instead focus on his beast and the knowledge I could provide. At the very least, I knew Kost would come running at the mention of more information, and Oz would follow suit. But Noc... He'd just have to listen and retain what I said. It wouldn't be the end of the world if he didn't end up with a Gyss, anyway. Better for everyone involved.

As Calem stood and walked toward the tents to wake the others, my mind flitted back to last night. To the way Noc had stopped me only to let me go once again. Frustration brewed in my chest. Better to not think of Noc. Instead, I let my thoughts wander back to the beast taming I'd be facing later, as I ran my hands down my arms. I'd dressed for function today, opting for tan breeches and a jungle-green camisole. Camouflage so as not to startle the Myad.

At the rise of grumbled voices behind me, I turned to find the men moving around camp in varying states of excitement. Remnants of sleep clung to Oz, making his movements sluggish, and he trudged toward the firepit to get a pot of water boiling over an open flame. Calem was about the same as he'd been only moments before—wary with furtive glances occasionally tossed my direction, but a grin on his face nonetheless. And Kost was beside himself. I rolled my lips together to keep from smiling as he ran his hands endlessly down his tunic, then righted his glasses, then smoothed his hair. Then started all over again. A fire lit in his green gaze, and he gave me a quick nod.

Meanwhile, Noc stood silently off to the side, his eyes cast toward the ocean. When I approached the camp, he barely deigned to spare me a glance, and my gut simmered. He was as cool as the sea breeze, and the hard set to his shoulders and obvious distance from his brethren told me that detachment was all I could expect for this morning's interaction.

"Leena, s'okay if I get some coffee going while you start?" Oz asked, a slight slur to his words.

"Sure, Oz. Just summon your beast first." I nodded to Kost and Calem as well. "You too."

Oz, Kost, and Calem extracted their bronze keys. As the door to the beast realm groaned open, a flood of light to rival the sun rushed over us. When it faded, their beasts appeared by their feet. Felicks wove his way between Kost's legs, letting out soft, chattering barks. As excitable as her master, Effie launched herself into the air and flew in circles above Calem's head before diving into his chest without caution, relying solely on him to catch her—which he did with a laugh before he nuzzled his nose in her feathers. Jax extended his long neck to the sky, silently asking for a scratch beneath his chin from Oz. Oz's thick fingers ran down his beast's scales before he flopped to the ground and eyed the warming pot of water.

Noc lowered himself onto some driftwood and clasped his hands together, gaze traveling from beast to beast. For a moment, he looked my direction, and just like that, a flicker of warmth danced in my chest. It was as if he felt it, because he immediately glanced away, expression hard. But now was not the time to corner him about his ever-shifting mood. Now was the time to teach these men about their beasts. Once Kost and Calem situated themselves on the ground, I followed suit and crossed my legs.

"As you've already figured out, all of your beasts have different abilities and quirks. The more time you spend with them, the stronger their powers will be." I reached my hand out to Felicks, and he complied by crossing over to me and plopping onto his haunches. I scratched the space behind his ears, and his eyes slipped closed just as his orb began to fill with a swirling mist. "Kost, you've already discovered quite a bit on your own. I'm impressed."

He nodded, eyes softening as he studied Felicks. "He's a fast learner."

"And so are you." My fingers moved to the underside of the beast's chin, and his orb cleared. "Right now, the images you receive are disjointed. The more you practice, the stronger the bond you forge with him, the clearer they'll become. They'll start to progress like an actual series of events you can see from beginning to end. Which might keep Oz from suffering any more accidental burnings." I gave him a sly look, and Oz laughed before patting Jax on the snout.

"It was worth it," he said. Jax let out a warble from the back of his throat in agreement.

Turning my attention back to Felicks, I moved one hand to the scruff of his neck and the other to his jowls. Then, I pulled up his lip to reveal his finely pointed teeth. He went stock-still beneath me, but didn't fight my touch.

"Poi venom is deadly, but slow-acting and only effective if it enters the bloodstream." With my pointer finger, I nudged a small duct at the base of his gum. A bead of viscous fluid dribbled down his teeth. "On rare occasions, his ducts can get clogged. If that happens, feed him some braskas leaves. The texture will naturally break down the buildup, and he'll be fine."

Kost leaned forward and pushed his glasses up the bridge of his nose. "I thought the realm healed all beasts."

"It does," I said, letting Felicks's lip fall back into place before giving him a pat. "They'll always have food and water, and wounds will naturally heal faster there. But a thorn in a paw or a clogged duct might need some extra attention. It's not like the realm is an actual person who can remove a foreign object."

"Noted. What about his ability to heal?" Kost extended his arms, and Felicks bounded back toward him, circling three times before nestling in his lap.

I smiled. "That's just in his saliva. He makes plenty of that on his own. He'll need attention and exercise, but more of the mental variety than, say, an Effreft." Shifting my attention to Calem, I gave a nod to Effie. "The healthier she is, the stronger her life magic. Make sure she gets all the exercise her little heart desires."

Calem's grin stretched from ear to ear. "We get plenty of that, don't we, girl?" Digging his fingers into the sand, he came up with a small pebble and held it out in front of her. Her eyes immediately went wide, and her tail started to shake in anticipation. "You want the stone? Yes, you do. Go get the stone!" He chucked the tiny rock as hard as he could, and Effie launched into the air. Her wings kicked up sand around us, and Felicks barked his displeasure.

"Calem!" Kost wrapped his arms around Felicks. "Was that really necessary?"

Noc chuckled, the first sign of life he'd given all morning, and my gaze riveted to him. A smile captured my lips even as I said, "It's all right. Sand won't bother any of your beasts. Especially not Jax."

Jax tilted his chin at the sound of his name, but didn't move from Oz's side. Oz had busied himself with preparing coffee, one eye on his creature and the other on the now-boiling pot of water. He wiped down some tin mugs before draping a filter across each one and pouring water over ground beans. Jax leaned closer, his nostrils flaring wide, and breathed in the heady aroma.

"Laharocks are extremely driven by food," I said. As if on cue, Jax curled his tongue around the beans and ate them in their entirety. And then shook his head in disgust, sneezing and backing away, as if he couldn't understand why Oz would ever produce something so foul. He scraped at his nose with his long talons and grunted. Coffee beans, it seemed, were not his favorite.

Oz looked appalled, but then reached forward and patted the Laharock's maw. "You don't like coffee? We're going to have problems." His smile was warm, and he simply refilled the filter with more beans instead of admonishing his beast.

Kost's brow twitched. "Both of you really need to control your beasts."

"Leave them be," Noc said, his words warming and his shoulders slackening just a fraction. At that same moment, Effie came soaring back. She landed in a heap in front of Calem, but instead of a pebble, she carried a twig complete with fresh leaves she'd ripped from a tree. Her whole body trembled with pride.

I bit my lower lip to keep my grin under control. Everything about these assassins and their wily new beasts reminded me of home. Of the times I'd sat with my own mentors and listened as they discussed beast knowledge with me. This was the first time I'd ever attempted to teach anyone about my world, and I caught myself mimicking their warm tone and gentle encouragement. "Effrefts, surprisingly, are less motivated by food, despite the taming process. They respond well to praise."

Calem obliged Effie, inciting a game of tug-of-war with the twig. "She deserves all the praise in the world, doesn't she?" His voice went uncharacteristically gooey, and I couldn't keep from laughing.

Leaning forward, I tried to call to her, but she ignored me completely. That seemed a good enough segue to add, "She's also steadfastly loyal to her master. Oh, and be sure to preen her feathers on occasion, as she's sure to get them dirty with all her antics."

"Is there a time limit for how long they can stay in our world?" Kost asked.

"Yes and no." Flexing my hand, I studied the multitude of

branches extending outward from my Charmer's symbol. "Some beasts have strict time limits, like Iky. No matter how often I train with him, he can only stay in this world for two hours. But your beasts…" I dropped my hand and glanced at each one. "None of them have time limits. It's entirely dependent on the strength of your bond. There are some beasts out there who can stay for extended periods of time in our world if they have a powerful master."

"Powerful master?" Noc asked, bracing his elbows on his knees and leaning forward. His dark gaze bore into me, and I wondered, exactly, what was running through his head. I'd already told him why I hadn't wanted to gift him with a Gyss. Because powerful people could do powerful things, and if they didn't care about ramifications…the possibilities were endless.

I swallowed. "Yes. Whatever that power may be to you—physical strength, mental fortitude, control over the shadows—that's an ability you've honed over the years. Some beasts can tap into that, as if they're sharing the same well of power, and are able to use that as a lifeline of sorts, granting them the ability to stay in our world much longer than other creatures."

Like the Gyss.

I didn't have to say it out loud for Noc to understand. He nodded once.

"What about Jax?" Oz asked, passing out coffees to each of us. I took mine and inhaled deeply, taking a moment to savor the scent.

"Jax won't be like his mother." I took a sip and sighed, practically melting into the ground. "Babies are empathic metamorphs. Had we never interfered, he would've grown up to be like Lola— fiery aura, face-melting heat, the works. But Jax's power manifested when he decided to protect you. It will require a bit of discovery on your end, but it appears as though those lava-rock walls are near-impenetrable and heat-proof, much like his scales."

Oz looked at him with pride. "Guess Kost and Felicks won't have to protect me from any errant fires after all."

"No." I took another long drink of coffee. I needed all the energy I could get before the Myad taming. "But keep an eye on him when he's out of the beast realm. Laharock scales are worth a lot of bits. If a poacher sees him, they might try to get their hands on some."

Oz's face darkened. "They could try."

A mixture of happiness and relief flared to life inside me. I so rarely felt *good* about giving away beasts. When this all started, I would never have guessed that these men, these *assassins*, would be so suited to beast care, but it was obvious that they loved their newfound family members. Calem would never stop playing with Effie. Kost would always challenge Felicks in the best possible way. Oz would always protect Jax. They would give anything to keep their beasts safe, and it was evident in the way they looked at them. Their love was palpable.

Smiling, I set my now-empty mug in the sand. If I died today, I could rest easy knowing these beasts were in good hands. "All beasts should be treated with respect and love, but you clearly have that covered. All beasts also have weaknesses you should be mindful of. Laharocks can't be in salt water for more than a few minutes. Effrefts are extremely sensitive to sound, and loud noises can damage their hearing. And Poi shouldn't be summoned in desert climates. Something about the heat mirages makes it hard for them to focus and clouds their ability to see the future."

Each one of them glanced at their creatures with a spark of worry. Kost cleared his throat first before meeting my gaze. "And if something should happen? What do we do?"

I bit the inside of my cheek as I searched for a response. The obvious answer was that the realm would provide. But if something more drastic happened, if they needed attention in our world before returning to the realm, or perhaps encountered a situation the realm couldn't fix—like clogged ducts or foreign objects in their bodies—then what?

Hireath.

I dropped my gaze to the ground. "Then you find a Charmer. No matter the circumstance, a Charmer will always help a beast in need. Even if they don't like you. Even if they don't *know* you. We place beasts' lives above all else."

For a while, no one spoke. Coals shifted on the fire, and a few soft bestial calls slipped from Effie's beak. I knew what I was suggesting was difficult. I was likely the first Charmer these assassins had met in all their years. But I couldn't send them to Hireath. They'd never get past the barrier. They'd have to scour the black market and listen for rumors of Charmers who were out on beast hunts. We flooded those spaces to acquire rare ingredients for tamings, and we never hid our identities. All it would take was one dealer to notice our necklace. Someone would know.

I only hoped it never came to that, and that if something perilous did happen to their creatures, that they'd be able to find a Charmer fast enough to help them.

Noc coughed, and my gaze snapped to him. He could probably read every emotion I was trying to hide on my face. "Thank you, Leena. I'm sure we can ask you more questions later if they come up."

If there is a later. My stomach turned to cement. "Yeah, of course."

Oz offered a broad grin. "Let's eat, yeah? Breakfast will only take a few minutes to whip up, and I'm starving."

One by one, they recalled their beasts to the realm and went about getting breakfast prepared. Only Noc remained seated, his stare trained on me. His brows started to creep together, as if he were trying to solve a complicated riddle but couldn't quite find the right answer. Heat crawled up the back of my neck, and I looked away. If I continued to pick apart the mystery that was Noc, I'd only end up lost. And for now, I had other things to focus on. More important things.

Somewhere in the distance, a low, feline yowl rattled the treetops and a flurry of birds rocketed into the sky.

The Myad was waiting. And I was ready.

TWENTY-FOUR

LEENA

Taming a Myad was a three-step process. Two were feasible, given my present company. The third, on the other hand, would be tricky. Casting a quick glance behind me, I watched as Noc tipped his head back and laughed with Calem. The two of them walked stride for stride in front of Kost and Oz. Kost's gaze was carving something vile into Noc's shoulders while Oz hummed to himself, hands plastered to the back of his head.

They wouldn't like step three.

Turning back to the dense jungle before me, I stepped around hollowed-out logs and roots thicker than arms. Rubberlike tree leaves blocked most of the morning sun's rays, and the density of the jungle kept the ocean breeze from piercing the grove. Birds cawed wildly above our heads, beady eyes tracking our progression. Insects competed for airtime, their drawn-out, grinding chirps thick in the air.

The vial of Noc's blood weighed heavy in the breast pocket of my tunic. There were rumors the offered blood affected the power of the Myad. The stronger the donor, the more amplified his magic became. There was no possible way of knowing for sure. No way to measure the fortitude of the beast before it was tamed. And yet, excitement hummed through my body. If there was any merit to the rumor, there was no better donor than Noc.

Calem caught up to me. A mosquito landed on the vein along his neck, and he slapped it. "I vote we get this over with. As soon as possible."

"We're almost there." At least I hoped we were. The Myad's den would be in the center of the jungle, a safe distance from the volcano and potential ferry traffic. A secure place to raise young away from disturbances. Palm trees loomed above us, heavy fronds weighed down by coconuts. There needed to be a break somewhere. A place for him to land.

Another twenty minutes stretched on until we stumbled upon a shallow pond with crystal-clear water. Roots from overgrown trees lined the bottom, and small fish huddled in shaded spots. I slowed to a stop, my gaze jumping from one edge of the clearing to the other. Above us, the heavy trees parted, their branches forcibly bent. Loose bark and twigs littered the ground.

My heart stilled at the deep, clawlike wounds gouging the base of a nearby tree. Sap leaked from the bark and coated the jungle floor, glue for a mixture of forest-green moss and iridescent feathers—the Myad's den.

He was out, but he wouldn't be gone for long.

"We're here." Trying to ease the tension in my muscles, I rolled my head from side to side. If this taming went wrong, my life was on the line—even with Noc and his brothers at my side. Turning to the men, I lowered my voice to a whisper. "He'll be back any minute. No matter what happens, I need you to stay here."

Noc narrowed his eyes. I envied the way he used them as weapons. He ran his fingers through his bed-head hair, halting for a moment at the nape of his neck. "I don't think that's a good idea."

"I'll be fine, I promise." I stared at each of them. My band of assassins. When had I gone from dreading this trip to dreading its end? Each one clad in black, they stood ready to disappear into the shadows at their backs. "Myads can be volatile when surrounded. We won't stand a chance if you don't let me handle it."

Oz frowned. "We tamed Lola and Jax together."

"I know, but this is different."

Noc's gaze slanted to the treetops. "If your life is in danger, we'll be forced to intervene. I'm still short a beast."

I balled my hands into fists. Why did he want a Gyss so badly? Was he only thinking of fortunes? Was that all that mattered? I could've sworn there'd been something between us when we'd kissed, but his detachment... Was I alone in my delusions? Was it wrong for me to want something that was so clearly bad for me?

My breathing hitched, and I turned away. "I'm aware." Flexing my right hand, I called on my power, and a cascading light showered the space around us. The door to the beast realm swung open, and out rolled Grundy, my Graveltot.

"Using him to tame the Myad?" Calem crouched to the ground and reached out to run his fingers along Grundy's rocky hide. No larger than the size of a desk globe, he bowled between their feet until he nestled into the ground an equidistant point from each of them. Slates shifted, and his head popped up. Red-rimmed, coal-like eyes targeted me.

"Something like that."

The jungle fell silent. Birds pressed themselves flat against tree trunks, hiding behind branches and burrowing into nooks. Craning my neck upward, I scoured the green blanket of leaves. Palm fronds quivered, and a low creak broke the quiet. A heavy branch smacked the ground. The Myad followed through, growling and dragging the limb off to the side away from his bed of feathers.

"Fuck me," Calem barely whispered, but the Myad froze.

Outstretched wings coated in vibrant teals and emeralds went taut, and he tilted his nose upward to sniff the air. Built like an oversize black panther, the lithe jungle beast exhaled, shaking his mane from left to right. The peacock streak running the length of his spine and tail shimmered in the sun. A plume of feathers exploded around his head, standing tall between his ears. Gold casings masked his ankles and heels, protecting the weak points of his legs.

I'd never seen anything so beautiful. Powerful. I took a small step forward. The brush crunched beneath my feet, and the Myad skewered me with his blazing gold gaze. Thin tendrils of blue light streamed from his eyes.

"Grundy."

Without further prompting, plates shifted along Grundy's body, and two fat arms pushed outward. Once his soft hooves met the earth, a shallow divot appeared in a circle around the men. As one, they gasped, crashing to the ground under Grundy's invisible weight. Calem sputtered, lungs working overtime to keep oxygen flowing through his body. Face flat against the earth, Oz groaned into the dirt. Muscles ticked along his back as he fought against the weight to no avail. Kost cursed and dug his fingers into the ground.

Noc alone managed to remain on his knees, palms pressed flat to the earth. Fissures of pressure cracked around his fingertips. Slate eyes lanced with frustration speared my heart, and a low snarl broke free from his lips.

Such power. I was wrong. The Myad wasn't the most beautiful thing I'd ever seen. Noc would always win that contest.

A rumbling growl sounded from deep in the Myad's belly, and heavy paws thudded against the banks of the pond as he stalked toward me. Fifteen minutes, and Grundy's gravity manipulation would fade. I mouthed an apology to Noc before turning to the beast. Palms outward, I slowed to a stop a few feet in front of the creature. *No weapons. No beasts. No threat.* A cool sweat misted above my lips. To be in front of something so powerful...

The Myad's tail flicked from left to right. Pulling back his muzzle to reveal a row of elongated teeth, he growled again. I willed my breath to remain steady. Blue wisps began to stream from the gold plates in his legs. He'd take flight or pounce if I wasn't careful.

Kicking on the charm, I knelt before him. Rosewood light spilled outward, but he didn't blink. My heart traded places with my throat, and I swallowed twice before exhaling deeply.

Step one: Blood of the murderer. With my eyes locked on his, I extracted the vial from my breast pocket. Another growl simmered in the back of his throat, and I paused.

Easy now. My heart thundered in my ears. I popped the stopper off and poured Noc's blood into my cupped hand. The Myad's nose twitched, and he lowered his head to sniff the substance. Slowly, his scratchy tongue grazed my skin. Sheer power thrummed from his touch. I'm sure he tasted the raw flavor of Noc's magic in the blood. The icy heat of it threatened to sear my skin, and the scent of burnt honey and hot metal tainted the air.

Once the beast licked my hand dry, he sat back on his haunches and studied me, the corded muscles of his legs rippling beneath black fur.

Step two: A token of loyalty. Proof that, if the taming were a success, I was as much his as he was mine. That we would never abandon each other. With bloody, shaking fingers, I took my opal ring off my hand.

"Your mother left this for you." My aunt had held out a tiny box with silver clasps. My eager fingers had wrenched it open. There, lying in a bed of violet silk, was the rose-gold ring my father had given to my mother as a promise of his love. The one I now wore at all times.

This ring was my last tie to Hireath. My last tie to a memory that I cherished above all else. My parents had died trying to tame a beast beyond their capabilities. It seemed fitting that, if this didn't work, I'd go out the same way.

Hot tears stung the corners of my eyes, and I bowed to the Myad, extending my palm toward him. Blue tendrils of vapor streamed from his eyes and looped through the ring, lifting it to the space before him. A crown of pure gold burst through his black fur. His feathered mane shot outward, and the tendrils carried the ring to the center of the headpiece. The gold rippled and molded, allowing for the jewelry to become part of his plumage.

Fighting back cries of joy, I tossed a quick glance over my shoulder to steal one more look at Noc. Eyes wide and jaw tight, he strained against Grundy's pressure. Muscles bulged along his neck, and his fingers trembled. The detachment he'd wielded earlier was gone, and there was nothing but concern shining in his intense stare.

My heart twisted. Too bad it took me putting my life in danger for him to look at me like that.

Turning back to the Myad, I slowly undid the belt from my breeches. The Myad tilted his head, eyeing the black leather contraption. A low warning growl rumbled at the back of his throat.

It's not a weapon. I promise. Folding my belt, I shoved it into my mouth between my teeth. *Not a single sound.* I breathed deeply and focused on the beast realm. My power flooded outward, pulsating to the cadence of my heart. The Myad stood before crouching low against the ground. Tension gathered in all his muscles, and he eyed my left shoulder. Screwing my eyes shut, I clenched down on my belt.

I heard the kick-up of dirt as he lunged. The back of my head smacked against the ground, forcing my eyes open, and a blinding heat surged from my shoulder as his fangs sank easily into flesh. The world slipped out from beneath me as pain blurred the lines of the trees and the sky, blending colors in ways that shouldn't have been possible.

Somewhere far off, Noc shouted my name. How he managed to work his vocal cords in spite of Grundy's gravity was beyond me. As long as it wasn't me screaming, it didn't matter. I was the Myad's prey. I had to submit. Let his viscous saliva ooze into my system and connect us so he could examine my past and determine my worth.

Step three.

Dark splotches bled across my vision. With his saliva came a slow-moving, searing agony that dredged through my veins. Heat rammed my skull and forced thick tears from my eyes. The jungle disappeared. All I could see were memories. Blue magic streamed loosely around me, formed raging fires that lined a long and endless path. Flames licked my skin, and I fought against the urge to scream. The only way out was *through*. I took a few careful steps, bit back cries as the fire burned through my mind. The Myad scrutinized my worst dealings. They played on repeat, and my heart shuddered as I watched every beast trade I'd ever made. Every innocent creature I'd placed in unworthy hands.

The violent blue flames burned brighter. Hotter. My insides cooked. The Myad was angry. But I had to keep going, keep sifting through every bad choice I'd ever made. If I couldn't face myself, my mind would be burned to ash.

Visions shifted. A bloodied Kost appeared, hundreds of shallow holes marring his arms. My own skin throbbed with mirrored pain. I'd done vile things to survive, and Kost hadn't been my first victim. Countless other visages appeared. Each hurt I'd inflicted sparked to life again in my own limbs. My body was battered and bruised, but it was nothing compared to what I'd done.

But I did it to survive. Tears flowed without restraint. It was such a hollow excuse. Even now, it felt fragile. So breakable and horrendous. Why was their suffering, their pain necessary?

I had to... If not for Wynn... The memories jumped as if they'd been electrocuted. Violent flames slashed against me, and suddenly I was there again. Standing in our bedroom while Wynn slept peacefully. We'd only just been together, and I was still warm from his touch. I'd slipped out of the sheets for some water when his journal caught my eye. He normally kept it locked away in his study, and my naive, younger self had hoped it would be filled with musings about me. About our love.

I was so utterly wrong.

I'd peeled back the leather cover and thumbed through the pages, pausing to read notes about beast-taming ingredients or foreign magic. But the further I read, the darker his entries became. Formerly beautiful handwriting turned cramped and erratic. His thoughts were incoherent, jumbled, dark. He wrote about failed tamings. About the impressive will of man.

I'd snapped the journal shut. Placed it back on his nightstand and crawled into bed without getting my drink. Squeezed my eyes closed and forced myself to forget, to willfully misunderstand. To curl against him and draw comfort from the only person I had left in my life.

If only I'd acted then, maybe that innocent man he'd tried to tame would've survived.

What had I done? How had I allowed myself to stoop so low? All the excuses I created, all the lies I spoon-fed myself—not one of them mattered. I couldn't take back what had happened with Wynn or Kost or all the others. I would live with those choices, repent in my own way. But my reason for selling beasts? It wasn't good enough, and I knew: When all of this was over, I'd never sell another beast. I'd go back to Midnight Jester and ask Dez for a job. Something. Anything other than what I'd become.

The darkness shifted, lightened. My memories stopped. Slowly, the surrounding jungle came back into view, and the weight of the Myad on my body lessened.

I'm so sorry. I bit down hard on the leather belt to keep my sob at bay. He retracted his fangs and growled, the sharp exhale blowing heavily in my ears. *On my life, I'll never stand idly by again.* He roared above me and I jolted in place, pain spiking. *I will protect you. I will protect all beasts, if I am able.* He dropped his forehead to mine. As I spit the belt from my mouth, adrenaline left me in a cool rush, and I began to cry.

He'd absolved me of my transgressions. Clean. I was clean. And worthy of being his.

Mine. The Myad purred, nuzzling my rib cage. *He was mine.* Slowly, I cupped the side of his face with my right hand. The rosewood emblem exploded. Tree roots dove toward my fingers, and branches reached across my collarbone and neck.

Losing my fingers in his fur, I choked back a happy cry. I had done this. Not anyone else. Not another Charmer. Me. I had a beast worthy of a member on the Charmers Council.

My gaze drifted to Noc. He stared at my wounded shoulder with horror, eyes flickering from the Myad to my face and back again. Shadows weakened by Grundy's power tried in vain to reach me. They dissipated and reformed, inching across the jungle floor, never quite reaching their mark.

Emotion strangled his voice. "Lee...na."

My stomach fluttered. "It's okay." With a nod toward my beast, I called off Grundy. He whined in answer, a coarse groan like two stones scraping together. His power gave out, and Noc launched toward us, slicing his hand open and summoning blood blades in an instant.

He poised them at my precious beast. "Get off her."

The Myad growled, protectively hovering over me. The barest

hint of his weight made my body protest, and I winced. Scooting out from under him, I cradled my left arm to my chest. "Noc, it's all right. I'm all right."

His jaw ticked. "You almost died." Calem, Kost, and Oz slowly picked themselves up, brushing dirt off their clothes as they walked toward us.

"No, I didn't." I leaned into the side of my beast, ignoring the sharp stab of pain. "But if I don't get some of those bandages we packed, we might have a different story."

"You're impossible!" The blood blades quivered before exploding in a sudden burst of rain. "Do you have any idea what that was like?"

I cringed more from his words than the pain in my shoulder. "Noc, calm down. Really, I'm fine."

"Well, thank the fucking gods for that." Without another word he stormed off into the jungle. Shadows curled around him, licking his rigid frame and pulling him away into darkness.

My heart ached at the sight. I didn't know what to make of this. Why had he reacted so strongly? "I'm sorry. I didn't think he would stay put if I asked."

"You're probably right." Kost braided his gloved fingers together. Hands tense, it was as if he did it to stop himself from throttling me. "Doesn't mean it was the right thing to do."

"I'll go after him." Calem followed Noc into the dark.

"You go, too." Kost tilted his head toward Oz. "Calem could accidentally set Noc off with one wrong remark, and that's the last thing we want right now." He brought his rigid stare back to me. "We'll meet up with you shortly."

Oz teetered in place, worry lancing his expression. "All right, but hurry." Dark tendrils consumed him, and he disappeared.

Kost knelt beside me, and my beast let out a low warning growl.

Unmoved, Kost lifted one brow. "I'm not interested in hurting her." The Myad huffed before shaking out his feathered mane.

"He's protective. It will take time," I said. Looking past Kost, I spied the abandoned bag on the edge of the jungle. "Bandages?"

"Felicks will seal it, but the puncture wound is deep. We should clean it first." He stood and retreated to the bag to riffle through its contents. After securing a clear glass bottle and a cloth, he returned. "Alcohol. Not the good kind."

"Kost..." I fumbled over words.

"Just tell me why." His words were brittle. With deft fingers, he unstopped the bottle and tucked the end of the rag into the liquid. Turned it upside down for a beat.

"Why what?"

He clenched his teeth. "Why you faced this danger alone."

"Because I had to. The taming required—"

"That's bullshit." He leveled me with a glare at the same time he pressed the rag to my wound. I yelped at the sudden sting, and the Myad growled. With my free hand, I stroked the side of my beast's face. He settled onto his haunches and watched, his wary gaze trained on Kost.

"How is that bullshit? I had to approach him alone. There was no other way."

Kost dug the cloth in deeper, and I screwed my eyes shut—only opened them when his seething words hurt worse than the burn. "Because you could have *told* us. You're supposed to trust us."

"Trust you? Just the other day you told me you hated me." Hurt sat heavily on my chest.

"I hate that you *fit*. I don't hate you." The pressure on my wound lessened, and with it, the sharp edge of his glare. "I wanted it to be me. But you can't jam the wrong piece into the picture if it's not meant to be there."

My response died. I struggled with his confession, uncertain how to answer. What could I even say? *I'm sorry?* It felt so hollow and meaningless in comparison to the love behind his words. He continued speaking anyway, voice painfully low.

"That's why I'm so angry. Because despite myself I do care, and you just put Noc—put all of us—through a terrible ordeal. You stripped him of his ability to choose. To react. To *protect*. You showed him that you couldn't trust him to listen or put your needs and wants first. When in reality, all he ever does is put everyone else's needs and wants before his own."

I swallowed. Hard. "I didn't think... I didn't think he cared."

The fight left Kost's eyes, and he snorted. "He cares too much. He just never shows it." Removing the rag, he inspected my injury. Traded the cloth for the bottle and doused the whole area in alcohol.

Tears stung my eyes. "How can you love someone who won't let himself love you back?"

Kost stilled, considered me. He pressed the rag back to my skin, mopping up excess liquid. "It's safer to love someone who'll never have the opportunity to break your heart."

My spine bowed at the weight of his words. "That's so... awful."

His smile was thin. "I said it was safe, not pleasant." He tossed the rag to the side and brandished his key so Felicks would appear. With a nod, he directed his beast to my wound. "Noc is brilliant. He's cunning and intelligent and an exceptional leader. Talmage made the right choice, putting him in charge of Cruor. No one else would sacrifice like he does to keep us safe."

Felicks's scratchy tongue raked over my skin. "But why? Why all the sacrifice and detachment?"

"That's his story to tell." Kost pinned me to the ground with his stare. "Maybe if you showed him trust, he'd share it with you."

My stomach curled in on itself. He was right. Kost was always right. "Okay."

"If you're going to love him, that means believing in him. In this family. When you finally do that, we won't have a problem anymore."

A dull ringing sounded in my ears. Love? I didn't love him. Right? *Could* I love him? I didn't know if I was strong enough. Not like Kost. I couldn't totally devote myself to someone who refused to reciprocate those feelings. But I did care—that much I knew. Maybe when this was over, I wouldn't have to leave. I could stay near Cruor. I could keep my friends and this...family.

A faint smile ghosted over my lips as I looked up at my unlikely ally. "All right, Kost. I hear you."

"Good." He stood and helped me up. Then, he turned to Felicks and opened his arms, allowing his beast to leap to his chest. Gentle fingers stroked the space between his ears. "Come on. We need to catch the ferry."

"Yeah." I reached for my Myad. He rammed his thick head into my healed shoulder, and I stutter-stepped to keep my balance.

Kost glanced at my beast. "What are you going to name him?"

I stared at the tree line where Noc had slipped away. Impossibly black wisps still clung to the trunks, working their way through roots and leaves. He'd disappeared into the obsidian void, but had left whispers of his existence.

Working my fingers through the Myad's ink-black fur, I let out a quiet sigh. If ever there was a beast made for Noc, it should have been him. "Onyx. His name is Onyx."

TWENTY-FIVE

NOC

By the time Leena and Kost boarded, I'd already holed up inside the wheelhouse with the captain. As soon as I knew they were safe, I gave him the signal to push off and left for a secluded, unused room in the bowels of the ship.

I relished the cobwebs clinging to the moldy rafters and endless crevices filled with darkness. The warmth of the deck was too much. I needed the steady lapping of waves against the thick paneling of the ship. The dank and musty aroma of salt and grime. I needed distance. Separation. Sitting on a wooden crate, I rested my chin in my hands. At least here I was hidden. At least here I was alone.

My fingers quivered, and I balled my hands into fists. The sight of that beast on top of her had ruined me. If she had failed, I wouldn't have been able to stop myself from bringing her back. And I don't know if she would have ever forgiven me. I don't think I would have forgiven myself.

By the time we hit the slick docks of Ortega Key, the sun had kissed the horizon. Still hidden, I slipped out onto the deck. A vibrant emerald flash dominated the sky for a breath before disappearing, and the bright excitement in Leena's eyes threatened to shatter my resolve. I was a brooding mix of furious and desperate, and that wasn't a combination that bode well for anyone.

"Are you guys going to be at the Drinking Mermaid tonight?" Corinne asked. Twirling her hair, she fished without looking. Not like she had to—Ozias was a marlin in a tiny barrel, and she wielded a harpoon.

Ozias grinned. "I think we're in the mood to celebrate."

Still lingering in the shadow realm, I winced.

Calem's eyes pinned me, seeing through the darkness before skipping toward Leena. With a careful smile, he rested his hand on her shoulder. "Sounds good to me."

I left before Leena could respond. Without looking back, I stormed through the streets and targeted the Roasted Boar. If they wanted to celebrate, then so be it. I was in no mood.

I barricaded myself in my room and threw open the double doors leading out to the beach. The ocean waves attempted to drown my emotions, but they refused to comply. When I slammed my fist into the wall, wood shavings scattered to the floor. The breeze carried in the salt of the ocean, and I closed my eyes. *Breathe.* This wasn't supposed to happen. *Breathe.* Why on earth did she have to fall onto my lap? *Breathe.* Did I really deserve this?

Yes, yes I did. My hands were bloody, and they'd continue to be that way for the rest of my ungodly existence.

I'd almost lost her today. It wasn't the wound but the way she stared into nothingness, as if slowly slipping toward insanity, thanks to the Myad's magic. I could revive a deceased body, but I couldn't mend a broken mind. She wouldn't have been dead, but not really alive, either. The very thought of her slipping beyond my reach had shattered my control. If she hadn't made it out...if I'd lost her to that beast...

Don't be ridiculous. She wasn't mine to lose in the first place. She never *could* be.

I uncurled my hands. Stared at the imprints of my nails against my skin. I was supposed to be stronger than this.

Behind me, a soft knock sounded on the door. Kost. He'd have waited for a time to slip away from the group to come and check on me. I rested against the doorframe, body still angled toward the ocean, and called to him without moving. "Come in."

A quiet click, and the hinges creaked as the door swung open.

Folding my arms across my chest, I let out a long breath. "You didn't need to check on me."

The door shut. "I just wanted to clear the air."

My pulse died, and I spun on my heels to find Leena, one hand gripping an amber bottle of spiced acorn whiskey by the neck and the other cradling two small crystal glasses.

"I thought you were Kost."

She shrugged. "Sorry to disappoint." *Disappoint?* I swallowed my laugh. Skin glowing from our recent time in the sun, wearing a thin peach dress that clung to her curves, she was far from disappointing.

Gripping the doorframe, I struggled to keep control over my composure. "What do you want?"

She winced. "To apologize." The washed-out yellow chandelier lit of its own accord as the night rushed in. She stood beneath it, carefully shifting her weight from one foot to the other, and she stared at my chest rather than meet my gaze.

"That's not necessary."

"Isn't it?" She speared me with her eyes, and my heart thundered against my rib cage. Slowly, she made her way across the room to stand before me. "I should have told you what I was planning. I blindsided you. You deserve to be mad."

Mad didn't begin to cover it. An image of Leena coated in blood surfaced in my mind, and a low growl forced its way through my pursed lips. "Do you have any idea how stupid that was?"

Her lips parted, ready to spew an angry retort, but she slammed them shut. Her stare devoured me, and the anger pulling at her brows faded. "I'm sorry. I didn't want to risk losing the Myad. If something had gone wrong, if any of you had interfered, it would have been impossible to make him mine. I would have lost him. Or I could have died."

She said that last part as if it were an afterthought. Like the very weight of her life was less than the worth of taming the Myad. I palmed my face, hiding my expression for fear of her unearthing the truth. "Why was this beast so important to you?"

She set the twin tumblers on the nightstand and poured the whiskey with a heavy hand. Ocher liquid splashed along the ridges, and she brought the first glass to her lips. "What do you know about the Charmers Council?"

I took the other glass from her. Our fingers brushed, and I swallowed the rock in my throat before sinking onto the bed. "Not much. They're more clandestine than Cruor."

"Right." She eyed the space beside me and opted to lean against the wall. "There are seven members total. Six High Charmers and one Crown of the Council. They are the strongest Charmers around with beast networks larger than all other Charmers combined. In order to be considered for a seat on the Council, you need to be more than an A-Class Charmer. You need to own beasts of a certain caliber that are nearly impossible to obtain."

"The Myad." I took a slow sip and watched as her face lit up.

"Yes." She drained her drink and a pink flush tinged her cheeks. "The Myad is one of ten legendary feline beasts. Each member on the Council has a legendary beast, though none have the Myad."

The Council. They had to be the one pulling the strings behind Leena's bounty. The mark on my wrist burned. I had no idea how to infiltrate Hireath. I wanted to leave Leena out of this, but it was becoming abundantly clear I might need her to end our predicament. Pushing off the bed, I reached for the bottle and poured more alcohol into her glass. "I didn't know you wanted to be on the Council."

She laughed up at me. "A long time ago, maybe. Now, I just need protection. To be honest, if I had never been cast out from Hireath, I probably would have lived a meek life, taming whatever beasts naturally came to our homeland. But now..." Her words died, and she touched the bestiary around her neck with her free hand.

"Will they think twice about attacking you now?" Hope. It was a dangerous thing. My fingers acted on their own, dancing across her collarbone to trace the links of her necklace. Goose bumps followed their trail, and Leena peeked up at me through her lashes. When she looked at me like that...

"It's a start. It'd be nice if I could clear my name." Gripping the rim of her glass, she dropped her hand to the side. Her other hand remained over her bestiary, her fingers tantalizingly close to mine. "Noc?"

"Yes?" I grasped my drink to keep a grip on reality. My mind warred with my heart, and I breathed deeply. Her scent tormented me. Every nerve ending sparked, a painful sort of burn that could only be alleviated by indulging in this. In *her*.

"I'm sorry. I really am." Forced out through shallow breaths, her words were raspy. They destroyed the meager restraint I'd been clinging to. I palmed her neck, caressing the line of her jaw with my thumb. Her chest heaved, and she rested her head against the wall, an unspoken question lingering in her eyes.

Resolve was a fragile thing. One moment it was there, and the next, it was wrecked by the simplest of looks. She was too much and not enough. In one rash moment, I tossed my drink to the side and pulled her face to mine. She moaned against my lips over the shattering of the glass, and her own tumbler crashed against the floor, spattering drops of amber liquid.

She melted into me, and everything that was Leena was suddenly mine. The feel of her breasts pressed flush against my chest. Her tongue twirling with mine. Her lips forming a language I so desperately wanted to learn. To keep private between us. Pressing her harder against the wall, I abandoned her mouth for her neck, trailing my way toward her collarbone, nipping skin and teasing flesh as I went.

"Noc." Her breathless exclamation killed me. The taste of her skin, the feel of her body—my wildest imagination couldn't have done her justice. How long had I longed to touch her? Feel her? I dug my fingers tighter into the soft curves of her hips.

She was trapped beneath me, and she did everything she could to encourage it. Slipping her hands under my tunic, she raked nails along my skin, exploring every inch and leaving a delicious sting in her wake.

Moaning into my ear and completely drowning out the sounds of the night, she clutched my back and anchored herself there. The weight of her against me sent a thrill through my spine. Pausing for a moment, I moved away from the swelling red mark on her neck. She let out an exasperated, defeated whimper, and satisfaction brewed in the pit of my stomach.

"What do you want, Leena?"

She leveled me with her heavy-lidded gaze and moved one hand to the side of my face. A wry smile captured her lips. "Isn't it obvious?"

But gods, I wanted to hear her say it. "Tell me."

"I want you."

And even though it was everything I craved to hear, it was the very thing that gave me pause. A selfish, reckless part of me begged to give her what she so obviously desired. But I'd listened to that voice before. It hadn't ended well. Achingly slow, I brushed my lips against hers. "I can't do this..."

Her breath hitched. "Why...?"

"It's not that I don't want to. Gods, Leena. I want to." I trailed my hand along the curve of her side. "You have no idea how badly I want to." I desperately needed to wrap myself in her scent, to have her on me, so when she left, I could taste her for days to come. But I couldn't give her what we both truly desired—not as I was.

Slowly, I took a step back.

The space between us cut like a blade, and she winced. "If you want to, then why do you keep pulling away? I know you're upset about the Myad, but—"

"It's not about the Myad." This wasn't her fault, not in the slightest. She was innocent in this, and if she started to blame herself for my actions... I couldn't live with that. She deserved better.

She deserved the truth.

Sinking to the edge of the bed, I gripped the back of my neck. I'd kept this secret for so long. It was too hard to explain. Curses, while not unheard of, were rare. Explaining that my detachment was necessary to protect others always sounded like an excuse. Far-fetched and unbelievable. The only thing that confirmed it would be their failing health, and I wasn't willing to put anyone in harm's way for the sake of proving a point.

"I think it's time we talked."

Her gaze narrowed, but she didn't move for the door or shout at me for leaving her high and dry. Again. I had her for the moment, and she *needed* to understand. *I* needed her to understand.

Swallowing, I stared down at my hands, at the lines of fate etched across my palms, and prepared to tell her about the curse I couldn't outrun. I only prayed she'd listen. That she'd hear it as truth and finally see that, no matter what, we couldn't be.

Not like this. Not without a Gyss.

TWENTY-SIX

LEENA

I leaned against the wall, watching Noc. I'd expected some reluctance, but his dismissal still burned. At least he was talking to me. Trying to explain whatever ridiculous reason he had for pushing me away. Folding my arms across my chest, I waited. Conflicting emotions broke over his expression. He pinched his nose. Sighed.

"I'm cursed."

It was an effort to keep my expression neutral. "That's the best you could come up with?" Hurt started to brew in my chest. I was no stranger to liars in my world, but a curse? He could've just told me he wasn't interested, instead of making up some far-fetched excuse.

"I'm not lying," he said through a sigh. And then he looked at me. Really looked at me. Pain and frustration and despair all mingled together in his intense gaze. It was so real. So *honest*. A curse... No. But, what if? It seemed ridiculous—impossible—but I could hear the truth in his words. Whatever Noc meant, he was in dead earnest. Even though it *had* to be a lie. Even though my own heartache had faded, leaving room for uncertainty, with his upending look.

Maybe. Just maybe... When he spoke again, his voice was

even, as if he were reciting some long-forgotten history and not the bitter truth that kept tearing us apart. "A high priestess did it. A long time ago, before I was raised from the dead. If I start to care about someone and they return my feelings, they die."

I took a careful step toward him, half expecting him to flee. "High priestesses only work for royalty and the gods."

His eyebrow twitched. "It's safe to say we weren't 'working' together."

"I see."

"This curse… It's made being around people difficult. I can't get close with my brethren. Forming new relationships is tenuous at best. Most of the time, people fade away because I'm too detached—or I'm too erratic, torn between wanting to be close and wanting to keep them safe."

Even as he said it, he pulled away from me. Called shadows to his form and surrounded his limbs in darkness. As if that would keep his hands from acting of their own volition. Slowly, his actions started to click into place. The detached demeanor. The contradicting nature of our conversations. His fiery curiosity that he constantly kept in check. The realization tugged at my heartstrings and threatened to bring tears to my eyes.

He kept talking, his words falling like weights. How it must have hurt him to carry the brunt of this alone. "I don't want to be like this. But if I let myself get that far, someone dies. Always. Staying one step ahead of my emotions, controlling my reactions and measuring others' feelings—it's a constant necessity. It's the only way to keep everyone safe."

"I couldn't imagine…" My throat thickened as my words trailed off. So *that's* why he pulled away. He *had* sensed that connection between us, the one that sparked fear and longing in my heart. The connection that shouldn't have been there. I swallowed. Hard.

"You should know, I don't do love—or anything remotely close to it, for that matter."

Something flickered in his gaze. Hurt? Happiness? I didn't know. "What?"

Noc had just shared something monumental with me. And I couldn't explain it, but I wanted to do the same. I wanted to show him that he wasn't the only one suffering. That we all had pasts that threatened to wreak havoc on our future. Slowly, so as not to spook him, I made my way to the bed and sat down beside him. "The last person I loved had me ripped from my home. You know that."

He braided his fingers together in his lap. "I do."

"How could he do that?" I wrapped my fingers in the chain of my bestiary. "I was dragged before the Council. He didn't...he didn't even *look* at me." A silent tear fell down my cheek.

Carefully, as if his touch would actually break me, he brushed it away. "I'm sorry, Leena."

"Don't be. It taught me a lot about people. About what they're capable of. After that, I made a promise to myself that I'd never rely on someone else again. Never fall in love again. Why get so invested when, in the end, they might still find you disposable?"

Noc's fingers stilled against my cheek. Then, he dropped his hand just inches from mine on the bed. "People can be cruel. Myself included."

"You? How?" I raised my brows and felt myself start to smile, despite the weight of our conversation. "If this curse is real, then everything you do is because you care. I'd hardly call that cruel."

"I haven't always been this...self-aware." His faraway gaze studied something I couldn't see. "I've loved before. Twice. And both times they died." With a heavy swallow, he lowered his chin to his chest. "I didn't know then that I was the cause, but I do now."

I'm especially good at killing people I love. His words rattled in my mind with all the weight I'd missed earlier, and my heart sank to my feet. To live with that knowledge... Reaching out, I skimmed my fingers along his cheek. Even if he was telling the truth, I couldn't keep my feelings in check. This was the most vulnerable I'd ever seen him. The most *real*. I wanted to wrap him in my arms and hold him close. "Noc, I couldn't even imagine. I'm so sorry."

He leaned into my touch, almost as if the action was inevitable. As if there was a magnet between us that pulled us together despite the danger. Shifting, he faced me on the bed. "Ozias told me something interesting."

My heart thudded wildly. "Yeah?"

"He said something about a Charmer's lure. Is that why I can't help myself?"

"Maybe." My breath was shaky, uneven. "It wouldn't make you fall in love with me, though. So we're safe."

"Are we?"

It was barely a whisper, and yet it threw my whole world out of balance. A rush of adrenaline surged through me, and I tried to ignore it. Tried to push it away. But his gentle gaze made it harder to focus. Hard to separate wishful thinking from the truth.

When I didn't answer, he shook his head and leaned away. "I want to blame my lack of control on that. But I fear it's something more. And if it is...I can't do to you what I've done to others."

"You don't have to worry about me." The words tumbled out before I could check them. I wanted his vulnerability, his honesty— everything. "Like I said, I don't *do* love. I don't have feelings for you."

Wary eyes tore me apart. "Leena, I don't know." He leaned back farther, trying to put distance between us. "It's not worth the risk."

"There's nothing to risk." I gripped his hand, threaded my fingers through his. "I don't do feelings. With anyone. Including you." It hurt to say it, but there was truth to that statement. No matter that I didn't want to picture a world without him. Without any of my newfound friends. But I'd pack up and leave if I had to.

He gave an inch and leaned toward me, as if we were both incapable of walking away. "I don't want to hurt you."

"You won't. I promise." He wouldn't hurt me because I *couldn't* love him. I couldn't be like Kost, offering affection and devotion only to be met with a cold shoulder.

I couldn't.

He dipped his head to mine, and his lips barely skated over my mouth. We stayed like that for what felt like an eternity, each of us giving the other a chance to back out...and then his hands were in my hair, his mouth pressed firm against mine. Hunger and longing taking over and tossing caution to the wind. Nothing else mattered except the feel of him against me. The languid brush of his hands as they dropped first to my neck and then my waist. He tugged my closer, and I complied, crawling into his lap. I needed him to know that this was okay. That I wanted this. That nothing bad would happen.

Wrenching my fingers in his hair, I tilted his head to deepen the kiss. Reveled in the feel of his tongue twirling with mine and the warmth of his breath. Every sensation centered around him. He demanded all my attention—and I willingly gave it to him. For a brief moment, he paused and cupped my chin. Studied me with those devastatingly beautiful pools of black ice. His intent stare set my heart racing. Never had someone looked at me like that before.

I turned into his touch, kissing his fingers lightly, and caught sight of the black tattoo on his inner wrist. There was something so delicate and yet so brutal about those sharp lines. I ran my fingers over it, feeling the grooves of his veins masked beneath the ink. I wanted to unearth all his stories. He touched my spirit without even trying.

I placed a soft kiss on the tattoo. Then my gaze flickered to Noc's unending eyes.

Something unreadable flashed over his face, and he pulled his hand away. Fingers trembling, he traced the length of my jaw before enveloping me in a heated kiss. Whatever that look had been, it was lost in the wake of his tongue. In the way we somehow exchanged thoughts and words with our bodies alone.

I didn't want to waste another moment in this stupid game of cat-and-mouse we'd been playing. Everything was on the table now. I knew of his curse, my feelings weren't strong enough to trigger it, and all he had to do was keep his emotions in line. We could do this.

It was as if he could feel my sudden determination, the heightened emotion between us, because he pulled away once more. This time, with more tension in his shoulders and a cautious look that sent panic racing through my veins.

Not now. Don't hide now.

"Noc?" I placed a hand against his chest and felt the erratic beat of his heart against my fingers. It was a cadence I never wanted to forget.

His voice was rough, gravelly. Full of unspoken emotions and desire. "Are you all right?"

"Of course I'm all right. I told you, we're safe."

And then I coughed. Just a small, weak thing. Apparently, our intense kiss had left me thirsty, and I glanced around the room for a glass that wasn't shattered against the floor.

He stiffened beneath me. "You sure?"

"Yeah, just need some water." Slipping out of his arms, I made my way to the bathroom. I turned the faucet and cupped my hands beneath the water. Refilled them twice.

Noc filed in behind me, shoulders stiff and gaze stricken. "Was there blood?"

I frowned. "What? Blood? No. I just had something in my throat."

Leaning forward, he pinned my chin between his fingers and angled my face toward the light. Brushed a cautious thumb along the underside of my eye. Powder smeared, revealing the dark bruises I'd been trying to hide, and he hissed.

"How long?"

The look in his eyes rattled my foundation. "How long, what? You're not making any sense—"

"Have your lips cracked, too? Or did you find a way to hide that as well?"

I strode past him into the bedroom. "So what? Kost packed nemla salve with my makeup. It works wonders on chapped lips. My skin just isn't used to this weather—it's not a big deal."

"Gods dammit, Leena. You're dying." Panic filled his eyes before his expression flipped into a hard-set grimace. "I've seen this before. I can stop it. But you need to get out. Now."

I barked out a shallow laugh. "You're joking, right?"

Silence bred unease, and then Noc spoke. "Leave. Now."

Anger flared deep in my bones. "Now I *know* you're joking. I'm not leaving, not until you tell me what the hell is going on." I placed my hands on my hips. He never met my gaze.

"It's for your own good. Please, get out of my room."

I took a step toward him and reached for his hand. The cool bite of his ring sent shivers across my heated skin. "You're serious. You really want me to leave."

Noc cut me off with icy finality. "Yes. This is over."

He might as well have buried one of his bloody knives deep in my heart. That was the problem—it was his blood, his breath, everything about him now wreaking havoc on my system. Permanently intertwining with my own, mixing and melding to be a part of me I could never extract.

"With time, this memory will fade," Noc said in a slow and

measured way, as if trying to convince both of us. "You'll forget about this mess. You'll forget about me, about Cruor, and it will be for the best." He made a move to the door, resting his hand on the bronze fixture so he could let me out.

My feet refused to move, and I spoke to his retreating figure, to the back I'd become so familiar with. "You're wrong."

I'd never forget him. He was a damn earthquake, and his aftershock would quake through me for the rest of my life.

Voice exasperated, he refused to turn back to me. "I wish I were."

"Is this because of the curse? Noc, I'm *fine*. I told you, I don't have feelings for you."

"Gods dammit, Leena!" He stalked away from the door, pacing at the foot of his bed. Wild black eyes full of fury and desire threatened to swallow me whole. "This isn't something you can just lie about! Hide it with some makeup and pretend everything is all right."

"For fuck's sake." I whirled on him. "Stop berating me and just *talk to me.*"

Noc rubbed his temples. Voice thick, he answered me without meeting my stare. "I am talking to you."

"You're yelling at me."

"I'm *protecting* you." He took a long, steadying breath. Sank onto the bed and cradled his head in his hands. "I need to be cold. The proof of my curse is already showing—the dark bruises. The chapped lips. The cough. We're dangerously close to the fever, and at that point, I won't be able to stop it."

My retort died as I recalled the first time I'd noticed the bruises. The cracking lips. Was I really that close to death? A chill swept through me. Voice soft, I studied my hands as the gravity of the situation took hold. "Your curse works in stages."

"Yes." Hard eyes skewered me. "And apparently, your feelings are stronger than you let on."

"Yours must be, too, then." It was stupid that, for a fleeting moment, I was happy. Elated to know that I wasn't alone in this swirling, confusing mess of emotions. But if he didn't shut me out completely, it wouldn't matter. My eyes burned with unshed tears. How cruel was this? Death or a broken heart. Why were those my choices?

His stoic face cracked, a glimmer of hurt streaking through his eyes, and he shook his head once. "It doesn't matter. Can't you see now why I need a Gyss?"

A Gyss. Of *course*. It was all beginning to make sense. Another option. One that hinted at a possible future, but held unknown and likely devastating consequences. "Isn't there another way? A safer way?"

"I've tried everything. Save this. If there's another beast that can do it, I'm all ears."

I didn't know of a beast that could eradicate a curse that ran so deep. Perhaps a Council member with a more robust bestiary would know, but since leaving Hireath, my resources had dwindled. "No. Not that I know of."

"Can we get on with it, then?" He stood and glanced out at the ocean. His sudden detachment after being so close cut deep. I knew if I reached out now, tried to touch him, he'd only move away. Reject me. If only to keep me breathing.

My heart twisted at the choices before me: death, heartbreak, or a Gyss. I couldn't even imagine the type of payment required to remove something like this. But it was up to him to decide if the risk merited the reward. If anything, wishing with the help of a Gyss would only protect me further if he did succeed. Maybe then we could have something more...

I coughed, and Noc's gaze riveted to me.

I didn't know what was worse—that these feelings could condemn me to death, or that I was about to do the very thing I'd promised myself I'd never do: give a Gyss to someone I cared for.

Dropping my gaze to the floor, I finally gave in. "Tomorrow. We'll leave at dawn if we want to catch one in time."

TWENTY-SEVEN

NOC

We rode hard into the late afternoon, veering off the beaten path to Eastrend and heading west toward Nepheste's Ruins. We only slowed to prevent our Zeelahs from snaring their ankles in gnarled tree roots. Lightwood was nowhere near as dense as the Kitska Forest, but that didn't mean traveling was smooth. Pine trees clambered together, low branches skimming the tops of our heads. Leena picked her way through it all, leading without ever looking back and pushing her mount to the limit. By the time she called it, a glossy sheen covered the flanks of her panting Zeelah.

Sliding to the ground, she surveyed the small meadow. Thick grass swayed against her leather breeches, and I was reminded of the first clearing where we'd made camp. Of the time she flexed her beast network and put Calem in his place.

Birdcalls, high and sweet, coursed through the air, and she tilted her head to the trees. How many bits would I pay to hear her thoughts, to know how she was reacting to the news of my curse? A million? More? Was there even a price?

She hadn't bothered with makeup this morning, and all I could do was cringe. Those dark bags and chapped lips were death sentences. She coughed into the back of her hand, and I held my breath. Searched for red droplets against her skin. Nothing.

I needed to push her further away. Kost had fallen this far, and I'd somehow managed to keep him breathing. I could do the same with her. I'd spent too many years searching for a cure only to come up empty-handed. If the Gyss didn't work, then she could still have a life elsewhere. Find someone else. No matter how much that notion made my teeth clench and stomach churn.

Not to mention the bounty. Gods. When it came to us, there were just too many thorns. But damn if I didn't want to cut them all down and see what grew.

Patting her mare on the neck, Leena led her away from the forest's edge. "Make camp here. I'll be back in a few hours with Noc's beast."

I barely had a chance to open my mouth before Calem and Ozias simultaneously protested.

"You shouldn't go alone," Ozias said.

Calem echoed him a breath later. "Let us come with you. You look...tired."

Strained smile on her lips, she glanced at Kost before turning her attention to Ozias and Calem. "I am tired, but I'll be fine. It's not that I don't trust you. It's just that this taming requires a lot of concentration on my part. There's no danger, I promise."

Kost studied her while Calem and Ozias shared a wearied look. Slowly, Kost's damning, horrified stare slid to me. He knew.

I couldn't let her go alone. Not when she was sick. "I'll come with you."

Leena's eyes devoured me. So many emotions, so little time to categorize them all, but the last thing I glimpsed was uncertainty. Fear. Of what? The curse or the Gyss? I wouldn't use the beast against her, even if it meant losing my curse. She had to know that.

She nodded once. A cool breeze swept over us, and she grabbed her jacket from the back of her Zeelah. With quick hands, she laced it up and pulled the hood over her head, obstructing the view of her face. Wisps of hair flirted with the edge of fabric. "Let's get this over with."

She walked away into the woods, hands shoved in her jacket pockets. Her light squandered, she was as cold as an assassin and dressed the part. What I would give to see her glow again.

Couldn't she see that I was doing this to protect her? To protect us both?

No. Gods damn it, I didn't *want* her to see. It was all a hopeless tangle.

Calem and Ozias dismounted, carrying saddlebags a short distance away to set up camp. Kost, on the other hand, remained seated on his Zeelah, the heavy weight of his stare still hammering into my back.

"She's dying."

I swallowed. Hard. "Yes."

His voice was carefully even. "Does she know why?"

"Yes. It's why she finally agreed to the Gyss taming." I hated that it sounded like I'd forced her hand. She had been so unwilling to trade me the beast before, and now, faced with an impossible fate I'd bestowed on her... I shivered. She didn't deserve this.

As I took a step to follow her, Kost's words rooted me in place. "Noc. Fix this."

I turned. "Everything is fine. No matter what, everything will *be* fine. I'll distance myself like I've done before. She's not too far gone."

"That's not what I meant." He slipped out of his saddle and strode toward me. "I want you to be happy. We'll find a way to make that happen. I promise."

Frowning, I studied the slight tremor to his hands. I'd told him about the Gyss's magic in passing—he knew of the risks and potential payoff. And yet...something about his unrelenting green gaze told me this was much deeper than a beast. A promise that, if this failed, he'd keep trying to fulfill.

Feeling swelled in my chest just as unease settled in my gut. He'd always been by my side, a friend who never faltered, despite my unpredictable emotions. He had no idea what that meant to me. How badly I wished I could reciprocate. When I went to grip his shoulder, I swore I saw a glimmer of darkness beneath his eyes. The first sign of my curse. I had to rein myself in. Letting my hand drop, I ignored the frustration, the longing, brewing in my chest. Leena was already ill. I wouldn't be able to handle it if he was, too. "What are you saying?"

He removed his glasses and stared at me without filter. Emotion flared behind his eyes, honest and, for once, unguarded. Love, pure and real. Pain, as deep and as dark as mine, and at once, I knew. I knew why he hated Leena—not her, but the thought of her. How long had he been silently suffering? Decades? Since the moment I set foot in Cruor?

I'd never once acknowledged his love. How cruel I was, even if it was better that I'd never said a word. Even if it had saved his life.

A fist wrung my heart. I cared for Kost in ways I was too scared to admit. I couldn't condemn him to death. Again. And still, through it all, he'd been there. A silent partner. A constant shoulder that I couldn't lean on, but offered just the same. Words faded, and I stood completely still.

I didn't just need this curse gone for Leena. I needed it gone for *him*. For Ozias and Calem. For me.

"Kost, I—"

"We'll talk later." He replaced his glasses and turned toward his mount. "You better catch up with Leena."

"Yeah." It was all I could muster, and it was impossibly lacking. A branch cracked in the distance, and I spurred into motion, tracking the imprints of Leena's boots in the grass. Only when I was hidden within the safety of the forest did I dare expel my breath.

Kost. Leena. I was more monster than man, and I didn't deserve either of them.

Moving quickly, I caught up to Leena and followed without uttering a word. She stiffened at my presence, but didn't turn to check. She didn't have to. There was an electric current between us, and it was impossible not to be aware of her.

I braved disturbing that connection first. "How do you know about Nepheste's Ruins?"

She halted to take a breath before she continued forward. "Everyone born on this continent knows about the ruins."

"About them, yes, but not where to find them."

"Beasts talk. No one knows our world like Charmers do." Quickening her stride, she leaped over a fallen tree covered in moss and miniscule magenta flowers. The forest watched us. Beady eyes gleamed from behind ferns and tree stumps, and soft calls questioned our approach. The deeper we got, the more insistent the sounds became. "Why do you ask?"

There it was. Affection. A desire to further understand, to learn more. It was small and repressed by pain, as if she was trying to stifle her own emotions, but the slight pique in her tone gave her away. I shouldn't have been happy, but I was. I'd shut down entirely after we'd kissed. Thrust her out and left her alone to sift through the weight of my curse. It was wrong, and yet somehow it was the exact right thing to do. The only way I could have kept her alive. The contradiction burned me up inside.

Quieting my heart, I moved closer to her. "Curiosity. I suppose aside from Charmers, the only other beings aware of the ruins' location are the royal family." It was a rite of passage for the future king or queen to visit the sacred grounds before accepting the crown. The first mages of Wilheim were buried there. Returned to the earth in ruins forged by the gods. There, an ascending prince or princess received the world's blessing.

"I suppose," Leena said. Another unspoken question. This one, I couldn't answer. My past was dangerous and buried with my former life—resurrecting it would invite war. Until I knew for certain the outcome of us, I couldn't utter a word.

Without warning, Leena came to an abrupt stop. She rested her hand against the ivory bark of a lumina tree. Lilac leaves drooped low to the base, and blooming saffron-colored flowers opened to the night. Touching her chin to her shoulder, she cast a slow glance my direction. "We're almost at the ruins. I need absolute stillness to attract a Gyss. If you can't manage that, hide until after I tame her."

"I can manage."

She blinked, and tension melted from her shoulders. "Noc... Are you sure about this?"

My world came to a standstill. There was so much behind that small question. I wanted to tell her everything—from the truth behind why the curse was placed to the reason for the heavy ring on my finger. But what good would it do if this didn't work? She deserved a life of happiness, and if she stayed with me, I'd never be able to provide that.

"Yes."

She sighed. Her hand fell to her side, and she moved forward through the brush. Lumina trees dominated the space before us, their gargantuan roots intermingling with boulders and slabs of glistening black granite. Weeping strands of leaves kissed the ground, and Leena pushed them aside like a curtain, revealing a magical oasis.

The placid water of the lake glimmered in the low lavender

light of dusk. Dusted-pink water lilies covered the surface, and the occasional ripple from a fish ghosted the water. It was said the gods had blessed five locations across our continent. Five sacred ruins carved from the heavens themselves. Staring at the altar resting in the middle of the lake on its lone island, I believed it. Pristine as the moon and lit the same, the structure glowed. The water around the island was pure mercury, a spectacular silver that bled into crystal blue the farther out it traveled.

A heartbeat pulsed from the ruins, and warmth spread through me, encouraging heat in places I hadn't even realized were cold. Eyes burning, I braved a glance at Leena. Other than the quiet smile on her lips, she seemed unaffected.

A gong rang true and deep, like a mallet striking a chime, and a pleasant hum vibrated through every muscle in my body. Hairs along my arms rose skyward, and emotion swelled in my chest. I'd never felt so alive.

Blessed.

Was that it? I stared at the ruins, at the throbbing glow pouring from the slabs, and my heart slowed to match the pace. Cursed was an everyday predicament, a constant drag on the soul. But this? My gaze lingered on Leena's back. Without knowing, she'd delivered a piece of my former life right back into my hands.

If the Gyss didn't work, I wasn't sure I'd be strong enough to leave her.

"Stay where you are." Frustration apparently forgotten, she smiled at me and pulled off her hood. Backlit by the glow of the ruins, by the ancient ties to my past, she stood like a queen. I'd given half of myself before, and in that moment, I contemplated giving her more.

All I could do was watch and break. Shatter into a million pieces and hope that all of this would work so she could put me back together again. Otherwise, she needed to run. Run far and fast, because these emotions were no longer hiding. They were climbing to the surface, reaching out toward her, and if she accepted them, if she admitted her love for me, she'd die.

I wouldn't let that happen. Not now. Not ever. Not again.

Kneeling against the water's edge, she tipped her face to the sky and illuminated my world with her glow. The ruins tried to compete, but she outshone them, radiating pure warmth from her skin.

My chest stilled at the first sign of the Gyss. She arrived quickly, parting blades of grass with her hands and floating before Leena's knees. Wild black hair dotted with tiny white flowers. Pointed nose and rosy cheeks. She looked past Leena to inspect me, her wide-set eyes assessing. Her stare hit me with the force of a train, and my heart trembled.

Leena poked her with a careful finger, and the Gyss giggled. Her wispy tail fluttered as she moved, and Leena pursed her lips. "She's ready. I'll take her to the beast realm, grab a key, and bring her back. Wait for me here."

Minutes passed. With every breath came an unstoppable wave of doubt. What if it didn't work? What if it *did*? How would I know? I paced along the shore of the lake, eyes drifting to the ruins. Everything about this place reminded me of the life I had before I died, the life I was *supposed* to live. Amira, my betrothed—dead. My brothers-in-arms—lost to my curse before I could even realize I was responsible for their deaths. My parents, gone. Died of broken hearts.

So much loneliness. Both before and after I'd been raised by Talmage. This place was heavy with it. Crushing despair settled deep in my bones. It was too much. I'd done too much. I didn't deserve this possible cure. I needed to live with my crimes. I couldn't endanger anyone else. I—

The groaning swing of a heavy door rushed over me, and Leena appeared in a shower of light. She smiled, and suddenly I could breathe again.

The Gyss floated by her feet. Twiddling the bronze key in her hands, Leena stood before me. "Last chance to back out."

"Never."

Her eyes bored into me as she delivered the key to my open hand. "You'll need to name her."

The Gyss moved toward me, expectant yellow eyes and wry smile already targeting the key. Cunning didn't even begin to describe the glimmer in her expression. Leena must have noticed it, too. She tensed, hands shaking at her sides.

Crouching to the ground, I held out my hand to the Gyss. "I think I'll call you Winnow."

She peeled back her lips to reveal sharpened teeth. *I like that name. Are you ready?* She glided into my open palm and placed her hands on her hips.

Tell me the terms. I stood slowly so as not to disturb her, and Winnow glanced back and forth between Leena and me.

"No matter what she asks for, you can't be mad at her." Leena wrapped her fingers in the chain of her bestiary. "That's just how it goes."

My pulse quickened. "Of course."

Can she hear you? I thought privately to Winnow.

Not unless I project my thoughts to her. She ran tiny fingers through her hair, wrapping it into a tight bun with a blade of grass. *You want your curse lifted? I can see it.* Floating down my arm, she pressed her finger to my chest just above my heart. *It's deep. Dark. Nasty.*

Leena watched with wide eyes, and I did my best to focus on Winnow. *I know. Can you do it?*

Winnow laughed, a high-pitched tinkling of bells, and Leena winced. *I can see you've tried in the past to no avail, but I can promise you: I'm much more skilled. A wish is a wish, a payment is a payment. Nasty retribution for nasty people who use their wishes foolishly.*

How do you determine payment? My mind raced. Leena said Gyss were cunning, but there wasn't much I wouldn't give to lift this curse. Leena. My brothers. Those were my limits. Beyond that... My gaze shifted to the Charmer I'd grown to care for, to the worry lines framing her eyes and the erratic rise and fall of her chest.

The gods determine payment. I'm simply a conduit. Winnow placed both hands on my chest, the tiniest pokes of pressure.

Then why does Leena care? It doesn't sound malicious.

Winnow looked up at me, pointed teeth on display, and tilted her head to the side. *Gyss have a special relationship with the gods. We can make a case for a less severe request, though the gods don't always listen. I also enjoy watching bad people endure deserved pain. Are you one of those people?*

My answer was swift. *Yes.*

She nodded, a satisfied look in her eyes. *Honesty will go a long way with me. To remove this curse...* She pressed her fingers deeper, testing, searching, for what felt like a very long time. My pulse was racing. *You must be willing to lose what you've worked so hard to achieve.*

Worked so hard to achieve? I paused, riffling through potential answers to that riddle. Only one stood out: Cruor. Unease coiled tight in me. The guild relied on me. I was responsible for protecting them, giving them a place to call home. What would they do without me? Could I really walk away? Talmage had given me a new purpose in life. I would die for them again and again without question.

My eyes slanted to Leena's worried face. My shoulders relaxed. For her, for my brothers, I could say goodbye. Cruor had existed long before I'd come along and would continue to survive without me. But...who would lead? I bristled. Not Darrien. If I had a say, Kost. But would I have a chance to appoint him as the next guild master? Or would the payment simply be taken and a new leader chosen at random?

"Noc, don't rush into this. Please. Think about the consequences." Leena's voice pulled me from my reverie. An errant tear broke free and rushed down her face. Without thinking, I brushed it away. I couldn't let her go.

Winnow. With great effort, I pulled my gaze back to my Gyss. *Is that all?*

Her smile deepened. *Yes.*

You can't change it?

Once the gods tell me the price, it can't be altered. Hope bloomed in my chest, and Winnow's eyes speared my heart. *What are you thinking, Noc?*

I'm thinking that the gods aren't too big on the details. I can lose it, and I can get it back. I'm nothing if not resourceful.

A wide smile split across Winnow's face. *I quite like you as a master. Shall we?* Flexing her hands against my chest, she closed her eyes. I stole one last look at Leena.

Do it.

Emerald light fractured from her fingertips and moved through me, piercing my chest with the sting of an electric current. Crying out in unexpected pain, I dropped to the ground. My heart shuddered beneath Winnow's touch, squirming and pumping at the intense burn.

Hold still. Winnow's voice surfaced in my mind, but it barely registered. Faces of long-dead loved ones flashed before me. So different and yet all the same—dark bruises beneath their eyes, cracked lips with flecks of blood dried around the corners, a sheen to their fevered foreheads. And then lifeless stares pinpointing nothing at all.

There was so much blood on my hands. All the good deeds in

the world couldn't wash away the stain of my actions. The deads' listless gazes burned into me, and then slowly, miraculously, their sickness faded. Color warmed their faces and smooth, unmarred lips turned up in smiles. Bright eyes shone with happiness.

A sharp crack like a glacier splitting rang in my ears. My frozen cage. Winnow tore through it all to get to the curse I'd kept locked away.

Leena sank to the ground beside me, lips parted and tears streaming down her cheeks. "Noc... Gods, please be okay. Please..." Her words ended in a sob.

The visions gave way, and she was all I saw. All I felt. The warmth of her touch. The heat of her breath. The fire in her eyes.

Gods, but I loved her. I felt a reflexive moment of panic at the thought, only to realize it was finally safe to feel this way. She'd saved me. Never again would I hurt someone I cared for. I was *free*.

The agony from Winnow's magic subsided to a dull burn, and my beast removed her hands.

Leena's watery gaze lingered on my chest. "You're okay. You're okay." I don't know if she was trying to convince herself or me, but the urge to comfort her outweighed every other sensation.

Tilting my head to the side, I pressed a light kiss against her thigh. "I'm fine."

Winnow moved away, and I pushed myself up into a sitting position. Wiping her hands across her makeshift leaf dress, she nodded her head once. *It's done.*

And it was. There was a lightness in the cavity of my chest, like nothing I had felt in decades. I hadn't realized the weight of the curse, the cracking, splintering feeling of it prodding against my heart. My gaze went to Leena's face. To the lightening circles beneath her eyes and her smooth lips. *Gone.* My curse was gone. Elation rushed through me, and I ached to hold her.

Winnow tapped my knee. *I have to go now. The gods want to discuss the terms of payment immediately.*

I didn't pull my eyes away from Leena's. She was incredibly still. Uncertain. *How long do I have before it's taken?*

I don't know. The invisible door to the beast realm groaned open. *I go to the realm, hear the full extent of their request, and act. It could be tomorrow or ten years from now, but it will happen.*

Thank you, Winnow.

Something soft broke through Winnow's voice. *Enjoy it while you can.* The realm door creaked to a close, and she disappeared.

"How are you feeling?" Leena made a move to worry the ring around her finger, but came up empty. She paused, hands stilled, before laying her palms flat against her thighs.

"Fine. Amazing, actually." I inched closer to her. I wanted to touch her. Feel her. Know what she felt like without any reservation.

Leena looked up at me through her lashes. "What did you have to sacrifice?"

"Cruor."

She gasped, the harshness of it slicing through the night and silencing the nightingales lingering in the trees. "That's your *family.* Do you know what I would do to have mine back?"

"Make a deal with a Gyss?"

Her glare threatened to murder me.

"Sorry, that was uncalled for. Can I explain? Please?"

She pressed her lips into a thin line. "Fine." Even in anger, she was a masterpiece. If I lost her, I'd never survive.

"I had to relinquish what I worked so hard to achieve. That doesn't mean I can't attain it again. It just means I have to let it go for a while."

Some of the anger fled from her gaze. "That's a huge risk. You might not get it back."

"It's worth it." I brushed my knuckles along her cheek, and she shivered. "You don't know what this curse has done to me."

"I can't imagine." Her eyes drifted to the place where Winnow had worked her magic. "Now you can love as you please."

"Indeed." I dropped my hands into my lap, uncertain. I knew I loved her—desperately. But her previous declaration sat heavy on my mind.

I don't do love.

Was that true? There had been a hint of conviction to her tone when she'd uttered that phrase. She'd gone through so much with Wynn. And I'd been so cruel to her, pushing her away when I wanted to pull her close, in order to save us both. But maybe, with time, she'd give me a second chance. I'd give her eternity if she needed it.

And yet... There were things she needed to know. Now.

I rotated my wrist and studied the oath inked into my skin. "There's still the matter of your bounty."

Her stare followed mine, and then she offered me a cautious smile. "I've delivered all four beasts, as promised."

I needed to tell her the full truth. It was long past time. "Yes. You did."

She pushed away from me. After finally ridding myself of the curse, the added space I would've welcomed earlier stung. "What aren't you telling me? What's wrong?"

"When we negotiated, I didn't tell you the full truth. You see this?" I pointed to the mark. "This is called Cruor's Oath. It's a binding magic that activates when we accept a bounty."

She frowned. "And?"

"And, it only goes away when the job is complete."

She froze. "We had a deal."

Panic spiked in me. "Leena, no. Don't worry. You're safe." I reached for her, stilled. Her eyes targeted my hands like they were weapons. "No one at Cruor will come after you. Not now, not ever. There's another way to remove the oath. All this means is that there's a little extra work involved on my end. Work I'll happily take on if it means keeping you safe."

She rolled her lower lip into her mouth. Looked up at me with wary eyes. "You promise?"

Reaching out, I rested my hand on her knee. "I promise."

"Gods be damned. You better not be lying." She pressed her palms into her eyes. "You were right—you're nothing but danger."

Pulling her hands away from her face, I forced her to meet my stare. "That's what I've been saying all along."

She tried her best to hold onto her uncertainty, but it slipped away with an exhale. "You make me tired."

Chuckling, I dragged my thumb along her jawline. "Just tired? Nothing else?"

Her eyes snapped to mine, a faint glimmer of heat already shining in her stare. "So damn dangerous." And then she laughed. It was pure and light and real. Trust. I felt it like I felt the hum of the magic bleeding from the ruins.

Closing the distance between us, I placed a gentle kiss on her lips. She caved beneath me, caved *in to* me, and I wrapped my arms around her. She trusted me. Despite everything. And I sure as hell was going to do everything I could to hold on to that forever.

TWENTY-EIGHT

LEENA

As the moon rose into the night, the forest came alive. Julips—miniscule jellyfish-like creatures—floated up into the air, leaving their homes in the dirt to soak their transparent skin in starlight. The delicate membranes of their bodies exploded in color, and the navy sky was suddenly blotted with electric aqua. Noc dragged his lips away from mine for a moment to watch as one crept upward between us.

"I've never seen this before." His voice was raw with a mixture of desire and awe, and his words rattled my heart. In the gleaming light of the Julip, his onyx eyes flashed and the angles of his face sharpened.

He was beautiful before, but even more striking now. Face tipped toward the heavens, gaze tracking the progression of a Julip, he rested his hands on his knees. Ease. It was the first time since knowing him I'd seen him so relaxed. Instead of a frown, his lips formed a genuine grin, and my heart gave up. I didn't mean to fall in love, but I did. Right there. I'd been fighting for so long that the feeling completely upended me.

A cool shiver raced across my skin. How long had I known but not been brave enough to think of the word? Loving Noc was like faith—a force that existed beyond my capabilities and drew me to him, an endless current between us.

There was still a sliver of me that burned with fear. Here I was, in love with a man who'd been willing to use a Gyss. It was all too familiar and all too terrifying...and yet, I understood. Wouldn't I have done the same, had our roles been reversed? The amount of pain he'd been living with for years on end was beyond my comprehension.

Noc stood and gently poked one of the Julips. The surface rippled from his touch, and the creature skittered away. Now at eye level, the affronting, cruel bounty mark laughed at me from Noc's wrist.

"How do we get rid of the oath?" I came to stand behind him, pressing my nose between his shoulder blades so I could breathe him in.

Noc glanced down at his wrist. "I need to unearth the true identity of the person who placed the hit. Cruor has resources."

"Even if you don't have Cruor anymore?"

He leaned into me. "I guess I'll know for sure when we get back. Even so, Kost, Calem, and Ozias will help. They're my brothers first, members of Cruor second."

Wrapping my arms around his waist, I held him closer. "It was probably Wynn. The man I told you about in the beast realm."

"I don't think so. The person in charge was female. When she placed the bounty with Kost, she was cloaked, masked, and never spoke, though there was a deep-red glow around her hand when she summoned a beast. She wrote all her requests on parchment."

"That would mean her Charmer's mark is the same hue." I fingered the waist of his trousers, feeling the waistband of his drawers and the velvet kiss of his bare skin. "That doesn't make any sense. Wynn would have the most to lose if he somehow thought the Council could decipher his lie. But a woman? I don't recall crossing anyone."

My fingers slid beneath his tunic, and Noc placed his hand over mine, stopping my progression. "Leena..."

"Yeah?" I couldn't stop the sudden swell of dread in my gut, and my body tensed. Why was he stopping me now when his curse was gone? Had it been a ruse all along? He turned to face me, and I was struck by the uncertainty in his gaze.

"I... It's been so long since I've felt this way. I don't even know how to act without the curse. What if I say too much? What if I say too little? I'm not sure—"

My unease died, and I pressed my finger to his lips, charmed by the nervous energy radiating off him. I supposed, in a way, this was all new again for him. It had been such a long time since he'd been free. "Take a dip with me."

His brow furrowed. "What?"

"You're thinking too much." I turned so my back faced the lake. Intertwined his hands with mine and slowly pulled him toward the water. "Let's just go for a swim. Enjoy the night. How does that sound?"

His easy smile broke my heart. "It sounds relaxing."

"Good." I laughed. "C'mon. It'll be fun." I snaked my hands beneath his tunic and lifted it off over his head. Everything in the world slowed. The casual flight of the Julips. The chirps of the nightingales in the wood. Even the breeze toying with the edges of the grass. Noc was statuesque, each cut definitive and sharp. Faultlessly proportioned. I traced the hard lines of his chest, touching the contoured V of his lower abdomen.

He snared my wrists and brought them to his lips, planting gentle kisses on my fingertips. "Tell me something."

"What do you want to know?" I cupped the side of his face. Trailed my thumb over his scar. His eyelids fluttered. Tender hands went to my jacket, unlacing it and pulling it over my head.

"Anything." He kissed my neck. "Everything."

I tilted my head back. I'd fallen fast and hard for this man, and I burned to tell him the depth of my emotions. To be the first person who shared their feelings with him now that the curse was lifted. But there was still a lingering thread of fear. One that was ice cold and reminded me of all the times he'd shut me out.

This is over.

I was scared that was the truth, not this newfound warmth.

. Something close, then. "I don't want to say goodbye."

His hands paused beneath my blouse, fingers tightening against my waist. "Me either." A deep heat bloomed in my stomach, and I lost myself in his eyes. He raked them over me, devoured me without even trying. Leaning in close, he dragged his lips down my neck toward my collarbone. Paused at the top of my cleavage and placed a delicate kiss on my bestiary.

"So maybe…"

"Stay." His voice was gruff. Slowly, he peeled off my shirt and bralette, let his hands roam over my skin. "With me. With us. If you want to, that is."

"I do." I'd never wanted something more in my life. A home. A family. *Him.* Toeing off my boots, I set them beside my discarded blouse and Noc's tunic. He did the same, dropping his trousers and drawers as I unlaced my breeches.

His fingers teased my hips. Toyed with the lace of my undergarments. He pressed his forehead to mine. "I'm glad."

With his help, I slipped out of my underwear. "I'm done telling you all about me. Tell me something about you."

A grin captured his lips. "But I'm not very interesting. You, on the other hand…" Gripping my waist, he lifted me and carried us into the lake. Even with the crisp fall air, it remained tepid. Water lapped against my back, and I wrapped my legs around him.

Leaning in, I kissed his sternum. "You don't have to hide anymore. Tell me as little or as much as you want. But tell me *something*."

Silence, save the trill of nightingales. Julips skated low over the water, their aqua bodies reflecting against the placid surface. Noc loosed a shuddering breath, and ripples traveled outward, jostling pale-pink lily pads.

He snuck his hands around me and stroked the small of my back. "I don't have any hidden talents like you."

I scoffed. "You can control the shadows. I'd call that talent enough." With water cupped in my hands, I drizzled streams over his shoulders. "C'mon. Dazzle me."

Raising an incredulous brow, he grinned. "Dazzle you?" He walked us farther into the lake until the water us up to our collarbones. "I'm gifted with a sword."

I rolled my eyes. "I could've guessed that. Tell me about your family."

He glanced down at me. Hesitated.

Gingerly, I skimmed my fingers across his cheek, leaving beads of water on his skin. I wanted him to see that it was safe. That I cared. Nothing he could say would change that. "It's okay."

He bent his head toward me and brushed his lips against mine. "There's not much to tell. My parents are dead."

My breath hitched. "The curse?"

His lips moved to my jawline. "Thankfully, no."

Dropping my hands to his chest, I felt his heart jump against my fingers. "Any siblings?"

"No." He stilled, smiled. "Okay, yes. Three annoying but loyal ones who have put up with my nonsense for the past several decades."

I couldn't help but laugh. "I bet they'll be pleased your curse is gone."

"They will." Noc drew me closer. "I can't wait to finally be myself around them. To tell them how much I appreciate their friendship. What it's meant to me, what it still means to me, that they stood by me despite everything. I owe them the world."

"I have a feeling they would've endured it for the rest of their lives if they had to. They love you, you know." Slipping out of his grasp, I sank beneath the surface of the water before I could finish that thought out loud.

I love you, too. I needed to know if he felt the same. I prayed he'd tell me. That we'd spend the night in the water, clearing away the lingering doubts and making room for true emotions. Hopefully, he hadn't perfected locking them away entirely.

Droplets dripped down my face when I came up for air, and Noc wiped them away. I nuzzled his fingers. "What else?"

"I'm fluent in six languages."

"Six?" My eyes widened. "That's so many."

Snaking his hands through the water, he wrapped me in his arms once again. "Not really. There are…thirteen known languages? I'm sure countless more. For example, that lovely script on your bestiary was foreign to me. The one along the binding." He pressed a finger to my necklace, lifted it to the moon.

"It's the ancient language of my people. We rarely use it for anything other than ceremonies." I rested my hands on his shoulders and felt the sharp cut of his muscles. Kneaded soft circles and felt those muscles loosen beneath my touch. His eyes fluttered close. After a moment, he dipped his head back, soaking his hair. Radiant, starlit water streamed over his face.

Peace. He was at peace. My heart trembled. "Say something to me in one of your languages."

Straightening his neck, he slowly opened his eyes. "Which one?"

"Your favorite one."

Lazy fingers explored the length of my spine, and he placed a searing yet gentle kiss at the hollow of my throat. "*Nae m'olluminé miele. Or, for short, nae miele.*"

A soft tingling spread over my skin. "What does it mean?"

He leveled me with one look. "One who fills my soul."

For a moment I let that phrase sit. Breathe. It settled deep in my heart and took hold, whispered of love. Of feelings I thought I'd never experience again. When my eyes burned with unshed tears, I brought my trembling lips to his. Inhaled as our breaths mixed and became one. I never wanted to exhale. I wanted to fill my lungs with him, with his scent, and keep a part of him permanently alive inside me.

"You do, you know." His gravelly voice shook my world. "It's because of you that I'm free." My hands trailed over the bare skin of his chest and felt his heart jump against my fingers. I needed this. Needed him. Needed to fall into the love I'd denied myself since leaving Hireath and Wynn behind.

"You freed me, too." My words came out rough with desire and emotion. I slanted my mouth over his. Ran my hands across the expanse of his back. "I didn't even know how bad it was."

He kissed my shoulder. The space beneath my ear. My cheek. "How bad what was?"

"My people exiled me, but I was the one who exiled myself from everyone else. You, Calem, Oz—even Kost—showed me that I didn't have to go through this alone. You saved me."

He cupped my face. "*You* saved *me*."

His ink-black stare held nothing but longing. And then he kissed me with devastating tenderness. His tongue mingled with mine, and he shifted in the water, bringing me close and angling my hips against him. He waited for a breath, asked for permission with his eyes, and I nodded. Achingly slowly, we became one. Every sensation seared itself in me: the splash of water against my back as we moved. The trills of nightingales in the swaying lumina trees around the lake. The whisper of a breeze licking our exposed skin. The Julips taking flight around our bodies. Magic. Everything about him was magic.

We pressed our foreheads together but didn't speak. We didn't have to. His gaze said everything, put every heated emotion on display. Longing. Passion. Devotion. Not a hint of despair or uncertainty. Soft moans were passed between us, and I clung to every feeling, every emotion, that flared to life.

We came undone together, and the ruins seemed to throb with the connection between us that I never wanted to lose. I could've stayed with him in that lake all night. He dragged a gentle thumb across my lips before dropping his hand to the water. "You're something else, you know that?"

"I know." I grinned.

"Should we head back?" He spoke against the shell of my ear, nibbling the lobe. Painting light kisses down my neck, he wrapped his fingers in my hair. My body arced into him.

I bit back a groan. "If we have to."

"If we take too long, they'll come looking for us." His devilish grin did delicious things to my nerves. "And I'm not sure you really want to be undressed when that happens."

Grumbling, I relented and let him carry us out of the lake. I used my jacket to loosely towel off my body before dressing. Clothes clung to damp skin, and I studied Noc with interest as he dressed. Itched to trace the cut of his figure even though I'd just done so without the barrier of fabric.

He caught me staring, and his mouth kicked up at the corners. "Enjoying yourself?"

"Quite."

He bent down, kissed me deeply. "*M'omu lieta ta braisée mon panua.*"

"What does that mean?"

"I'm glad you walked through my door."

My heart warmed as I laughed. "And I'm glad you didn't kill me when I did. Why do you speak so many languages, anyway?"

Crouching before me, he intertwined his fingers with mine. Tension gathered in his shoulders, along with a familiar glimmer of uncertainty in his stare. But then he gave a faint nod as if making a decision. "My father made me. A good leader never knows who he'll have to negotiate with. One of his many lessons."

I tilted my head to the side. "What exactly did you do before—"

The brush beside us exploded with movement.

Appearing with the lethal precision of assassins, a group of men encircled us. The earthy browns and mossy greens of their clothing lent to their ability to blend in with the surrounding forest. Power, untapped and hazardous, poured from them, washing over us and suffocating the air in my lungs.

In a mercury robe, one man stood out from the rest. The edges of his cloak flared with the passing gust of wind, and his Charmer's emblem bled with vibrancy in the dark of the night. Fear spiked in my veins, stabbing my heart and rendering me completely useless.

Before I could react, a Graveltot rolled out and planted itself in the ground before Noc. Just like when I'd used Grundy, the Graveltot targeted Noc with his eyes and gravity took hold, pushing him deep into the soft earth of the lakeside.

The robed man stepped forward, a wry smile peeking through a trimmed beard, and the Charmers at his back shifted as he came to stand before me. Slowly, as if the very motion caused him joy, he drew back his cloak.

Wynn.

TWENTY-NINE

NOC

I strained furiously against the weight of the beast's gravity manipulation. But with one creature dedicated solely to me, I could barely lift my chin to see the scene unfold before my eyes.

The robed man stretched his arms wide. "Leena. It's been a long time."

She stood impossibly still. "I haven't done anything wrong."

The man chuckled. I recognized the deep timbre of his voice. This was the lackey who I'd met in Midnight Jester and Devil's Hollow. Agony splintered my lungs, and I screamed with every ounce of strength I had, but only a suppressed moan escaped my lips. Where were my brothers? I desperately tried to call forth my shadows, to send a message to bring them here, but they were weak in the presence of the creature.

"Don't bother." The man's gaze slanted to the faint wisps trailing about my frame. "If you're trying to contact your friends, they're stuck like you. Wouldn't want reinforcements slinking in now, would we?"

Leena's voice trembled. "Please, don't hurt them, Wynn."

The way she whispered his name wrecked me. This man had hurt her. He was the reason for her heartache and mistrust. The reason she no longer had a place to call home.

Pure, unadulterated fury spiked in me, and I managed to brace myself on my forearms.

Wynn turned to me, brows lifting to his hairline as he assessed my strength. With a nudge, he toed the side of my wrist to reveal the tattoo. "I see I wasn't wrong in entrusting the job to you."

Leena flexed her hand. "Leave him alone." Her Charmer's symbol started to glow.

Wynn ran his fingers over his clipped brown hair. "He was supposed to kill you."

"But why? I haven't told anyone about what happened with the Council. I swear."

Fear threaded through my gut. If he found out she was lying, that she'd told me, what would he do to her?

Crossing over to her, Wynn sighed. "Desperate times call for desperate measures. We're on the cusp of something big, Leena. I never meant for you to get caught in the cross fire." He grasped her arms and pulled her close. "You're different. Stronger. How did you shatter the taming bond between me and my Scorpex? Not to mention taming a Myad and a Laharock."

Her eyes went wide as the rosewood light sharpened. "How did you..." I could see her quick mind turning. Processing. Calling forth a beast now would be futile. There were so many Charmers surrounding us, guaranteeing that her creature would suffer. Perhaps die.

Not to mention what they could do to her.

"*Tsk, tsk.*" Wynn shook his head and released her. "Leena, I taught you better than that. Beasts talk. But this does put us in a bit of a predicament." The way he inspected her made my skin crawl. Her face paled, but she gripped her hands in fists and stood tall. Wynn didn't seem to notice—or care. "With the Myad's taming, you're no longer fit for her needs. Which means if I don't present her with another fallen Charmer, then I'm the one she'll want. And that can't happen. I wonder, what would become of your newly cleansed soul if I forced you to relinquish the Myad?"

Leena leaned away from him. "What are you talking about? You can't force me to do anything."

"We'll see. Change is coming. Someone has to be the sacrifice. The catalyst."

She bristled. "If you take me back home, I'll tell everyone what you did. I'll tell the Crown of the Council."

He laughed. "Who would believe you? Trust me, my way is easier. You won't feel a thing in the end."

Leena spat at his feet, a glimmer of the fire I fell for shining bright, and my heart rammed against my rib cage. "I'd sooner die."

The smirk dropped from Wynn's face. "Yes, well, that's the plan." He signaled to the group of Charmers, and they tightened their ranks, edging toward Leena. "You don't know what we're up against. I'm doing what's necessary to protect our home."

She barked out a sharp laugh. "Sure, Wynn. You keep telling yourself that."

"How are my actions any different than his?" He gestured toward me, and Leena pursed her lips.

"What do you mean?"

Wynn snapped his fingers. "Bring me the Gyss." One of the Charmers stepped forward and handed Wynn a transparent box with golden trim. The air inside the cage shimmered, and Winnow banged her fists against invisible glass. Staring at me, she mouthed words I couldn't hear.

Leena's resolve cracked. "Winnow?" Winnow turned, a single tear trailing down her cheek, and rested one palm against the pane. Horror racked Leena's frame, and her fingers trembled. "Let her go."

"Nifty contraption, isn't it?" Wynn tapped on the glass, and Winnow covered her ears. "Another one of my experiments you'd probably disapprove of. But don't worry. It won't hold her for long. The beast realm will call her back within the hour. I just wanted to make sure she didn't slip out before then."

He handed the gilded cage to one of his lackeys. The panes of glass magnified Winnow's fear, and her wide eyes threatened to break me into a million pieces.

"Imagine my surprise when she appeared in my chambers with your exact location." Wynn shook his head. "After you'd stolen my Scorpex and murdered my Femsy, I wasn't sure how to proceed. I couldn't send another beast in case your charm somehow broke the bond again, and I knew you wouldn't stay in Ortega Key long."

Fury stoked fire in my veins, and the weak shadows leaking from my frame desperately tried to lash out.

With his back to Leena, Wynn offered me a private smirk. "But the solution fell right into my lap in the end. Noc *wished* for this."

My world went cold.

Leena's voice wavered. "No, it was his guild. He had to give up—"

"Did you even consider he might lie?" Wynn's grin deepened, and the veins on my neck bulged as I tried to scream. None of this was true. But I could see the flicker of doubt in Leena's wounded gaze.

Wynn extracted heavy metal shackles from his robe and latched them on her wrists. She didn't even fight back. She only stared.

He brushed a stray lock of hair out of her face. "Look at the facts. He made a wish, and now here you are. Back in my hands."

Tears endlessly spilling down her face, her eyes silently accused me of everything I knew I was.

Filth.

Scoundrel.

Liar.

"Leena," I croaked, the harsh weight of the gravity beast's magic threatening to smash my vocal cords to oblivion. "I didn't know. I swear."

Her chest heaved. How on earth could I make her believe me when we both knew her greatest fear was once again being collateral damage at the hand of a Gyss?

Each tear that fell from her cheek was shattering, my heart aching for everything I'd gained and destroyed in such a short time. I should have known. Because whether he knew it or not, Wynn was *right*.

Cruor wasn't something I'd achieved—it was gifted. A rite of passage from one leader to the next. I had formed the ranks, built a family. But nothing in this world was more precious than what I had built with Leena: trust. Love. A future.

Gods, I should have known.

Wynn yanked on Leena's chains. Blazing white, his Charmer's symbol erupted, and the same lizard beast he'd summoned in Devil's Hollow appeared by his feet. A fresh portal sparked to life in its unhinged jaw. "Come, Leena. As you've said, you know what happens when you put your trust in a man who is willing to wield a Gyss." He turned to the stone beast beside my head. "Hold him until your time runs out. Then, return to the beast realm."

Pushing Leena into the swirling gateway, he offered me a parting sneer. Shadows tried in vain to reach him, but the rock beast's unending gravity buried me deeper and deeper into the earth, and the lizard beast disappeared before I could even dream of getting close.

THIRTY

LEENA

Manifesting through the portal, we landed at the foot of the glistening falls on the banks of my former home. Hireath was everything I remembered it to be—and more. Gargantuan trees lined the clearing, and their branches reached across the pool of water to form a network of interconnected walkways and bridges for Charmers to cross. Alabaster platforms and buildings suspended against trunks were full of people. Of laughter. Flush with the mountain, a castle of white marble reached toward the clouds. The Beast City. A sanctuary birthed from the earth itself to provide haven for Charmers.

All I could see were Noc's wide, pleading eyes. Damn him. I'd trusted him.

Wynn nudged me in the back, and I walked along the edge of the lapping waters toward the glittering steps. A fine mist from the falls lingered in the air, and the taste of minerals coated the back of my tongue. *Home.* I swallowed hard, ignoring the hot sting behind my eyes. It was all too much.

Walking in silence, I followed the Charmers under Wynn's command past the watchtowers into the open gardens of the Beast City. Trickling water sang from the fountain in the middle of the clearing, a maiden upending a vase into an endless pond. Plants with vibrant pink, pastel purple, and hypnotic blue flowers clustered along the marble path. Beasts and Charmers alike rambled down walkways, quiet murmurs just audible over the water's call.

Maintaining a tight circle, Wynn's guards hid me from any wandering eyes. As one, we hit the smooth stone slabs of the keep and navigated corridor after corridor. Swinging lanterns with soft blue flames marked our progression as we climbed higher until we reached a lone floor dedicated solely to Wynn.

He dismissed the attendants standing post outside the double doors of his room and led me in. "What do you think, Leena? It's quite the step up from our home before."

Our home. Floor-length windows thrown open to the sky, the constant rushing of the nearby waterfall ricocheted off the slick marble stone. A four-poster bed large enough to sleep six dominated the wall to my right, tulle curtains flapping lazily in the breeze. Clean lines. White furniture. Open space. It was the picture of innocence, and the very thing Wynn could never be.

"Making a show before you kill me?"

Wynn turned to face me, a controlled smile revealing perfect teeth. "While that's the most plausible outcome, I might have an alternative. She won't like it, though." Only an arm's length away, the familiar aroma of bergamot was heavy on his tunic. He hadn't changed. Same clean-cut brown beard and hair, oozing arrogance and authority.

He paled in comparison to Noc.

Noc. My heart squirmed, and I dropped my gaze from Wynn. "Who are you talking about?"

"That's none of your concern." Wynn folded his arms across his chest. "How did you break my bond with the Scorpex?"

"I don't know." I edged closer to the door.

His eyes narrowed a fraction, and a slight tremor worked its way through his right brow. I knew that look. That intense curiosity that led to questionable experiments. He took a few quick steps to position himself between me and the door. "Interesting."

"What are you going to do with me?"

"That depends." Thick fingers brushed the length of my jaw. "But if you don't cooperate with me, I'll have to turn you over to her. And she will kill you."

Growling, I snapped at him, "Cooperate with you? I will never forgive you for what you did—to that man or to me. You stole my home!"

"Perhaps." He went back to studying me. Back to assessing every inch of my frame, sending thousands of insects crawling across my skin. "But that was then, and this is now. She has plans that need to be realized."

"Who are you talking about? Someone on the Council?" I bit back fear. Not many citizens knew of my banishment. I needed *out*.

Wynn hummed to himself. "Like I said, it doesn't matter. It's me or her."

"You just want to see if you can charm me. Like you did with that man."

Wynn grimaced. "You make it sound so horrid." He reached out again to touch my face, and I jerked forward, head-butting him as hard as I could. He reeled, and I dashed for the doors before he could react. Gripping the handles, I pulled them, only to have his hands come down hard against the wood, slamming the doors shut. He yanked me back and threw me into the wall. My head smacked against the granite, and stars danced across my vision. "Careful, Leena. You're in my home now. Don't act out."

Grasping the chains, he dragged me toward the far side of the room. As he pressed his hand flat against a smooth slab of ivory, a network of cobalt lighting shot out from his fingertips. A hiss of escaping air whispered through cracked seams, and a hidden door swung open.

He hauled me, struggling, into the low-lit, windowless room. It was whitewashed and stinking of lemon—a feeble attempt to cleanse the obvious horrors that occurred in this tomb. Weak candles flickered in chunky marble fixtures cemented to the walls, illuminating a steel cot soldered to the floor. A chain hammered into the floor with thick links wrapped across the tile, ending in an empty ankle shackle.

The memory of the man Wynn had imprisoned flashed in my mind. The ultimate crime. Taming a person was strictly forbidden. There were stories of a handful of Charmers over the centuries who had tried, unsuccessfully, to make a human theirs. The people in question never survived. Something about our charm always turned their brains to mush.

I still didn't know why Wynn had risked it. He'd always been curious, but nothing compared to this degree of insanity. How many others had he detained after my banishment? And for what purpose?

"The way I see it, there are three possible outcomes here." Quiet frustration seeped through his words, and he pushed me to the floor. I tried to kick him in the gut, but he trapped my legs in a vise grip, and my bones shuddered. "You fight me, and I take you straight to her, where you *will* die." Quick hands yanked off my boots, and I thrashed in vain against him as he shackled my ankle. "Option two, you play by my rules. The charm works, and she finally sees that my way is the best option for protecting our people." He crouched low into his heels, once again studying my face.

I strained against the chains. "And what's option three?"

"The charm works, but she still wants to move forward with her plans. In which case..." He tipped his head to the ceiling and rested his hands on his thighs, drilling his fingers against his knees.

"I'll force you to relinquish your Myad. Its blessing makes you unsuitable for her needs, but without it... True, you'll die. But it will be painless. You'll simply slip away."

"You're a lunatic."

"If that's what it takes." He shrugged. "And don't hold out any hopes for that assassin. He's no better than me. Maybe worse."

Noc. He'd promised he wouldn't risk eliminating his curse if it put me in danger. But how could he not know? I had *warned* him. Told him Gyss were mischievous, their offers not to be trusted, and he didn't listen. I was still here. Still the brunt of a wish, still alone and unsure of whom to trust.

A lump formed in my throat as I replayed every interaction in my mind, every nuanced look. It wasn't just me he was detached with, but everyone around him. How far would he go to remove that barrier? To actually be himself for the first time in years? Was I worth losing if it meant he could be free?

Wynn had sacrificed as much. But Noc... My head throbbed.

It couldn't have been deliberate. He wouldn't do that to me. He *wouldn't*.

Satisfied with my prison, Wynn removed the cuffs from my wrists. "He used you for his own purposes."

"Liar." Noc was cunning and dangerous. Yes, his curse consumed his focus and likely had made it difficult for him to see through the Gyss's trap of words. But to use me? Never.

Voice soft, Wynn shook his head. "Whatever he told you, whatever you thought you found, it was all fake. He won't come for you."

A breath caught in my chest. Wynn was wrong. I had to hold on to what little piece of life I'd found outside Hireath.

"I'll give you some time to adjust." He stood and moved toward the doorway.

With a slow but definitive groan, the thick slab of wall closed behind him, and for the first time since spying Wynn in the ruins, I screamed.

The sharp wail rang through the room, shaking the chains and echoing endlessly around me as the walls of my prison crept closer. Jagged edges ripped my already tattered insides, and a heavy fist wrenched my heart tight.

Noc.

———————◆———————

Noc was a constant in my dreams. An immovable force I couldn't escape. The feel of his skin on mine. The burning need to bury my head in his chest again. His stare leaving marks along my skin. Sleep was a reprieve because it meant I got to see him. Got to live in the delusion that I was his and he was mine. But waking... Waking was designed to break even the strongest spirit. Reality clawed at my fragile peace and yanked me back into despair.

Eyes forced open, all I could see was him, and the agony started all over again.

I slept in short intervals and quickly lost count of how many times I gained and lost Noc all over again. Just as I realized I was sleeping, my mind revolted and the glaring truth of his absence shocked me into heart-wrenching awareness.

Not to mention true sleep was next to impossible, thanks to a beast stationed on a small, metal perch fastened to the ceiling. Pear-shaped and covered in tiny green feathers, it sat without moving—but it was far from quiet. A staticky, dissonant sound constantly streamed from its trumpetlike beak. Just low enough to be mistaken for white noise. Just loud enough to scrape along my nerves and steadily drive me insane.

Wynn would try anything to subdue me. He didn't know what kind of fight he had coming.

Somewhere amidst that, I tried in vain to summon Onyx. Hand splayed out, I focused on the symbol and willed every ounce of remaining power I had into that tree. Pictured Onyx's lithe body. His ink-black fur and explosion of peacock feathers. He could get me out. He could save me. But with the flux of power came an instant reprimand, a stabbing and violent pain reminiscent of needles hammering into my bones. Whatever Wynn had done to enchant this room, it worked.

Food appeared on sterling silver platters, carried in by a low-level Havra, a beast with gangly limbs and the ability to materialize through walls. I didn't dream of eating it. There was no telling what kind of drug Wynn could have slipped in there. So the Havra would wait for an hour or so, and then disappear with the platter, food entirely untouched.

The buzzing continued. Sleep came and went. So did Noc.

I didn't know how much time had passed until Wynn visited me again.

Marble slab groaning open, Wynn stepped through the threshold into my hell. Casting a quick glance between me and an untouched tray, he shook his head.

"It's been two days. You need to eat."

Crinkled white cotton tunic. Loose-fitting trousers. Black boots. He wore *approachable* like a garment—except I knew it was all an act.

When I didn't respond, he sank to the floor, kicking his feet out in front of him. "We need to discuss your future here."

"I'm not interested." I met his gaze with as much ire as I could summon. Staring him down was all I had left.

He flexed his hands before settling them in his lap. "Here's the deal—you're living on borrowed time. The woman who placed the hit doesn't know you're here. If she did, she'd demand your head, and I wouldn't be able to deliver you to her, what with the Myad deeming you worthy. You might be a criminal in the eyes of the court, but your spirit says otherwise."

"The only criminal here is you."

"That's exactly my point." The vibrant Charmer's symbol on the back of his left hand taunted me. "The spell requires a fallen Charmer. If not you, then it's me. She's tired of waiting, and I refuse to be her fallback."

My aching muscles protested as I pushed myself into a sitting position. "What, you're protecting your own hide? How very courageous of you."

Wynn's eyes flashed. "You don't understand. This is the only way. So I *am* going to charm you, ensuring all of your beasts will be at my command. And if that's not good enough for her... Well, like I said, we'll do away with your Myad, and you will revert to the pitiful state you were in before its blessing. Your death will be painless."

I laughed. Hollow and sharp, the sound skittered around the room like a frightened spider. "You're out of your damn mind. You couldn't charm a human, so now you're trying your hand at a Charmer?"

Nails scraped along his beard. "Not quite. Humans are beyond the realm of taming. Like Zeelahs—all of the magic is bred right out of them."

My lungs came to a standstill.

"That's the theory, anyway." Crossing his ankles, Wynn continued to speak more to himself than to me. "Her spell won't save us from our fate. But our people are in danger, and this is the only way."

I finally found my voice. "Her spell? What are you talking about? And how will taming me protect our people? It's not even possible."

His temple throbbed, and for the first time in years, I saw a glimpse of the man I used to know. "Breaking the bond with my beast shouldn't have been possible. And yet you did it."

My gut churned. "What danger?"

He tilted his head to the ceiling. "We're outnumbered. And after what happened in the First War, with so many beasts slaughtered, they're unwilling to fight. But if I can force them to act, take control of their beasts and protect Hireath, we'll survive. The spell she's relying on, it's too much of a long shot. Bone of a tainted Charmer, blood of an undead prince...these things don't exist."

"Wynn." I scooted closer to him and prayed I could break through to the man who'd once claimed to love me. "Tell me what happened. What's going on?"

"I tried. I really did. If I could've tamed a human, we would've been saved..." When he brought his gaze back to my face, I didn't recognize him at all. Standing, he brushed his hands along his trousers. "But I couldn't, so here we are."

My mind lurched, regurgitating images of the injured man stapled to the wall in Wynn's basement. Dead and soulless eyes. Fluttering, erratic heartbeat. He had moved his chapped lips as if to speak, but nothing more than a wheeze left his lungs.

Was that my fate? First Cruor, and now this?

A cold shell of the man I used to know spoke over his shoulder as he left. "I have Council meetings to attend today. Tomorrow, we work."

Thirty-One

NOC

Two agonizing, never-ending days. That's how long it took us to make it back to Cruor. Every minute that crawled by was a cut against my skin. A reminder of what I'd done. I traveled without stopping, dragging my brothers day and night toward our home. Toward the only glimmer of hope I had at getting Leena back. We didn't sleep. We didn't eat. No one complained. No one said a word. They didn't have to—I felt every ounce of their sorrow, witnessed anger brimming in their eyes, heard every unspoken truth waiting on their tongues.

Leena was family. And that family was gone.

We burst through the double doors of Cruor just as the moon ascended to the heavens. Emelia had spotted our return from her post, and before joining us, she'd sent a series of shadows ahead to spread the word—Noc was home.

When I stormed into the foyer, every assassin was already waiting. Eyes diligently trained on me, they stood without moving. Only Darrien stepped forward, his weary gaze darting from tendril to tendril. My shadows hadn't receded once. We'd already wasted so much time on travel. We needed a plan. I needed to get to Leena before it was too late.

"We have a job." Anger simmered heavily in my chest, but I

forced my voice to remain steady. Even. Assassins sidled in closer with questions brewing in their eyes. "We don't know the exact location of Hireath, only that it's northwest through the Kitska Forest. If we leave now, we should be able to—"

"Wait a minute... Hireath?" The muscles running along Darrien's neck stiffened. "The Charmers' den that has *never* been infiltrated? Who gave us such a dangerous job?"

"I did."

Throughout the foyer, mouths fell open and small gasps sounded above the hearth's crackling fire. Darrien blinked several times before squeezing his eyes shut. "Why?"

Grinding my teeth, I fought to keep control over my building emotions. I needed immediate action from my brethren, not a million questions. The longer this took, the more danger Leena was in.

Kost laid a gloved hand on my shoulder and stared down Darrien. "One of our own was taken. If we don't act quickly, she will likely die."

Die. Leena's stricken expression surfaced in my mind. Anger and agony fought to consume me, but if I was going to rescue her from an impenetrable fortress, I needed to keep my wits. To maintain control.

"Who was taken?" Darrien fingered the leather strap across his chest holding the bow on his back in place. Assassins rustled against the railing, each one eager to know who was missing. Who I was willing to go to war for.

I reached for the ring on my finger and spun it the way she would have. "Leena."

Voices competed against one another, complaints lost in the cacophony of shouts.

"She's not one of us. Why does it matter?"

"She tried to kill Kost!"

"Noc, what has she done to you?"

I slammed my fist against the wall, silencing them all. "Leena is one of us. End of story."

"You raised her?" Darrien crossed his arms. Hard amber orbs unearthed the truth before I even had the chance to speak, and he grimaced.

"No. She is not an assassin. But I love her." The words were out before I could question them. They felt so incredibly right, and the weight in my chest both lessened and intensified. The truth was finally out there, only to be squandered by the reminder that she wasn't here with me to hear it. That my brethren heard my confession first when it should have been her.

Quiet murmurings rolled through the hall. Darrien hissed, running a hand through his curled locks. "Are you suggesting we wage a war simply because you fell prey to a Charmer? What kind of precedent will this set for Cruor? Murdering the people who contracted the hit?" Whispered agreements sounded from a number of assassins, and Darrien grew more confident with their support. "How many contracts will we lose because of this? How will you keep our guild afloat?"

My entire world narrowed to the smirk lingering on his lips and the arrogance twisting his clenched jaw. One wrong move, and I'd end him. "I am your leader, and I'm issuing an order."

He took a careful step toward me, and his eyes narrowed. "And I'd say that's a gross abuse of your power. We may not fear death, but I won't let you lead this clan into a war of your own making. You're nothing but a fool."

Pulse speeding, I sliced an elongated nail down my palm and called on the dormant power in my blood. The power bestowed to me by Talmage and the leaders before him. The power of Zane, first of our kind.

The air in the room disappeared, suffocating the remaining embers of the dying fire. Blood blades rose in unison around me, glistening in the light of the swaying chandelier. The sharp tips angled in Darrien's direction, and shadows crept from my frame to slink along the floor and snare his ankles.

"Remember who you're talking to." Excess blood dripped from my palms to the stone below, a steady cadence that rocked the very foundation of our home.

"You've gone mad." His wild gaze tracked the blades. "You're asking us to risk our lives for some mindless fling."

My hand curled into a tight fist. She wasn't a fling. She was my *only*. Something Darrien couldn't comprehend.

And yet, I couldn't force him or anyone else to fight for something, someone, they didn't know or believe in. Not without using my blood, and something about that action felt...wrong. My gaze drifted to a few of the assassins who'd spoken against me. Some had been warriors in their former lives, but most were just people. Gardeners. Tailors. Artists. Forcing them to fight would be cruel. Something the old me might have done, but Leena had changed all that. She'd brought me to life once again.

My blades melted to a pool at Darrien's feet. "Leave. Start your own guild. Take the members who desire to join you, and get the hell out of my home."

No one moved.

I stepped in close, bringing my nose inches from Darrien. "This is your only warning. Stay if you'd like, but if you ever speak out of turn again, it won't be your picture on the wall next to Talmage. It will be your head."

Straightening my back, I eyed all my brethren.

"This is the only offer of free passage you'll get. Leave now, or consider yourself a permanent member of Cruor. Stay, and help me build something new. If you don't want to take on bounties, don't. If you do, fine. But I'll never force your hand again. Cruor's Oath should be a decision you make, not one I dictate. We'll find a way to survive, because our strength comes from each other." I toed the pool of blood before me, reminding them of the power I could've used—and never would. Not against them.

The old ways were officially over. It was time to start anew.

Silence stretched on for minutes. Then, a flurry of movement and shadows exploded around us. Darrien stormed from the building, sweeping out onto the lawns with enough darkness in his wake to make up half the guild. The rest of my brethren remained in place, cautious smiles pulling at their lips.

Emelia approached me from the foot of the stairs. "I'm not sure what this means for the guild in the long run." She glanced back to the top of her stairs where her twin brother, Iov, leaned against the railing. Born together, died together, and born again—together. "But I always thought it was stupid to pretend that I didn't fear death— for myself or those I love."

I nodded once to her and the rest of the assassins lingering along the staircase, fidgeting and waiting for guidance. Looking to the oil painting on the mantel, I could've sworn Talmage was smiling.

Iov slunk down the stairs to stand by his sister, dark feathered hair teasing his forehead, and offering the broadest grin I'd ever seen. "What's the plan, boss?"

I took a steadying breath and faced what remained of my family. "First, we need to find Hireath."

THIRTY-TWO

LEENA

I'd once thought the shadows around Noc were the ultimate void, but the sheer whiteness of my cell, the total absence of color, was even more chilling. It was impossible not to cry. And yet, I couldn't give up. Even if I died in this prison, I'd never let Wynn use me. Turning my focus back to my chains, I set to work on the screws. I'd been twisting them nonstop since he'd left me, and while only one had shown the tiniest movement, it kept my hands busy. Gave me purpose and direction.

I will make it through this.

The constant droning from the bird beast continued. His cacophonous call made it hard to focus, to *think*. But I could move. Turn a screw a little at a time.

The far wall shuddered, and the slab of stone leading to freedom cracked open. Morning. I stopped toying with the shackle and hid my hands. Disgust rippled through me as Wynn closed the door behind him.

He frowned, stepping across the room to crouch in front of me. "You've been crying." Thick fingers wiped salt water from my cheeks.

My stomach twisted, and I jerked my chin away. "Don't touch me."

He dropped his hands. "You know how tamings go. Every beast is different. I might have to touch you to win you over. There will be some trial and error, of course."

Wynn snapped his fingers, and the Havra who served me food appeared with a white cloth in her hands. Four blue eyes blinked at me, and she placed the fabric at my feet before disappearing.

Alone. We were alone.

With his weight on the balls of his feet, Wynn leaned over to unlock the shackle on my ankle. "Change."

Momentary hope crested in my chest. *Freedom.* I lunged without thinking, bolting straight for the sealed door. Wynn snared my ankle with his hand, and I tumbled to the floor. Rolled onto my back and kicked him square in the jaw. Fury burned in his eyes. He pinned me and smacked my temple so hard my ears rang. Heat settled across my cheek, and he grimaced. Flexed his hand twice before dragging me back toward the chains.

"That was stupid. Change. Now."

Bile soured my tongue. "No."

"Now, Leena. Unless you'd prefer my help."

He wanted me bare. Humiliated. Completely destroyed so it would be easier to break what little resolve I had left. He'd test out every emotion necessary to try to get me to submit.

He would not win.

Brown eyes narrowed with intrigue as I stripped, piling my clothes on the floor. I tried to be fast. Tried to give him as little time as possible to take in my flesh, but his piercing stare couldn't be altered, and the burn along my breasts remained long after I'd donned the white shift dress.

"Good."

If running won't work... Before he could read the shift of my weight, I barreled into him, raining punches down on his face.

Prayed for at least one solid connection. My fist glanced off the hard bridge of his nose, and he trapped my wrists with thick hands. One hard twist, and my muscles gave. I caved beneath his grasp, weak from lack of food and sleep.

"You really should stick to summoning beasts."

"Fuck off," I spat out.

He reattached the shackle on my ankle and pulled a second one out from under the bed, securing it to my other foot. "Let's get to it. We'll start with the obvious. If you feel any inkling to submit, I'd suggest you do so early."

Ravenous light showered from his frame, reaching out toward me and licking up my exposed legs. I hated that something so beautiful felt all too violating. Transforming into a statue, he sat mere inches from me. Palms up toward the heavens. Chin angled to his chest.

His light turned smothering, flattening me against the smooth wall of the cell. My mind rewound to the first time I'd seen Wynn tame a creature. His light had been so entrancing. A reminder of the sun-kissed afternoons we used to spend lying in the open wheat field beside our cottage. When had his buttery, yellowed-white light shifted to something so stark? It used to be so calm. Soothing. Now…it was almost sinister. As if something had tainted the purity of his color.

Burying the memory, I tipped my head to the ceiling. "Either you've gotten worse, or you've forgotten how to tame."

His light slashed against me. Heated welts rose to the surface of my forearms. Still, he didn't speak. We sat like that for hours. Me, entirely unaffected by his attempts. Him, burning like the center of the sun. His light was all wrong. Intense from sheer power, but completely devoid of love. Devotion. He was trying too hard to snuff out my last shred of humanity with false brilliance.

Sleep teased my senses, but the incessant static from his beast would not allow a respite. So my mind wandered where it shouldn't have—right back to Noc.

My chest heaved, and Wynn twitched. A misperceived sign of submission. Closing my eyes, I rested my head against the wall. The gaping hole in my chest was endless and ribbed with bloodstained daggers. Being with Noc in Nepheste's Ruins was unlike anything I'd ever experienced. We had merged. A true and real connection. A bond stronger than anything I had with my beasts. With any other person.

But he hadn't listened. His actions had brought me here. And the very thing that gave me hope was now a snaking, angry current pulling me under. I was drowning in him.

Tears squeezed through my tightly pressed lids. I wanted to rip my mind apart and remove every image of both these men who'd hurt me so badly.

The sudden absence of light brought me back, and I peeled my eyes open. Before I could react, Wynn pulled handcuffs from his belt and locked my wrists together. Guiding them above my head, he attached them to a metal hook in the wall.

I jerked against him, glaring. "Was that really necessary?"

He snarled back, "I can't have you fighting me. You've done enough of that already." Reaching for his other hip, he pulled a curved blade from a worn leather sheath. Polished clean, the silver edge taunted me.

As if the blade wasn't threatening enough, he pulled another vial out of his pocket. Viscous liquid glowed an eerie scarlet, and he doled a small amount over the knife. It sank into the silver and left an iridescent gleam. "Uloox venom. I'm sure you know what it does."

My blood ran cold. Uloox venom was downright lethal. That damn poison would cause my muscles to seize and cloud my mind. Between that and the jarring static still pealing through my cell, there was no hope of holding on to my thoughts. And I had no way of stopping him.

He reignited his lure, and the stone walls reverberated with the sudden influx of light. The carving knife glimmered.

"When she found the spell for saving our kind, she also discovered a number of forbidden texts. Scraps of dark practices and magic left behind from some of our exiled brethren. Bloodletting to weaken the resolve—a reminder that the world outside the realm is a cruel and unfair thing. It was used to tame a monster from Kitska Forest." Eyes devoid of emotion, he met my gaze head-on. "Certainly a crime, but I'm running out of options. Let me in, and this will all be over."

I bucked against him, but his fingers were shackles of their own, and the blade sliced my skin. A perfect half-moon cut. I screamed and jerked my chained wrists. But the venom was fast, and soon my limbs were lead. My cries fell on deaf ears, and Wynn made another cut an inch above the first. A torrent of pain arced through me, burning in heated waves up my legs and pushing water through my eyes.

Again and again his blade pierced my flesh.

Vision swimming in a series of stars, I prayed for darkness. For my subconscious to break and pull me under. But when it was tantalizingly close, when stars turned to black dots and my fractured sight slipped into indeterminable swirls, Wynn stopped.

"I can't have you passing out. No one has ever tamed an unconscious beast." He summoned a Poi from his unending network of beasts. Without prompting, the Poi moved to my weeping wounds, and a scratchy tongue methodically coated every nick. Once done, the Poi sat back on his haunches and looked up at Wynn. Sighing, he leaned over my leg again. "Whenever you're ready, Leena."

The second time around was worse. Agony crushed me, shattering my ribs and making it impossible to breathe without sobbing.

Wynn's voice seemed to drift from a thousand miles away—and yet in this moment, he was so monstrously close. "Why don't we try a different tactic? Maybe associating pain with a memory, a reason for abandoning your ties to this world. How about…Noc?"

His name spoken aloud was harsher than the blade against my skin. Shuddering, I tried to press myself into the wall. To disappear completely.

Wynn paused. "What a selfish thing for him to do."

Selfish. The venom clouded my mind and whispered about things I didn't want to believe.

Wynn picked up the blade again. The tang of iron skirted through the air. "Is it worth staying here? With this pain? There is no agony in the realm. You've been there. You know."

Noc. It was so wrong and so right to still want him, to still hope that we had a chance.

Wynn murmured, "Leave him behind, Leena."

My back arched into the wall. *Noc.* In my mind, I reached for him. Spoke to the shadows lingering in the recesses of my brain in the hope he'd hear me. I cursed him for—willingly or not—using me as a bargaining chip and then begged him to come back and prove everything I'd seen wrong. There weren't any dark corners in my chamber, though, and the barriers of Hireath would make it impossible for him to find me.

"You've still never wished on a Gyss, am I right?" Wynn set his blade to the side. "Your knowledge is all theory, not firsthand experience. Did you know they don't *have* to speak in riddles? That sometimes the payment is as simple as the wish?"

I tried to pull away from that taunt, even as I felt compelled to ask, "What are you saying?"

He signaled his Poi to attend to my wounds. I barely registered the lick of the beast's tongue. Leaning closer, Wynn brushed hair away from my face. "I'm saying there's a chance Noc knew he'd be sacrificing you. Just like I did. After all, it was your life or his."

Fresh tears fell from my eyes, and I fought against my heaving chest. "What?"

My thoughts slipped through my fingers like water. I couldn't hold on to a solid memory. He'd promised he wouldn't use the Gyss against me, hadn't he? He wouldn't have knowingly sacrificed me.

The buzzing intensified, and the burn in my legs crawled higher. Nothing felt right.

"If he didn't kill you, then he'd die. It's the magic behind Cruor's Oath." Wynn pressed his lips into a fine line. "Everyone has their own agenda, Leena. Some are just nobler than others."

The poison settled thick in the crevices of my brain, but even so, I could hear truth in Wynn's words.

Noc. He'd told me that the oath still needed to be fulfilled, but he hadn't told me about the cost. He might've been willing to sacrifice some bits for my life, but this? He wouldn't give up his own head in exchange for mine. I'd pegged him as dangerous from the moment I set foot into his house. And yet I'd trusted him, fallen for him, and forgotten just how deadly he could be.

"He was nothing more than a murderer for hire, and you were the easiest mark he ever saw." Wynn's fingers fell to my chest, and he rested his palm against my heart. Searing fire spiderwebbed outward from his fingers, burning through my veins in an attempt to cleanse the very thought of love.

I was spinning. Or maybe that was the room. The ceiling and walls converged and separated.

Wynn moved his hands to cup my face. "Let go."

Rivers spewed from my eyes, salt water crashing against the marble. Broken. I felt so *broken.*

"That's it, Leena."

I'm trying so hard, Noc. I want him to be wrong, but it just sounds so right. I'm lost. So lost.

"Leena. Let go."

No.

Wynn's light flared, and the smallest pricks of warmth ignited in the column of my spine. A glimmer of a world without this shattering, rupturing pain.

Wynn smiled, and darkness swam before my eyes as blood loss finally pitied me. Right before the room winked out of existence, I could've sworn I heard Noc bellow my name.

THIRTY-THREE

NOC

The Kitska Forest worked against us. Even with the shadows on our side, we couldn't avoid the watchful eyes of untamable monsters. Their guttural howls were a haunting ballad that never ended; one screeching call grating along bone bled into another. A phantasmal mist hid thick vines crawling across the mossy earth. Thorns snagged our trousers, tearing through fabric and nicking flesh. No one complained, but it made progress slow. Darkness, which we normally welcomed, was steeped in danger. Only the occasional glimmer of moonlight sliced through the knit treetops, a dim and filtered glow.

The farther northwest we traveled from Cruor, the worse it got.

Kost flanked my right, and a strange chill clung to his breath. "Nothing yet."

Nothing other than the terrors of the forest, and Leena's pained face consuming me. I could've sworn I'd felt her earlier in the day. Nothing more than a twinge, a searing and sudden twist of agony, but it was there.

The connection vanished within a breath, and the startling lack of her presence had shattered my control. I'd torn deep into the woods and followed the low-pulsing heartbeat in the hope of finding her.

Hours later, we were lost. Twenty-five assassins strong, and we still couldn't navigate the enchanted forest. I had contemplated bringing all fifty remaining members, but Kost advised I leave some behind in case Darrien returned. Or, in case we didn't.

The dark wood had a heart and mind of its own. It was a perilous, endless maze, but it was the only way to Leena and the hidden city. Brushing aside a dead branch, I kept my voice level. "Hireath is northwest."

Kost shot me a sidelong glance. "It would help to know more."

Coils of shadows burst to life in front of us, and as one, our brigade came to a halt. Calem manifested from the dark, chest heaving and running his hands through his dampened locks, retying his bun. "I think I found something."

Hope detonated in my chest. "What is it?"

Calem grimaced. "I'm not sure." He extended one hand to show me a trail of receding red marks. "I ran into something."

"Take me there."

Calem turned on his heels, leading the way around monstrous boulders and dense trunks. He had more tears in his clothing than the rest of us, and lines of blood smeared along exposed portions of skin.

"It's here." He kept his voice low, as if that would somehow keep the lurking monsters from attacking. Pointing to nothing more than continued darkness and wood, he slowed to a careful stop. The space before us appeared no different, just a repeated scene of clambering trees, darkness, and vines. "Look at the mist."

Dropping my gaze to the forest floor, I studied the swirling vapor at our ankles. Milky-white and thick with the scent of dirt. I stepped forward, and the mist lazily shifted with the momentum of my step, crawling over snarling roots until it curiously crashed into nothing.

I blinked. "A wall?" My assassins stirred, peeking around our shoulders to get a glimpse at nothing.

"Watch." Flexing his hands, Calem shrouded one arm in shadows and left the other exposed. He rammed them forward and screwed his eyes shut. A sharp hissing trilled through the air, and I winced. When Calem pulled his hands back, both were covered in shiny red welts. "I was hoping we'd be able to sneak through." He stared at the curling darkness clinging to his fingertips. "I was wrong."

Kost picked up a twig and shoved it through the invisible wall. Nothing happened. "Curious."

Ozias grimaced. "This has to be the way."

"Make camp here," I said, pressing my back firmly against a tree so I could study the barrier. "I know it's not ideal, but we've yet to come across a clearing."

Urgent whispers snaked through the group in hushed undertones. Emelia crept to the front of the line, dark eyes skittering left and right. "I'll watch for danger. If I could have one or two others assist me, we can take turns guarding our own."

"I'll help," Calem said.

Emelia pivoted in place, and her black ponytail swept the air behind her. "Great."

Kost spoke to Emelia, but his gaze lingered on my face. "I'll help in a moment."

I nodded. "Thank you."

With her face angled toward the interlocking branches above, Emelia leaped. Tree leaves floated to the ground with the force of her jump, and she launched around branches, finding height and a point of lookout with lethal precision. Calem did the same, disappearing without words.

"All right, let's clear away some of these vines so we have a place to rest." Ozias clapped his hands together and ushered the assassins to his side.

Kost took a small step toward me. "How are you holding up?"

"Not great." I gripped the back of my neck and stared at the wood. Leena was out there. Somewhere. And I couldn't get to her. "How did this happen? How the hell did we end up here?"

Kost adjusted his glasses, avoiding my gaze. "You fell in love. That's how we ended up here. At least she's alive, Noc. It's not like before. You have a chance to be with her..." His voice trailed off. Beside us, assassins worked to uproot vines from the depths of the earth. Occasionally, they'd snap a root in half, showering the ground in a vile purple substance. Their grunts punctuated the silence that stretched between us.

"I'm sorry, Kost."

His shoulders tensed. "For?"

"For not reciprocating." My hands fell to my sides. He'd been with me for so long. Too long, he'd waited for something I couldn't give, something I'd refused to see, only to watch as I fell for someone else. "After you got sick the first time, I didn't dream of expressing myself at all. I think that made me blind. What I've put you through... It's not right."

Finally meeting my gaze, he offered a strained smile that did nothing to mask the hurt. "You did what you had to. The sacrifice you made to keep me alive... No one has ever done something like that for me. Your love is complex, Noc. Leena is fortunate to have it."

A lump formed in my throat. If my emotions were complex, then Kost was a riddle I didn't have the dexterity to solve. Had timing been different, had my curse never come into play, perhaps I would have found myself enjoying an entirely different puzzle. "I love you, too, Kost."

"I know." He cleared his throat to hide the dip in his tone. "We're brothers, and your curse is gone. I'm so glad."

I pushed off the tree and wrapped him in a hug. He smelled of mint and leather, and even though he stiffened against me, I couldn't let go. We'd been through so much. For decades, I'd kept my feelings beneath a layer of ice, and now I could finally tell him everything. *Show* him. I hoped he could feel it. I hoped he understood what he meant to me. What he'd always mean to me. My grip tightened.

Slowly, Kost melted, and he pressed his hands against my back. Voice thick, he spoke in a whisper. "Thank you."

"Don't thank me. I didn't do anything." I released him, and he stepped back, a slight flush to his cheeks.

"You've done everything—and then some." Idle hands smoothed his vest, and he looked away. "I'm going to help Emelia. I'll let you know if we see anything."

And with that, he disappeared.

Sighing, I went back to leaning against the tree and staring at the hidden wall. Mist plumed at the base and crawled upward. The surrounding air rattled like mucus trapped in lungs, and I shivered. If I were in the business of erecting barriers, I'd block out the Kitska Forest, too. Cruor technically resided in the enchanted wood, but we were close enough to the edge that we only experienced the occasional disturbance. Nothing like this.

A shrill wail screeched in the distance, and there was no escaping my thoughts of Leena. Of the beast realm and the quiet love she showed all of her creatures, regardless of their abilities and subsequent consequences.

Consequences. My fingers brushed against Winnow's bronze key in my pocket, and I hesitated. Even if she'd been the conduit, she wasn't responsible for what had happened. The fault was all mine. I held out the key. My last tie to Leena. A groan much warmer than the errant calls pealing through the night scraped through the air, and my Gyss appeared at my feet.

I didn't expect to see you any time soon. She pressed her arms to her chest and studied me with guarded eyes. *I'm not responsible for the payment.*

Slumping to the ground, I rested my hands on my knees. *I know.*

She tilted her head, some of the unease escaping her frame. *Then what do you want? I can't give you another wish. Not for six months.*

Reaching out my palm, I beckoned to Winnow. She was more important to me than any of my possessions because Leena had gifted her. *Comfort. You're here for comfort.*

Sadness touched the corners of her eyes. She floated toward me, her wispy tail bleeding through foliage as she went, and she nestled into my hand.

Despite everything, it was because of Winnow that my curse was gone. That I was able to embrace Kost and express my devotion. That I could acknowledge my love for Leena without fear of losing her. As dangerous as Winnow's magic was, it was the very thing that had saved me.

Winnow and Leena. Together.

For a while, we simply sat in silence and stared at the wall. Her tail was a different kind of mist, a gentle warmth rolling down the lines of my future, and my eyes grew heavy. I hadn't slept in days. Leena made it impossible. Every minute of every day was spent devising a way to save her. To prove that none of this was intended.

I'd told her about my curse, and she'd witnessed the darkness of that firsthand. It wouldn't be a stretch for her to believe I'd give up anything to rid myself of that.

She'd be wrong, but it wouldn't be hard.

Rough bark from the tree scratched the back of my neck. *Leena.* The weight of her absence smothered my lungs. At some point, Winnow left my palm. The wetness of her touch faded, but the door to the realm never groaned. Peeling open my eyes, I watched her gliding across the forest floor, cutting through the mist and heading straight for the barrier.

The barrier.

"Winnow, stay back!"

My heart slammed into my throat. My last tie to Leena, burnt to a crisp. I could already imagine the tracks of tears that would mar her beautiful cheeks when I told her.

But Winnow wasn't burnt—she was floating above mist-free dirt with a surprised smile on her face. *Look, Noc!* Twirling in place, she floated back and forth across the barrier, each time her smile growing broader. *I'm a beast. Charmers would never want to hurt me.*

Hope splintered through my heart. *Winnow, how long can you stay outside the beast realm?*

Her eyes lit up. *A long time. I don't require as much recovery as other beasts, and I have a powerful master.*

Long enough to get to Hireath? To find Leena and give her a message?

That depends on where they're keeping her. I don't know Hireath. But I'll try, Noc. I promise.

My pulse raced. *Promise me: If it's too risky, if they find out you're not one of theirs, you'll go back to the beast realm. Leena or not.*

Winnow paused. *After everything, you'd care for me?*

Of course.

A wide smile stretched across her face. *What's the message?*

Tell her I'm coming, and I won't stop trying to reach her.

I only prayed she'd believe me.

With a nod, Winnow turned her back to the barrier and sped away from the darkness of the Kitska Forest in the direction of Hireath.

All I could do now was wait.

THIRTY-FOUR

LEENA

S leep died with the scent of honey, and the sudden, throbbing ache in my chest had me bolting upright. Head swimming, I white-knuckled the sides of the steel cot and steadied my nerves. Dull pain simmered along my legs, and I released the bed frame to peel back the sheets. Countless faint-white scars crisscrossed skin. Lightly, I ran my fingers along the network of ridges. And then I vomited off the side of the bed. The saliva of the Poi hadn't been enough to permanently eradicate the signs of Wynn's torture. Not with him ripping each wound open over and over again.

I stared at the clear mixture of bile seeping across the floor. Hunger had finally made me cave, but I'd barely managed to keep anything other than soup down. Wynn had put me to bed without the shackles on—no doubt thinking me too weak to attempt escape—and I rotated my ankles in tiny circles. Cracks and pops ricocheted off the walls. My knees protested when I stood, but I couldn't dally any longer. Wynn would return. I'd recognized that fleeting glimmer of warmth at the end of our last session, and I didn't want to welcome it back.

Running my hands along the smooth walls, I searched for

hidden seams. Cracks. Secret passages. Anything. The drowning static buzz from the bird beast followed me as I worked, and my already fried nerves threatened to short-circuit entirely.

Between the bed, toilet, and silver anchors along the walls and floors, Wynn had created an inescapable prison. Slumping to the floor in the middle of the room, I fingered the hem of my shift dress. Speckles of dried-on blood dotted the edge, courtesy of Wynn's wandering blade.

I needed to fight back. I couldn't let him win. But between his beasts and his knife, I was sorely outmatched. If I wanted out, I had to catch him off guard. Knock him unconscious, and drag his hand to the magical wall to unlock the door.

I'm too weak. I'd already tried a physical assault, to no avail. He'd always been strong, but now, with my muscles racked by fatigue, he was an immovable force. I needed a weapon. Something to defend myself.

My gaze drifted to the shackle attached to the floor. One screw stood a few inches taller than the rest, thanks to the hours I'd spent loosening it.

Better than nothing. I scooted toward it and started twisting again. Getting more movement out of it the farther it pulled from the floor. Finally, it gave. I tugged it out of its hold and studied the pointed tip. It would have to do.

The cell door scraped along the floor, and I hid the screw in my hand. Wynn stood at the threshold. Beige linen pants. Faded blue tunic bordering on white. Shoeless this time. A reminder I was indeed in his home. He tried so hard to be light. To convince me this was for the greater good—no matter that he wouldn't tell me about the cause.

Reaching for the door behind him, he paused when he noticed the puddle of vomit near the bed. "Not feeling well today?"

When I didn't respond, he poked his head out the crack and called his Havra. She snaked between his legs, tattered rags in hand, and mopped up my mess. Rather than inspect his beast's work, he studied me, as if searching for signs of weakening resolve.

I rolled the screw between my fingers. I wasn't about to give in. When his Havra finished her cleaning and left, he didn't notice that she'd forgotten to close the door behind her. Used to materializing through walls, she probably didn't think twice.

Now is my chance.

"C'mon, Leena." Wynn reached for me, and I lunged. Drove my makeshift weapon into the thick muscles of his neck. Stumbling backward, he cursed and clapped a hand over the screw. Blood leaked between his fingers.

Run.

I bolted for the door, but my muscles shook from lack of food and sleep. I only made it a few steps before Wynn caught me by the arm. My bones threatened to snap beneath his grip, and I tumbled to the floor. He jerked me toward the chains. Thrashing against him, I attempted to knee him in the chest. He responded with a swift punch to my gut, and the wind abandoned my lungs. Body shuddering for air, I wheezed in place on the floor, and he made quick work of shackling me in place.

Thick fingers extracted the screw, and it clattered to the floor. He wiped excess blood off on his tunic, scowling at the shallow wound. "And here I thought I would go easy on you today." Painful breaths stabbed my throat until my chest relaxed. Wincing, I leaned against the wall. Wynn tacked my wrists above my head and once again settled down in front of me. The leather sheath on his hip dominated my vision.

"I saw it, you know." He scratched his beard while studying me. "You gave out at the end. You were almost mine."

I went completely still. He could never know. "You're imagining things."

Reaching for the blade at his side, he frowned. "I don't think so." He coated it with more Uloox venom and ignited his internal glow, kicking on his charm and meeting my gaze head-on. "Ready?"

I didn't have time to answer. The sharp bite of his blade split open my skin, and agony lanced through me. I shrieked with all the force I could muster. In the corner of my vision, I kept the open door in mind. But either the rushing falls backing the tower were too great, or there simply weren't any Charmers to hear. Aside from my crescendo of screams, each one louder with the tinge of raw pain, I heard nothing. And no one came.

I don't know how long I lasted. I just know that at one point, the sound of my voice escaped even my ears, and the steady flow of my tears dried altogether. The static buzz droned on, and the venom settled thick in my veins. I couldn't move. Couldn't think. Couldn't act. I was never getting out. My only option was the curious ball of warm light illuminating Wynn's frame. A solace of sorts. A promise.

I was sick of this room. Of the revolting mixture of lemon and bleach failing to mask metallic blood and bile. I needed out. I needed a way to escape the pain.

"They have us." Wynn's strained voice cracked, as if it were a struggle to utter those three words. "They want our beasts to fight for them, no matter the cost."

His words were a fogged string of nonsense I didn't have the fortitude to dissect. Who had us? We were all here. Safe in Hireath. The venom settled like a fog in my brain. I didn't bother to try to wipe it away.

"We need to fight, but no one wants to leave our sanctuary."

His voice went in and out, one minute glaringly loud and the other muted as if spoken through cotton. The murmurings of a lunatic. Charmers didn't fight. The only time we'd taken up arms had been for the First War, and the casualties had nearly destroyed us. Our pain had been a sign from the goddess Celeste that our creatures were meant to be companions, not weapons. We'd never militarize again.

The world spun, white walls converging with the expanse of the ceiling into a swirling mess of sickening light. Framed by the stone door, a Gyss appeared. One of Wynn's. Wild black hair fanned her shoulders, revealing a smattering of tiny white flowers. She had eyes like the sun. And she looked horrified.

That was odd.

Leena. Faint and hushed.

Did I know that voice? It was painfully familiar. Her shaking timbre cut through the fog and begged for recognition. I'd seen her somewhere before...on the banks of Nepheste's Ruins.

Winnow. It was Winnow.

A hysteric laugh bubbled in the back of my throat. *Not real. She's not real.* I mouthed the words endlessly to bury hope before it even had a chance to breathe.

She pressed her hands to her face, capturing tears with her fingers. *Leena, what do I do?*

Uloox venom was a cruel, wicked thing. Hallucinations of escape when I was on the cusp of giving in. The light in the distance grew in intensity. A tangible and soft promise. I wanted to touch it. It was almost within my grasp.

Winnow dared to pass through the crack. *Tell me what to do. Noc's at the barrier. He can't get through.*

I never wanted something to be true so badly. I clung to it, knowing that when I closed my eyes the illusion would fade. Winnow traded for Wynn. Love for torture. My chest tightened and suffocated my heart.

I indulged her anyway—nothing left to lose. *Visitors need permission from the Kestral. It lives in the sacred tree straddling the river.*

Another deep gash from Wynn's blade, and I speared my lip with my teeth. Winnow swam out of view with the sudden burst of light. Otherworldly warmth chased away every remnant of pain, condemning my agony to a world far away.

Free. I was free—and in the end I didn't care if my limbs were mine to control or someone else's.

THIRTY-FIVE

NOC

Winnow appeared more than a full day later, just as night crept toward dawn. She sped through the barrier, hair wildly dancing behind her, and fell into my open hands. Fresh tears brimmed from her yellow eyes, and her tiny chest heaved. It took me a full minute to speak. A full minute to determine if I wanted to hear what she had to say.

Swallowing hard, I met her gaze. "Tell me."

It's bad. More tears squeezed between her fingers. *He's torturing her.*

Shadows erupted around me, responding to the violence of my fear and fury. I wanted to vanish into them. To slink through the dark and slaughter Wynn. Drain him of blood and watch him beg for his life. I wanted it slow. Painful. And I wanted it now.

Teeth bared, I snarled. *How do I get to her?*

Winnow turned back to the invisible wall keeping me from Leena. *The Kestral is coming. She can lift the barrier.* In the distance, a faint light glimmered through a break in the trees. Too slowly it grew, crawling toward us, until a bird appeared on the other side of the forest.

Wings stretched wide, they barely flapped as the creature glided through the dark. Long tail feathers drooped behind it, and a serene glow stemmed from the core of its paper-white body. Oval blue orbs spied me, and the bird paused at the threshold. Cradling Winnow to my chest, I brought myself inches away from the searing wall.

How does this work? I glanced down at Winnow, but she only shook her head.

I don't know. Leena didn't have a chance to say. I found the Kestral, and she followed me here. She doesn't speak, but I think she understands.

The bird flapped her wings once, and a dust of magic shimmered beneath her. Tilting her head to the side, she waited.

"Please." I pressed my hand against the barrier, ignoring the searing heat. "Take me to Leena. She needs our help."

A soft coo hummed from the back of her throat. She twitched her head from me to Winnow. My Gyss burrowed her head against my chest, hiding her face in the soft fabric of my tunic. I brought my blistering hand away from the wall to stroke her hair.

It's okay, Winnow. You did everything you could.

She only cried.

I'd asked too much of my beast. First by having her remove the curse, second by having her search for Leena. Both tasks she'd executed perfectly, and both times we'd still come up short. If the Kestral wouldn't let us through, we'd find another way. We'd have to.

"Noc, look." Kost appeared beside me, his gaze glued to the now-retreating bird. Clenching my teeth, I raised my hand again to test the wall. And pushed right through. My heart lunged into my throat, and I followed the slow-moving Kestral with my forces in tow.

I wanted to speed through the thinning wood, but the beast floated at a consistently unhurried pace. Agitation mounted in me with every step. With every errant beat of the beast's wings, Leena was being tortured.

As I gripped my hands into fists, my nails bit into my palms.

Blood swelled between the cracks and dripped to my sides, naturally forming slick, hovering blades.

"Noc." Kost placed a hand on my shoulder. "Put those away. We don't want the Kestral to view us as a threat."

It pained me to dismiss them when all I could think about was slitting Wynn's throat. But I did—if only for Leena. Calem and Ozias stayed close on my left, each one occasionally tossing quiet commands to the creeping assassins at our backs. Like me, they kept their shadows at bay. There would be a time to sneak. A time to kill.

The barrier must have acted like a sieve because the air was crisper here. The cursed woods gave way to vibrant, healthy trees that grew to impossible heights the farther we traveled. The dark calls of monsters disappeared entirely, and we were left with a reverent silence, the kind saved for ceremonies before the gods. This was hallowed ground.

Blush dawn light sliced through the trees as we stumbled upon a river. An impossible mixture of green, blue, and orange, it trickled past us, and the Kestral turned to follow it north. The muddy banks were covered in ankle-high plush grass, and sturdy tree roots climbed over the edge to douse themselves in the babbling water.

Eyes tight, I watched the sunlight shift to warmer hues. Too much time. We were losing too much time.

Ozias stepped closer to me. "We'll get her. She'll be safe." His words were steady, but strained muscles ticked along his neck. No matter where I turned, we all wore the same fear. Calem would clasp his hands together only to let them fall by his side. After a minute, he'd start up again, eyes straining for a city we couldn't see. Emelia and Iov shared quiet glances and stuck to my heels. Kost kept clearing his throat. The rest of what remained of my family walked in silence, hushed murmurs occasionally shattering the quiet of the forest.

Every footstep was a hammer nailing in the truth—I had caused this.

Following the curve of the river, we came upon a colossal willow tree. Branches bent at crooked angles from the weight of leaves seeking the forest floor. Roots larger than grown men delved deep into the earth and anchored the tree directly over the river. An arched passageway formed in the base of the smooth trunk.

The gateway to Hireath. The Kestral circled her tree once before nesting in a crook at the point of the arch. This was as far as she'd take us.

Stepping in front of my brethren, I bowed my head. "Thank you."

Soft chirps lilting from her beak, she preened her feathers. Her blue eyes never wavered from mine. Taking a steady breath, I led the way through the archway, picking around lichen-covered roots and slick river stones. I'd sent Winnow back to the realm to keep her safe, but not before she told me the way.

Follow the river. Leena is in Wynn's quarters of the keep.

My nostrils flared. *I'm coming, Leena.*

The moment we passed through the gateway, we called on our shadows. We slunk in a realm of darkness, stalking the river's edge with quiet speed. A distant roaring called. The heavy beat of water crashing over rocks.

Closer. We're getting closer.

Morning ushered in a symphony of bestial cries. Bird screeches chimed in the breeze, and the banks grew heavy with hooved beasts emerging from caves to drink. Their rumbling growls vibrated my bones, but we went unnoticed. The river pooled outward and came flush to a monstrous mountain of pure-white stone. A vast waterfall poured over one of the highest peaks, crashing against the basin in a billowing shower of mist.

As one, we stopped and stared.

A marble castle carved from the mountain beckoned to us. The gargantuan oak and white ash trees surrounding it were laden with houses, and stone homes stood sturdy on the climbing walls of the falls. A few of the larger estates and communal buildings dominated the forest floor with cavernous structures crafted in tree trunks. Charmers milled about, crossing the network of ladders and vines tying the city together, the keep pressed flush against the smooth mountain wall.

Leena.

Gripping my hands into tight fists, I turned back to my brethren. "Let's keep our presence hidden." I rolled my head from side to side, stretching my neck. "We hit the keep first. If she's not there, fan out to the rest of the city."

Emelia stepped forward, gripping the hemline of her tunic. "About that." With one pointed nod, she directed our attention to the guard towers stationed on either side of the lake. Snaking vines crawled over slabs of smooth stone piled high. The flat platforms of the strongholds were littered with beasts of a single make.

Every one of them stared at us.

With heavy talons, they clung to the lips of the towers and speared us with oval black gazes. Their deerlike bodies were as still as statues. Even their impressive wings, the color of the mountain, were taut. I'd passed right over them, but now I saw the twitching. The occasional flick of an ear. Heavy antlers crowned their heads, and they angled their faces toward us, lances at the ready.

"Do you think they can see us?" Calem asked, voice low.

Kost grimaced. "Most certainly."

The closest beast reacted then, its stomach contracting and forcing air up and out of its throat. A deep whistle started low before screeching in a high-pitched tone and stretching on for what felt like an eternity. A second one followed. And a third, until the whole colony of creatures whistled, sharp bugles slicing through the tumbling crash of the falls.

Hireath stilled. Charmers stopped and turned toward the towers.

My brethren cringed. We'd been outed. If we'd been able to rely on our shadows, I had no doubt we could've snuck through the buildings without repercussion. But now... A memory of Leena calling forth three beasts at once flashed before my eyes. There were hundreds of Leenas here, each with arsenals as vast as hers. Some even larger. Some even stronger.

Taking flight, the sentry beasts formed a tight circle over our heads. Fear threaded through my insides. Fear for the lives my family might lose—all for me.

Jaw set, eyes level, I turned to my men. "Go back. Leave the rest of this to me."

No one moved.

I snapped, "That's an order."

Ozias looked past me to the Beast City. "You know damn well we're not going anywhere, so stop trying."

Calem bounced on the balls of his feet. "I know it isn't our forte, attacking straight on like this, but you gotta give us more credit than that."

Enthusiastic nods from the rest. Slowly, I turned to Kost. He didn't meet my gaze. "You already know my answer. Till the end, Noc."

Soft. His words were so soft. Reaching out, I placed a firm hand on his back. "I know."

Green eyes speared me from behind thin lenses, and he righted his tunic before willing the shadows at his fingertips to form blades. "Shall we?"

"No need for subtlety, I guess." I stalked toward the gathering congregation of Charmers and stepped out from the darkness. We manifested in a cloud of black, letting the onyx tendrils of night cling to our wrists and ankles. Blades dipped in ink melded from nothing.

With a careful finger, I slit open my palm and let the blood flow.

THIRTY-SIX

LEENA

Blanketed, comforting warmth. I could stay in this cocoon forever. But there was something odd scratching my brain. A bug skittering around on the grooves and crevices that I couldn't quite catch or kill.

Pillars wrapped in rose vines and blush moondust flowers marked the entrance to the throne room. Wynn had left me on the steps with an order not to move. My limbs obeyed. Even my head locked into place. My mind didn't care much, either.

Charmers passed through the manicured courtyard without acknowledging my presence, too busy with their day-to-day lives to notice a once-exile literally in the heart of their home. I couldn't place any of their faces. It was like peering through a chiffon veil, textured and out of sorts. I knew they were there, could feel their presence and see the outlines of their bodies, but details were lost in the fabric of Wynn's hold.

His quiet voice reverberated through the alabaster halls, momentarily breaking through the cotton in my ears. "I have her."

"Here? Now?" Female, but the tone was foreign to me. "Why isn't she dead?"

Wynn fumbled for words. "The assassin failed to kill her, so I took matters into my own hands. She tamed a Myad."

The woman hissed. "Gods be damned. She's unsuitable?"

"For the moment."

"Explain." Her singular order crashed like a cymbal.

"I've tamed her. She's more formidable than we realized. We could use her. I'm not sure death is necessary—"

"And why is that?"

I wanted to turn my head, to move my chin even a fraction of an inch and get a glimpse of the woman who wanted my head. But Wynn's order held strong. Would I even recognize her? Or had new Council members already come and gone since my days in Hireath?

"Tell me, Wynn, do you still have feelings for her?"

"No." Zero hesitation. "But you need to see what I've done. She's the perfect soldier. If I can do it to her, I can do it to anyone. And that means we'll have an army instead of a foolish spell."

Her voice dropped an octave. "This spell is the only way to save us. But we need tainted bones, Wynn. I'm running out of options, unless you'd like to volunteer."

His voice was tight. "She's under my command. If you still want to proceed with the spell, it will be easy enough for me to force her to relinquish the Myad."

"And if that doesn't work?"

"I'll set up another Charmer to take the fall. But Leena *will* work. I know she will."

Whining bugle calls from the Dreagles stationed atop the sentry towers cut through the air. Everything stopped. Intruders. A first for Hireath.

The once-still city erupted into panicked shouts and jostling feet. We were an army-less people. Protected by our beasts and living in heaven, there was no need to prepare for invasion.

Wynn's voice skirted above the chaos. "Cruor. It has to be."

"I'll find the Council. Now's your chance to show me what she's worth. We can talk about the spell later."

One pair of hurried footsteps took off in the opposite direction, and then Wynn appeared, thick hand wrapping around my wrist. "C'mon."

We moved as one until we reached the open lawn spreading between us and the Kitska Forest. A cloud of black curled around the roots and spread like a disease across the earth. Sickening darkness poisoning our land. It was grotesque and...and...

Beautiful.

The leech on my brain stilled, and for a moment, I could see. Hear. Breathe. Swirling onyx shadows beckoned from the wood, calling me home.

Noc.

As if I'd summoned him, the glittering dark receded, and there he stood. A harbinger of absolute terror and wrath, blood leaking from open wounds on his palms and dripping down his fingers. If I didn't know him, I'm not sure I could have separated the undercurrent of worry in his black gaze from the fury. But it was there. And it was the very thing that made my heart sing.

"Leena." Wynn cupped my face, forcing my gaze to meet his. Soothing white light pulsed from his fingertips, and the chiffon veil pulled tight around my face. "You will obey."

The moment of clarity escaped, taking my thoughts and care with it. "Yes." When I looked back at the looming forces, all thoughts of Noc disappeared. There was only vicious darkness and a man at the helm. The center of it all. Wynn's voice whispered in my mind that it was him or me, and my hands twitched.

It wouldn't be me.

THIRTY-SEVEN

NOC

We were monsters, and the Charmers knew it. A cacophony of groaning doors broke over us, and fractured rainbow light tore through the clearing, each vibrant shade a testament to the color inked into the Charmers' hands. Creatures appeared from the beast realm, and my heart sank. I didn't want to fight them, but there were two things I knew for certain. First, there was no way to beautify war. Innocents would die by my hand. And second, I would condemn every one of them to the afterlife to get to Leena.

Fire sparked in my veins and I stormed forward, teeth bared.

A magnified masculine voice boomed over the frenzy. "Citizens of Hireath, please return to your homes. The Council will protect you."

The sea of bodies parted, and Wynn appeared with seven people in tow, including Leena.

All sights and sounds faded except for her. Gaze hollow and unfocused, she stood limply by his side in loose-fitting linen pants and a flowy blouse. A strong breeze threatened to topple her, and Wynn placed a hand on her shoulder to steady her. She was ethereal in the worst kind of way.

"Wynn!" It was more of a roar than a word.

He angled his chin high. "Welcome to Hireath, Noc. To what do we owe the pleasure?"

Charmers barricaded themselves in nearby buildings, but they kept their windows thrown open. Heads peeked through curtains and surveyed the standoff. Wynn sauntered a few more steps forward and tugged Leena along. Behind him, six Charmers remained in place. The Council.

I looked directly to them. "I'm here for Leena."

A few curious glances were shared among them, but no one spoke.

Wynn glowered. "How did you get past the barrier?"

"Give me Leena, and we'll leave in peace." Not before I turned his insides into a meal for the monsters in the Kitska Forest, but details were details.

"Leena doesn't want to leave." Wynn glanced at her. "Tell them."

Leena's broken voice carried across the clearing. "I'm fine. Please go."

"Leena..." Her name burned my tongue, and I dropped my hands to my sides.

"She's not herself," Kost whispered. His fingers twitched, and a dark blade inched closer to his palm.

That much I could see. I might have scarred her beyond repair, broken her last chance at believing in trust, but even when she was furious or hurt or happy, there was always a light burning behind her eyes. Now, her gaze was blanched. A milky fog of what it used to be.

Sheer hatred ravaged my heart, and I dug my feet into the soft grass, ready to pounce. "What have you done to her?" It took time for a Charmer to call forth a beast. I had seconds, maybe less, to end his life before a creature arrived. Assuming he hadn't already summoned one.

"She wants to return to Hireath and live among her people. Would you take that from her?"

His words briefly rooted me in place. What if he was right? What if I put something into motion that—

Calem barked out a laugh. "Does that silver-tongued bullshit work often for you? It must if her own people can't see what you've done."

Errant grumbles snaked from the lips of the Council.

Calem. He nodded at me once before crouching low into his heels. Ready. He was always ready to fight. I wasn't much for prayer, but in that moment, I hoped the gods were listening. I hoped they'd spare my brothers.

"I'll give you one more chance. Give. Me. Leena." The dark part of me hoped Wynn wouldn't comply, only so I didn't need an excuse to carve him into a million pieces.

The gods, it seemed, were on my side. Wynn placed a possessive hand on the back of her neck. "No."

Rational thought shattered, and I exploded. The Council didn't bother to move.

Driven by the desire to murder Wynn, I didn't stop to think why. I streaked forward, crashing into him in a snarling mess of shadows and blood and rage. I was immediately thrown back. My spine cracked against the earth, and I slid across the clearing to the feet of my brethren.

There, lingering in the folds of every Council member's putrid silver cloaks stood an army of Asura. A single milky eye shuttered close, and Wynn's beast sighed. While Calem had never gotten Leena's Asura to ten, she had shared what would've happened if all those eyes closed.

Flanking my right, Kost barked out orders. "Count the eyes to determine the remaining hits necessary to break the shield. Do it quickly!"

We never got the chance.

A rainbow of colors shone from the Council members' hands and mixed together into a blinding prism, making it briefly impossible to see. Invisible doors creaked open, and beasts crawled from the realm to stand before their masters. The air shivered, danger rolling heavy and electric off their bodies. Seven massive catlike monsters pawed to the front of the lines, sharp claws piercing the earth and rumbling growls simmering in the back of their throats.

Leena's voice drifted through my mind. *The Myad is one of ten legendary feline beasts.* The quake of power snapping against my skin couldn't have belonged to anything else. She might have been the only one with a Myad, but these other beasts were just as dangerous.

Flexing my hands, I eyed the white one at the head of the pack. Wynn's. Violet and emerald wings sprouted from its front and hind legs, and the scaled plates of its chest glistened with each echoing breath.

"Good luck getting to us." With the stroke of his forefinger on Leena's jaw, Wynn gave her a disastrous order. "Summon the Myad. Prove to the Council you'll fight for your home."

She didn't hesitate. Empty gaze trained on my heart, she splayed out her hand and called to her most prized beast. Even now, in the face of battle, the dark fury of the Myad stilled my chest. Following his master's stare, his streaming blue eyes were riveted on me.

In that moment, I realized we were fucked.

I couldn't kill him. I couldn't murder the very thing she'd worked so hard to achieve.

Wynn waved his hand. "Raven, if you'd please."

One of the Council stepped forward, her crushed-copper hair

sweeping across her face. Sunken yellow eyes slid to her cat, a slender slate-gray beast with twin tails tipped in arrowheads, and she let out a bored drawl. "Mika, end this quickly."

The cat shuddered, and every hair on its body rose to the heavens and solidified into sharpened points. It shuddered again, and an exact replica of Mika shimmered to life beside her.

And another.

And another.

Perfect copies littered the clearing, and we were surrounded. The other legendary felines sauntered in behind them, crouching low to the ground and waiting for the opportune moment to pounce.

"Enjoy the true strength of Hireath." Wynn dismissed us with a wave, and the cats lunged.

I barely had time to dodge. The first copy streaked past me, and I dropped to the ground while slicing a blade upward. Flesh tore open, but instead of showering me in a spray of blood and guts, the beast disappeared into a puff of gray smoke. Another sped toward me, and I crossed my forearms to block its gnashing fangs. Teeth skewered my arms and I bit back a cry, writhing in place under the weight of the monster. My blood responded. Fine blades sprung from my wounds and scraped into the soft flesh of its throat. Once last gurgle, and it too vanished into mist.

Kost, Calem, and Ozias dashed toward me, and we pressed our backs together. Blood along my arm stretched and coagulated, forming a deadly weapon from elbow to fingertips. The more they ripped me apart, the easier it was for me to attack.

Calem swiped a blade at a copy, only to have his hands shredded by its fur. A gaping wound marred Kost's calf. He grimaced, studying the furling shadows of our brethren. Between their enraged roars and the earsplitting yowls of beasts, it was impossible to tell who was winning.

"Stay together," Ozias growled, and pummeled the face of a copy. With slick blades wedged between his fingers, his shadow knuckles ripped through the beast at his feet. But his skin shredded upon impact, too, and couldn't heal fast enough before the next beast pounced.

Kost willed the darkness to form a slender rapier. Gripping it in his right hand, he speared the neck of the nearest feline. Safer than Ozias's approach, but it took a considerable amount of energy and power to contain shadows in one form for so long.

A copy hurtled toward me, and I sent a flurry of blades directly into its open mouth. Smoke leaked from the wounds, and the beast winked out of existence. Peering through the throng of cats, I spied the watching Council. With the Asuras' shields still in full effect, they didn't bother to distance themselves from the carnage.

Dodging another beast, I shouted above the snarls, "The only way we can stop this is if we get to them!"

My brothers dipped low in their stances in preparation for the next round of attack. The legendary beasts slunk around the copies. Calculating. Waiting while we fought off illusion after illusion, our defenses weakening and our muscles giving. Then they'd strike. Lethal and fast.

Darting closer to the Charmers, I sent a wave of blades aimed directly at Wynn.

Only one smashed against his shield, sending a spiderwebbing ripple in the energy field before the surface returned to normal. Flinging themselves before the Council, the copies willingly abandoned their pursuit of the assassins to take blades to the gut, and the rest of my arsenal disappeared.

Ozias followed suit, peeling off behind me to get a better angle at Wynn. But as he wound his arm back to unleash a fistful of blades, one of the legendary felines intervened. Russet-brown with bone spikes along its spine, it slammed into Ozias and pinned him to the earth.

"Ozias!" I lunged, but a series of copies lashed out. Smooth claws ripped into my thighs, and I whirled in place, swiping my elongated forearm blade along their hides. Smoke escaped and I was free, but not fast enough to get to Ozias.

Devil-red eyes burned bright, and the beast reared its head back, teeth exposed. There was no saving him from those yellow fangs.

Sounds faded; my heart was in my throat as I ran.

A sudden fracture of light cracked in the space around Ozias, and the beast recoiled.

Jax emerged, lumbering beside Ozias with ire in his glowing white gaze. He'd come of his own accord, wasting no time in sinking his teeth into the beast and tossing it back into the throng of monsters.

As one, the Council's eyes widened. I sent another barrage of blades at Wynn's face. This time, two struck home.

Six more to go.

Wynn's white legendary feline emerged, running side-by-side with the russet demon, and they launched at Jax. Volcanic walls shot from the ground, sizzling the air with their red-hot veins, and he let out a roar from the pit of his belly. The legendary beasts smashed into the rock and hissed, leaping aside as the smell of burnt hair singed the air. Ozias slipped behind one of the walls. With his blind side protected by Jax's defenses, he began attacking another brigade of beasts.

We were making a dent in the copies. Their numbers started to dwindle to the point where I could breathe for a moment before a fresh one lunged. Kost and Calem worked back to back, facing off with a liquid-blue legendary beast that had snaked through with the ease of water.

The beast slipped through their defenses, and thick claws sank into Kost's thigh. His shout cut through the backdrop of cries, and I froze. Calem yanked him back out of reach, but not far enough. The water legendary crouched. Launched into the air.

The ground rumbled, and a vein of red streaked beneath my feet, rushing toward Calem and Kost. A rock wall exploded from the earth. The legendary crashed into it, his watery skin erupting into steam. With a violent yowl, he retreated and slunk back into the throng of copies.

"Jax, there!" I turned to see Ozias pointing at another fallen assassin. Jax glanced between me and Calem and Kost, and then focused his power across the clearing. Another one saved. Ozias gave him a proud grin before lunging back into battle, taking down what beasts he could while keeping an eye on Jax.

And the rest... Not all of us were warriors before the transition, and it showed. It was one thing to kill with the element of surprise, and another thing entirely to wage a war.

Gone. So many were gone. Eleven men and women lay strewn about, bodies snared in tree roots or beaten senselessly into the earth. The fields were more red-brown than green, and the slush of our steps in the grass had little to do with the mist of the falls.

"Watch out," Emelia shouted, diving to her left to spear a copy at my rear. Smoke crawled up the edge of her glittering halberd, and she offered me a fierce grin before spinning on her heels to parry another monster. Iov flanked her side, and he buried his ax without fault into the forehead of a copy.

I grunted my thanks before shooting another flurry of blades. Another showering of smoke as copies faded. A few snuck through and battered against Wynn's shield, and four eyes closed.

Two left. My gaze slid past him to Leena. Motionless aside from her eyes, she followed the path of her Myad across the battlefield.

Crouching low into the ground, I prepared to sprint toward Wynn, delivering a series of blades along the way so when the barrier broke, I would already be on top of him.

I never made it.

The sick splattering of claws embedding in flesh sang through the air. A few feet away, Iov dropped to his knees. With a heavy roar, a beast retracted its nails from his shattered shoulder and reared back to finish the job.

"No!" Emelia shrieked louder than the falls. Gripping her halberd with two hands, she propelled herself forward and impaled the beast's side.

Instead of mist, blood poured to the earth. The force of the blow knocked the cat to the ground, and the remaining copies shattered.

Leaving Mika pinned, Emelia retreated to her wounded brother. "Iov. Iov, no. Iov..." Tears bisected her face. A dribble of blood trickled from his mouth to his chin, but he managed a shaky wave as he slumped into her body.

"Mika!" Raven bolted from her place behind Wynn, rushing to her beast's side and casting the air around her into deep-red light. The rest of the Council froze, their beasts slinking back to their masters. Instead of returning to the Council's side, Raven and Mika vanished. Sanctuary. The beast realm would provide.

My assassins didn't have that luxury. I couldn't raise them again.

Rage fueled me, and my blades flew true, crashing into Wynn's shield and breaking it entirely. He stumbled, wild eyes spearing me from across the clearing, and I couldn't help the manic grin tugging at my lips. "Got you."

Wicked and dark, he laughed. "Not yet."

Barreling toward me with otherworldly speed, seeming to burst from the shadows themselves, the Myad launched himself into the air. Wind pulsing under his wings, he gained momentum and targeted my chest, fangs and claws readily poised. He must have thought I was aiming at Leena, because nothing but sheer rage burned in his eyes. It was the kind of fierce loyalty reserved for protecting his own.

Time slowed to a standstill as I realized there was no escaping this. I had only enough time to get my blades up to skewer the beast—and that I would never do.

Glancing back at Leena, I drank in the sight of her one last time. *I'm sorry. For everything.*

Bracing for impact, I kept my weapons at bay—but the hit never came. Flesh ripped, but no pain arced through my body. No lancing heat. Only the dank and metallic smell of blood coupled with a body slumping to the ground at my feet. The Myad retreated out of reach before I could fully understand what had happened. My gaze dropped to the ground.

Calem.

My entire existence narrowed to him. To the stupid grin on his face and his brilliant-red hands as he held his abdomen together. Intense ringing seared through my ears, and I sank beside him in wounded shock.

"What are you doing?" Veins twitching along his neck, tears brimming in his eyes, he gripped my hand. "Go get her."

A sob caught in the back of my throat. Kost and Ozias sped toward us, sliding on their knees as they dropped beside him, everything else forgotten. Agony, hot and terrible and all-too consuming, burned me from the inside out.

Not Calem. Not my brother.

Life dwindled from his gaze, and his head sank heavily into the ground. The pocket of his jacket sparked to life, and Effie appeared in a fluster of shrieks and mint-green magic. She took one look at me—one piercing look filled with heated betrayal—before positioning herself over Calem's wound.

The Council murmured, but none of it mattered.

All I could see were Calem and Effie. She wailed, clacking her beak to the heavens and spilling tears across his chest. Trying to save her master, she desperately poured magic from her wings.

Calem didn't move.

Earsplitting shrieks pealed from her small body, and again she showered him in magic and tears.

He stayed still. Silent. Dead.

"Calem, quit kidding around." Ozias spoke around tears, the soft words breaking my heart.

"Get up. Please, get up." Kost. Soft. Pleading.

Nothing happened. Effie never stopped. And Calem never opened his eyes.

He was gone.

THIRTY-EIGHT

LEENA

Effie's agonizing wail shattered Wynn's hold. The veil that had pulled tight across my eyes dissipated, leaving before me a devastating and bloody scene of death. Each beat of Effie's wings was an unyielding tornado of anguish—a mother helplessly begging for her child's life.

Regaining control of my limbs, I sprinted toward my family.

My family. For that is what they'd become. They were here for me. To save me. And I'd led them to this.

"Leena!" Wynn yelled at my back. He'd never again own me. Never again touch me.

As I slid to the ground to cradle Calem's head in my lap, Noc disappeared, trading sunlight for shadows. I knew exactly where he was going as all eyes fixed on us.

Running my fingers through Calem's knotted hair, my chest shuddered. My beast had done this. Onyx lingered on the fringe of my vision, his worried gaze shifting between Calem and me. He hadn't known. How could he?

I did this.

Effie cried, laying tired wings across the expanse of Calem's wound before dropping her head to his chest. Tears streamed from my eyes.

This is my fault.

Calem. Shameless flirt Calem. Tactless Calem. Caring Calem.

"Those kids need you," I whispered, pressing my lips to his forehead. "You can't leave them behind. Not yet."

Oz cradled his head in his hands and Kost simply stared, face bone-white and sweat-slicked. They would blame me. For the rest of my life, I would be a source of pain and suffering. They'd endure me for Noc, but they'd never forgive me.

I wasn't sure I'd forgive myself.

Wynn took a few steps toward us. "Leena. Get back here."

Slowly, I rotated my head to give him the full weight of my stare. "No."

His jaw twitched. "No?"

"You'll never charm another human again." Gently moving Calem's head out of my lap, I stood and stormed toward him. Rosewood light ruptured from my symbol. Onyx snapped to attention and flanked my side, teeth bared.

Wynn thrust his hand forward, white light sharpening around his fingers. "Stop, Leena."

My body tightened. Froze. I fought for every twitch of my finger. Ground my teeth and glared at him with all my worth. "You will *not* control me again."

The Council stilled. Accusing gazes slipped from me to him.

His charm faltered, and I gained an inch. And another. My muscles protested as I forced them to push beyond his control. To listen to me instead of him.

"Leena." He used my name as a warning.

"No!" Everything ached. I was a trembling mess, but it was my body to control. Not his. My mind and my thoughts and my feelings. They were *mine*. He'd done enough. "This ends now."

Wynn flexed his hand, preparing to command his beast. "We'll see about that."

Noc appeared from the shadows behind Wynn. "No, we won't."

As he sank a blade into Wynn's back, a splintering crack split the quiet clearing. Blood shot from Wynn's mouth on the tail end of a gurgling cry, and Noc twisted the blade deeper. With deadly precision, he extracted it and made a clean swipe across Wynn's throat.

The whole thing took less than a second.

Noc stared at the decapitated body with enough disgust to send chills down my spine. Turning on his heels, he stormed back to us. Pain shredded his features. Red-rimmed and heavy, his gaze found mine. And then I ran. Right into his open arms and clung to him with everything I had. He'd come for me. All those awful things Wynn had said, the poison that had steeped my mind and manipulated my thoughts, were gone. Noc loved me. And I loved him.

Noc pressed his forehead to mine. "Leena." So much weight in my name. We had so much to fix. But I knew Noc had fought for me, that he would've given his life for me, and I was ready to fight and die for him, too, if that was what it took.

Lips trembling, I placed gentle kisses on his cheeks to catch his tears. "I'm here. I'm sorry. I love you."

He broke then, a low cry ripping from his lungs and disturbing the quiet horror of the clearing. Slowly, I kissed his tears away. Gave what little solace I could and held him close. The remaining assassins wept around the fallen—some near Calem, the rest around members I didn't know. Who I'd never get to know. Wrapping Noc's hand in mine, I guided him back to Calem. We slumped to the ground by his head, and Kost and Oz looked up with bleary eyes.

What have I done? Throat thick, I swallowed and stroked the side of Calem's face.

"Leena Edenfrell."

My head snapped to the woman who spoke my name. She'd crossed the clearing to stand a few feet from us.

Dark eyes rooted me in place, and I sucked in a breath. "Kaori."

"Wynn charmed you? Is that why you've returned despite your banishment?"

I nodded. "Yes. He brought me back a few days ago without notifying the Council." A few of the members flinched, and angry scowls touched their faces.

Kaori studied me for a long moment before her pensive stare shifted to Calem. She scrunched her thin brows together. "An Effreft?" Effie snapped her beak and sank lower into his wound. Kneeling on the ground, Kaori extended her hand to Effie. Her sapphire symbol glittered against her skin. "May I?"

Kost, Oz, and Noc stiffened. Murderous stares targeted Kaori, and dark tendrils crept near their fingers. Effie eyed Kaori's hand for a moment before gently clucking and moving aside.

My stomach threatened to upend itself. Mincemeat. My beast had turned him into mincemeat.

Kaori studied the damage. "If not for the Effreft, he'd be beyond repair. Even now, though, I can't make any promises."

"What are you saying?" Noc croaked.

Slowly, Kaori reached up and removed a white-gold leaf pin from her black hair. "Stella." One of the legendary beasts moved toward her. Dipped in silver, the beast could've been carved from metal. Harsh lines. Daggerlike teeth. Piercing amethyst eyes. Stella brought her twitching nose inches from Calem's wound. Kaori tilted her head toward Noc. "He will be different."

"You can bring him back?" Noc gripped my hand.

"I can try. I can't with the others, though." She looked past Noc at his fallen brethren. "They're too far gone and without the lasting life magic of the Effreft."

Noc swallowed. "I understand."

Tristan, one of the original Council, stepped forward. "Kaori, these people barged into our home—"

"That's enough, Tristan." Yazmin. Crown of the Council. She'd been away on a beast hunt during my first supposed transgression. A breeze swept her long, platinum locks across her face, and she brushed them aside. "We can debate later. If we can spare a life, it's what the goddess would want. We aren't meant to be at war."

Stabbing the hairpin into the center of her palm, Kaori pressed her hand flat against Calem's wound. "To ease the beast inside him, a bit of Charmer's blood."

Noc's grip on my hand tightened. "The beast inside him?"

"It's a condition of Stella's gift." Kaori shifted, making room for her beast. Stella dipped her head low and cracked her jaw wide open. As she positioned her fangs over the gaping wound, a thick silver substance dripped from hidden glands behind her teeth. A sharp heat cooked the air. "Stella's saliva is a potent healing balm that has been known to bring back those on the brink of death. However, something so powerful requires sacrificing a sliver of humanity."

I studied the faint track-work of silver veins on her hands. "You speak from experience."

She nodded once. "It was a requirement for taming her. My blood should ease the pull, but it will still be there."

Kost wrung his hands together, his voice breaking. "What kind of pull?"

Stella sat back on her haunches, licking her lips, and the gash nearly severing Calem in half sewed back together.

My heart stilled. *This has to work.* A soft purr brewed from Onyx's throat. He waited in the background, heavy eyes tearing my soul in two. To love the thing that stole my family... They would never understand. I would never ask them to. Without looking away from Calem, I summoned my power and sent Onyx back to the realm. He didn't need to feel guilty for my actions.

"The effects are different for everyone." Kaori dipped her nose closer to Calem's face. "For instance, I—"

Calem gasped, eyes flying open and chest heaving. His gaze bounced wildly from face to face until he spied Kaori kneeling over him. Confusion tracked canyons in the plane of his forehead. We all froze, shocked, hopeful, fearful—waiting. He had come back to us, but what would the change be? Would we know him anymore?

After what felt like an endless stretch of time, a lopsided grin teased his lips. "Well, hello there. I don't believe we've had the pleasure of meeting."

Oz choked on a laugh through a fresh stream of tears, and Kost slumped in place. Noc stared without speaking. He reached out and placed a hand on Calem's shoulder.

Kaori smiled. "No, we haven't met. My name is Kaori."

Calem blinked away the remnants of death, and that teasing grin grew. "What are you doing later?"

A faint blush touched her cheeks. "Um."

A bellowing laugh escaped Oz's chest. "Gods, Calem."

Calem grinned, dropping his hand and pushing himself up into a sitting position. "What's with all of you?" He turned his face my way. A rock wedged itself tight in my throat, and I dropped my head. I couldn't bear to look at him.

My beast... The deep red of Calem's wound stained the back of my eyelids.

A quick finger snaked its way around my chin, Calem angling my face to his. "Leena. It's good to have you back."

Tears broke through my lashes. "But—"

"Not another word." Calem glanced up at Noc. I tried to pull away, but he gripped me tighter. "I'd do it for you, too."

My heart split into a million places, and my body shook. Noc cradled me against his chest, wrapping his arms around my waist and placing a quiet kiss on the crown of my head. "I've got you," he murmured.

Burying my head into Noc's collar, I wept. He smelled of battle, of blood and grime and death. And honey. Always honey. I gripped onto that familiar scent and told myself that somehow, we'd put ourselves back together again.

I registered the groan of the beast door opening and glanced up to see Raven return. Her eyes were guarded, but not tearstained. Mika must have survived. Yazmin glided toward us with the others following close behind. Offering a slight bow, she inclined her head toward me. "Leena."

I rubbed my cheeks with the backs of my hands. "Yes?"

"I hate to break this up, but we need to speak. Now."

Fear and relief warred with each other. How long had I waited to gain an audience with the Crown of the Council? The opportunity to tell my side of things was here, and yet Wynn couldn't contest or confirm my words. Would they believe me? Would they banish me yet again? Worse?

Gaze roaming to Noc, I intertwined my fingers with his. At least I wouldn't be alone this time. "Of course."

Pinning Noc with her authoritative stare, Yazmin clasped her hands together. "Your people are safe. We'll help the wounded any way we can." Charmers leaked from buildings, summoning beasts to put the clearing back together. Stretchers for the wounded appeared, and the brave jogged toward the fallen assassins.

Noc stood and pulled me up with him. "Do you want me to go with you?"

"Council hearings are typically closed." I placed a gentle kiss on his lips. "I'll be okay."

"Actually, that won't be an issue." Yazmin brushed a finger against the glittering crown of gold woven into her hair. "As your *anam-cara*, he's permitted to attend. Plus, we have questions for him."

Tristan balked at her statement, muttering unintelligible words beneath his breath. Yazmin simply turned, a glimmer of mischief lifting the corner of her mouth.

Anam-cara.

The truth of that word branded my heart. There was no higher relationship for our people. To be chosen was the greatest honor, a declaration of true love. It wasn't a term we doled out lightly, and yet hearing her say it… She couldn't have been more right. From the moment he'd kissed me, I'd changed. Something had shifted for the better, something only he could have influenced.

Yes, I would name Noc my *anam-cara*. I just prayed he would accept me as his.

I caught one of his stray tears with my fingers. I wanted nothing more than to ease his pain, to fill his days with light and love. Noc looked at me, a question burning in his eyes. But with the Council eager to get started, explanations of the weight of that single word would have to wait. Now was my chance to prove I had been innocent all along. I needed to take it before they changed their minds.

I squeezed Noc's hand, and we followed the retreating Council members to the keep.

The ceiling was open to the network of tree branches tangling above, and natural light spilled over the marble floor between pockets of leaves. Seven chairs, each a mixture of roots and stone and pure earthly beauty, sat in the middle of a raised dais. As one, the Council members took their seats. Above them, a beautiful statue burst from the wall like a figurehead on the prow of a ship.

Celeste. Her face upturned, her half-open eyes stared into the future. A rose-gold crown dipped across her forehead, her stone hands cradling a platinum harp wrapped in golden roses and vines. As if she were caught in a perpetual wind, her long dress fluttered outward.

Her harp and crown were the only remaining artifacts of her existence—one of the most powerful gods to grace our continent, and it wasn't hard to see why. Emerging from the wall above her head was Ocnolog, an ancient dragon that once preyed on the people of Wilheim. Eyes shut in peaceful slumber, his thick neck curled around his master.

Dragging my gaze away from the masterpiece, I returned my attention to the Council. Yazmin sat in the middle throne reserved for the Crown. To her right, Kaori, Raven, and Eilan, the longest-sitting member. Appearing molten gold, his stern gaze burned into my chest. To Yazmin's left, Tristan and Gaige. Tristan leaned forward, pressing his elbows to his knees, and steepled his fingers together.

The empty chair next to Gaige dominated my vision.

Wynn. The fog of his charm had faded, but there were still lingering tendrils in my mind. Wisps of uncertainty and muddled thoughts that made it hard to focus. Who knew how long that would last—or whether I'd ever fully regain the days he stole from me.

My fingers trembled, and Noc glanced down at me before gently squeezing my hand. Wynn was gone. Noc was here. Everything was fine. Safe.

Biting my lip, I steadied my erratic breaths and forced my gaze to the waiting Council. A Nezbit sat to the side of Yazmin's throne. Its long ears formed sizeable feathered wings that stretched outward to the ceiling, and the extremely rare rabbit beast studied us with unblinking intensity. Teal feathers shivered along its haunches.

Yazmin leaned forward, her mercury cloak open to reveal her black, high-necked dress. "All right, Leena. We're all aware of your first transgression."

"Alleged transgression." I couldn't help myself.

Yazmin's smile was kind. "Alleged." Ears twitching, the Nezbit straightened. Yazmin reached down and rubbed her fingers along its scalp. "Nessie can help with that."

Noc shifted closer to me, shielding me partially from view. "What does the beast do?"

Stepping around him, I pressed a hand against his chest. "She listens to your heart. Right now, she's familiarizing herself with our cadences. She'll then be able to detect when our pulse races, determining lie from truth."

"Though we won't be able to do the same with Wynn," Tristan mused.

"Is Leena's word not good enough?" Noc demanded.

Tristan ran his fingers along his scraggly beard. Harsh brows angled down toward the bridge of his curved nose. "You want me to make a ruling without hearing both sides?"

Noc simmered. "You did before."

I didn't know much about Tristan, other than he was rugged and difficult, and entirely dedicated to nature. He would have valued the Gyss's tale above my own any day.

Eilan leaned forward, his baritone voice vibrating from deep within his chest. "We're listening now."

Raven placed a hand on Eilan's leg. Cloak rolled past her elbows to reveal bronzed skin and inked forearms, her deep-red symbol sparked with the promise of power. Her fiery eyes targeted Noc. "Mika was hurt because of you."

Warning bells sounded in my ears. Raven was a new member. The sheer anger in her voice caused me to pause and reminded me that Wynn had been working with a woman. Someone whose motives I couldn't quite grasp, but that I knew weren't good.

My gaze riveted to the emblem gleaming on the back of her hand. Noc had said the bounty had been placed by someone with a red Charmer's symbol. It couldn't be a coincidence. But there were hundreds, thousands, of Charmers living in Hireath. Which meant she likely wasn't the only one with a shade like that. And even though Wynn had hinted that the woman was on the Council, I needed proof. More concrete details.

A heavy fog settled in my mind as I tried to recall the memory. What exactly had I heard? Something about a spell? My thoughts were slippery, and I struggled to remember what had happened before I'd been charmed.

"You slaughtered my people." Noc's voice was cold as ice. "I think injuring one beast is a pale comparison at best."

Raven simmered. "We'll have to disagree."

I shot my arm out against his chest to keep him from engaging. "Mika is fine, right?"

She didn't spare me a glance. "Yes."

Eilan placed a heavy hand on Raven's. "It's okay, Raven."

Noc cast me a quick glance before straightening the hem of his bloodstained tunic and slipping his hands into the pockets of his black trousers. I knew that look of ease. A pretense so he could strike on a whim and leave the target reeling.

I took a small step forward, and he tensed. "Thank you, Crown. Let's begin."

Yazmin inclined her regal head. "All right." Nessie's wet nose twitched, and Yazmin folded her hands in her lap. "Recount the events leading up to your banishment."

I did. I described the night I'd found the human stapled to the wall in Wynn's basement. How he'd dragged me before them and claimed it was *my* doing. How he'd used a Gyss wish to convince them I was lying when I swore I was innocent. That it was him, not me. That wish prevented them from discerning truth from lie back then, but it held no baring over my words now. Every vivid detail

burned against my tongue, and the Council winced. Kaori dropped
her gaze entirely when I spoke of being torn from my home and cast
out as an exile. Of the things I'd had to do to survive.

Yazmin tilted her head to her beast. "Nessie?"

Nessie's clear opal eyes flashed a vibrant green. Truth. Tristan
dropped his head into his burly hands. Raven settled back into her
chair, mouth open and hand squeezing Eilan's tight. And Gaige...did
nothing. His steel-blue stare was locked on Noc.

Yazmin's voice was soft and full of anguish. "I'm so sorry,
Leena. The Council will take steps to ensure that nothing like this
ever happens again." Somber eyes met mine from across the dais,
and I nodded.

"What about Wynn?" Tristan clasped his hands together.
"Since he's not here to answer for his actions, what can you tell us
about his motivations? Why would he charm you?"

Clouds formed thick in my mind, and a dull ache throbbed
behind my eyes. "I'm...I'm not certain." My gaze slanted to Raven.
She was watching me with an intensity that left me shaken. Was she
really behind this? If so, she wouldn't want me spilling plans, no
matter how half-baked and convoluted they were to me. Yet, she
hadn't flinched at my words. Hadn't moved to keep me from revealing anything. Nothing added up.

Tristan scrunched his nose. "His grip must have been strong."

"I'm having a hard time sorting through it all. I remember
him capturing me. I remember him locking me away. But once he
started poisoning me with Uloox venom..." My fingers trembled
and ghosted the hidden scars along my thighs. Noc's brows drew
together as he tracked the action. "Between that and his charm, I
can't seem to clear my head."

"Call on your Myad." Kaori cupped her face. "Perhaps his
magic could help."

Onyx. Maybe he could eradicate the lingering threads of Wynn's charm. Heal my memories. Flexing my hand, I focused on the rosewood symbol and welcomed the flush of power that came with my beast. Onyx appeared, uncertainty still readily visible in his gaze. But he nudged my hand just the same.

No matter what, he'd always love me.

The Council had seen him on the battlefield, but there was still a quiet murmuring from a few of the members. Even though Nessie had heard truth in my words, there was something to be said for a Myad finding me worthy. He'd weighed all my transgressions—supposed or otherwise—and found me suitable to be his master.

Closing my eyes, I pressed my forehead to his. His breath trickled over my skin and settled deep in my bones. Heat traveled through me much like it had before, but the intensity was gone. Onyx had already cleansed me. All that was left was to destroy the tainted remnants of Wynn. Fog evaporated in my mind, and I craned my neck to the ceiling. Weights lifted from my limbs, and I rolled my shoulders to loosen my muscles. Slowly, I opened my eyes. Listened to the steady thrum of my heart. Felt the soft fur of Onyx's hide beneath my fingers. Smelled the fresh scent of roses and moondust flowers.

My senses were my own again. Fully. Truly. *Mine.*

But my memories... I tried to sift through the days, but the muddied images of Wynn had disappeared with his charm. Only whispers of what had happened remained.

"Well?" Tristan prompted, eyes locked on the space where my hand rested on Onyx's head.

"Nothing. I'm sorry."

Yazmin sighed. "It can't be helped."

Gaige leaned forward. "But perhaps Noc could share his side of things? That might provide some much-needed insight."

Noc met his gaze head-on. "I accepted a bounty for Leena. She bartered for her life with beasts, and I accepted."

Nessie's nose twitched, her eyes flashing green.

Gaige scratched his jaw. "What next?"

"I fell in love with her."

My heart came to a standstill. I hadn't realized how much I'd wanted, *needed*, to hear those words.

He offered me a heartfelt glance. "But we still had a deal, and I wasn't sure what I was going to do about the bounty. I wanted to keep her out of it. She gifted me with a Gyss, and I used a wish to take care of a private issue. I had no idea that would backfire and land us here. Otherwise, I never would have put her through this."

My eyes burned from the lack of blinking. Nessie was all I saw. The twitching of her nose. The fluttering of feathers along her ears. I knew in my heart what Noc said was true, but to have affirmation... To know without a doubt he hadn't known about the outcome of his wish...

Green light showered from her gaze, and my chest heaved. Noc looked at me, really looked at me, and my heart throbbed in my throat.

Gaige prodded further. "Why did you need a Gyss?"

Noc's eyes formed narrow slits. When he didn't answer, Nessie stood on her hind legs, wings shooting straight toward the sky. No matter how collected he appeared on the surface, there was no telling if his heart had given him up. Even one infinitesimal flutter would alert Nessie.

Yazmin rested her fingers at the point of tension between her beast's ears, and a faint glimmer of pale-pink light emanated from her emblem. "What are you hiding?"

"Something that doesn't concern Hireath."

Silence stretched on until Gaige spoke. "I see. Has anyone ever told you that you have a famous dead doppelgänger?"

My nose scrunched. "Doppelgänger?"

Noc brushed his comment off with a belittling chuckle. "You wouldn't be the first, and I'm sure not the last."

Gaige's grin only sharpened. "I'm somewhat of a historian. Forgive me. I spend too much time with my books."

Yazmin stiffened in her throne, turning her soft smile into a grimace. "Gaige, is your probing really necessary?"

Gaige tossed up his hands. "I digress."

"Thank you." She surveyed the Council, studying their faces and weighing minute nods of consent. After another stretch of silence, Yazmin's expression turned remorseful, and she met my stare. "It's obvious you're not at fault here; between Nessie's verdict and the Myad, you have been absolved in the eyes of beasts. As such, you will be absolved of all crimes in our eyes, too." Relief made me light-headed, and I slumped against Noc. He pressed a feathery kiss to the top of my head.

But Kaori's light voice sliced the happiness in my heart with the ease of a knife. "There's the matter of Calem."

Noc tightened his grip on my hip. "And?"

"If his symptoms become too much, send him here. I will teach him to control the feral magic in his blood."

Yazmin braided her fingers together. "Speaking of feral..." She nodded toward the entrance of the grand hall where Wynn's legendary beast, the Mistari, glowered at us.

Unlike the Scorpex, whose bond had been weak, the Mistari's had been strong. Sheer agony dripped from his gaze, and a smeared path of wet fur lined the underside of his eyes. He wouldn't know what his master had done, wouldn't be able to comprehend the disastrous pain he'd caused. He only knew loss.

Unlike the rest of Wynn's beasts residing in the realm, free to live out their days without returning to our world, the Mistari was stuck. Bond shattered, he would wander. He would never be the same as he was when he was wild.

I knew what Yazmin would ask before she spoke.

"He needs a home. A way back to the realm. Noc technically owns the claim, but as he is not a Charmer and already owns a Gyss..." She trailed off, and my knees trembled.

Noc hissed. "You'd ask her to care for the beast that belonged to her torturer?"

Torture. That's what I saw in the Mistari's eyes. I wasn't sure I'd ever be able to call on him, but I could offer him a reprieve. "I'll take him."

Noc looked as if I'd slapped him. "What?"

"Look at him." I turned to Noc, tears already heavy on my lashes. "He didn't know. He didn't do this to me. Just like Onyx isn't responsible for the order I gave when he brought Calem to the ground."

Noc stared at me for a long moment, and then brushed his thumb along my cheek. "You're amazing, you know that?"

Leaning into his hand, I smiled, soaking in the warmth of his forgiveness. His *love.* "I try."

"It's settled, then." Yazmin stood, beckoning to the Mistari, and the beast padded toward me. Heavy white paws smashed against the tile, and he paused before me to angle his forehead to mine. Light sparked in the air between us, and a door to the beast realm opened. A glimmer of relief chased away some of his pain, and the Mistari disappeared. A careful smile stretching her lips, Yazmin approached us. "What now, Leena?"

I blinked. "I'm not sure what you mean."

"Your name is clear, and the Council is short a member." Her smile deepened. "A Mistari, a Laharock, and a Myad. You're more than qualified to petition for the seat."

The Council. It was something I'd strived to attain from the moment they banished me. Proof that I was right. That I was strong enough. My gaze skipped to Raven. She refused to meet my eyes. I wasn't sure I'd be entirely welcome, but if she was up to something, then maybe I needed to be here. Needed to help protect the Council from whatever she had up her sleeve.

One look at Noc told me he wouldn't say no. He wouldn't stand in the way of the dreams I'd been chasing. But to accept such an offer meant I'd spend less time at Cruor. Less time with him.

"I'm not sure."

Yazmin didn't falter. "Think about it. We won't decide for a few weeks."

Noc reached for my hand, and the jet-black oath on his wrist blared up at me. My gaze darted to Raven, needing to see her reaction. "The oath is still in place."

Six pairs of eyes slanted to his wrist, none of them betraying even a sliver of damning evidence. Yazmin's brow furrowed. "We'll conduct a search on our end to find the culprit. Rest assured, you've been pardoned."

Exhaustion racked my body, but unease simmered in my veins. Raven still avoided my prying eyes. "Thank you, Yazmin."

She nodded. "For now, get yourself cleaned up. Breathe. A lot has happened." With a soft smile, she placed a hand on my shoulder. "And be sure to consider our offer."

THIRTY-NINE

NOC

Kaori whisked Leena and me away from the grand hall toward the first floor of the castle. As we broke out into the gardens, I glanced back to the battlefield where my brothers waited. Basins of water and platters of food were spread out between them, and they rested with wary eyes. Save Calem. He met my stare across the clearing with his signature grin, unaware of the newly formed silver line threading around his pupil.

What have I done?

Leena's hand found mine. "He'll be okay." She hesitated at the bottom of the stairs leading to the keep. "He has to be okay."

"He'll be fine," Kaori said. She had decidedly fox-like features with sharp, inquisitive eyes and a slender face. She affixed her black locks on top of her head with the leaf pin she'd used to give Calem her blood.

Leena cast her eyes to the ground. "Your Ossilix saved Calem's life, and for that, I am in your debt."

Those should have been my words. I pulled Leena close. "Leena, you are not at fault. This is what happens when people fight." My mind rewound to the days before my death, to the years spent on the battlefield watching my friends and family die.

This wasn't any different.

"He's right." Kaori turned to study the Council members disappearing down a corridor of marble stones and ash-tree roots. Only Yazmin had returned to the battlefield. "Don't worry about Calem. Right now, I can still feel him. He's got a strong mind. If anyone can learn to manage with a monster in his veins, it's him."

A monster in his veins and a void in his heart. Kaori couldn't have heard my thoughts, but her head turned toward me, a knowing look touching her expression before she continued down the hall.

We followed in silence to a wing in the castle reserved for guests. She showed us to a heavy plank table overflowing with a variety of food and an ornate armoire packed with clean, fresh clothes. After pointing out the bathroom, Kaori left, shutting the door to the outside world and leaving Leena and me alone for the first time in days.

Yazmin's words rang in my brain. *As per our customs, your* anam-cara *is permitted to attend the hearing.*

Anam-cara. I knew the word from my studies. Like *nae miele*, it spoke of a deeper connection, but there was something feral and ancient about the Charmer's tongue, and my insides delighted with the possibility of being hers.

But Leena hadn't said a word about it.

"Leena—"

"I need to bathe." She spun on her heels, heading straight for the bathroom. "I need to burn every memory of him from my skin."

Rubbing my neck, I followed behind her. The moment she set foot in the room, water sparked to life. Cascading streams dripped from the ceiling like rainfall, snaking between slabs of marble, and steam curled along the edges of the floor-length mirror stretching along the far wall.

Leena peeled off her blouse and bralette, but her trembling fingers hesitated at the waistband of her pants. I caught the glimmer of a tear escaping down her cheek as she touched her chin to her shoulder. In one swift movement, she dropped her pants and underwear and stepped into the waterfall.

A knife stabbed my lungs.

Her legs.

She stood trembling with her back to me as if she were afraid to see my reaction.

I stripped and stepped into the water beside her before dropping to my knees. She turned at the touch of my hands, eyes wide and full, and wrapped her arms around her chest as if to hold herself together. Pain scraped along the back of my throat. With deliberate slowness, I placed a soft kiss on the first bone-white scar I saw.

She let out a ragged whisper. "Noc."

Another kiss. "I'm not done." Running my fingers across the expanse of her legs, I felt for every hidden lip of scar tissue, and kissed each one.

When her trembling faded, I moved my hands upward to her hips and stood. She pressed her forehead to my chest and wrapped her arms around me. For a while, we simply held each other, and I kneaded soft circles down her spine.

"Want to tell me what you're thinking?" I asked.

Tilting her face upward, she took a steady breath. "I'm thinking that I love you. That I'm a terrible person because I'm so glad Onyx didn't make it to you. I'm not sure how to forgive myself for Calem. For any of this. And"—her voice cracked, and she speared her lower lip with her teeth—"I'm thinking I'm not sure if I'll ever be able to look at my own skin again without thinking of Wynn."

Moving my hands to cup her face, I placed a faint kiss on her lips. "Four things. First, I love you, too." I paused a moment to let those words sink in, to revel in being able to *say* them so openly. "Second, you're not a terrible person. There's nothing I wouldn't do for you, so don't think you're the only one who would protect the one you love at the cost of everything else. Third, if you don't learn to forgive yourself for Calem, he'll pester you for the rest of your damn life. Do you really want that?"

She laughed, closing her eyes and tipping her head upward into the water. The sound didn't hold its usual warmth, but it was still the most beautiful thing I'd heard in days.

Palming the back of her neck, I stroked her jaw with my thumb. "And as for your scars..." I angled her face toward mine. "Don't think of who gave them to you. Think of how strong you are because you survived. You broke free."

Tears welled and rolled down her cheeks. With one hand, she traced the angles of my face, lingering on the scar on my cheekbone. My chest cracked open wide, and I swore I could feel a tether surging between us.

Shuddering, I dug my fingers into the flesh of her hips. She was my everything. And I was finally able to acknowledge my love. Express it.

"You're real, right?" she whispered, tracing my face with light fingers. "This isn't a dream?"

"I'm real. I'm here."

A wet sob ratcheted through her chest, and she pressed her lips to mine. "I missed you. Gods, Noc. It was so hard. I didn't...I didn't know if I'd make it out alive."

My fingers worked their way through her hair, massaging her scalp. "I missed you, too. I was a wreck. I had no way of proving to you that I didn't know Winnow would take you as payment. And after everything you'd told me about Gyss...I should've listened. I'm so sorry, Leena."

"I believe you." She leaned her head into my hands, and some of the tension in her shoulders eased. "And you're right—you should've listened." She glanced up at me, the hint of a smile teasing her lips.

Just that glimmer of her old self broke me, and I slanted my mouth across hers. "Forgive me?"

"Always." She trailed kisses along my neck, dug her hands into my back. "What kind of *anam-cara* would I be if I didn't?"

The pattering of the water falling around us dulled in the wake of her words. Cupping her face in my hands, I begged her to meet my gaze. "Tell me what that means for Charmers."

"It means I've chosen you. And I will continue to choose you every day of my life, through the good and the bad, because I can't imagine loving anyone else but you." Her eyes were full. Shining. "For Charmers, no bond is more cherished. It's more revered and protected even than the connection we share with our beasts."

Slowly, I brushed my knuckles over her cheek. I didn't seem worthy of such devotion, but I would spend my life trying to be the man she thought I was. I would devote myself to her like she did to me, because choosing her was the easiest decision I'd ever been faced with.

We still had so much to discuss, so much to *learn* about each other, but for perhaps the first time in decades, I wasn't afraid.

"In Wilheim, two people who choose each other are called pair bonds. I'll gladly be both your pair bond and your *anam-cara*—and anything else you need me to be—for the rest of our lives." I ghosted her lips with mine. "You have no idea… Every day around you was a struggle. A constant battle between what I felt and what I didn't want to admit. Saying it now, *feeling* this way… It's the most amazing thing I've ever been able to experience. And that's all thanks to you."

A beautiful look of relief washed over her face. "I love you, Noc. With everything that I have."

A deep groan shattered my chest, and I buried my face in her neck. "I love you, too." Gripping her waist, I pulled her close. Felt the steady beat of her heart against mine. To love and be loved, after

I'd locked away my emotions for so long... The feeling shook my world and tied me to her. Forever.

Together, we exited the shower and dried off, neither of us saying a word. We didn't have to. Only after we dressed did I pull her toward the bed. We laid down together, her back pressed against my chest. Her breaths were shaky, uncertain. I smoothed her damp hair. Pressed soft kisses to her shoulder. Worked my knuckles into the tense muscles along her spine.

After a while, she summoned a beast I didn't recognize. A small, round thing that looked like a puff of cotton with eyes too big for its head. Gently, she ran her fingers through its fur. "This is Poof."

"Poof?" I smiled into the crook of her neck. "That's a cute name."

She relaxed beneath me and pulled her beast to her chest. "He's a cute beast."

"What does he do?"

"If I squeeze him just right, he produces a powerful mixture of lavender and valerian that aid with sleep." She snuggled him closer, and he let out a soft coo.

"You can sleep if you want, Leena. It's all right." Planting a gentle kiss on her shoulder, I let out a long, tired sigh. "We don't have to leave right away. Take whatever time you need."

"I just want a minute." Touching her chin to her shoulder, she looked up at me through the tops of her lashes. There was so much love, so much *trust*, in her gaze that it made my heart tremble. With a light touch, she traced the scar on my cheek. "I love you."

"I love you, too." Gently, I pressed my lips against hers. She melted into me, and a wondrous warmth spread through my chest. Never again would I lose her. Never again would she endure the horrors still lingering in her teary gaze. Never. She was mine to protect and love.

And I would follow her anywhere.

FORTY

LEENA

I never wanted to leave the safety of the room, but while Noc would never say it, I could see the anxiety in the depths of his eyes. He wanted to get back to his people. To check on Calem. To assure himself that his brothers were safe like the Council had promised. So we abandoned the bed and ate in hurried silence, each of us consumed by the unknown path our future would take.

When we emerged from our room, Gaige was already waiting for us. Dressed in a cranberry-colored tunic, a black vest, and slim-fitting trousers, he wore a nonchalant smile that didn't match the curiosity burning behind his steel-blue gaze. "Ready to go? I'll be accompanying you."

Tension sparked like an electric current between the men. Noc's lips pressed into a thin line. "Thank you."

Gaige didn't falter. "Shall we?"

Waiting at the edge of the forest, our assassins lingered in a darkness of their own making. Standing near Oz and Calem, Kost said something to his brothers and smiled. Then he turned, caught me with his stare. His smile strained but didn't disappear completely. With a pointed look between me and Noc, he nodded, just the slightest tilt. I wasn't sure he'd ever count me as a friend, but at least he seemed to accept my relationship with Noc. There was hope yet.

I glanced at Noc in time to see a pained tightening to his jaw, and he sped up to meet Emelia and Iov. He could finally feel again. Show the breadth of his emotions. And not a moment too soon, because his brethren needed comfort. He placed a gentle hand on Iov's forearm, worried eyes inspecting the bandages clinging to the wound just above his heart.

Morbid silence deafened the life of the wood, drowning out birdcalls and keeping beasts away. Beds of furling shadows carried our dead. Assassins walked beside them, eyes tight and focused on the path before us. I couldn't bring myself to look at them for more than a moment. Noc floated between them all, whispering condolences and soothing whatever pain he could with his words.

The gate to Hireath appeared on the horizon before Gaige spoke, breaking the reverie. "He's a good leader."

Dragging my gaze away, I studied our escort. "Can I ask you something?"

"Of course."

"Any sentry could have escorted us to the border."

He smirked. "That's not a question."

"Why you?"

Running a hand through his windswept brown locks, he shifted his stare to the assassins walking in front of us. "I'm an ambassador for Charmers. Prior to this whole debacle, Yazmin had tasked me with a quick errand into Wilheim. Taking you to Cruor is simply on the way."

"Sure. And this sudden journey doesn't have anything to do with Noc's supposed doppelgänger, right?" Unease flared in me, and I reached for the ring on my finger, only to come up empty-handed.

"Right. Though admittedly, there are other things prompting

me to escort you." Gaige's eyes bounced to Kost, walking a few feet
behind Noc, along with Calem and Oz. Kost cast a cursory glance in
our direction. Light glinted off his glasses, and he smoothed his hair
before looking back to the path ahead of him.

Gaige's smile deepened, revealing small dimples.

I couldn't stop the laugh from escaping. "You've got your work
cut out for you."

"Good." He winked.

My gaze traveled back to Noc, to the strong, corded muscles of
his back peeking through his thin tunic. We'd gone through a special
kind of hell to find each other, yet here we were. It wasn't over yet,
either.

As my hazy memories slowly showed signs of returning, I was
increasingly sure Raven was the one behind Wynn's delusions and
the oath still lingering on Noc's wrist. But why would they need an
army for anything? The last war the continent of Lendria had seen
was some fifty years ago when the prince of Wilheim murdered the
princess of Rhyne. A lovers' quarrel gone wrong, and we weren't
even involved in that skirmish. So why did Wynn think the Charmers
needed to protect ourselves? And what did this mystery woman's
spell entail?

Gaige whistled beside me, tipping his head to the heavens. The
gods only knew what he kept hidden in that library brain of his.

"What exactly are you doing in Wilheim again?"

Gaige waved away my question with the brush of his hand.
The jeweled, citrine shade of his symbol reflected in the sun. "Just
research. Join the Council, and I'll be able to share every lovely detail
with you."

I folded my arms across my chest. "Maybe. I need to see what's
happening at home first."

Gaige's brows disappeared into his hairline. "Home?

Interesting." But he didn't push the matter. Instead, his gaze shot back to Kost. "Guess I'd better get to know some of your new brethren." Straightening his vest, he quickened his pace and left me alone with my surprise.

Home. Not Midnight Jester. Not Hireath.

Cruor.

Oz. Calem. Even Kost. But most importantly, Noc. They were my family. My home. We'd endured so much over the past few weeks, and we were finally done.

Noc peeled away from his brothers to return to my side. Harsh obsidian eyes trained on Gaige, he wrapped an arm around my waist. "Something I should be concerned about?"

"I'm not sure. But Kost, on the other hand..." I bit my lower lip to keep my grin masked. Gaige was already rubbing elbows with him, talking with animated hands and a wry smile.

Ease wiping the wrinkles from his forehead, Noc smiled. "I guess we'll leave him to Kost for now."

I nodded. "He can handle himself. If Gaige really is a historian, I'm sure they'll have plenty to talk about. Speaking of, what was he getting at with that doppelgänger bit?"

Noc's gaze flashed to Gaige, as if worried he'd hear our low conversation. "It's tradition in Cruor to leave your past in the ground when you're raised. Most of us don't talk about the lives we had before."

"But what does that have to do with Gaige?"

"Nothing. Possibly something. Look, Leena," he paused, interlocking his fingers with mine, "some things are better left buried. I wasn't the greatest person before I was raised. I made...horrendous mistakes."

I squeezed his hand tight. "That won't change how I feel about you."

Something darted through his dark eyes. "Maybe. I haven't talked about it in *so* long. My past could invite...problems. And there's already so much to do here. I need to make sure Cruor is safe from Darrien. I need to find a way to sustain the guild without bounties." He dipped his head low, whispering against my temple. "And I need to enjoy what I've found with you."

Leaning in to him, I let out a contented hum. "Fine. But after everything at Cruor is settled, we're revisiting this. You're not the only one who wants to solve this puzzle."

He chuckled. "Understood."

"I just hope things settle down for a while. I want happiness—for all of us."

He brushed tender knuckles along my jaw. "We are happy, Leena. So long as we're together, that's how it's going to be." Placing a gentle kiss on my lips, he stole my breath away.

Happiness. *Yes.* This was it. I pressed my forehead against his, closing my eyes against the wellspring of hope opening up inside me.

No matter what the future held, we would tackle everything—together.

EPILOGUE

NOC

Returning to Cruor—our home—with my brothers and Leena filled my soul with a kind of warmth I'd long since forgotten. Before, it'd been a place of refuge. A sanctuary. It was still that, and yet it was so much more. Full of potential and life. After checking on the wounded, we'd each retreated to our quarters for a while, Leena following me to my room and picking her side of the bed. She'd made a big show of testing out the pillows before laughing and throwing them at my face. I had no choice but to fight back, and the sheets were quickly covered in feathers. She'd collapsed into the bed and they billowed around her, caught in her hair. One stuck to her nose. It was the most innocent thing I'd ever seen, and after everything we'd been through, it was exactly what I needed.

For a while, we simply lay together without saying a word, until our stomachs protested and we met Kost, Calem, and Ozias downstairs for dinner. It was so good to simply *feel* again. To talk with them, to listen and answer and not worry that my words might condemn them to death. The laugher of our conversation lingered long after we'd cleared our plates, and we sat together around the crackling hearth, finding joy in each other's company.

Reclining on the couch, I draped my arm over Leena's shoulder, and she leaned in to me, eyes light and glued to the tiered game board erected on the table before us. Klimkota. She'd mentioned seeing a handful of assassins playing it when she'd first arrived, and Ozias and Calem were eager to teach her. Even Kost joined, after some dogging from Calem, as they needed four players. I'd settled for being Leena's partner. It wouldn't have been fair otherwise.

"This is futile." Kost studied his emerald knight on the lower level of the board and scooted the armchair an inch closer. "We're not playing against Leena—we're playing against Noc. He's never lost."

Leena raised her brows. "You've never lost? Not once?"

I grinned. "Never." Lazily, I dragged my fingers across her hand and guided her toward an obsidian crown. "Move this one three spaces up and one to the left."

"How is that even fair?" Calem griped from his seat on the floor as Leena moved the piece on top of a gleaming ivory sword. She knocked it off the board with the flick of her wrist and a giggle.

"But I'm not *really* playing. Just offering suggestions." I nuzzled the side of her neck, and gooseflesh bloomed down her throat and across her collarbone. She spared me one heated look before batting me away.

"Not now, I need to win."

Gods, I loved this woman.

Kost lifted a brow. "If you tell her every move, then it's the same thing." He dove his fingers into his breast pocket and pulled out a bronze key, summoning Felicks from the realm. "Seems fair to even the playing field."

His beast let out a happy bark before jumping into his lap. After two quick circles, he nestled against him and turned his sharp stare to the board. The gem atop his head clouded.

Calem threw up his hands. "Yeah, because that's *fair*."

A grin tugged at my lips. What kind of challenge would this pose? Would I still be able to outmaneuver them? My gaze tore apart patterns across the board, searching for viable outcomes. Of course I'd let Leena make the moves, but I was eager to see what would happen if I ever truly played against Kost and Felicks.

The orb cleared, and Kost offered a wry smile. "Assassins don't fight fair, Calem. You can thank Noc for teaching us that." With light fingers, he snared his knight and moved it a few spaces up. Safe from Leena's lingering ebony shield. He was the only one who ever came close to besting me in a game.

Seated beside Calem, Ozias chuckled. "I'm just here for moral support." He toyed with his last ruby tower, finally moving it diagonally across the board. "You guys always beat me."

Calem pounced, careening an ivory archer toward Ozias's tower. With an unnecessary flourish, he sent it flying across the room. The two of them laughed, and Leena quickly joined them. Kost sighed, but his eyes were light. Warm. Together, we were whole.

A strand of hair fell across Leena's face, and I reached out to brush it away.

My fingers never made it.

Searing heat scalded the inside of my wrist, and my hand froze. The oath pulsed with magic. Reverberated through my bones and drowned out the beat of my heart. Somewhere in the distance, I swore I heard a feminine laugh. Haughty. Low. I dropped my hand into my lap, and Leena frowned at me.

"Everything all right?"

The pain died as quickly as it had appeared. I offered her what I hoped was a reassuring grin. "Of course. It's your turn. Why don't you decide where to move?"

She studied my face for a moment longer before giving up and returning to the game. Ozias and Calem watched her ponder her moves, but Kost stared at me with unveiled concern. I shook my head once. We already knew the culprit was still out there. Bringing it up now wouldn't solve anything. For a moment, we had peace. A little slice of happiness.

A dull ache throbbed around my neck, reminiscent of a noose. The Charmers would come through. They'd locate the woman and force her to remove the hit. If they didn't... No one had ever denied the call of Cruor's Oath. We had no records. No plans. No idea what would happen or how long it would take for my life to be sacrificed in exchange for Leena's.

I gripped the side of her waist, and she placed a hand over mine. We'd find an answer. Before anything bad could happen. Before I lost the chance to be the man she thought I was. I'd promised forever. And no one was going to take that from me.

But even as my resolve rang true, the laugh in my ears sharpened, and magic branded my wrist like a shackle.

Time, it seemed, was running out.

BESTIARY

Asura

Pronunciation: *ah-sur-ah*

Rank: B-Class

Description: An Asura is the size of a small child, with an upright, humanlike torso, cow legs, and a cow head. Its body is covered in tan hide, and it sports six humanlike arms. It also has ten milky-white eyes, which correspond to the number of hits that can be absorbed by its shield. When activating its impenetrable defensive shield, the Asura holds two hands palm up toward the heavens, two flat and parallel to the earth, and two pressed firmly against the ground. The invisible, bubble-like dome this creates can withstand any attack for up to ten hits. The number of closed eyes indicates the number of hits sustained at any point during the battle. Asura are slow to move and incapable of physical attacks. Their shields will remain intact if they travel with their Charmer, but since movement requires them to remove their lower two hands from the earth, this weakens the shield.

Taming: Taming an Asura takes considerable time. The Charmer must sit cross-legged before the beast, with arms extended outward, and activate charm. This position must be held for several hours while the Asura chews on wheatgrass and evaluates the Charmer's power. If it finds the Charmer unsuitable, the Asura will walk away and become untamable for seven days.

Bone Katua

Pronunciation: *bone cat-ew-ah*

Rank: A-Class

Description: The Bone Katua is one of the ten legendary feline beasts and is russet-brown in color with bone spikes protruding along its spine. Its devil-red eyes have the potential to cause paralysis in prey, making it a supreme hunter. Since the Bone Katua can heal itself by rubbing its fur against trees, it's difficult to kill. Its yellow fangs stretch past its maw and can pierce thick hides with ease.

Taming: Bone Katua are difficult to locate, often living reclusive lives in mountains populated by dense forests. The Charmer must discover the Bone Katua's den and take up residence near it, demonstrating a willingness to live fully with nature by eating and drinking only enough to survive and maintaining no contact with the outside world. After several months, the Bone Katua will approach and paralyze the Charmer with its stare. It will then sniff and lick them from head to toe, determining whether they've truly dedicated themselves to nature. If it believes the Charmer has, it will sit before them until the paralysis wears off and then allow them to tame it. If it feels the Charmer does not value nature, or has contacted another human or indulged beyond what's necessary during those few months, it will kill them.

Canepine

Pronunciation: *cane-pine*

Rank: C-Class

Description: Canepine are wolf-like beasts with ivy-green fur and powder-blue eyes. Male Canepine have small white flowers that grow naturally along the undersides of their bellies, neck, and around their faces, while females have indigo flowers. They live in packs deep within the woods and are peaceful in nature. They have excellent tracking abilities, making them sought after by Charmers who frequent beast hunts. In addition, they can purify any water source, making it safe for consumption.

Taming: Taming a Canepine largely depends on whether or not the beast is attached to its pack. It is impossible to convince a Canepine to leave if it has already mated or birthed pups. Therefore, it's easier to tame youngsters than adults. Once a Charmer has caught the attention of a Canepine, they must play fetch for as long as the beast desires. Once the Canepine is satisfied, it will take an item off the Charmer and run away, returning sometime later. At that point, the Charmer must find the missing item. If they're able to track it down, the Canepine will allow itself to be tamed. If not, the Canepine will leave.

Dosha

Pronunciation: *doh-sha*

Rank: D-Class

Description: Dosha are no bigger than teacups and have exceptionally long tails and large hands. They're generally tawny-colored, with slight coat variations between males and females. While all Dosha have three eyes, female eye color is blue and male eye color is green. The adhesive secreted from their palms is so strong that a single finger attached to a branch could keep them from falling. When they wish to unstick themselves, a secondary dissolvent secretion is released from their hands, granting just enough movement for them to dislodge themselves. They live high in the treetops to avoid predators and eat a variety of leaves and fruit to sustain themselves. Thanks to a special lining in their digestive system, they're immune to any poison they might consume. As such, they're useful for detecting whether or not food is safe for human consumption.

Taming: Dosha never leave their treetop homes. To tame one, the Charmer must climb as high as the tree will allow and present the beast with a ripe coconut. If the Dosha accepts, it will glue itself to the Charmer's body while consuming the fruit. Once the Dosha is finished eating, the Charmer should initiate charm.

Dreagle

Pronunciation: *dree-gul*

Rank: B-Class

Description: Dreagles live in flocks atop mountain peaks and form deep bonds with their family. As the seasons change, the coats of their deer-like bodies adapt to match the environment—dirt brown and black during the warmer months and snow-white during the winter. With powerful, eagle-like wings, they can fly for hours without tiring. They use their antlers and sharp talons to catch small game or unearth grubs. Their incredible eyesight cannot be fooled by magic, and they're able to detect threats from great distances.

Taming: Dreagles have a unique relationship with Charmers. So long as high peaks are provided for them to stand guard—as well as more secluded mountaintop perches to nest and birth young—they'll watch over a designated area without needing to be tamed. They can be tamed with standard charm, but it's generally not recommended to separate a Dreagle from its flock, due to their highly social natures.

Effreft

Pronunciation: *eff-reft*

Rank: B-Class

Description: Effrefts are roughly the size of small dogs, with falcon heads, long, feathered tails, and wings. Their mint-green coloring and pink eyes make them easy to

spot during the day, so they typically hunt at night. They can shower the space beneath their wingspan with magic, encouraging plants to reach maturity in seconds, and the soil left behind is regarded as the most fertile in the world.

Taming: The Charmer should find an open field on a moonlit night and prepare a cornucopia. After overflowing it with a variety of food, they must initiate charm and wait. A successful taming may take several days, because Effrefts have unknown migratory patterns and might not be present. More sightings have occurred in the south, as they seem to prefer warmer wind currents.

Fabric Spinner

Pronunciation: *fabric spinner*

Rank: B-Class

Description: Fabric Spinners are reclusive beasts that live deep in caves far from civilization. While they're skittish in nature, they've been known to attack anything that strays into their territory. The wrap their prey in a web and slowly devour its organs over a period of time. They have humanoid heads with insect features, and human torsos that end in bulbous abdomens reminiscent of arachnids. With eight hairy legs, two pincers at the space where the torso transitions to abdomen, and two spiny, human-like arms, they're exceptionally talented at snaring prey. The ducts on their inner wrists shoot an endless supply of near-unbreakable silken thread. Their fingers are coated in tiny, retractable barbs that allow them to slit their webs if need be. The spinner that protrudes from the beast's rear produces a single thread that tethers the Fabric Spinner to its lair. If it senses danger or wants to return after a successful hunt, it will retract that thread and be pulled at immense speed back to safety. Given they're solitary creatures and rarely mate—females often attempt to eat males after copulation—not many Charmers own this beast. Those who do own the beast are often tailors, using the silk threads to craft immensely sturdy clothing or other sought-after materials, such as fishing line.

Taming: After finding the lair of a Fabric Spinner, the Charmer must bring several buckets of fresh organs to present to the beast. It will examine each offering one by one, and if it finds the organ appealing, it will wrap them in webbing for later consumption. If one of the organs has gone foul, the Fabric Spinner will become enraged and attack. Assuming all organs are satisfactory, the beast will then weave an intricate web. The Charmer must willingly ensnare themselves and wait patiently while the Fabric Spinner eats the provided organs, symbolizing the patience the beast exudes while hunting. The Charmer must remain completely still for the entire duration of the meal, otherwise the Fabric Spinner will attack. Once the beast has finished eating, it will cut the Charmer down from the web and allow itself to be tamed.

Femsy

Pronunciation: *fem-zee*

Rank: D-Class

Description: Like the sparrow, the Femsy are small and flighty. They travel in flocks and rarely hold still, making it difficult to snag one's attention long enough to charm it. They're steel gray in color with violet breasts. When one is tamed, a yellow film slides over its three black eyes, marking it as owned. After a successful taming, the Charmer can tap into the bird's eyesight for short intervals by concentrating on the bond. Because there are no distance limitations to shared sight, the Femsy is often used for reconnaissance. However, the act is quite draining on the bird and can only be used three times before it must be sent back to the beast realm to recover.

Taming: No additional taming requirements are needed aside from standard charm.

Graveltot

Pronunciation: *grah-vul-tot*

Rank: D-Class

Description: The Graveltot is a small, spherical beast covered in slate and rocks. It moves by rolling across the ground, only popping out its head and feet when prompted to activate its power. When its hooves meet the earth, it manipulates the force of gravity in a perfect circle around it, making it impossible for anyone caught in its trap to move. It only lasts for fifteen minutes, and the Graveltot must rest for several hours before it can use its power again.

Taming: No additional taming requirements are needed aside from standard charm.

Groober

Pronunciation: *groo-ber*

Rank: E-Class

Description: Groobers are round, fluffy beasts with white fur softer than a rabbit's fluff. They have stubby arms and legs and circular eyes. When squeezed tightly, Groobers emit a mixture of lavender and valerian to aid with sleep.

Taming: No additional taming requirements are needed aside from standard charm.

Gyss

Pronunciation: *giss*

Rank: C-Class

Description: Gyss are the size of coffee mugs, with human torsos and misty, wisp-like tails for the lower half of their bodies. They can only be found in sacred sites and often adorn their hair with flowers or leaves. Their sharp, pointed teeth are used to crack nuts, one of their preferred food sources. Exceptionally cunning and mischievous, they like to talk in riddles and are the only known beast with an active relationship with the gods. Male Gyss have been spotted but not tamed. Gyss have the ability to grant one wish every six months. There are no limitations, so long as payment is met. However, the breadth of their ability is dependent on the master's power and intelligence. While Gyss can use their relationship with the gods to argue for less severe payments, they often don't, as they take joy in using their power to the fullest extent of their abilities. As such, they are rarely, if ever, called upon. Many Charmers feel Gyss should be ranked higher, but their restricted conditions for wish-granting caused the Council to rank them as C-Class beasts.

Taming: Gyss can only be found at sacred sites and require utter stillness to tame. Otherwise, standard charm is all that's needed.

Havra

Pronunciation: *Hav-rah*

Rank: E-Class

Description: Havra are small and slender in stature with gangly limbs and knobby fingers. They have long faces with four deer-like eyes. They are solitary creatures who live in forests and survive off berries. While holding their breath, they are able to materialize through objects. Because of this and their bark-like skin, they were initially thought to be tree spirits.

Taming: Havra can only be found in dense wood. The Charmer should place a basket of fresh berries at the base of a tree and wait. Once a Havra is spotted, the Charmer must hold their breath and initiate charm.

Iksass

Pronunciation: *ik-sass*

Rank: B-Class

Description: The Iksass alters its constitution to suit its master's needs. Generally, though, they appear to be tall and slender and take human shape, but are faceless. Despite that, they have excellent senses. Limbs appear and disappear on a whim, and they prefer invisibility, making them difficult to locate. They lurk unseen and hunt small game or steal food from wandering travelers. Needing vast amounts of sleep to power their ability, they can only be called upon for one two-hour stint during a day once tamed. Many Charmers use Iksass for protection, as their shape-shifting abilities make them formidable opponents.

Taming: The key to taming an Iksass is locating it. Without a known preferred habitat, the only way to tame one is for the Charmer to catch it picking their pocket in search of food. When this happens, immediately activate charm to keep the beast from fleeing, and maintain it for two hours or until the beast tires.

Kestral

Pronunciation: *kes-tral*

Rank: Unknown

Description: The Kestral is an untamable beast that magically appeared when Wilheimians forced Charmers to flee after the First War. The Kestral emerged and created an unbreakable border around Hireath to keep the dark magic of the Kitska Forest out. The beast maintains the threshold at all times, only allowing Charmers and those it deems fit to cross. It has incredibly long tail feathers, a large wingspan, and a slender, paperwhite body with blue eyes.

Taming: Not possible. Trying results in the beast casting the Charmer across the threshold, only allowing them to return after an undetermined length of time.

Krik

Pronunciation: *crick*

Rank: D-Class

Description: Krik are pear-shaped birds with tiny green feathers. They have small, trumpet-like beaks that emit a staticky, dissonant sound known to steadily drive those who hear it insane. The Krik's lungs operate independently of each other, allowing the bird to inhale fresh air while still exhaling to maintain its call.

Taming: No additional taming requirements are needed aside from standard charm.

Laharock

Pronunciation: *la-ha-rock*

Rank: A-Class

Description: Larger than an elephant and built like a wingless dragon, the Laharock is one of the largest beasts in Lendria. It uses its thick claws to traverse the rough volcanic terrain of its preferred habitat and is surprisingly nimble. The bone mane around its crown acts as an extra layer of protection for the head, and large, pupil-less white eyes glow with the intensity of fire. Red scales rimmed in gold cover the Laharock's spine, neck, and legs, making the underbelly the only unprotected portion of its hide. These scales are easily corroded by salt water, which can cause damage to the Laharock. If the Laharock grows up in the wild without threat or human interference, it will develop magic that allows it to summon scalding fires and intense heat. Offspring, on the other hand, are empathic metamorphs, susceptible to an outside trigger that could alter their power. Once the trigger event occurs, the power solidifies.

Taming: Laharock absorb minerals from the volcanoes on which they live. Charmers will need to seek out an active volcano and bring a freshly caught marlin. Once the Laharock spots

the Charmer, they should leave the fish on a slab and take several steps back. While the Laharock is eating, the Charmer should insert ear plugs, then summon a Songbloom and use its lullaby to put the Laharock in a stupor. The Charmer must remember to approach slowly and find sure footing along the mountain, because one loose rock or loud noise can break the trance and enrage the Laharock. Regardless, the Laharock will produce an intense aura of heat as a means of protection. Being burned is unavoidable. To avoid severe damage, Charmers should immediately summon a Poi afterward to tend to their skin. Once upon the Laharock, Charmers must place a hand on its snout and initiate charm.

Alternative method (discovered by Leena Edenfrell): Find a Laharock with her recently birthed young. Separate the mother from the child. Carefully approach the offspring and tame it first (no additional requirements outside of standard charm). Be careful not to spook it, as that might cause a flood of unstable powers to occur. Once the offspring is tamed, the mother will call off her pursuit and willingly allow herself to be charmed in order to stay with her young.

Mistari

Pronunciation: *mis-tar-ee*

Rank: A-Class

Description: The Mistari is one of the ten legendary feline beasts and has a white coat and scaled crystal plates over its chest. Four wings sprout from each of its ankles, resembling jagged pieces of precious gems. They enable the Mistari to propel itself forward, even gliding over short distances. The crystal feathers are highly valuable and, when dropped, can be broken and embedded in the skin of two people, granting them the ability to share thoughts. Mistari live in small prides scattered throughout the plains. Due to their wings and speed, they are difficult to track.

Taming: Charmers should approach with caution and begin the following sequence: First, encircle the Mistari with a mixture of highly valuable gems and stones while half crouched and chuffing to symbolize deference. Then, lie facedown on the ground and remain completely still. If the Mistari does not approve of the Charmer's offering, they should run. Taming will not be successful and could result in death. If the beast does approve, it will pick the Charmer up by the scruff (Charmers should wear thick clothing to prevent injury) and bring them into the circle. Charmers should stay limp until the beast begins to lick them, then initiate charm.

Myad

Pronunciation: *my-ad*

Rank: A-Class

Description: The Myad is the largest of the ten legendary feline beasts, with a panther-like build, black fur, and a mane comprised of peacock feathers. The same vibrant teal and emerald feathers travel the length of its spine and tail, as well as onto its wings. Gold casings protect the weak points of its ankles and appear around the crown of its head. When the Myad is about to take flight, blue magic streams from its feet and eyes. The Myad has the unique ability to place its prey in a stupor while prying into their deepest memories. The person in question is then forced to

face the horrors of their past, which often results in insanity. If the Myad finds them unworthy, the person's mind is burned to ash, leaving them in a comatose state for the rest of their lives. Because Myads are carnivorous, they are likely to consume their helpless and unfeeling prey.

Taming: Taming a Myad is a dangerous three-step process. First, the Charmer must acquire the blood of a murderer, freely given, and present it to the beast. Second, they must offer a token of loyalty with high personal value. And finally, they must allow the beast to bite them, thus spurring a connection that enables the Myad to review memories and determine worth. Throughout the entire process, the Charmer must not scream, because that will break the Myad's concentration, causing it to either flee or attack. If the Charmer can survive the evaluation of their past, the Myad will grant permission to tame.

Nagakori

Pronunciation: *na-ga-kor-ee*

Rank: B-Class

Description: Nagakori mate for life at a young age and, as such, are always found in pairs. They are twin serpents that float in the air with dragon-like heads and whiskers that trail the length of their bodies. Females are electric-blue in coloring and can spew water from their unhinged jaws, while males are snow-white and shoot frost. When tamed, they must both be summoned at the same time, as they refuse to be separated.

Taming: Pairs can be found in cold areas near bodies of water. They're attracted to pleasant sounds, so Charmers should lure them out with a musical instrument or by singing. While maintaining the music, the Charmer must then perform a ribbon dance. The Nagakori will begin to mimic the flourishes of the ribbons, eventually surrounding the Charmer and allowing charm to be initiated. The Charmer cannot falter with the music, as this will cause the Nagakori to freeze them and flee.

Nezbit

Pronunciation: *nez-bit*

Rank: C-Class

Description: Nezbits are small, have rabbit-like builds with brown fur, and are coated with teal feathers. Exceptionally rare, they're near impossible to find because of their low numbers and their preference for living underground. They form small colonies and create large networks beneath the soil, only poking their wing-like ears up once every few days to absorb nutrients from the sun. Their ears can hear sounds from miles away, and they track reverberations in the earth to avoid danger. When tamed, they're used to listen to people's hearts and determine lies from truth. Their opal eyes flash green for truth and red for lies.

Taming: As they live underground, the Nezbits have no known preferred environment. Finding a colony involves luck and careful examination of the earth, because Nezbits leave behind small mounds after sticking their ears up from the ground. Once a possible mound has been sighted, the Charmer should remain still for several days until the ears appear. The Charmer should then quickly yank the beast up from the dirt and immediately initiate charm. It's important to note that the mounds in question are extremely similar to those left by prairie dogs, and because of that, reports of colonies are often inaccurate.

Ossilix

Pronunciation: *oss-eh-lix*

Rank: A-Class

Description: While Ossilix are the smallest of the legendary feline beasts, they exude a calm fury and are lethal, using size to their advantage to outmaneuver prey. Slightly larger than an ocelot, they have lithe bodies coated in metal, giving the appearance of silver and making their hide near impenetrable. They're known to be incredibly intelligent, displaying exceptional tactical thinking and striking only when they see the possibility of a killing blow. Ossilix saliva is a potent healing balm with the capability of bringing someone back from the brink of death. However, accepting this gift requires the recipient to sacrifice a sliver of humanity in exchange. The effects vary from person to person, but largely involve a physical transformation to that of a beast.

Taming: After finding an Ossilix, the Charmer must allow it to inflict a life-threatening injury and then accept its healing balm. If the Charmer does not accept, it will kill them quickly. If they do accept, the Ossilix will retreat and watch from a distance as their humanity slips away and they transform into a beast. This transformation represents the constant fury the Ossilix feels and, as such, is incredibly difficult to control. The Ossilix will study the Charmer's behavior, killing them if they're unable to withstand the burning rage, or accepting them as its master if they're able to revert back to human form.

Poi

Pronunciation: *poy*

Rank: B-Class

Description: Poi are solitary creatures that often establish territories over small clearings in the woods. They have fox-like bodies with white fur and a single black stripe running the length of their spines. Their most identifiable feature is the jewel-like amethyst orb nestled between their ears, which turns cloudy when a prediction is brewing and clears once the future has been set. Poi bites are venomous and will slowly kill, but the poison can be removed by the beast if tamed. Their saliva can close minor wounds and alleviate burns, though their true power lies in their ability to predict outcomes two minutes into the future. When tamed, the Poi can share its visions with its master.

Taming: No additional requirements are needed outside of standard charm, but the Charmer must hold their charm for several minutes while making no sudden movements, allowing the Poi to perform a series of predictions and determine the outcome of being tamed.

Scorpex

Pronunciation: *scor-pex*

Rank: B-Class

Description: The Scorpex is a dangerous beast that can grow to roughly thirty feet in length. Its wormlike body is plated in thick orange scales and coated with a shimmery mucus. It has four legs, each ending in hooked fingers, and a barbed tail with a stinger like that of a scorpion. Its poison is painful but not incurable. With six eyes, three on either side of its mandibles, the Scorpex is difficult to catch off guard. It is carnivorous and uses its eight tongues to strip carcasses down to the bones in a matter of minutes.

Taming: Scorpex are rarely owned, because taming one requires collecting carcasses for weeks to accumulate enough food to entice the beast. The smell alone dissuades most Charmers, not to mention the danger of the Scorpex itself. After presenting the pile of carcasses, the Charmer should wait until the beast has finished eating to initiate charm. If the Charmer has not provided enough to satiate the Scorpex's hunger, it will strike. A relatively "safe" number of carcasses to present is somewhere in the high twenties.

Songbloom

Pronunciation: *song-bloom*

Rank: D-Class

Description: The Songbloom is a relatively harmless beast found in rosebushes in remote parts of Lendria. The lower half of their bodies mimic the petals of a flower, and their human-like torsos bloom out of the center of the bulb. They can detach and float from plant to plant, reattaching via miniscule roots at the base of the petals that allow them to pull nutrients from the plant. Male Songbloom are ivy-colored and camouflage with the leaves, whereas females take after the actual roses. Both male and female Songbloom spend their days singing in an unknown language. There are a variety of tunes, and each one has a unique effect on the listener, ranging from feelings of elation to causing temporary slumber. Charmers frequently use Songbloom to elicit feelings of joy and love during ceremonies between mates.

Taming: Find a Songbloom colony by listening for their voices while searching through rosebushes. Once found, the Charmer must seat themselves before the beast and listen to a song of the Songbloom's choosing. Once the tune is complete, they should offer applause and then initiate charm. If the Songbloom elects to perform a sleeping tune, the Charmer will fall into slumber and be unable to offer applause, and the taming will fail. As the effects should only last a few minutes, the Charmer is free to try again once waking, assuming the Songbloom has not fled.

Telesávra

Description: *tell-eh-sav-rah*

Rank: D-Class

Description: The Telesávra is a lizard the size of a small boulder and has a rocky hide. It can detach its jaw to suck in air and summon a flickering white portal that will transport any beast or person with Charmer's blood to a designated location, referred to as a hearth point. The Telesávra can only remember one hearth point at a time. Many Charmers set Hireath as their hearth point for efficient and safe travel home.

Taming: No additional taming requirements are needed aside from standard charm.

Uloox

Description: *oo-locks*

Rank: C-Class

Description: The Uloox is a black snake found in caves with yellow eyes and three fangs. It can eat prey up to five times larger than its body size, thanks to its unhinging jaw and fast-acting digestive system. Tiny ducts are found along the roof of its mouth, just behind its fangs. Uloox venom is dangerous, and is known cloud the mind and cause hallucinations, as well as weaken the body. Muscles will seize and become nearly immobile until the venom fades. Very few Charmers own one, as they're known to be temperamental and find little joy in being summoned from the beast realm.

Taming: To tame an Uloox, a Charmer must allow themselves to be bitten as many times as the beast deems fit. This is highly dangerous, as multiple bites can result in death. Once the Uloox is satisfied that the Charmer has become immobile, it will wait until its venom has cycled out of the Charmer's system. Only then will it allow itself to be tamed. However, if the beast becomes hungry during the taming process, it will slowly devour parts of the Charmer, such as fingers or toes, until it is either full or the Charmer is able to move. It's recommend that several field mice are brought along to the taming to prevent this.

Vissirena

Pronunciation: *vis-sy-reen-ah*

Rank: B-Class

Description: Vissirena have human torsos and fish-like lower bodies that end in long, colorful tails. Iridescent scales varying in color cover the entirety of their figure, and their hair is a mixture of seaweed and tentacles. Their faces also share similar structures to those of fish, and additional fins often develop along the forearms. Vissirena live in schools in the waters to the west of Hireath. The fleshy voids on their palms can open and close, altering currents to bring prey in their direction. When tamed, they can channel powerful streams of water with immense force. Vissirena can only be summoned in bodies of water.

Taming: Do not attempt to charm a Vissirena underwater. At the first hint of danger, they will send the threat to the bottom of the ocean via an unforgiving current until drowning has occurred. Likewise, do not attempt to catch from a boat, as they'll simply destroy the ship. Instead, a Charmer should fish for one from the shore. Only a magically reinforced pole, coupled with fishing line made from Fabric Spinner silk, will hold the Vissirena's weight. Preferred bait is tuna wrapped in orange peel. Once the Vissirena is hooked, the Charmer should prepare for a fight that could last several days. After the Charmer has reeled one in, they should initiate charm.

Xifos

Pronunciation: *zy-fos*

Rank: A-Class

Description: Because of its replication magic, the Xifos is regarded as one of the most difficult legendary feline beasts to tame. It has a slender, slate-gray body with twin tails that form sharp arrowheads. When the Xifos is activating its power, all the hair on its body stands on end, solidifying into fine needles, and then it shudders, creating an exact replica of itself. The number of copies one Xifos can maintain varies, though the recorded high is two hundred and three. Each copy can attack with the full strength and force of the original. If a copy is injured or otherwise incapacitated, it will dissolve into smoke. Xifos are solitary, yet they usually have a pack of copies flanking them for protection.

Taming: A Xifos will only bond with a master cunning enough to separate the original from the copies. Simply approaching the beast and initiating charm will cause the beast to activate its power, surrounding the Charmer with copies. After the copies have shuffled, the Xifos will wait until the Charmer touches the one they believe is real. If they're wrong, the copy disappears, and all remaining forms attack. No one has ever guessed correctly via this method. Instead, after locating a Xifos, the Charmer should study it for several months to ensure they have the original version pegged. Charmers should find a cavern that can be used as a den, and construct an elaborate display of mirrors. They should then lure the Xifos to the cavern with the mating call of a pheasant, their preferred prey. If arranged correctly, the mirrors will trick the Xifos into thinking it has already summoned copies of itself. While it's searching for the pheasant, the Charmer should slowly approach. Thinking the Charmer is already surrounded by copies, the beast will sit and wait for them to choose. Touch the original Xifos, and initiate charm.

Zystream

Pronunciation: *zy-stream*

Rank: A-Class

Description: The Zystream is the only legendary feline beast that prefers water to land, though it's capable of breathing in both environments. Liquid-blue, its coat is a mixture of water-resistant fur and scales. It has a long tail that ends in fins, as well as finned whiskers lining its jaw and throat. Fluid in nature, it's nearly impossible to pin and can shoot immensely powerful jet streams from its mouth. It's stronger in water and can summon small rain clouds to follow it when on land.

Taming: The Zystream can be found in fresh or salt water during the warmest month of summer. A Charmer must approach while the beast is swimming, where it will assess the Charmer by circling them several times. At some point, it will dive beneath the surface and snare the Charmer's foot, dragging them into deep water. It's imperative that a Charmer does not resist. If they do, the beast will become irritated and either kill them or release them and flee. If the Charmer remains calm, it will continue to swim until it senses the Charmer's lungs giving out. At that point, it will leap out of the water and place the Charmer on the bank. Then, it will press its snout to their chest and use magic to coax any water from their lungs and encourage them to breathe. Now that the Charmer has become one with the water in its eyes, it is ready to be tamed.

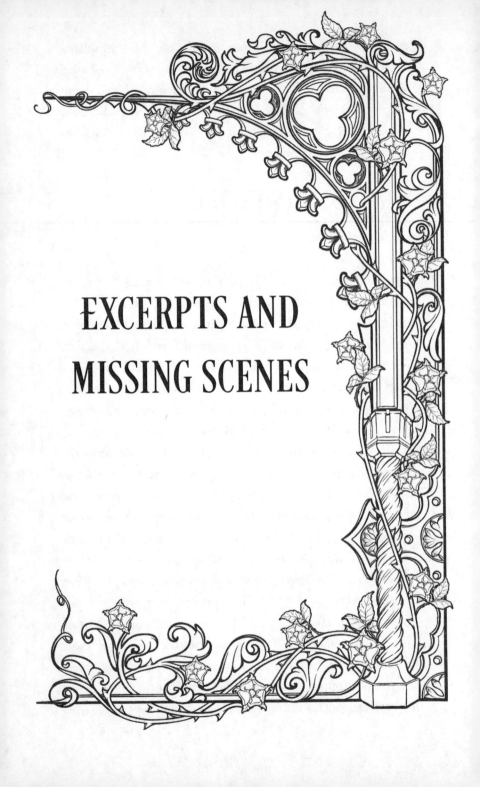

EXCERPTS AND MISSING SCENES

Keep reading for a glimpse into Noc's past...and a hint of what's to come for Noc, Leena, and the assassins of Cruor in

THE FROZEN PRINCE

ONE

THE FROZEN PRINCE
50 YEARS AGO

T he heavy beat of the approaching army's drums echoed through my rib cage. My horse shifted beneath me with a nicker, and my grip on the reins tightened. Not for the first time, Rhyne's forces had crossed the sea between our countries and landed on the flat edge of Penumbra Glades. Our armada had lost, and now the small town of Moeras was counting on me and my men to protect them. The people may have fled for safety, but their homes were here. Their *lives* were here.

And if I couldn't save them, then I didn't deserve to call myself their prince.

"Ready yourselves!" I urged my mare forward, and her hooves churned through the soft muck of the marshy battlefield. Thick cattails battered her legs, and the harsh breeze carried the swampy stench of salt and earth. Flat and treeless, the expanse stretched before us, giving my troops full view of the amassing army. Glinting in the morning sun, their severe jade armor sent a chill running down my spine.

For years now, that color had haunted my dreams. But no matter how many times I tried, no matter how many letters I sent in hopes of negotiating peace, the royal house of Rhyne would not listen. All they wanted was my head on a pike: a life for a life, a prince for a princess.

Amira. I pushed away the memory of her golden hair and gentle smile. War was no place to get lost in the past. I had other lives depending on me.

With a sharp click of my tongue, my horse leapt into a canter and made for the front line. Thousands of men and women clad in steel armor stared back at me, the griffin crest of Wilheim etched across their hearts. They stood at the ready, their backs ramrod straight and gazes locked forward, the white banners with their purple emblems snapping in the wind. We had no drums. We had no horns. We had no need to declare our presence. This was our home, and the quiet town at our backs was the only reminder we needed.

We would not lose.

As I came to a halt, one man broke rank and guided his stallion to my side. A scraggly beard crawled down his neck, and when he tipped his head my direction, umber eyes locked with mine. He gripped my shoulder with a smile.

"Let's get this over with. There's an ale with my name on it waiting back at camp." A laugh rumbled through his chest, cut short by a wet cough.

Dread stirred in my gut. "Thaleus?"

My general waved me off. "It's nothing a little ale won't fix. Best get on with this so I can wet my whistle." Straightening, he pounded a closed fist to his chest a few times, seemingly loosening whatever had caught in his throat. The coughing died, but my unease didn't. He touched a finger to his cracked lips and winced. No doubt there were purplish bags swelling beneath his eyes, too.

This plague—or whatever it was—was just as skilled at killing my men as Rhyne had proven to be, and if we didn't get out of this gods-forsaken marsh soon, I wouldn't have a kingdom left to defend.

Before I could say anything more, a low horn sounded from across the marsh. It picked up an octave right at the end before dying completely, signaling Rhyne's attack. The ground rumbled from the sudden quake of hooves and feet, and thousands of jade soldiers crashed through the muddy banks toward our ranks.

Beside me, Thaleus took charge. "Archers!" His voice rang out loud and clear. Maybe this plague hadn't marked him for dead quite yet. The tiniest sliver of relief settled my fear. We'd live to fight another battle together. We had to.

Archers raised their bows to the skies at his command, and Thaleus unsheathed his sword. "Nock!" His bellow was followed by the stretching of string and arrows clacking against wood. Shoulders tense, they held position without wavering. I turned my back to them and faced the oncoming threat. Tightened my grip on my sword.

"Steady," Thaleus called. Blood rushed to my ears, carrying with it the frenzied beat of my heart. I took in a slow breath. Let it out. Repeated the action. Sounds dimmed, and all I could feel was the steady vibration of pounding feet. The time was here.

"Loose!" Thaleus's order preceded a volley of arrows that blackened the sky. The sun winked out, and our world was cast into temporary shadow. The low whistle of wood and feathers sung through the air...until metal-tipped heads clanked against armor or sunk into flesh, and the definitive sound of bodies hitting the earth interrupted the steady cadence of Rhyne's war drums. Angered bellows answered our attack, and they broke formation to charge.

Thaleus signaled for another round of arrows before yanking

his own sword out of its sheath. Turning to the men at our backs, he raised his weapon high. "Infantry with me. Riders with Prince Aleksander. We will not fall!"

The company of horsemen to my left waited with baited breath, their mounts pawing anxiously at the ground. Among them were three imposing figures clad in mercury armor. Sentinels. Wilheim's elite force of soldiers tasked with protecting the city and the royal family. An army of them would have destroyed Rhyne's men in a matter of days. Instead, thousands of men and women, soldiers I'd grown to love over the years, were forced to give up their lives so that my home could remain protected.

Despite the war, despite my arguments with Father, the Sentinels of Wilheim remained stationed atop the gleaming diamond and marble walls—save these three. My royal guard.

Frustration brewed in my chest, but I bottled the anger tight and focused on Rhyne's forces. Father might be able to deny our troops the aid of Sentinels, but he'd never stop me from leading the charge.

"For Lendria!" My war cry burned my throat at the same moment I dug my heels into my mare's sides. She rocketed forward, and my riders followed. Spears and swords glinted in the sun as we charged toward the thick of the enemy ranks. With every pounding beat of my horse's hooves, my pulse jumped higher. We rode without fear. We rode without hesitation. We rode without thinking of anything except what lay before us. Our horses crashed into the first wave of men, and soldiers crumpled to the ground as we effortlessly broke the line.

Spears shook and splintered against shields, swords clashed against armor and men. Blood sprayed all around us, and the earthy scent of the marsh was soon coated with a copper tang. And still we rode. I arced my sword high and crashed it against a solider, meeting the soft spot between neck and shoulder. He fell to the earth only to be replaced by another, and another. Swinging to my left, I caught sight of the morning sky aglow with something other than pale sunlight. Enemy arrows soaked in oil and licking flames careened toward my battlement.

"Shields!" With my free hand, I stripped a shield from my horse's side and flung it over my head. Arrows thumped into the soft wood, cooking the iron holds and heating my skin. I winced with every hit as each vibration shook through my bones. Once the rain of arrows died, I lowered my arm and continued to push my mare forward. The jarring clatter of armor meeting metal filled the air, and I swiped my blade at an advancing jade-clad soldier. His head hit the ground.

Part of me felt sick. The spray of blood against my horse's legs turned her snowy white coat a speckled red, and the sound of death was everywhere. But war was never pretty, and I'd be damned if I left my men to fight a battle I'd started, intentionally or not.

Beside me, the Sentinels were making easy work of our enemies. They'd dismounted and were cleaving through the ranks. Bodies fell in heaps around them, but they did not flinch.

Stomach churning, I stared out over the blood-soaked expanse. The muddy banks and shallow pools of water had turned a murky reddish brown, and the lifeless eyes of many, so many, stared up at me as I passed. It didn't matter if their armor was jade or steel, their expressions were the same: lost. I hated it. This was a useless war with no end, but one side had to win eventually. One side had to cave.

We would persevere. *We* would win. We had to.

An enemy rider bolted toward me, and our swords met with a harsh clang. The scrape of metal rang through my ears as I thrust my blade against his thigh, knocking him off balance. He slid in his saddle, and his horse veered. I was about to lunge after him when a brilliant orb of sparking magic careened between us. It singed the air with electricity and cooked everything it passed until it crashed into the ground. My gaze snapped to the enemy forces and the singular woman standing clear in their midst. She'd opted for leather armor that mirrored the drab browns and sage greens of our surroundings, keeping her position camouflaged until she struck. But now, with a burnt path of grass and cattails leading directly to her feet, she was all too visible.

Mage.

Flexing her fingers, she brought her hands before her chest and summoned another crackling ball of energy. It raged between her palms and sparked outward like lightning, and she looked up with a ferocious grin.

Thaleus galloped toward me like an arrow loosed from a bow. "How did Rhyne manage to get their hands on a mage?"

My gaze dropped to the ashy earth before us. "Explains how they tore through our ships so easily." Mages didn't trifle with the wars of Lendria. And yet there she was, summoning another sphere of lightning that could annihilate our forces without consequence. She had to be stopped.

Leaning into my mare's neck, I nudged her sides and called over my shoulder as we galloped forward. "You take command of the riders. I'll deal with her."

"Aleksander!" Thaleus shouted at my back. Enemy forces surged toward me, and I cut them down, ignoring the rising bile in my throat as more blood spilled. Blessed by magic of their own, the Sentinels chased after me with breakneck speed. For the first time since they'd been assigned to my guard, panic flickered through their barely visible gazes. Their movements were jerky, their kills sloppy and reeking of unease. Just how dangerous was this mage?

As if in answer, the glowing orb between her fingers finally reached its pinnacle. She thrust it from her hands directly toward me. Her cry rose above the trumpeting horns and beating drums, and I swerved my horse to the side. The snarling mass of energy streaked by, searing the left side of my armor. Heat cooked my skin, and I cried out even as my mare let out a frightened squeal and reared onto her hind legs. Fumbling to grip the reins in time, I lost my balance and smacked into the earth, reddish muck squelching through the slits in my armor and coating my skin. Black dots danced across my vision as the cattails swam in and out of focus. A dull ringing reverberated in my skull.

Somewhere behind me, the Sentinels shouted. We'd separated ourselves from the majority of our forces, and a barrage of enemy foot soldiers converged to take advantage. Rolling to the side, I avoided the deadly arc of a sword and swept the feet out from a jade warrior. He responded with a swift punch to my jaw. Pinning me beneath his weight, he brought his sword down fast. I countered with my blade and grimaced as the lingering burn from the magic transformed into a bone-deep blaze of pain down my arm. Grunting, I forced all my strength into my hands and pushed. He fell onto his back, and my blade met his jugular. A wet gurgle spewed from his lips, and then he went limp. Dead. I scrambled to my feet and stumbled forward a short distance until a familiar swell of static electricity clouded the air.

From a few feet away, the mage smiled. "And now this war will finally end."

I had no time to dodge her attack. My strength was already waning, and while her first attempt had missed, this one wouldn't. The last thing I'd see was the slash of her grin across blood-stained skin. Gritting my teeth, I crossed my arms in front of me in a futile, last-ditch attempt to protect my heart.

And then a blade so black it must have been carved from the night itself exploded through her ribs. Her magic died in an instant, and she sputtered, wild hands flailing against an attack neither of us saw coming. She took one look at me, blood staining her lips, and crashed to her knees, then to the ground.

Gone.

With a slow blink, I glanced at the space behind her. A man clad in sable clothes stood without moving, his gloved hand holding a black blade dipped in red. Confusion dulled the threat of battle, and I took a careful step forward. He wore the attire of a Wilheimian noble, with filigree patterns and brocades etched in fine stitching along his vest. His shoes were somehow remarkably clean, his clothes only showing the faintest signs of dirt and blood. Helmetless, his styled pompadour was on display, and not a single hair dared to jut out of place, despite the wind.

With a belabored sigh, he righted his silver-rimmed spectacles. "Thank you for distracting her, Prince Aleksander."

"It's you I should be thanking." I did a quick glance behind me and saw my guard had taken care of our nearby enemies and were waiting, gauging the distance between me and this mystery assassin. Threat or no? He wore no affiliating emblem. No colors from either army. Still, he had saved my life. As a show of faith, I sheathed my sword. "Why kill the mage? Are you Lendrian?"

"Lendrian?" The man raised a careful brow. "I suppose by geographical terms, the answer is yes."

Geographical terms? My brow furrowed. "I see. Then you should return to camp with me. I'd like to reward you for your courage."

"There's no need." With a flourish of his hand, the blade disappeared. Into a hidden sheath? I couldn't tell. It was as black as his clothing, so perhaps. The man ran his hands over his vest until they came across a stray piece of lint. He flicked it away. "It seems as though this victory is yours."

He gestured to the fields. Sometime during my standoff with the mage, the drums and horns had been silenced. There were still cries of agony rising and falling with the wind, but the anxiety of battle had diminished. The roar, gone. Penumbra Glades was a wasteland of blood and bone. We'd held the line and protected the town of Moeras, but not without casualty. As the last bit of adrenaline fled my body, fatigue settled deep in my bones, and I let out a quiet sigh.

Slowly, I turned back to the man. "So it seems."

He nodded once, a curt jut of his chin, and stepped back. "I must be going. Stay vigilant, Prince Aleksander."

My gaze dropped as he stepped back into something dark as an oil slick. Rhyne must have been in a rush to douse their arrows. Taking a few quick strides, I closed the distance between us. "Wait. I insist you return to camp so I can properly thank you."

Something flickered through his ice-green gaze. "As I said, that's not necessary. I am a member of Cruor. The mage was a job. I can procure proof if necessary."

Cruor?

My father had once mentioned a guild of elite assassins living on the fringe of our country, but I'd never paid him much mind. The rumors surrounding their abilities were exactly that—rumors. No one could move with the shadows. No one could form weapons out of night.

And yet...

I stared at the dark patch beneath his feet. Shiny like ink and yet wispy as mist, it curled up in small billows. And the blade, had that been one of their famed weapons? Something truly crafted from death itself? Curiosity burned deep in my chest, and I removed my helmet. Shock-white hair spilled over my eyes, and I brushed it to the side. "Proof won't be necessary. But I'd still like you to return to camp with us. Both as thanks, and so I can learn more about you and your work." I waited for a beat to see if he'd answer, but he only stared at me with a look of disbelief. "What's your name?"

The man's gaze faltered. "Kostya, my prince."

I grinned, extending my hand. "Call me Aleksander. There are enough people around to call me *prince*."

He pressed his lips together in a fine line, as if contemplating the request. Finally, he shook my hand. "I couldn't possibly deny a request from the royal family. Shall we?"

"No, you couldn't," I joked. I gripped his shoulder, and he stiffened beneath me. I instantly let my hand fall away, but stayed by his side as we strode across the marsh, casting him the occasional curious glance. A man born of shadows. A man born of death. The gods only knew what kind of life he led—but I was eager to discover that for myself.

———◆———

As we hit camp, evidence of our battle was everywhere. People hurried about while commanders barked orders to establish a night patrol. Others still carried armor and weapons to the temporary blacksmith for repair. More were heading toward a line of campfires where pigs roasted on spits, the scent of ale and smoke already thick in the air. A smile tugged at my lips. I'd have to introduce Kostya to Thaleus.

Turning to the assassin, I was about to offer him a place by the fire when a foot soldier from Thaleus's unit rushed toward me. He came to a screeching halt and offered a haphazard bow before righting himself.

"Sir, Thaleus has been injured."

All thoughts of ale and good conversation fled in a breath. "What happened?"

The man fumbled for words. "I... I don't know. I didn't see. He just collapsed."

My world narrowed, and I barely tossed Kostya a glance before pushing past the soldier and sprinting toward the medical tent. The white canopy dominated my vision. "Where is he?" I burst through the open flaps, only to find rows and rows of bodies strewn on cots. Some were covered head to toe in sheets, a ghastly declaration of death. Others were propped up on pillows, bandaged and bleeding, with frantic attendants rushing from bed to bed. I snared the first one who hurried by and forced her to meet my gaze. "Where. Is. He?"

She paled but nodded toward the far end of the tent. I released her the moment I spotted Thaleus's scraggly beard. He laid quietly between two cots. The man on his left screamed wordlessly as healers attempted to set his broken leg. The cot on his right was silent, the outline of a body decipherable beneath a sheet. I hated how close they put him to those who'd already passed through to the realm of the gods. Crossing the tent quickly, I came to his side and gripped his clammy hands in mine.

Weak eyes framed by ever-darkening bags stared up at me. "Aleksander."

I swallowed the rock in my throat. "What happened to that ale?"

A brittle laugh scraped through his chest, followed by a wet cough flecked with red droplets. "Might have to wait on that."

"Where are you hurt?" I scoured the length of his body, searching for wounds or bandages only to come up empty-handed. And yet, the ashen tint to his skin spoke volumes, and I tightened my hold on his fingers.

"Nowhere. You think some Rhyne soldiers would get the best of me?" He coughed again, and I ignored the sticky feel of blood on my hand. "I'll be fine come morning. Just need some rest."

My heart gave a pitiful thud. Not a single soldier had survived the plague. The symptoms baffled even our best healers. Priests and priestesses were brought in, and still no one could get a grip on the sickness rampaging through my camp. And while I couldn't possibly be held responsible for something as uncontrollable as this, I couldn't help but blame myself. This entire war was because of me. Because I'd fallen in love with a Rhyne princess and slighted the High Priestess who'd coveted me. Her curse had killed my one true love, and yet Amira's parents hadn't believed me. No one believed me. Even now, when the battles were done and men crowded around fires with ales in their hands, there were whispers. Frustrations. They had all believed my claim once. But too much death soured their perceptions. I didn't blame them—curses were rare and hardly left proof. Whether or not I had ended Amira's life, I was responsible for her death.

"Hey, stop that." Thaleus wrenched his hand free to place it gently on my forearm. "I can see those wheels turning. This isn't your fault. I'll be fine by morning, just you wait. Now, get out of here. You don't need to see," he winced as a piercing shriek split the air, "or hear any of this."

"Thaleus..." Words failed to form, and my chest tightened. What would I do once he was gone? Who would I joke with or share ales with or let myself just *be* with? No one wanted to brush elbows with the prince who started it all. If I were in their shoes, fighting a war I didn't understand, I'd be hesitant to rally to my side, too.

Go home. I clenched my jaw tight. Returning to Wilheim and the safety of my castle would only cause more discord. I needed to be here, fighting with them. Not commanding from afar.

I owed them all so much.

"Go on. I need to sleep." He slapped my arm with a slackening hand that lacked any semblance of strength.

I turned without another word and slipped through the tent. My heart was as heavy as the dead weight of each body I passed. When I broke out into the camp, I gulped down air...and fled. Broke into a sprint and ran toward the fringes of our settlement, ignoring the pensive stares of my royal guard as they decided whether to follow. I prayed they didn't. I needed space. Room to breathe. And so did my men. They needed time away from *me*, time to vent their frustrations and speak their minds without fear of the royal house coming down on them. There was too much death hanging low over us all.

I didn't know how long I ran, only that I did until the sounds of camp faded in the distance. Slumping to the ground, I worked muck and grime between my fingers as I sought for a grip on reality. And then I crumbled. Because I knew. I knew Thaleus wouldn't make it. I knew this war, all this death, was on me. No matter what lies I told myself, this was *my* doing. A sob cracked my chest, and I held my head in my hands. Thaleus wasn't the first brother or sister I'd lost over the years. There was Helena. Broderick. Parvis. Amira... So many more. There was no solace to be found, but at least it was quiet out here. At least there were no whispers or false smiles. At least death was stuck in that gods-awful white tent.

Hours ticked by until the faint light of dusk claimed the sky and the first brave stars dotted the horizon. Behind me, someone cleared their throat.

I jumped to my feet and reached for the small blade I kept on my hip.

Kostya eyed my hands. "Decent reflexes, though it would've helped had you known I was here to begin with."

My hand wavered. "I heard you approach."

Kostya sighed. "Because I alerted you to my presence. How long do you think I'd been waiting?"

Everything left me in a rush, and my shoulders slumped. I didn't care if he'd been there since the beginning. I didn't have it in me to try to pick apart my surroundings in my grief. And I didn't rightly care. Running a hand through my hair, I gave him a weary glance. "Sorry I took off like that. You're free to leave if you'd like."

Kostya studied me for a long moment before removing his glasses. Slowly, he pulled a cloth from his breast pocket and began polishing the lenses. "What's wrong?"

"What's wrong?" I barked out a harsh laugh. As if it wasn't glaringly obvious.

"Something is troubling you." Kostya replaced his glasses.

Giving way to absurdity, I tossed my hands to the sky in exasperation. "Of course something is troubling me. Were you not there today? Didn't you see the battlefield? How many people, on both sides, had to die for this endless fight?" I started to pace, acutely aware of the way his gaze tracked my progression. "I've tried to negotiate with Rhyne. I've tried to explain what happened to their princess. I've tried everything I can think of to bring this to an end, and nothing is working.

"And what's worse is my men are paying the price. If they're not dying with a sword in their hands, they're dying with their backs on a cot, courtesy of a plague no one can cure. It might look like Lendria is winning, but everywhere I turn, we are losing *everything*."

Kostya was silent for a long breath, as if waiting to see whether I'd continue. Only when I finally came to a stop did he fold his arms across his chest. "You said you've tried everything?"

"Yes. Everything."

"And you're sure about that?" His harsh green eyes softened before he looked away to the night sky.

The raging pulse that had been building inside me quieted. "What are you saying?"

Kostya cleared his throat. "What does Rhyne want? All wars boil down to what one side desires but isn't getting."

"Vengeance, I suppose." I went to slip my hands into the pockets of my trousers but failed. I hadn't even had time to toss aside my armor. The metal gauntlets covering my fingers scraped against my plated thighs.

With a deliberate slowness, Kostya dragged his gaze back to mine. "Specifics matter. What *exactly* do they want?"

It didn't take long for me to answer. "Me. They want me."

Kostya said nothing, but his stare was so damning I had to fight to keep my chin held high. Shadows started to fester in the space around him, and he dipped his hands in the abyss. Onyx tendrils pooled in his palms before spilling out between his fingers. "Then you haven't tried *everything*." With that gut-punch, he added, "I'll be going now, Prince Aleksander. I wish you luck with your never-ending war."

Before I could clear my throat to speak, a vacuum of darkness swallowed him whole, and he was gone. If it weren't for the way his words lingered in the air, I could've convinced myself he'd never been there at all. But he had been there. He'd listened. And he wasn't wrong—all Rhyne wanted was my head on a spike. I'd been fighting against my own death for so long that the concept of giving in had always seemed foreign. Like admitting defeat. And yet… I slumped back to the ground and stared out over the darkening marsh, my world reorienting around the assassin's parting words.

Thaleus would soon be gone. Amira was gone. Nearly everyone I loved, gone. They were only blips of brightness in my life, stolen away before I was ready to say goodbye. How many other families and loved ones were suffering through the same heartache?

Maybe Amira was waiting for me in the gods' realm. Maybe a world without me truly was better. Those deathly shadows that had swallowed Kostya whole hadn't seemed so dangerous. He'd almost seemed to welcome the way they moved, the way they cocooned him in a solitary reprieve reality couldn't offer.

Think of your parents. I pictured my father's eyes, a frozen blue that mirrored my own. The stern gaze that turned soft with wrinkles when he smiled. My mother's warm embrace that always welcomed me home. The smell of fresh-baked bread somehow constantly present in the folds of her clothes. If I were to die, they'd be heartbroken. I was their only son. And yet...

This war would never end while I still breathed.

Rocketing to my feet, I stripped the armor from my body and cast it to the ground. In a simple tunic and light breeches, I was entirely unprotected. A gentle breeze kissed the exposed skin of my arms, and it felt like home. Like affirmation. With my armor went the blade, and I paused for a moment at the lack of its weight. But no—where I was going, weapons weren't needed. And then I started walking with more purpose than I'd felt on the battlefield that morning. This war would end tonight. I'd make sure of it.

I walked until the muddy marshland shifted to sediment-filled banks of black sand. We hadn't destroyed the entirety of Rhyne's forces, and those who'd retreated were in the midst of loading gear and bodies onto ships. Flickering fires cast the beach in an orange hue, and the quiet murmurs of soldiers created a lull that competed with the ocean waves. For a moment, I paused and focused on that sound. On the ebb and flow of the tide creeping over the sand and washing away the remnants of the war. Of the blood and horrors these people had faced.

Raising my hands above my head, I walked to the first campfire I could find. I had no delusions they'd take me alive. I'd offered my imprisonment before to end the war, and they'd spit on the letter and sent it back, sealed with the wax and emblem of the royal family.

This would be different. A strange sense of peace flowed through to my fingertips, and for the first time in years, relief relaxed my lips into a gentle smile.

———◆———

The first thing I saw was darkness. A maelstrom of shadows that varied from slate to onyx to sable, all somehow unique. They were gentle in their touch, and it was then I realized I could feel my fingers. My limbs. My body. There wasn't any pain. There wasn't much of anything at all. The total and complete silence was deafening and yet comforting. The sounds of war and death, gone. Here there were no whispers or judgments threading low through conversations.

And then there was a pinprick of light—a pale gray that hinted at smoke. It grew until it devoured the expanse, blanketing out the darkness and bringing with it sounds. A rustling of bodies and hushed words. Voices I didn't recognize and couldn't piece together through the veil of mist. And then a fiery heat bloomed in my chest, and my heart, which had been still, beat once against my ribs. Searing pain cracked through me like a hammer battering brittle wood. Light blossomed behind my eyes and white sparks danced in my vision. Again my heart beat, this time with less anguish but more vigor, and more flickers of light erupted in the gray.

The voices grew impossibly loud, and suddenly I could *feel*. I was flat on my back somewhere, blades of grass tickling my neck. My clothes were damp, as if my body had been soaked at one point and was only beginning to dry. The cool air was thick with pine, and as I took a staggered breath, the fresh scent of earth and blood skated along the back of my tongue. My eyes flew open. The world of gray traded for an indigo expanse dotted with millions of stars. Treetops towered high like jagged spears against the sky. And darkness. Thin tendrils of shadows unrelated to the night snaked through my peripheral, as if they'd always been there. As if they *belonged*.

Someone knelt beside me and placed a hand over my chest. A man I didn't recognize peered down, his curling hair the color of weathered bark falling about his shoulders. Framed by heavy wrinkles, his dark eyes held nothing but wisdom—and perhaps a glimmer of pity.

"Where am I? What happened?" My words were a harsh rasp, and I desperately wished for water.

The man didn't move. "You're safe. You're still in Lendria."

"Did you heal me?"

"No, I didn't heal you. You died as you intended, and I merely brought you back." His gruff voice was oddly soothing, but his words set me on edge. I shouldn't be *back*. Prince Aleksander *needed* to stay dead to end the war. It was a decision I'd made of my own volition, and apparently it had been ripped away from me without my consent.

Curling my hands into fists, I stiffened in place. "Who are you? Why did you resurrect me?"

"My name is Talmage. I'm the guild master of Cruor. You're alive because of Kostya." With a nod, he indicated a man standing to my left wreathed in shadows. Just like outside the camp, he hadn't made a sound. But this time, I could hear the subtle inhale and exhale of breath, the minute scraping of cloth on cloth as he straightened his tunic. The way his swallow seemed forced. Death had done something to my senses, and the unease in my gut ratcheted up several notches.

"I don't want to be here." Anger colored my voice. I hardly recognized it.

Talmage clasped his hands together. "That can be arranged. I won't force you to live as an assassin of Cruor if you don't want to."

I ignored him entirely and glared at Kostya. He averted his eyes, unwilling to meet my gaze.

"I felt responsible for your death. I... I fear my words may have driven you to take such extreme action." He cleared his throat and gripped the back of his neck. A beat later, he dropped his arms to his sides. "While it may have ended the war, you didn't deserve to die. I thought, if you wanted a second chance..." His low voice was clouded with guilt, and some of my anger fled. Perhaps his words had been the catalyst, but the decision was my own. *Mine.*

"You chose your death. Kostya found you without armor, without weapons, and with a smile on your face. I can't say this life will be easier, but it will be new. You can move on. You can forget. We leave everything from our past in the ground." Talmage's words hinted at a possible new beginning, at a life outside of the wars I'd grown so used to. But that was the thing—no matter how alluring it sounded, no matter how much he promised my previous life could be left in the dirt, there was simply no way a prince of the realm would be forgotten.

There was no outrunning who I used to be. Who I was.

Pushing myself into a sitting position, I bit back a growl. "I don't get that choice. So long as I live, Rhyne will continue to fight. I died so my men could find reprieve. I died so all of this would end. You might as well kill me now, because I'll walk right back to their forces if I have to. I won't let my country suffer any longer."

"We have ways of hiding your identity." Talmage's words were so soft I barely heard them. "The only people who would know of your past would be myself and Kostya."

"And what of my body? I'm supposed to be *dead*. Rhyne won't accept my disappearance as proof, and the war will continue."

"About that." Kostya gave a curt nod to my wet clothes. "They were transporting your body to the main ship on a rowboat when I came to...extract you. During the confrontation, the boat capsized. No one was seriously injured, but your body was lost to the depths of the ocean. Or so Rhyne thinks."

"One of the men transporting your body was a high-ranking official. His word will be good enough for Rhyne." Talmage steepled his hands together, and I pursed my lips. I wanted to believe in this absurd possibility of a different life, but what if they were wrong? What if Rhyne continued to fight?

"Aleksander." Kostya crouched before me and leveled me with one look. "You've done enough. You've done more than any prince has ever done for the people of Lendria. You don't owe this world anything else. If you truly wish to die again, then I'll do it myself. But if you want a chance at living, at being someone other than the Frozen Prince of Wilheim, then take it. If at any point you change your mind, I'll end it quickly. This I promise you."

Silence stretched on for an eternity. Part of me was livid. I'd found peace in death, and they'd brought me back to a world where I'd done nothing but cause others pain. I wasn't sure I could live with that knowledge. But another smaller part of me burned with a new hunger I'd long since forgotten: hope.

Hope was a funny thing. All it took was a moment of reflection. One second of attention. And then it was blooming and burning in my chest, overtaking the fears and doubts I'd carried with me to the grave.

Kostya stood and offered me his hand, already reading the answer on my face. "Well?"

I took it after only a breath of hesitation, and he pulled me to my feet. "If I change my mind, you end it. No questions asked. Understood?"

"Understood."

Talmage straightened. "Before we take you to Cruor, we've got to see a mage about your appearance. But first, you'll be needing a new name. You're not a prince anymore, Aleksander Nocsis Feyreigner."

You're not a prince anymore. Nothing in my life had ever sounded sweeter. It would grieve my parents to no end that their son had died, and they'd probably spend weeks, maybe months, dragging the ocean for my body only to come up empty-handed. Guilt flared for a moment in my chest, but I buried it deep. A world without the man who sparked a never-ending war with Rhyne was surely better off. They'd find a suitable replacement to take the throne once they passed, and life would go on. This would be but a small note in history, and my new life was just beginning. With a tentative smile, I glanced between my newfound brethren.

"Noc," I said. "My name is Noc."

THE FROZEN PRINCE

Noc is living on borrowed time. With the dark magic of Cruor's Oath testing his control, he has to fight with everything he has to keep Leena safe...but when his true identity is discovered, there's no manner of beast that can save him.

Coming February 25, 2020

MISSING SCENE: OZ'S CHAPTER

Author's Note:

This scene was originally intended to come after Leena leaves the Drinking Mermaid with Noc, and it shows a game of getsa ball between Ozias, Calem, Corinne, and her friends. As the sport touches on some new magic that won't be seen until much later in the series, though, I decided to remove it. However, for those who love a good match of Quidditch, this will be a fun look into this fantasy game.

I had no idea how we'd gotten here. Yeah, there'd been a few drinks. Yeah, Corinne had this dimpled grin that made it impossible to say no. So when a group of her friends strolled into the tavern and suggested we take the party elsewhere, I'd gone along with it. But still... I ran a hand over my scalp and stared at the predicament before me. I'd forced Calem to come with me, but judging by his dark glower and balled fists, he wasn't too excited with the prospect of a game of getsa ball.

"I don't know the first thing about this," Calem said. He stared at the seemingly normal arena. Oval in shape and covered in cropped grass, it was the very definition of unassuming. But I knew what would happen the moment the game started—this placid terrain would shift to something formidable. A canyon with rocky outcroppings. A turbulent ocean with nothing more than stepping stones stretching from one end to the next. Perhaps something with fire.

"Sure you do. We've gone to a game together. What was that, five years ago outside of Wilheim?"

Calem's jaw tightened. "One match, Ozias. One. I don't know the rules or how to play this thing." He expelled a heavy breath before rounding his gaze on me. "Look, I know I was supposed to help you get a date tonight, but this? This is insane." He gestured to the empty stadium surrounding us. Tiered bench seating rose high into the sky, allowing for thousands of bodies to pack in and watch the event. Ortega Key had a professional getsa ball team that played against the other cities of Lendria, and they frequently won. Even competed in something called the Realm Championship against other countries.

Pinpointing Corinne's animated form a few feet away, my brows drew together. I only hoped we were playing with minor leaguers instead of the real deal. If we were, well... Calem would kill me. Even if he didn't know how to play the sport, he wouldn't do well with losing. Especially not if it was a sound defeat.

"We needed another player—otherwise the teams would be uneven."

Calem's glare only deepened. At that point, Corinne skipped toward us carrying a trunk with brass latches and buckles. Two women followed in her wake, one with warm, golden-brown hair that fell in a ponytail to her midback, and the other with long sable hair done in twists and fashioned into a bun atop her head. While I didn't recognize anyone else from Corinne's group, it would be impossible not to place this woman. Slender with toned muscles and rich, dark skin, she stood tall. Impassive eyes studied us, and then she folded her arms across her chest.

Awe welled up inside me, and I barely managed to eek out her name. "Dominya."

Corinne's smile stretched from ear to ear. "Oh, good! You know her."

Calem raised a questioning brow as I extended my hand her direction. "Not in the slightest. I know of her, sure. Best spotter in Lendria." Dominya shook my hand, her grip firm. "Pleasure."

"Gods." Calem pinched his nose. "I thought this was supposed to be a low-key game for fun. Not that we'd be playing with professionals."

"What, scared of a little competition?" The brunette placed her hands on her hips, her blue eyes lighting up like the stars in the sky.

Something in Calem's gaze shifted from disappointment to interest, and he straightened slightly. "Hardly."

Her answering grin was wicked. "Good."

"Zenna, please." Corinne shot her a stern glance before softening her expression and turning to Calem. "Dominya is the only professional. The rest," she gestured to the retreating group of five behind us, three men and two women, "are part of my league. We play for fun, and Dominya occasionally drops in to offer pointers. She's a friend of the family."

"Not to mention I own the place, and you needed me to get in here." Dominya let out a sigh that pretended at exasperation, but carried far too much warmth. "You're lucky I had nothing better to do."

"Semantics." Corinne set the box at her feet and crouched before it. "Anyone need a refresher?"

"Please." Calem inched closer. "I've only ever seen one match."

"Great," muttered Zenna. Calem tilted his chin to the side, eyes crinkling at the corners. He always did love a challenge.

"The rules are fairly simple." Corinne unlatched the trunk to reveal an array of belts and something that looked like a leather cannonball. She picked it up and held it before her with two hands. "Get the getsa ball across your opponents' line three times and you win."

Glancing down the field, I spotted two poles on either side of the field dotted with rycrim cores. They glowed a faint green, but when the ball passed the invisible line stretching between them, I knew they'd flash red, signaling a goal.

"There are five players on each side." She handed the ball to Calem, who tested its weight by tossing it gently from hand to hand. Returning to the crate, she began to sift through the leather belts until she found one of each color: navy, burgundy, and emerald. "You can have as many attackers or defenders as you like, but only one spotter."

Dominya reached down and stole the navy belt. The gold buckle gleamed in the moonlight, and she ran her fingers over the eye sigil etched onto it. "I'll be taking that."

"What do the different roles mean?" Calem asked.

"The belts give buffs to the wearer. Attackers are granted additional strength and accuracy, defenders are near impossible to take down, and spotters receive increased agility and map knowledge."

Calem handed the getsa ball to me, and I tucked it beneath my arm. His gaze slanted to Dominya. "Map knowledge?"

"The trickiest part about getsa ball is the terrain." She jerked her chin over her shoulder. "It shifts every five minutes to keep the game interesting. When the magic of the belt activates, information about the environment becomes available to me and it's my job to guide you across the line. If it weren't for me, you'd be trying to learn about the terrain at the same time your opponents were attacking you or stealing the ball."

"Right. And the ball itself changes each time the arena does. If it shifts to, say, a metal environment, the ball might become magnetic and damn near impossible to move," Corinne said. Suddenly, the leather ball in my possession felt significantly heavier. I let it drop to the ground and roll between us. She looked knowingly at me before tossing the burgundy defender belt my direction and handing the emerald attacker belt to Calem. Then, she fished out two more green belts for herself and Zenna.

"An offensive strategy, then?" Zenna asked, studying the etching of crossed swords on her buckle.

"They'll go heavy on the defense. They always do. We're faster, and we've got Dominya on our side." After a moment, she rounded her gaze on me and broke out a dimpled grin that did weird things to my insides. "Plus, Ozias has played defender before. I have a feeling he'll be protection enough."

I studied the grass beneath my feet and ignored the crawl of heat up my cheeks. "We'll see."

"Okay, so three attackers, one defender, one spotter. Let's get this show on the road." Calem looped the belt around his midsection and fastened the buckle, yelping only slightly as a wave of iridescent magic rippled across his skin. A small, drawstring pouch appeared on his right hip. Corinne and Zenna didn't bother to hide their laughs at Calem's surprised reaction, and I rolled my lips together to keep from grinning too broadly. The belt's magic didn't hurt, but he'd jumped the gun like always instead of waiting for an explanation.

Zenna fashioned her belt in place, and once the magic settled, patted her pouch. "Careful with this. You only get so many pagdas, and they're needed to stop the other team." With dexterous fingers, she slipped into the pouch and extracted one gleaming, oily black ball the size of a marble. And then she tossed it to the side of the arena. When it smacked into the earth, it immediately started to expand until it stopped just shy of knee-level.

"They're activated the moment you touch them. You have roughly three seconds to throw them before they start growing in your hand, and you don't want that." Corinne slipped on her own belt. "They're sticky and weighted. The only person who can remove them if you happen to get hit with one is the defender."

Calem met my gaze, his brow twitching just a hair. "You follow me, got it?"

I couldn't help but laugh. "Sure thing."

"A better strategy would be to just not get struck." Zenna flicked her ponytail to the side. "Ozias should protect Dominya. If she goes down, we're screwed."

Dominya's lips quirked into a smile as she fastened her own belt in place. The same magic rushed over her, but instead of a pouch, she was granted a pair of goggles with green lenses and a black choker necklace with a gem positioned right at the center of her throat.

She tapped it with her middle finger. "This allows me to project my voice directly into your minds so I can share map information with you. The traps are endless."

Shrugging my shoulders, I gave Calem a pat on the back. "They know what they're doing. Just don't get hit. And don't get disqualified."

"How would I go about doing that?" Calem asked.

Corinne frowned. "There aren't many ways, but to name a few: outside magic, causing severe bodily harm, stepping out of the arena. Think you can manage?"

"Yeah." A small part of Calem deflated. No doubt he was thinking he could use the shadows to hide from potential pagdas. It was probably for the best, anyway—the last thing we wanted was to out ourselves to them.

Turning to me, Corinne nodded to the unattended belt in my hand. "Go on. Let's get this game started already."

Looping the burgundy belt around me, I fastened the gold buckle carved with a shield into place. Tingling magic reminiscent of a cool breeze poured over me, and suddenly I felt heavier. Sturdier. Like a tree rooted deep into the ground that could withstand a hurricane and come out unbroken. Then, a weight settled along my forearms and hands. Polished metal gauntlets and vambraces appeared, and I felt the beginnings of a smile on my lips.

Corinne reached for the getsa ball and tucked it beneath her arm, and Zenna closed the trunk before setting off to the side of the field. Then, as one, we met in the center of the arena before our opponents.

Zenna's eyes sparked with anticipation. "Friendly match, as we have no referee and newbies on the field. Wouldn't want anyone getting hurt, now would we?"

One of the men grinned. "Not our fault you went with an imbalanced strategy. But sure, we'll even let you start with the ball."

Dominya snorted. "That was a mistake." Raising her hand to the open roof of the arena, she snapped her fingers once. While the stars and moon had provided decent light, they were nothing compared to the sudden glow of floating orbs in the night. Enchanted globes on taut wire strings flickered to life, casting the ground in a harsh glow that illuminated every blade of grass. With a curt nod, she turned on her heels. "To your lines, then."

We retreated to our end of the field, each one of us stationed just behind the gleaming poles dotted with rycrims. Our opponents did the same. Beside me, Calem crouched low into his heels, and I watched as his muted-red gaze turned fiery and determined. They didn't know him, and thus underestimated him. All I knew was, I was sure glad I wouldn't be the one getting pelted by pagdas, courtesy of his arm. His aim was lethal.

"Normally the referee does this, but as I'm the one with the keys to the kingdom, I'll get things started." Dominya fished a small chain out of the back pocket of her breeches. She draped it over her head and let the oval pendant settle beneath her collarbone. Then she pressed the sky-blue button centered within. The mages had created some truly magnificent things in our world, but I'd always thank them for this sport. They'd even made it so the magic of the game was confined to the arena itself, meaning it'd never be weaponized for wars.

The ground trembled beneath my feet, and suddenly the grass disappeared, and the ground shifted to hard, red clay. Mountains sprung to life around us, each one redder than the last. Boulders burst into existence, blocking our view and creating narrow paths from one end of the arena to the other. Jagged outcroppings threatened to shred skin and clothes alike. And then a soft whirring sounded from Dominya's goggles, and she riveted her head toward one of the towering mountains.

"I'm getting a better vantage point. Calem and Zenna, stay as far left as you can. There are pitfalls scattered down the main paths. Corinne, hang back for now with Ozias. Keep my position secure." Without waiting to see if we followed her orders, she backed up a few feet and then took a running start toward the mountain, launching herself into the air. She gripped one of the small ledges along the rocky surface and found holds for her feet. Her muscles strained as she worked, climbing higher and higher without glancing once at the ground.

"Gods," Calem said, staring up after her.

Zenna grinned. "Spotters have to be able to do all sorts of things. Now, c'mon, you heard her. Let's go." With the getsa ball firmly in her grasp, she took off, Calem sprinting behind her with a look of pure excitement on his face.

Corinne crept around a cluster of rocks to sidle up next to me. With her sunset-red hair pulled back, I could see the eagerness in her gaze plain as day. This was her passion. Her sense of purpose. She cracked her knuckles and rolled her head from side to side, determined grin pulling at her lips. Winning would make her happy. And I wanted to make that feeling come true.

"What now?" I asked, scanning the rocky terrain. It was really something. I'd never been to the Gaping Wound to the southeast of Wilheim, but I'd heard tales of the red sands and mountains that dominated the landscape. I imagined it looked like this.

Corinne's shoulder brushed against my arm, and a chill raced over my skin. "I'm going to find a hiding spot close to the base of Dominya's outlook. You stay here and guard the line. If anyone comes running…" She made an x in front of her chest by crossing her forearms, and then grinned. "You know what to do."

A chuckled rolled through me. "Got it."

"Good. We've only got a few minutes left before the landscape shifts. Stay vigilant." And with that, she jogged away toward Dominya's mountain, finding a camouflaged position between two boulders and disappearing from view.

Glancing from post to post, I dragged my heel through the muddy red dirt to create a line to guard. A reminder to ensure I'd be in the right place if someone came streaking through the mountains with a getsa ball in their hands. Zenna's voice crackled into awareness in my mind. Staticky and rough, it was a bit on the choppy side, but I got the gist of what she was saying. Calem and Zenna were making progress and had encountered one of the team's defenders. Dominya was giving them orders to lure the man into a pitfall while progressing toward the opponents' line.

A physical shout echoed through the canyon that was full of frustration, and my gaze snapped skyward to track a black ball increasing in size as it arced through the air. It dropped down somewhere I couldn't see, but another disgruntled yell shook the loose rock along the ground. And then I heard Calem laugh.

My grin split my face. At least he wouldn't kill me later.

Dominya's voice prickled to life in my mind. "Nice work, Calem. Zenna, you're in the clear. Go, go, go!"

Within a minute, a loud gong sounded throughout the arena, signifying a getsa ball had crossed the line. I did a quick sweep to make sure it wasn't a sneak attack on our end, and then once again turned my gaze skyward. Calem, Zenna, and even Corinne—though she'd only been a short distance away—were thrust high into the air, thanks to the magic of their belts. The other team also floated high above the scenery, and then as if pulled on invisible strings, each party was returned to their line and dropped safely behind it.

Calem's blond bun was disheveled and there were a few scratches marring his face, not to mention the layer of red dust that had caked along his skin, but his wide grin outweighed it all—even the two pagda balls clinging to his back.

"Reset ends in three... two..." Dominya's voice snapped to life in our minds. As the spotter, she was the only one not forced to return to the line when a goal was scored. The getsa ball was now in enemy hands, and they'd be coming for our line. Calem, Corinne, and Zenna needed to steal it while I protected our side.

"One."

Right as she finished the countdown, I reached for Calem and wrenched the pagda balls from his back one at a time. The fingertips of my gauntlets glowed, successfully separating the strange oily sphere from his clothing, and I tossed them to the side. Zenna hopped my direction, three balls of her own across her thighs and calves.

I raised my brow. "I'm impressed. How did you even cross the line to score?"

She stuck out her leg and waited patiently as I worked. "I didn't. I distracted them, then tossed it to Calem. He scored. They only managed to hit his back as he crossed the line."

"You should see the other guys." Calem started to move

forward when once again the ground trembled. Mountains collapsed around us, spraying the air in a thick dust as trees, brush, and water sprouted to life. The dank scent of salt hung in the air, and tall cattails whipped against our legs.

"Marshland." Corinne studied the fog rolling across the new terrain.

"Gathering information, hang tight." Dominya's voice seemed further away somehow. Her mountain had disappeared, and now she was somewhere in the thick of the marsh, separated from us and vulnerable. My feet itched to move, and I glanced at Corinne.

She grimaced. "Trust her. She wouldn't—"

A loud scream carried through the air, followed by a series of thuds—thuds that sounded eerily like wet blobs smacking into something hard, and I feared she'd met one too many pagda balls to do her job.

Corinne leaped into action. "Calem, Zenna, stay back and protect the line. I'm taking Ozias with me." She gripped my wrist and tugged, a bit of frenzied excitement to her stare. "We're gonna save our girl."

Calem crouched low into his heels, his hand poised over his pouch. "Fine by me." Zenna nodded her agreement, taking up a similar stance and doing a sweep from left to right with trained eyes.

Corinne and I bolted, weaving around ankle-deep ponds and low brush. And because we didn't have Zenna telegraphing information to us, we were springing traps left and right. Our feet narrowly missing jawed snares that sprung out from beneath piles of leaves, or weighted nets dropping from the branches of overhanging trees.

"Dominya!" Corinne whisper-yelled as we scoured the area. She slowed her pace to a brisk walk and crouched low, eyes tearing apart the landscape. But she didn't spy the hidden lever beneath her right foot. One she accidentally triggered, which sent a volley of pagda balls flying toward her like loosed arrows.

I leaped in front of her and crossed my forearms before my chest, and iridescent magic rippled to life in the shape of a square that stretched from head to toe. The pagda balls crashed into it, and I planted my feet firmly to keep myself from sliding back. I felt the reassuring surge of magic as it trickled through my veins, coursed down my legs and into the earth, rooting me into place. I wouldn't budge, and Corinne was safe behind me. When the barrage finally stopped and a pile of pagda balls were clumped together before me, I dropped my arms. The shield disappeared.

"Nice work." Corinne's hand touched the small of my back, and I fought the urge to jump. A faint blush touched her cheeks. "Now we just need to find Dominya."

I swallowed hard as my gaze swept up and away. I needed to look anywhere but at her reddening cheeks. As I turned my chin, I spotted a strange figure tacked up against a tree. All feelings of shyness abandoned me. "Found her."

Dominya had been secured to a nearby tree, thanks to a pagda ball on each hand and foot. A fifth one was stuck to her center, and a sixth attached to her neck, blocking out the choker and her ability to communicate with us. Even through her goggles, I could see the wild fury in her gaze.

I wrenched the one from her neck first. "Are you all right?"

"Fine," she practically spat, muscles trembling. "They just got the jump on me. I made a foolish mistake. Won't happen again."

"We'll get them, don't worry." Corinne went to pat her shoulder, but right before her fingers could make contact, a loud gong crashed through the air.

My head whipped back to our line, and I heard Calem's enraged shout. "That answers that, I guess."

Dominya's face blanched, but she nodded. "Come back for me. Have the other two come with you. You've just about triggered all the traps on this side, and I can get them to the line in a heartbeat."

"Come back for you?" The words barely left my mouth before I was thrust high into the air with Corinne at my side. Behind us, three of the opposing team members were also careened into the air and were being pulled back to their line. They were grinning like madmen, but I took satisfaction in the sheer amount of pagda balls clinging to their frames. They had two defenders on their side, but it would still take them an extra minute to remove all those balls. Which would give us time to get to Dominya and attack.

When we dropped behind our line, I only had to remove two pagda balls from Zenna and one from Calem. Zenna swept the now fern-colored getsa ball into her arms, and a slick mucus coated her clothing where it touched her.

She groaned. "Slimy."

"Just hang on to it. Don't worry about attacking, we're moving as one this time," Corinne commanded with the authority of Dominya. We all nodded, and then we were off, racing toward our spotter with sure feet, getting to her in record time. I stripped the remaining pagda balls from her arms and legs, and we waited for her to gather herself.

Teeth bared, she snapped her gaze toward our enemy's line. "Only a few more traps. This time, we stay together. Ozias, stick with Zenna no matter what. We need to get that ball across the line."

With Dominya leading us, we deftly navigated the remaining traps and came upon our opponent's defenses. The two defenders were already in position, arms crossed and shields stretching between them. Their two attackers were positioned in trees on their flanks, and they let loose wave after wave of pagda balls the moment we came into view. But their aim wasn't as true as Calem's and Corinne's. They struck hard and true, hitting the throwing arms of our opponents and stopping their volley of attacks. One toppled to the ground, and Calem tossed a few more on top of him to hold him in place.

And then they distracted the defenders so Zenna could toss the getsa ball high above their heads, successfully crossing their line. The gong sounded, and Dominya immediately sprinted away to hide as the rest of us were thrust into the air and sent back to our side.

Calem laughed the whole way back. "This is the best night of my life."

Zenna grinned. "I don't know what else you had planned, but I'm glad Ozias dragged you along."

As we touched down, he tossed her a sly grin. "I still intend to make those plans come true."

"Easy, killer. Let's make it through the match first." But I chuckled regardless, turning my attention back to the terrain before us. The ground trembled, signaling a shift, and we braced ourselves as the marsh disappeared. The entire arena turned to ocean, and only a handful of stepping stones and small, treeless islands stretched between us. Waves lapped against the rocks, and I blinked as I stared at the open advance. Dominya was clearly visible, as well as the opposing team.

Her voice crackled into our minds. "Well, not much of a strategy here. Don't fall in the water, obviously. And stop them from scoring."

At that, the opposing team launched toward us, leaping across stones and making quick gains our direction. They didn't even bother to stop and pelt Dominya with pagda balls. And why would they? The trap was the water itself. There was no need to waste ammo when the layout was so clearly defined. Instead, we crouched low in our stances and waited as two attackers and two defenders rushed toward us.

"Ozias, this is mainly on you." Corinne didn't tear her gaze away from the attackers. They were nearly within striking distance. "Keep that ball away from our line."

My gaze snapped from opponent to opponent until I spotted a defender carrying the getsa ball. Now bright blue and covered in scales, it was hard to miss. And so were the sudden onslaught of pagda balls flying from their attackers' hands. Calem, Corinne, and Zenna responded in force, their arms churning air and unleashing fury so fast it was hard to keep up. A few struck home on their attackers as well as ours, and I crossed my arms before me to protect my face from a rogue sphere. It sunk into the ocean and disappeared, but not before another one hit my shield and then swiftly met the same fate.

"Here they come!" Corinne shouted, drawing my attention to the defenders. The one not cradling the getsa ball had braced his arms in front of him and called forth his shield, creating a battering ram that was aimed directly at me. There weren't many spaces to land on our island, and rather than risk getting caught by the ocean, they were going to try and push through. The female defender was following a breath behind him, safely protected and with two hands securely holding the ball in place.

"Calem!" I crossed my arms in front of me and felt the magic rush into my legs, rooting me in place. Calem jerked his chin my direction, taking in my predicament, and then launched toward me.

"What are you doing?" Zenna shouted.

Calem ignored her, instead crouching behind my back and directing his question to me. "You sure you got this?"

I didn't have time to answer. The opposing defender crashed into me, and an earsplitting clash sounded as our two shields met. Fire burned through my muscles as my legs threatened to buckle, and I let out a wordless grunt as I fought to keep my arms crossed. The other defender glared at me, the iridescent magic of his shield doing odd things to the gray of his eyes, and he leaned into his attack.

My legs quivered. "Here she comes!"

As expected, the ball carrier leaped from behind her defender, ready to fly through the air and cross the line with the getsa ball in her arms. But Calem was ready, and he pushed off my back to launch into the air and chuck a pagda ball directly into her gut. She let out a strangled gasp as it knocked the wind out of her, and the getsa ball fell from her hands into the ocean waves.

And then the damn thing started swimming. It zigzagged like a frightened fish with no real sense of direction or purpose, and panic spiked in me. It could still cross the line of its own accord, and then they'd score.

Calem didn't hesitate. He dove into the water, trapping the thing with all the years of training he had as an assassin, and emerged from the ocean waves with it safely in his hands. Dominya shouted, arms high, and he cocked his arm back before launching it toward her. She snagged it from the air and skipped across the small stones, completely unobstructed, to cross our opponents' line.

I barely heard the gong above the excited whoops and hollers from our team. We'd won. The terrain shifted back to one of flat-cropped grass, and instead of treading water, Calem was sitting firmly on his butt. Pagda balls disappeared, and the magic in my belt left in a rush. With my shield gone, I stood before the opposing defender and grinned. He gave a begrudging nod before turning and stalking away, grumbling something about beginner's luck.

Our team came together in an excited huddle, Corinne bouncing on her feet and fist pumping the air. "Okay, I'm not saying you guys are naturals, but you're naturals!" She rounded her warm gaze on me and gripped my hands. "We have to do this again."

Heat traveled up the back of my neck. "Sure thing."

"I think even my team would be wowed," Dominya said, her grin lighting up the night. "We just might have to call on you if one of them ever gets injured."

As they traded play-by-plays of the night's game, Calem getting more and more animated with every passing moment, my smile deepened. I wasn't sure we'd be in Ortega Key long enough for me to really take Corinne up on another game, but I'd helped win this one. And judging by the way she kept dancing in place, that was enough.

QUIZZES
AND MORE

QUIZ: WHAT BEAST WILL YOU CHARM?

In Lendria, there are a plethora of magical beasts with fantastic powers and unique personalities. And while Charmers can catch 'em all, answer the following questions to find out which one would *best* suit you!

1. What is your Hogwarts house?
   a. Gryffindor.
   b. Ravenclaw.
   c. Hufflepuff.
   d. Slytherin.
   e. The Sorting Hat just couldn't decide.

2. What is your favorite Marvel movie?
   a. *Captain America: The First Avenger.*
   b. *Spider-Man: Homecoming.*
   c. *Doctor Strange.*
   d. *Deadpool.*
   e. *Thor.*

3. What place appeals to you?
   a. A tropical jungle.
   b. A forest.
   c. Rolling fields with lots of room for activities.
   d. Sacred ruins.
   e. Somewhere warm with lots of sunshine.

4. **What leisurely activity do you enjoy the most?**
   a.   Reading.
   b.   Gardening.
   c.   Sports of any kind.
   d.   Puzzles.
   e.   Sunbathing.

5. **What is your greatest asset?**
   a.   I'm loyal to my core.
   b.   I'm a great listener.
   c.   I'm a caring person who always tries to help.
   d.   I'm cunning and great at weaving stories.
   e.   I'm really, really strong.

6. **What is your greatest weakness?**
   a.   I tend to hold a grudge.
   b.   I'm not great at understanding shades of gray.
   c.   I'm not good at taking care of myself.
   d.   I occasionally like to bend the truth.
   e.   I'm a bit hard-headed.

7. **What is your greatest fear?**
   a.   Being unworthy in the eyes of someone I care about.
   b.   Misunderstanding someone's intentions and reacting poorly.
   c.   Not being able to help someone who's dying.
   d.   Saying the wrong thing to someone I love.
   e.   Not being there to protect the ones I love.

8. **What is your favorite color?**
   a.   Black.
   b.   Teal.

   c.   Green.

   d.   Blue.

   e.   Red.

9. What is your favorite food?

   a.   Meat. All the meat.

   b.   Veggies.

   c.   I'll literally eat anything.

   d.   Nuts and fruits.

   e.   Fish!

10. What is your favorite Pokémon?

   a.   Persian.

   b.   Diglett.

   c.   Eevee.

   d.   Clefairy.

   e.   Charizard.

Ready for your results?

If you picked mostly A...

Congrats, you charmed a Myad! You're brave and fiercely devoted to those you love. Once you've deemed someone worthy, you'll do anything to keep them safe and happy, so long as they return your feelings.

If you picked mostly B...

Congrats, you've charmed a Nezbit! You're a great listener, and you've got a knack for always knowing what's in someone's heart. People come to you with their problems, and you have little patience for liars.

If you picked mostly C...

Congrats, you've charmed an Effreft! You're a caring individual who loves to give back to others. You're the type of person who strives to end world hunger, and you have a soft spot for kids. Plus, you love food. (Who doesn't?)

If you picked mostly D...

Congrats, you've charmed a Gyss! You're cunning, intelligent, and great at telling stories. A good puzzle never scared you, and you love picking the exact right words to garner your desired reaction in others.

If you picked mostly E...

Congrats, you've charmed a Laharock! Family is important to you, and you're always willing to protect the ones you love. Spending time outdoors in the sun is your jam, which meshes with your warm personality.

KINGDOM OF EXILES
DISCUSSION QUESTIONS

1. Considering Leena's experience with betrayal, do you think her reaction to Noc's Gyss wish—and the inevitable fallout—is realistic? How do you think this plays into Wynn's ability to charm her?

2. Leena places the lives of her beasts above all else. Considering she sells creatures who are unbonded to her on the black market, how do you think this makes her feel? Have you ever had to make the right decision for the wrong reasons, or the wrong decision for the right reasons? How does something like that shape her character?

3. Both Leena and Noc struggle with forgiving themselves for transgressions they've committed in the past. How do you think this shapes their character development? What does it mean to forgive yourself?

4. By the end of the story, do you think Leena has more in common with her newfound family, the Cruor assassins, or her pre-existing family, the Charmers from Hireath? Do you think she'll be able to honor both ways of life? Have you ever felt pulled between two seemingly conflicting sides of yourself?

5. Both Leena and Noc are exiles in their own right. What characteristics do they share that help them survive? How do they differ?

6. Leena is forced into exile by circumstances beyond her control. How does she take charge of her situation and rise above said circumstances? What kind of life do you think she would've led had she not been exiled?

7. Leena places a high value on being able to rely on herself throughout the story. Do you think this helped during her journey? Or would she have been able to achieve more if she'd opened up sooner, perhaps with a friend like Dez?

8. Noc places his emotions in a cage to protect those he cares about. How do you think this affects his friends and family? Would he be better off telling them, or do you think keeping his curse a secret was the right thing to do? Why?

ABOUT THE AUTHOR

Maxym M. Martineau is an article and social media writer by day and a fantasy author by night. When she's not getting heated over broken hearts, she enjoys playing video games, sipping a well-made margarita, competing in just about any sport, and, of course, reading. She earned her bachelor's degree in English literature from Arizona State University and lives with her husband and fur babies in Arizona. Connect with her at MaxymMartineau.com or through Twitter and Instagram @maxymmckay.